The Fiction of the 1940s
Stories of Survival

Edited by

Rod Mengham
Senior Lecturer
Faculty of English
University of Cambridge

and

N. H. Reeve
Lecturer in English
University of Wales
Swansea

First published 2001 by
PALGRAVE
Houndmills, Basingstoke, Hampshire RG21 6XS and
175 Fifth Avenue, New York, N. Y. 10010
Companies and representatives throughout the world

PALGRAVE is the new global academic imprint of
St. Martin's Press LLC Scholarly and Reference Division and
Palgrave Publishers Ltd (formerly Macmillan Press Ltd).

ISBN 0–333–91885–1

This book is printed on paper suitable for recycling and
made from fully managed and sustained forest sources.

A catalogue record for this book is available
from the British Library.

Library of Congress Cataloging-in-Publication Data
The fiction of the 1940s : stories of survival / edited by
Rod Mengham and N.H. Reeve.
        p. cm.
    Includes bibliographical references and index.
    ISBN 0–333–91885–1 (cloth)
      1. English fiction—20th century—History and criticism.
    2. World War, 1939–1945—Literature and the war. 3. War stories,
    English—History and criticism. 4. World War, 1939–1945—Great
    Britain. 5. World War, 1939–1945—Influence. 6. Psychic trauma
    in literature. 7. Nostalgia in literature. 8. Survival in literature.
    9. War in literature. I. Title: Fiction of the nineteen forties.
    II. Mengham, Rod, 1953– III. Reeve, N. H., 1953–
    PR888.W66 F53 2001
    823'.91209358—dc21
                                                              00–068195

10   9   8   7   6   5   4   3   2   1
10 09 08 07 06 05 04 03 02 01

Printed in Great Britain by Antony Rowe Ltd, Chippenham, Wiltshire

Contents

Notes on the Editors

Rod Mengham lectures in the Faculty of English at Cambridge University, where he is also Director of Studies in English at Jesus College. He has written *The Idiom of the Time: The Writings of Henry Green* (Cambridge University Press, 1982), *'Wuthering Heights': A Critical Study* (Penguin, 1988), *The Descent of Language: Writing in Praise of Babel* (Bloomsbury, 1993) and *Charles Dickens* (Northcote House, 2001). He has also edited the short stories of E. M. Forster, *An Introduction to Contemporary Fiction* (Polity, 1999) and, with Jana Howlett, *The Violent Muse: Violence and the Artistic Imagination in Europe 1910–1939* (Manchester, 1994). He is currently working on *Upward Spiral: Edward Upward and the Politics of Writing* for Oxford University Press. He is the editor of the *Equipage* series of poetry pamphlets and co-organiser of the annual Cambridge Conference of Contemporary Poetry; his own poems have been published under the title *Unsung: New and Selected Poems* (Salt, 1996; 2nd edition, 2001).

N. H. Reeve lectures in English at the University of Wales, Swansea. He is the author of *The Novels of Rex Warner* (Macmillan, 1990), and co-author, with Richard Kerridge, of *Nearly Too Much: The Poetry of J. H. Prynne* (Liverpool University Press, 1995). He edited *Henry James: The Shorter Fiction – Reassessments* (Macmillan, 1997) and has written numerous articles and essays on nineteenth- and twentieth-century fiction and poetry. He was the founding editor of *The Swansea Review*. He is currently completing a book on the late fiction of D. H. Lawrence.

Notes on the Contributors

Gerard Barrett is a graduate of University College, Galway, where he wrote a thesis on Henry Green. He is currently writing a study of the American novelist John Hawkes at St Edmund's College, Cambridge.

Maud Ellmann is a University Lecturer in English and a Fellow of King's College, Cambridge. Her books include *The Poetics of Impersonality: T. S. Eliot and Ezra Pound* (1987), *The Hunger Artists: Starving, Writing, and Imprisonment* (1993) and *Psychoanalytic Literary Criticism: A Reader* (1994). She is currently writing a book on Elizabeth Bowen.

Howard Erskine-Hill is Professor of Literary History in the Faculty of English, Cambridge University, and a fellow of Pembroke College. Among his books are *The Augustan Idea in English Literature* (1983) and *Poetry and the Realm of Politics: Shakespeare to Dryden* (1996). *The Selected Letters of Alexander Pope* will appear shortly.

Barbara Hardy is an Emeritus Professor of the University of London and Honorary Professor at the University of Wales, Swansea. She has written extensively on the novel, on narrative, and on lyric. Her most recent critical works are *Shakespeare's Storytellers* (1998), *Thomas Hardy: Imagining Imagination* (2000) and *Dylan Thomas: An Original Language* (2000). She is also the author of *Swansea Girl* (1995) and *London Lovers* (1997). Her *Selected Poems* will be published in 2001.

Phyllis Lassner teaches Gender Studies and Holocaust Studies at Northwestern University. She is the author of two books on Elizabeth Bowen, many articles on inter-war writers and women writers of the Second World War, and most recently *Battlegrounds of their Own: British Women Writers of World War Two* (1998). She has reintroduced the Danish feminist novel *The Dangerous Age*, by Karin Michaelis (1910; new edition 1991) and has collaborated in the reprint and new introductions to two novels by Phyllis Bottome, *Old Wine* (1924) and *The Mortal Storm* (1937). She is currently serving as co-president of the scholarly society 'The Space Between: Literature and Culture 1914–45'.

Peter Mudford is Professor of English and European Languages at Birkbeck College. His book on Graham Greene was published in 1997. His other books include *The Art of Celebration: Literature and Belief in the* *late 19th and 20th centuries* (1979) and *Making Theatre: From Text to Performance* (2000).

Mark Rawlinson lectures in English at the University of Leicester. He is the author of *British Writing of the Second World War* (2000) and is currently writing a study of the effects of the Second World War on British culture since 1945.

Lyndsey Stonebridge is Senior Lecturer in the School of English and American Studies, University of East Anglia. She is the author of *The Destructive Element: British Psychoanalysis and Modernism* (1998) and co-editor with John Phillips of *Reading Melanie Klein* (1998). She is currently completing a book on anxiety, history and psychoanalysis.

Geoff Ward is Professor of English at the University of Dundee. The author of *Statutes of Liberty: The New York School of Poets* (1993) and the forthcoming *Gates of Eden: A Cultural History of American Literature*, he has also published chapters and articles on Henry James, James Joyce, Romantic poetry and many other nineteenth- and twentieth-century developments. Currently he is the holder of a major Leverhulme Trust award, researching a critical biography of John Ashbery.

Introduction

The 1940s as a literary period is only now beginning to receive the kind of attention regularly afforded to decades such as the 1910s and 1930s, and to movements or phenomena such as Modernism. A vigorous interest in the literature of the first half of the twentieth century, specifically in relation to the cultural history of that period, has both required and sponsored a new and different quality of close reading, exploring the rhetorics not just of individual texts but of interanimating genres, media, discourses and ideologies. It is especially appropriate that in the study of the 1940s – for much of which the entirety of British society was engaged in a total war – literary criticism should be careful to open itself and be porous to the methods of cultural archaeology. A significant amount of the writing of the 1940s understood itself to be raw material to which later construction would bring a necessary finish; such writing predicted that its real, underlying meanings would only become apparent once the mystifying fog of historical circumstance had been dispelled. One of the most useful jobs the literary critic can do, paradoxically, is to link this projection, this desire and its motives, to the historical conditions that gave rise to it.

This is one of the ambitions of this collection of essays. The relationship of the 1940s to earlier and later phases of British history was a current anxiety of the period. One way or another, the eleven contributors to this volume have considered the persistence of certain historical continuities as understood by some writers, in relation to the overpowering sense of discontinuity that dominated the work of others. Howard Erskine-Hill's essay on Joyce Cary shows how Cary's development of his novel sequences allowed him to suggest the subtlety and complexity of historical process by locating the same characters and relationships within the changing constellations of a series of texts, making the connections between different historical moments liable to constant revision. Phyllis Lassner, in her study of Rosamond Lehmann and Kate O'Brien, is concerned with nothing less than the relations between history and narrative, between myth-making and its preconditions, between ballads and their sources. An understanding of the terms of these relations is vital to an appreciation of how fiction exploits and modifies the rhetoric of national identity. Lassner's particular comparative study includes a revealing discussion of the crisis in

Anglo-Irish relations during a war in which political neutrality is held in a tension between anti-fascism and anti-imperialism.

This dimension is also present in an important aspect of Maud Ellmann's comprehensive treatment of the fiction of Elizabeth Bowen. Bowen's partial dislocation from both English and Irish identities is only the most obvious form of doubtful inheritance that her work perpetually encrypts. Hers is a fictional environment in which characters are weighed down with the burden of a past they can neither decipher nor rationalise, for whom the presence of the past is as inevitable as it is baffling. Barbara Hardy's critical estimate of the achievement of Ivy Compton-Burnett focuses on a related disjunction between the awareness that is shared by author and reader and the total ignorance of characters as to the chains of causality in which they are bound. Hardy stresses the degree of contrast between Compton-Burnett's fictional practice and the 'flattering and consoling lies literature usually tells'.

The anachronistic redundancy, not just of traditional methods of story-telling, but of the novel itself, is an issue for many writers faced with the Blitz. Rod Mengham's essay analyses the short-story alternatives which many novelists adopted and gauges the degree of their conformity to a new paradigm of documentary realism. His thesis is that the overwhelming experience of the Blitz is what provoked the collapse of this realism, instigating something like the slow retaliation of modernism to the challenge to fictional form laid down by history itself. Neil Reeve scrutinises a similar transformation of structure in the immediately post-war fiction of William Sansom and Elizabeth Taylor. He concentrates on the period fetish for an 'estranged absorption in detail', interpreting this symptom as a sign of the mind's attempt to 'reclaim in one area the control which is dissolving in another'. The historicising of an almost clinical extreme of mental dislocation is a major theme of several essays in this book; the rather daunting conclusion of Peter Mudford's discussion of Evelyn Waugh and Graham Greene is that military victory in 1945 brings no guarantee of allaying the psychological conflicts engendered by the history of the previous six years. The fiction of the immediate post-war period brings out the intricacy of emotional scar-tissue.

Geoff Ward and Gerry Barrett are both struck by the intensity with which the theme of homecoming galvanises some of the key novels of the late 1940s. Ward examines the structures of addiction in the work of Malcolm Lowry, Patrick Hamilton and Anna Kavan, assessing the weight and value of repetition in a trajectory where both home and the hero returning to it have been ineradicably changed by the passage of history. Barrett shows how the echo-chamber that is the text of Henry Green's *Back* offers a formal parallel to the protagonist's paranoid delusions; demobilisation is primarily an experience of lack, of the loss of relations for which only fantasy can provide substitutes. The feverish intertextuality of the writing in *Back* is the equivalent in aesthetic terms of the post-traumatic stress disorder afflicting its main character, Charley Summers.

Lyndsey Stonebridge pursues a parallel investigation into the textual system of Green's earlier novel, *Caught*, whose obsession with a narrow range of images is accounted for psychoanalytically in terms of a defence mechanism against the return of trauma. Observing that trauma is 'less the effect of shock than an anticipated repetition of primal separation', Stonebridge alludes to the contemporaneous evacuation of children as a psychic event often experienced as equivalent in its violence to an abduction, and insists on the extent to which Green's text intertwines the historical and the psychic.

Mark Rawlinson deals with an author, Jocelyn Brooke, whose work is, if anything, even more obsessively repetitive. Although Brooke's novels and fictionalised autobiographies were composed after the Second World War, they reach back imaginatively to the psychic landscape of the First World War in an extraordinarily potent account of the willingness with which English literary culture has pastoralised its memory of conflict. Brooke makes war an inevitable element in the English landscape, portrays servicemen as 'native fauna', and makes the Home Guard seem like the latest efflorescence of an 'autochthonic myth' of the defence of the island realm. Brooke's curiously elegiac celebration of the militarising of Englishness, like so many of the novels discussed in this volume, correlates political and sexual identity, makes inextricable from each other the historical and the psychic.

The period from the Blitz in 1940 to the onset of the Cold War at the end of the decade was of exceptional interest in the reconfiguring of desire and betrayal, of retrospection and anticipation, of deferral and loss: all items in a vocabulary appearing in several registers, whose interdependence in the fiction gives us the measure of its formal complexity, its emotional layeredness and its psychological depth.

1
Elizabeth Bowen: The Shadowy Fifth

Maud Ellmann

'No, there is no such thing as being alone together,' Elizabeth Bowen writes in *The Heat of the Day* (1949):

> Daylight moves round the walls; night rings the changes of its intensity; everything is on its way to somewhere else – there is the presence of movement, that third presence, however still, however unheeding in their trance two may try to stay. Unceasingly something is at its work.[1]

What is this 'something', this mysterious third presence? Here Bowen identifies it with the 'time' – a time of war – that impinges on lovers' intimacy: 'Their time sat in the third place at their table' (p. 194). At this point in the novel the time is 1942, two years after the Blitz, when Londoners, no longer traumatised by nightly raids, were growing acclimatised to ruin. It was during the Blitz (we subsequently learn) that Stella Rodney and Robert Kelway fell in love, their first words silenced by aerial bombardment – 'the cataracting roar of a split building: direct hit, somewhere else' (p. 96). Deprived of a beginning, their love affair is also robbed of its conclusion, when Robert, exposed as a fascist spy, falls to his death from the roof of Stella's flat. Was it an accident, murder, or suicide? We never know – and the 'unfinished haunts', as Stella says (p. 321). So does the unbegun: the beginning of this romance, 'from having been lost', has acquired 'the significance of a lost clue' (p. 96). Bowen deprives the reader of beginnings too: the novel opens in an afterworld, the first Sunday of September 1942, when the 'great globular roses' in Regent's Park have reached 'the height of their second blooming', and the death-like 'trance' of love has already been eroded by the time that it strives to hold at bay (p. 17).

1

Noise obliterated the beginning of the lovers' story, and noise is the guise in which the time asserts itself throughout the novel: the screech of sirens, the crash of bombs, the 'sting' of telephones, the striking of clocks, the peal of victory bells and, most memorable of all, the 'icelike tinkle of broken glass... swept up among the crisping leaves' (p. 93). These noises burst through bolted doors and blacked-out windows, penetrating all enclosures in which lovers try to be alone together. This is a novel about leaks, about the porousness of architectural and psychic space, about the failure to keep secrets in, intruders out. Both war and love conduce to leakage by breaking down the boundaries between solid objects: 'War at present worked as a thinning of the membrane between the this and the that, it was a becoming apparent – but then what else is love?' (p. 195).[2] Robert Kelway is a 'leak' in human form who peddles secrets to the enemy (p. 35); in this sense he embodies the osmosis that pervades the narrative from the beginning. The novel's opening scene, an outdoor concert in Regent's Park, abounds with images of infiltration and diffusion: the 'smell' of evening steals out of the thickets, 'blades of sunset' flicker through the crowd, and hints of music escaping from the 'muffled hollow' of the orchestra enter 'senses, nerves, and fancies... drop by drop' (pp. 7–13).

This general invasion of the senses sets the scene for local, personal invasions which follow like a chain-reaction: for the plot of this novel – like a Racinian tragedy – is propelled by serial sexual harassment. First Louie Lewis (Bowen's rather patronising portrait of the 'factory girl'), discarded by her latest pick-up, intrudes on Harrison, a stranger she encounters at the concert, interrupting his theatrical display of 'thinking in public' (p. 14). Harrison is brooding about Stella Rodney, or rather, his mind has been invaded by the thought of her: for Bowen's characters do not exactly think, in the masterful Cartesian sense; their minds are passive vessels blitzed by thought. Next Harrison intrudes on Stella, 'forcing his way back' into her home (p. 22) – although Bowen makes a point of detailing each door that Stella has left open for him: 'she had left the street door unlatched and the door of her flat, at the head of the stairs, ajar...' (p. 23). Having invaded her flat (an enclosure that expands and shrinks with disconcerting elasticity), Harrison proceeds to invade Stella's mind with knowledge about Robert's treachery. Robert (she is told) is spying for the 'enemy', but he is also being spied upon by the authorities at home, and thus revealing secrets to both sides: he is a leak that spills in both directions.

Stella is placed in a diabolical dilemma: either she dumps Robert and prostitutes herself to Harrison in return for Robert's temporary safety, thus admitting Robert's culpability; or else she interrogates her lover, knowing that his knowing that other people know will drive him to betray himself, should he be guilty. As Harrison puts it: ' "I've never yet known a man not change his behaviour once he's known he's watched: it's exactly changes like that that are being watched for" ' (p. 37). Caught in these (Jamesian) wheels of surveillance – watching the watched watch the watchers – Stella has no choice but to become a spy herself, although her method of investigation, unlike Harrison's, is diachronic rather than synchronic: she seeks the origins of Robert's alleged betrayal in Holme Dean, his garden-gnome-infested family seat. Yet Harrison's accusation, whether true or false, is enough to destroy the lovers' trance, shattering the illusion that the couple had ever been alone together. If Robert is a double-dealer, the lovers could never have been merely two: Robert himself is that 'third presence', the foreign body at the heart of love, the enemy within. (In the closing pages of the novel Harrison divulges that his own first name is Robert too, thus reinforcing the suggestion that the lover and the third presence are one and the same.) Stella's suspicion of Robert's double-dealing, whether justified or not, makes her double too. Two and two make four.

Let's worry about four-ness later, though, and stick to three-ness for the time being. 'The apparent choices of art are nothing but addictions, pre-dispositions,' Bowen wrote in 1946. 'The aesthetic is nothing but a return to images that will allow nothing to take their place; the aesthetic is nothing but an attempt to disguise and glorify the enforced return.'[3] With the incantatory repetition of the term 'nothing', this passage performs the 'enforced return' that it describes. For what returns in Bowen's fiction is precisely nothing – 'love's necessary missing part' (p. 320) – a thirdness that makes two-ness possible but also sabotages its exclusiveness 'unceasingly'. In *The Heat of the Day,* as we have seen, the third presence is identified as the 'time' – but I suspect that this is an attempt on Bowen's part 'to disguise and glorify the enforced return' of a presence – or an absence – more archaic than any liveable historical event. As Harrison puts it, ' "War, if you come to think of it, hasn't started anything that wasn't there already" ' (p. 33). By invoking the archaic, though, I do not mean to de-historicise *The Heat of the Day* which, together with the family chronicle *Bowen's Court* (1942), is Bowen's most strenuous attempt to show how the political is implicated in the personal – a project (she complained) that 'presents every possible problem in the world'.[4] Her difficulty was to squeeze the panorama of an international conspiracy into the compass of Stella's flat, so that everything that happens outside the 'hermetic world' of love is acknowledged only by its impact on the inside (90). This obliquity of perspective seems to inform the very sentence structure, notoriously twisted with inversions, passive verbs and double negatives, in which every effort is made to avoid a 'direct hit'. For instance: 'not knowing who the dead were you could not know which might be the staircase somebody for the first time was not mounting this morning...' (p. 92). It was sentences like these that prompted Virginia Woolf to quip: 'I feel like you're somebody trying to throw a lasso with a knotted rope.'[5] The 'conflict' that Bowen found essential to her creativity asserts itself within the prose itself, which seems to be contending with an unseen obstacle, 'a never quite dislodgeable something to push against': a something that haunts Bowen's syntax much as the third presence haunts the trance of love.[6]

Thirdness takes many different forms in Bowen's work, ranging from the ominous to the hilarious, and it would be misleading to attempt to pin it down. Enough to say that there is always one too many, an uninvited guest at every table, or as Lacan would describe it, an 'inmixing of an otherness' in every structure. In his famous Baltimore address of 1966, Lacan asks his audience to consider the genesis of two. 'The *two*,' he argues, 'is here to grant existence to the first *one*: put *two* in the place of *one* and consequently in the place of *two* you see *three* appear.' At the risk of over-simplification, I would venture this translation: by establishing one, you thereby establish that-which-is-not-one, the 'necessary missing part' of one, the unaccountable remainder. Two, therefore, consists of two plus that-which-is-not-one, an absent third; three implies an absent fourth, four a fifth, and so on. Lacan continues: 'When you try to read the theories of mathematicians regarding numbers you find the formula "*n* plus 1" ($n + 1$) as the basis of all the theories. It is this question of the "one more" that is the key to the genesis of numbers...'. I wish to argue that the 'one more', the one too many, also provides a key to Bowen's fiction. While Lacan boasts that he has taught his students how to count to five, Bowen's writings of the 1940s teach us how to count at least to four, by alerting us to the one more that leaks out of any structure of containment.[7] To reach four, however, we must first return to Bowen's earlier fiction to trace the emergence of the shadowy third.

'The Shadowy Third', first published in 1923, is the story of a serial killer. Yet Martin, the protagonist, is an unlikely Bluebeard.

> He was a pale little man, with big teeth and prominent eyes; sitting opposite to him in a bus one would have found it incredible that

there could be a woman to love him. As a matter of fact there were two, one dead, not counting a mother whose inarticulate devotion he resented, and a pale sister, also dead.[8]

The very blankness of this pale commuter is his murder weapon: the women who have loved him have been vampirised by it, and left as white as he. But it is difficult to tell the living from the dead in Bowen's awkwardly contracted sentences: one wife, never named, is dead, another, named Pussy, still alive; but there is also a pale sister, who is dead, and a silent mother, who is scarcely living. The syntax forewarns us, in the words of Antonia in *A World of Love* (1955), that we are 'far too quick to assume that people are dead' – but also far too quick to assume they are alive.[9] In 'The Shadowy Third', the dead wife, known only as 'She' or 'Anyone', makes her absence felt in furnishings long since removed: absent curtains flutter in the windows, an absent *portière* blocks the hall, and an absent clock, with an infuriating tick, torments Martin with its silence:

> As they passed through the archway into the hall he put out his hand to sweep something aside; then smiled shamefacedly. It was funny how he always expected that *portière*. *She* had declared that a draught came through from the kitchen, and insisted on putting it up. *She* had filled the house with draperies, and Pussy had taken them down … Funny how he could never accustom himself to the changes; the house as it *had* been was always in his mind, more present than the house as it *was*. He could never get used to the silence half-way up the stairs, where the grandfather clock used to be.
>
> p. 78

Here, as in Daphne du Maurier's *Rebecca*, the dead wife asserts herself in furniture, but in Bowen's story it is not the things themselves, but the abysses that they leave behind, that haunt the living tenants of the house. Poor Pussy's efforts to redecorate are hopeless: they vandalise the old rather than create anew, leaving gashes and silences where furniture had been. In the garden, too, her flowerbed looks 'scratched-up and disordered' (p. 75): a wounding rather than a fecundation of the earth.

If the dead impinge upon the living, the living also impinge upon the dead, assuming both the immobility and the restlessness commonly attributed to ghosts. Bowen's characters are frequently transfixed, struck dumb, emptied out, and 'at a standstill', yet they are also constantly in motion.[10] Pussy's restlessness, her habit of pacing round the house, alarms her husband, who attributes her disquiet euphemistically to her 'state of health' (p. 77). He means, of course, that she is pregnant, but this state of health is figured in the story as a state of death, of purgatorial noctambulation. Later we learn that her predecessor, too, was always in 'an aimless bustle', rummaging through drawers in the upper reaches of the house, until her child came, unnamed and presumably still-born, after which 'she did nothing, nothing at all ...' (p. 81). There is a strong suspicion that Pussy, too, is destined to give birth to death. In her 'morbid' thoughts at the end of the story, she foresees her own nemesis: ' "I think," she said, "that not to want a person must be a sort, a sort of murder. I think a person who was done out of their life like that would be brought back by the injustice much more than anybody who was shot or stabbed" ' (p. 82). Unwanted in life, Martin's murdered wife is wanted painfully in death, in the sense that she is lacking, missing, gaping. One might say she is the gap that gapes – like the hidden skull in Holbein's painting *The Ambassadors*, which gapes at its unseeing spectator. Even when she was alive, her husband's emotional anaemia had sentenced her to ghostly vigilance: 'All the time he had felt Her watching his face; always on the verge of saying something ...' (p. 81).

Yet Bowen does not let us get away with dismissing Martin as a fiend. She forces us to feel his inability to feel, the torment of knowing he is missing something, which makes his vampirism almost poignant: as Hermione Lee points out, Bowen has the rare ability 'to persuade the reader of what it feels like to be a damned soul.'[11] Prey to what Bowen calls 'the inconvenient cruelty of passion', Martin cannot choose to be enchanted by Pussy's horticultural incompetence or infuriated by his dead wife's squint.[12] Nor can he control the paling of his own desire, destined to reduce Pussy, like her nameless predecessor, to a watchful shadow: ' "Just the littlest differences in you would make me eat my heart out," ' Pussy cries. ' "I should never be able to ask you for things. I should just look and look at you, trying to speak, and then you would grow to hate me" ' (p. 82). At this juncture the reader realises that Pussy – like the last duchess of this 'coldly distempered' house (p. 75) – is doomed to dissolve into the furniture.

'The Shadowy Third' is an immature work, but it nonetheless taps into the 'addictions' that fuel Bowen's art and give it truth. Among the most conspicuous of these addictions is to killers of the heart: bloodless Martin anticipates the ruddier monsters of her later novels, like the callous Eddie of *The Death of the Heart* (1938), or the satanic Markie of *To the North* (1932). The couple, Pussy and Martin, offer prototypes of 'the kid and the cad' (in Sean O'Faolain's catchy formula) whose lethal passion dominates the plots of her novels.[13] Both kids and cads, however, are subordinated to a third presence, which in this early story, as in many of her other works, manifests itself as furniture. In *The Hotel* (1927), Sydney speaks of people 'living under the compulsion of their furniture', and wonders if the human race were created 'for beds and dinner-tables and washstands, just to discharge the obligations all those have created'.[14] In a paranoid exaggeration of Merleau-Ponty's theory that the visible world reciprocates the gaze of the spectator, furniture in Bowen watches people, unnerving them with its reproachful stare.[15] ' "You know how it is about other people's belongings" ', says the narrator in the story 'Pink May' (1944), ' "you can't ever quite use them, and they seem to watch you the whole time" ' (*Stories*, p. 712). Matchett, the housekeeper in *The Death of the Heart*, works on furniture in order to protect herself from its uncanny scrutiny: ' "If I just had to look at it and have it looking at me, I'd go jumpy" ', she declares (p. 81). Yet she also praises the vigilance of furniture as evidence of its 'moral superiority'.[16] ' "Unnatural living runs in a family, and the furniture knows it, you be sure. Good furniture knows what's what. It's made for a purpose, and it respects itself – when I say *you're* made for a purpose" ', she rebukes Portia, ' "you start off crying" ' (p. 81). Matchett herself is portrayed as a household fixture: a 'living arch' (p. 77), a 'wall' (p. 79), a 'caryatid' (p. 312), her creased and padded body seems upholstered rather than enfleshed, her 'vein-marbled eyelids' petrified. We are told that she was moved to Windsor Terrace 'with the furniture that had always been her charge' (p. 23). ' "When they made a place for it," ' she explains, ' "they made a place for me" ' (p. 82). The sentence structure here suggests the interchangeability of it and me, of it-ness and me-ness, in a world where things and people, like the living and the dead, are constantly encroaching on each other's territory.

To infer that furniture is anthropomorphic, however, is to underestimate what Bowen (anticipating a buzzword of our day) describes as the 'sheer "otherness" of surroundings' (*Heat*, p. 318). For the threat of furniture lies precisely in its impassivity to human feeling, human meaning. If Matchett boasts that one can see one's face reflected in her highly polished surfaces, this does not mean that furniture is stamped with human feeling but rather that the face – traditionally the window to the soul – has been absorbed into the 'thingitude' of furniture. In her insistence on the thingitude of things, Bowen anticipates Robbe-Grillet, who deplores the traditional novel for its 'anthropocentric atmosphere, vague yet all-encompassing, that confers on everything its so-called "meaning" ', and sends out 'through the interior of everything a more or less crafty network of feelings and thoughts'. Objects, Robbe-Grillet declares, must be 'there' before being 'something'.[17] Bowen, too, affirms the thereness of objects, their opacity to the pathetic fallacy, their indifference to human sensibility. Yet there is something elegiac in her treatment of objects and appurtenances – this verbal caressing of the stuff of life. In Bowen's work, thereness is uncomfortably close to not-thereness, being to non-being, presence to 'no-presence' (*Friends*, pp. 33, 91). In 'The Shadowy Third', it is the absence, rather than the presence, of the banished furniture that bullies the protagonists, whose life together is depicted as a brief commotion in the chill repose of inorganic things. These things, moreover, offer none of the expected comforts of solidity; they stand, like Freudian fetishes, as monuments to lack and loss. Nothings, by contrast, bear down on Bowen's world with a weight more oppressive than materiality.

This nothingness is temporal as well as spatial: a sense of trance pervades her fiction, the feeling of a world transfixed and spellbound, as if time had stopped and left her characters suspended, in 'abeyance'.[18] Life is already over: this is a 'post-mortem' world where action is a fading memory and the living can scarcely be distinguished from the dead.[19] Her characters seem sleepwalkers, their torpor lifting only when besieged by the passions that destroy them. In her novel *The Last September* (1929), an autopsy of Anglo-Irish civilisation, the following sentence typifies the characters' paralysis: 'There was to be no opportunity for what he must not say to be rather painfully not said.'[20] In *A World of Love* (1955), her second novel set in Anglo-Ireland, the hero Guy is dead before the book begins; but his survivors seem more tenuous than his loitering ghost, which lounges amongst them at the dinner table, assuming the extra seat, the $n+1$ or place too many. Guy's counterpart in this novel (the name suggests) is Gay David, Maud Danby's imaginary sidekick, whose absence often seems more palpable than other people's presence. In the car-drive that concludes the novel:

> Maud's duality as a passenger became oppressive... Each time the child slid down on the seat she'd seemed to be dragging with her another entity, whom she kept down with her in a grapple; and each time she'd reared herself up again she'd done so with an oblique bullying hoist, forcing whatever it might be to sit still more erect, take still more furious notice than she had decided to do herself. She and her familiar would have been matched but that Maud always came out on top. This preoccupation with Gay David, whose

chastening if mindbroadening outing the afternoon evidently was, had relieved the others of much of Maud, at least up to now; but it had rattled Harris [the driver], particularly up here in the mountains...unnatural occupancy of his van he had not foreseen, nor would he stand for it.

World, p. 123

In this claustrophobic space, emblematic of the psychic terrain of Bowen's fiction, Gay David's absence threatens to overwhelm the presence of the other characters: only Maud can keep his nothingness subdued.

'Nothing can happen nowhere', Bowen declares – a resounding double negative that virtually undoes its own assertion (*Mulberry*, p. 39). Her novels fend off nothing and nowhere with an anxious solicitude for place, surreal at times in its intensity of focus. Whatever happens in her fiction is determined by its setting: by the houses, furnishings, and knick-knacks described with such exactitude that people, by comparison, seem ill-defined. Not that much does happen: on the rare occasions when acts are carried out, they detach themselves from their performers and hover in the past-clogged atmosphere. In *The Last September*, Gerald's kisses, wasted on Lois, float suspended in the living-room or 'asterisk' the evening sky (p. 158). In Danielstown, the Anglo-Irish Big House that dominates the novel, past acts lie petrified in household objects, like the imperialist loot bestrewn around the stately rooms: the exotic animal skins that Lois trips over, or the ivory elephants arranged in diminishing order on the bookcases. 'What she had done stretched everywhere, like a net,' Lois muses. 'If she had taken a life, the simplest objects could not more have been tinged with consequence. The graded elephants on the bookcases were all fatality' (p. 162). Such objects often show more sentience than their possessors: chairs are 'dejected', beds 'confidently waiting', and the dinner table 'certain of its regular compulsion' (p. 34).

Because nothing can happen nowhere, Bowen frames her characters within their habitats, but this framing often takes the form of an entombing: Bowen's interiors, like Dinah's cave in *The Little Girls* (1964), bear a sinister resemblance to crypts or mausoleums. These crypts, moreover, are always 'pre-inhabited' (*World*, p. 48); their living inmates find themselves hemmed in by other people's things, which are imbued with secrets of preceding generations. Bowen studies the effect of 'drastic passions' on posterity, passions that inhere in furniture long after their human performers have departed.[21] Matchett remarks in

The Death of the Heart: ' "Furniture like we've got is too much for some that would rather not have the past" ' (p. 81). Walter Benjamin, in his book on Baudelaire, argues that 'living means leaving traces', and that the stuffed Victorian interior was cunningly designed to retain the traces of the human form in velvet and upholstered surfaces. The detective novel, which deciphered these traces, came into being in the same period.[22] Gertrude Stein, on the other hand, regards the detective story as the only truly modern form of fiction because the hero is dead and the event is over before the narrative begins.[23] Bowen's protagonists resemble detectives insofar as they retrace the footsteps of their absent predecessors; but the clues encrypted in their furniture hark back to ancestral mysteries rather than to a decipherable past. Events, if they occur, tend to be re-enactments of deeper dramas of the past; and heroes, rather than initiating actions of their own, are compelled to undergo the aftershock of the suspended passions of their forbears. A sense of belatedness and anti-climax permeates her fiction. ' "How are we to live without natures?" ' cries the heroine in 'The Happy Autumn Fields' (1944). ' "The source, the sap must have dried up, or the pulse must have stopped, before you and I were conceived. So much flowed through people; so little flows through us. All we can do is imitate love or sorrow" ' (*Stories*, pp. 683–4). Ancestral secrets, if revealed, tend to be banal, like the toothbrushes that Dinah, in *The Little Girls*, buries in her cave for future generations to discover. Yet secretiveness pervades Bowen's world, creating an uneasiness too deep to be dispelled by revelation.

In this world, furniture embodies the unknown but resurgent past. It corresponds to Susan Stewart's definition of the relic, which she opposes to the souvenir. The souvenir, she argues, marks the transformation of matter into meaning – a paperweight purchased at the seaside evokes the vanished holiday. Conversely, the relic marks the transformation of meaning into matter – the holiness of Christ is condensed into a hair, a rag, a tooth.[24] Given this definition, furniture in Bowen represents a relic of the past, whose meaning is effaced in matter, sense in substance. Yet furniture also haunts its owners with the future: that is, with the past they are compelled to re-enact. 'Movable' in both the temporal and spatial sense, furniture resembles the 'phantom', as Nicolas Abraham defines the term:

> The phantom is a formation of the unconscious that has never been conscious – for good reason. It passes – in a way yet to be determined – from the parent's unconscious into the child's ... The

phantom's periodic and compulsive return lies beyond the scope of symptom-formation in the sense of a return of the repressed; it works like a ventriloquist, like a stranger within the subject's own mental topography.[25]

In Bowen, furniture assumes the role of phantom, inducing characters to re-experience a past that they have never lived, ventriloquised by the relics that surround them.

Absence makes these relics more coercive. In *The Heat of the Day* Stella, having stored her possessions in 'limbo' and moved into a rented flat, finds her relations with her son Roderick sorely strained by 'the absence of every inanimate thing they had had in common' (pp. 49, 55). Harrison, when he first enters Stella's flat, compliments her on her taste in ornaments, only to be told that they are not her own. This is reminiscent of a Jewish joke discussed by Freud, in which a marriage-broker invites the prospective groom to examine the rich possessions of the family of the bride:

> 'But,' asks the suspicious young man, 'mightn't it be possible that these fine things were only collected for the occasion – that they were borrowed to give an impression of wealth?' 'What an idea!' answered the broker protestingly. 'Who do you think would lend these people anything?'[26]

Similarly, Bowen's objects, neither owned nor borrowed, are foreign bodies in the heart of domesticity: if anything, it is the characters who are on loan to *them*.

In Stella's flat, the boundaries that define familial space are over-thrown: 'rooms had no names; there being only two, whichever you were not in was "the other room" ' (p. 51). There is 'no one right place to put a tray' (p. 52); and the sofa, which doubles as a bed, 'might have been some derelict piece of furniture exposed on a pavement after an air raid or washed up by a flood on some unknown shore' (p. 55). The dissolution of spatial boundaries suggests a loosening of moral bound-aries too: in this world where rooms have no names, and men's names are disconcertingly alike, personal identities dissolve into incestuous proximity: there is 'so little space left' between them (p. 46). Two Roberts figure in this novel, plus two Victors, one dead (Stella's hus-band), the other newborn (Louie's lovechild); 'Roderick Rodney' is vir-tually the same name twice over, like the curiously androgynous name 'Louie Lewis.' Through the power of the name, twos become ones; but at the same time, ones split into twos, individuals divide into opposing halves. Harrison is distinguished by his strange duality of vision – 'his ununified way of regarding you simultaneously out of each eye' (p. 75) – which gives Louie Lewis 'the feeling of being looked at twice – being viewed then checked over again in the same moment'. Harrison's 'inequality' of gaze (p. 12) finds its counterpart in Robert's 'inequality' of gait: his limp, which Stella puts down at first to 'the general rocking of London and one's own mind' (p. 90). Robert's legs, like Harrison's eyes, move at cross-purposes, somatic symptoms of psychological duplicity. Yet in spite of their divided bodies and divided loyalties, both characters merge into one 'Robert' at the end. Dividuals rather than individuals, both are two-in-one and one-in-two.

Nor is Roderick, Stella's son, firmly distinguished from this force called 'Robert' that threatens to absorb all men into one name (it is worth noting that Bowen herself, had she been born the boy her parents were expecting, would have been named Robert[27]). The encounter between Stella and her son bristles with incestuous innuendo: Roderick, having donned his mother's lover's dressing-gown, reaches his hand into its 'slippery pocket' and comes upon '*something*... pulped by age in its folds, limp from being in silk near a body's warmth'. This is not what it sounds like, but a piece of paper 'long ago folded' and possibly harbouring a secret message. Having 'twiddled it round and round', Roderick yields the object to his mother who, holding its 'dynamite... between her fingers and thumbs', undergoes a sharp moral crisis as to whether to unfold it or to tear it up. Finally she succumbs to her suspicions, peeks inside and finds 'nothing at all' – nothing, that is, that she is willing to divulge to Roderick (pp. 62–4). The reader, placed in the same position as Roderick, never discovers whether any message was actually secreted in those warm limp folds. It is not what this paper says that matters, but what it does – the way it circulates between the mother, son and absent third, implicating everyone (including the reader, the fourth party to this guilty transaction) in a conspiracy of secrecy, suspicion and betrayal. Here persons are reduced to junctions in the orbit of the Thing, concatenated into its mysterious trajectory.

Bowen attributes her attachment to things and places to the successive dislocations of her early life, when she was shunted back and forth from Cork to Dublin; then to England when her father had a nervous breakdown; then to boarding school and finally to a consortium of aunts after her mother's early death from cancer. Even when her family was still united, her parents' incommunicativeness, their retreat into their independent 'private kingdoms', created an ethereal atmosphere in which their daughter learned to cling to things. 'I find myself writing now of visual rather than social memories. On the whole, it is things and places rather than people that detach themselves from the stuff of my dream' (*Seven Winters*, p. 10). Given this preference for things over people, it is logical that Bowen, when writing the history of her family, should choose their house in County Cork as her title and her main protagonist. Her chronicle, *Bowen's Court*, tells the story of ten generations of an Anglo-Irish family in County Cork from the Cromwellian settlement until 1959, tracing the links between the fall of the house of Bowen and the self-destruction of Anglo-Irish civilisation as a whole. Bowen, the last inheritor of the Big House, was forced to sell it in 1959; shortly afterwards, to her dismay, the purchaser razed it to the ground. The book *Bowen's Court* therefore stands as funerary monument to the house Bowen's Court, demolished without trace four years before the second edition had been published.

In a literal sense, then, *Bowen's Court* is a book about nothing. And Bowen likens the Big Houses, imposed upon the island by her English forebears, to Flaubert's ideal book about nothing, which 'sustains itself on itself by the inner force of its style'.[28] The motifs of nothingness, silence and erasure reverberate throughout the chronicle. The prevailing impression of the countryside around the house is 'emptiness' (p. 3). Here 'history evaporates': in this 'country of ruins', abandoned dwellings, grappled by ivy and corroded by storms, vanish rapidly into the landscape, their human stories blotted out (pp. 15, 78). Bowen's Court (the house) was never actually completed, for resources were exhausted before the northeast corner could be built. This missing corner, with its implication of unfinished business, seems to represent the incompleteness of the English conquest of Ireland, the amputation of the Anglo-Irish people from the land. The lopped-off house is also reminiscent of the famous gnomon – an oblong with a missing corner – that glimmers in the first paragraph of James Joyce's *Dubliners*:

> Every night I gazed up at the window I said softly to myself the word *paralysis*. It had always sounded strangely in my ears, like the word *gnomon* in the Euclid and the word *simony* in the Catechism. But now it sounded to me like the name of some maleficent and sinful being. It filled me with fear, and yet I longed to be nearer to it and to look upon its deadly work.[29]

Whatever Joyce himself had in mind, these three terms, gnomon (the missing corner), simony (the traffic in sacred things), and most of all paralysis, with its double sense of immobility and dissolution, seem to encapsulate the history of the Anglo-Irish, their irresistible 'descendancy'. Strangers in a subjugated land, the Anglo-Irish needed an *'idea* of living' in order to embrace their isolation; integrated they could never be. It was the Big Houses, Bowen contends, that embodied this idea of living: each of these 'house-islands', with its intense, centripetal life, placed a 'frame' around the lives of its inhabitants, providing an aesthetic in default of rootedness. Within these frames, the Anglo-Irish lived like single children, 'singular, independent, and secretive' (p. 20). Whereas the English landowner was 'indigenous', the Anglo-Irish was 'imposed', gratuitous, installed by a divine caprice rather than a moral master plan, and hence a true aristocrat, free of purpose or responsibility (pp. 125–6). Abstracted from the world of fact, he tormented himself with fantasy.

Julian Moynahan has remarked that 'the Irish Big House is about as convincing a symbol of community as the House of Usher.'[30] And the fissures in the Big House began to show long before the fantastic imposition was destroyed. From 1800 onwards the Act of Union meant that Ireland, ruled by Westminster, was forced to yield much of its wealth in taxation to the English state in return for the 'protection' of a small minority (*Bowen's Court*, p. 260). It was at this juncture (Bowen argues) that the Anglo-Irish, long established in the lands their ancestors had seized by force, came to be resented as an alien garrison. Their society broke up: although it persevered 'in detail – comings-and-goings, entertainments, marriages', the 'main healthy abstract' was gone (pp. 258–9). In this sense the Anglo-Irish died before they became extinct, haunting their ancestors' crumbling demesnes, their civilisation frozen in the state that Yeats described as 'death-in-life and life-in-death'. Their moribund persistence could be summed up in the last words of Beckett's *The Unnameable*: 'I can't go on, I'll go on.'[31] The marmoreal atmosphere of Bowen's novels also evokes the paralysis of Anglo-Irish civilisation, its spellbound afterlife. '*Farouche*, haughty, quite ignorant of the outside world', and handicapped by their 'divorce from the countryside', the Anglo-Irish were 'driven back upon a tract of clouds and of obsessions which could ... only be solitary'.[32] 'The sense of dislocation', Bowen writes, 'was everywhere' (p. 258).

This picture of the Anglo-Irish mentality offers some insight into Bowen's own imagination. For the 'dislocation' endemic to her people's plight, with its compensatory dreams of integration, is the theme and motor of her fiction. It is a tale she tells time and again, particularly in her stories of the Blitz, in which the fact of upheaval repeatedly engenders fantasies of perfect worlds. For instance, in 'The Happy Autumn

Fields', the narcoleptic heroine, dislocated in the war-torn present, takes refuge in a dream world conjured up out of a family photograph. A similar sense of dislocation must have prompted Bowen herself to resurrect her family history: the composition of *Bowen's Court* began in the early summer of 1939 and was completed during the Blitz, in 'the savage and austere light of a burning world' (*Bowen's Court*, p. 454). During this time Bowen was serving as an air-raid warden in London, where she revelled in the fellow-feeling of a city under siege, so different from the 'cut-off life' of the Ascendancy in Ireland (*Bowen's Court*, p. 126). At the same time, however, she was spying on her native land – although 'spying' is perhaps too strong a word for her well-observed reports on shopping, rationing, black-marketing, and travelling in wartime Ireland. The British government, suspicious of Irish neutrality, urged her to gauge the Irish people's true allegiances and those of their incalculable leader Eamon de Valera. She gathered enough information to warn the Coalition Cabinet that a British take-over of Irish ports would be disastrous. But she also insisted that Ireland's neutrality – its 'first *free* self-assertion' – was 'positive, not merely negative'.[33] Some uneasiness about her undercover operations may have influenced her portrait of the double-agent Robert Kelway in *The Heat of the Day*. But Bowen struggled to stay loyal to both countries, defending Ireland's neutrality as ardently as she supported Britain's war-effort. 'Heart-cloven and split-minded' with regard to her two nations, Bowen found herself in the position of the shadowy third; like a child jostled between warring parents, her loyalty to each implied her betrayal of the other.[34]

In her extraordinary Preface of 1945 to the American edition of her wartime stories, *The Demon Lover*, Bowen describes their cumulative effect as 'a rising tide of hallucination':

> The hallucinations are an unconscious, instinctive, saving resort on the part of the characters: life, mechanized by the controls of wartime, and emotionally torn and impoverished by changes, had to complete itself in some other way. It is a fact that in Britain, and especially in London, in wartime many people had strange deep intense dreams.
>
> *Impressions*, p. 49

Characters require frames; but it is when these frames collapse, and walls come down, that dreams are born. The ruins of the Blitz, like the ruins of the Irish landscape, open up a missing corner in the real for the imagination to complete. We have seen how the shadowy third invades the frame of passion, destroying the illusion that lovers can ever be alone together. But the missing corner of Bowen's Court suggests a shadowy fourth more vengeful than the third, a fourth that disrupts the symmetry of the Oedipal triangle. This missing corner, this shadowy fourth, emerges most conspicuously in Bowen's early novel, *Friends and Relations* (1931).

Friends and Relations is not a good novel, but perhaps for that reason Bowen's addictions surface more clearly here than in her more accomplished works. The novel opens with a wedding, ominously marred by rain, in which Laurel Studdart marries Edward Tilney. The groom bears a striking disresemblance to the famous Tilney of *Northanger Abbey* who demystifies Gothic conventions for the naïve heroine's edification. Bowen's Tilney, by contrast, is a hysteric who embodies his creator's taste for melodrama, cramped by her commitment to the comedy of manners. Among the wedding guests is Laurel's sister Janet, who tends to be depicted as a ghost or sleepwalker: 'a positive no-presence' (p. 33); 'almost utterly silent' (p. 41); 'dead, but not disembodied' (p. 128); 'oblivious sentinel of oblivion' (p. 58); possessing the 'power of being nowhere' (p. 57). These epithets warn us not to be too quick to assume that 'heavy-lidded' Janet is alive (indeed, she bears a strong resemblance to the faraway mother of Bowen's abbreviated childhood [p. 10]). Some weeks after Laurel's wedding Janet marries Rodney Meggatt, heir to his uncle's large estate at Batts Abbey (like many of Bowen's protagonists, Rodney seems to have mislaid his parents). This uncle, absurdly named Considine, and even more absurdly represented as a former big game hunter, was once the lover of Edward Tilney's mother, Elfrida. Their scandalous affair, though long since extinguished, overshadows the marriages of their descendants. To avoid their elders' catastrophe, both the younger couples have foresworn the 'inconvenient cruelty of passion' for the sake of a 'miniature happiness' (pp. 104, 119). ' "Life after all," ' thinks Edward, 'hearing tea approach, the gay dance of china on the silver tray, "is an affair of charm, not an affair of passion" ' (p. 99).

In the second part of the novel, ten years have passed and each couple seems to have produced the other's children: the Tilneys' sturdy youngsters resemble Rodney, whereas the Meggatts' hysterical daughter Hermione – 'a preposterous child for Janet' (p. 56) – takes after the troubled Edward. These changelings deepen our suspicion that their parents could have been, or should be, recombined. A crisis is precipitated when Janet, overriding Edward's long-standing taboo, invites Elfrida to rejoin her former lover Considine at Batts Abbey. When Edward finds out about this invitation, he storms into his elders' bittersweet reunion, bent on rescuing his children, also visitors at Batts, from the corrupting influence of the ex-lovers. To his astonishment – and ours – he finds himself overwhelmed instead by his long-suppressed love for Janet. At this point, 'the present relaxed its grip on the house' (p. 71), and Edward and Janet are compelled to re-enact the dead-end passion of their fore-bears. Their love, never consummated, is renounced in a few weeks, after which the 'dear conventions' close again over the wound (p. 145).

The present relaxes its grip upon the reader, too, forcing a reversion to the past. For in order to reconstruct the chain of intimations that lead to 'this large non-occurrence' (p. 131), we are driven back to the beginning of the text. Only then do we discover – or rediscover – that Theodora Thirdman, a juvenile guest at Laurel's wedding, has already intuited the novel's plot. 'Theodora, intently listening, inferred that Janet loved Edward, that his mother preferred Janet; that for Janet this was a day of chagrin, possibly of despair' (p. 13). But because this insight is attributed to the boorish Theodora, whose 'personality was still too much for her, like a punt-pole' (p. 13), the reader is inclined to overlook the premonition. Reading backwards, other hints emerge: we are told that Edward 'was determined that his wedding, like the execu-tion of Julien Sorel, should go off simply' (p. 9); and a few pages later we find the newly-weds separated by a 'chasm' in single beds compared to 'tombs' (p. 21). All this sounds fairly inauspicious, but the narrative is so elusive that such portents can easily be missed. Nonetheless, when the crisis finally erupts, it is presented as a kind of *déjà vu*: Janet and Edward had always been in love, if only they – and we – had spot-ted its pre-indications. Oddly, Theodora alone, 'intently listening', is granted this power of decipherment: the other characters either read too quickly (like Elfrida, 'a rapid and superficial reader' [p. 17]) or too slowly (like Janet, who 'read, at all times, with an annoying slowness' [p. 93]) to penetrate each other's secrets, or their own.

Yet in spite of these clues, the climax flops: this 'belated flowering' of passion leaves us embarrassed rather than convinced (p. 120). Inert and undeveloped, Edward and Janet cannot carry off the repetition of their elders' downfall, and their elders also seem too nonchalant for tragedy. What is striking, though, is that the outbreak of romantic pas-sion is accompanied by the emergence of a shadowy third: in Bowen, a coupling need only be mooted in order for a tripling to occur. Janet, rushing to London under the hypnotic compulsion of her love for Edward, feels she is fragmenting into a third person:

> These weeks, a grotesque, not quite impossible figure, had come to interpose between herself and Laurel. A woman, an unborn shameful

sister, travestying their two natures, enemy to them both…Where had the three met, how did the two, innocent, recognise the third? We know *of* her, we do not know her. Never overt, less than a sinner, worlds apart from Elfrida, she was the prey of all speculation, the unpitiable quarry of talk…this horrible illusory figure had materialised on the upward train journey. The porter shutting the door shut Janet in with it; while the train ran down through a cutting they shared darkness…the figure, feeding on day itself, enlarged, took Janet within its outlines, occupied finally her own corner place…Janet's dismay was formless. 'Surely,' she thought, looking out at herself – for the train running under a bank, the window became a mirror – 'there is nothing with me but what I am?'

pp. 122–3

Clearly Janet is projecting on to the third sister her guilt for her betrayal of the second. But this apparition really represents a fourth presence rather than a third, a fourth that turns the triangle of Edward, Janet and Laurel into an oblong with a missing corner. That this fourth presence is associated with Elfrida is only reaffirmed by Janet's disavowal: 'worlds apart from Elfrida', she protests – too much. Elfrida's position in the novel resembles that which Freud, in his case history of Dora, assigns to Frau K., the missing corner of the rectangle that he initially misrecognises as a triangle. Only in a later footnote does Freud acknowledge Frau K. as the strongest love of Dora's life, stronger than any of the girl's triangular attachments; and elsewhere he likens this homosexual love for the mother to the Minoan-Mycenean civilisation buried underneath the patriarchal culture of Greece.[35] Elfrida, the shadowy fourth, also functions as a kind of footnote to the younger generation's love affairs, in that she marks a debt to something lost, archaic, matriarchal.

It is Elfrida's visit to Batts that brings Janet and Edward together, but she also functions as a prohibition on their love. She resembles other older women in Bowen's fiction – Mrs Kerr in *The Hotel*, Lady Naylor in *The Last September*, Lady Waters in *To the North*, Madame Fisher in *The House in Paris* – who at once inhibit and elicit the passions of the rising generation. They also tend to captivate young women, deflecting their erotic interest away from suitable young men. Bowen's critics associate these older women, rightly I believe, with Bowen's mother, who died of cancer when her daughter was only thirteen. Afterwards Elizabeth 'could not remember her, think of her, speak of her or suffer to hear her spoken of'.[36] Bowen's famous stammer, which emerged during her father's mental illness, consistently balked on the word 'mother'.[37] The bereavement that scarred her speech, however, also fuelled her writing, for the dead mother haunts her fiction in many guises and personae. But Elfrida's significance is not exhausted by the biographical connection. Bowen also associates her with Dickens's Miss Havisham – that great manipulator of the younger generation – through mischievous allusions to stale or ruined cake: 'the half-ruined cake went golden; the faces flame-coloured – Lady Elfrida's was for a moment ravaged: she had this less than moment for consternation, her own life was ruined, ruined – The moment went unseen' (p. 14). Later, in Bowen's most gnarled syntax, we are told that Elfrida 'disturbed the stale enclosed afternoon that like a cake under glass night after night had covered without renewing' (p. 86). Unlike Miss Havisham, however, Elfrida was not jilted: it was she who jilted Edward's father, but when she found herself alone with Considine at last, both lovers suddenly experienced a 'stupefying cessation of love, positive as the passion itself' (p. 82). The failure of their passion seems to corroborate Bowen's dictum that there is no such thing as being alone together: the couple, released from the interference of a shadowy third, or a shadowy fourth, cannot sustain what Bowen calls its 'trance'. ' "You and I are no longer two of three," ' Stella says to Harrison in *The Heat of the Day*. ' "From between us some pin has been drawn out: we're apart…The pattern's been swept away so where's the meaning?" ' (p. 320). Unpinned by a third presence, twosomes fall asunder.

Her own great passion may have fizzled out, but Elfrida's conception of love as 'a very high kind of ruling disorder' still looms over the younger generation like an unpaid debt, reproaching them for their erotic poverty (p. 104). In fact Elfrida comes to represent what everybody thinks they haven't got. Thus Laurel cries:

> '[T]his idea of Elfrida, what she had, what she was, has been fearful; it's ruined us all. We've been certain of missing something, we've all watched the others. Like that game, a ring going round and round on a circle of string under everyone's hands – you never know where it is, who may have it.'
>
> p. 129

Elfrida, like a fetish, stands for something missing, for a sense of lack that circulates among the other characters. It is this missing something (Laurel's simile suggests) that strings the characters together, creating geometries of love – like the purloined letter, in Poe's much-psychoanalysed short story, whose orbit constellates the characters in doubles, triangles, rectangles – and gnomons.[38]

Like Elfrida, Theodora Thirdman serves the function of disrupting erotic triangles. It is Theodora as a child who intuits – or perhaps invents – the passion between Edward and Janet; and it is Theodora as an adult who stage-manages its 'belated flowering'. Herself infatuated with Janet, Theodora descends on Batts during the elderly lovers' reunion and, miffed by Janet's *froideur*, writes a letter to Laurel revealing Elfrida's presence in the Abbey. It is this letter that exasperates Edward into his confrontation with Janet, which concludes with the traumatic disclosure of their love. The name "Thirdman" smacks of sexual ambiguity (neither man nor woman but "thirdman") as does Janet's characterisation of Theodora as the 'odd man out' (p. 94). Through 'one or two vital interpolations' (p. 119), Theodora engineers a plot out of ingredients remarkable for their inertia; without her intervention, combined with 'the Elfrida business' (p. 138), there would be nothing to galvanise these torpid thirty-somethings into passion.

It is worth noting, though, that Theodora's interference tends to be associated with communication at a distance, particularly with the letter and the telephone. As a child her favourite pastime is impersonating adults on the telephone:

> The telephone became at once her distraction and torture. She would not go out with her parents, but solitary in the flat remained for hours with the directory.... Then, having bolted the door, she rang up several prominent people and, skilfully passing secretary or butler, maintained with each a conversation of some seconds, under the pseudonym of Lady Hunter Jervois. She had a pleasant, mature voice: an asset. Passionately passing along the wire she became for those moments the very nerve of some unseen house.
>
> p. 28

The French word *parasitaire*, denoting the corrosive work of parasites but also interference on the telephone-line, encapsulates the role of Theodora: the sponger, 'bounder', stalker who devours her protectors and prevents them, through telephonic or epistolary terrorism, from cocooning home or self against the other.[39] Since her role is to disrupt relations between couples, she holds the place that Freud assigns to the castrating father, the shadowy third who shatters the primal dyad of mother and child. But the thirdman in this novel really represents a fourthman, a shadowy fourth who shatters triangular relationships and reveals another configuration of desire older than the threesomes of the Oedipus complex.

Older, but also newer. The shadowy fourth emanates from the archaic mother, like the Furies of Aeschylus's *Oresteia*; but there is something startlingly modern about Bowen's Furies, particularly in their penchant for the telephone. Theodora combines primeval vengeance with cutting-edge communicational technology. Sean O'Faolain, in a wonderful study of novelists of the 1920s, *The Vanishing Hero* (1956), marvels at 'the lengths to which Miss Bowen will go to deprive her characters of autonomy'.[40] It is the telephone, however, that causes their autonomy to leak away. In *The Hotel*, Tessa confesses that she is often surprised, when the telephone rings, to discover that she still exists: the subject seems to depend for existence on a 'call'. Similarly Cecilia, in *To the North*, is 'tempted to feel that she [does] not exist' unless she is connected to the telephone; only then can she 'crystallize over the wire' (p. 29). Her phone bill grows enormous because she cannot wait to be rung up: she must be plugged in or dialled up lest she should vanish 'into abeyance' (*Friends*, p. 82): a constant risk in Bowen's world. Recurrent metaphors of 'shadowy nets' suggest that Bowen's creatures are enmeshed in systems of communication-at-a-distance – 'hooped round with roads and netted with railways' (*Friends*, pp. 99, 136). These shadowy nets – the post, telephone, telegraph, roads, railways, airlines, and shipping-routes – usurp their users' agency, creating mysterious and uncontrollable relations of dependency. The characters' nervous systems seem to represent extensions of these networks: Cecilia's nerves are 'a living tissue of shadows and little insistent sounds' (p. 132). Nervousness is not unique to her, but spreads through *To the North* like an infection: even Lady Waters's dog is 'nervy' (p. 155).

Emptied of agency, plugged into unknown frequencies, human brains begin to buzz like telephones. Emmeline overhears 'some humming at the back of her mind that was not a mind' (p. 117); while Markie appeals to her precisely because he deprives her of autonomy and functions as white noise, a kind of dial tone: 'He had the effect of suspending her faculties not unpleasantly, like some very loud noise to which one becomes accustomed' (p. 49). Bowen's characters are 'wired' in every meaning of the term: entrammeled in clandestine networks, traversed by energies beyond control, they are jittering wrecks whose only respite from neurasthenia is numbness. In this respect they resemble Simmel's depiction of the metropolitan subject, dazed into apathy by constant bombardment of the nerves. For Simmel argues that the nerves, when agitated to their strongest reactivity for too long a time, finally cease to react at all, producing what he calls the 'blasé' attitude – a kind of Bowenesque insentience.[41]

Stella, in *The Heat of the Day*, seems automatised by her own telephone, lifting the receiver with 'a mechanical reflex ... to a mechanical thing'. Yet this mechanisation is curiously erotic: the telephone stands in for her lover's body, and Stella raises its receiver in the dark 'with the unfumbling sureness of one who habitually answers a telephone at any, even the deepest, hour of the night. Her hand would have reached its mark before her eyes opened; before her brain stirred her ear would be ready, so that the first word she heard, even the first she spoke, would be misted over by some unfinished dream' (p. 44). With telephones like that, who needs lovers? (In point of fact, it is her son who is on the line.) In *The Heat of the Day*, much of the contact between Stella and Rodney takes place over the telephone, which asserts itself throughout the novel as a supplementary, incalculable presence, both fetishised and feared. The fetishism is apparent when Stella fondles the receiver, but the telephone also precipitates her lover's death. At the end of the novel Robert, visiting his family at Holme Dean, is alerted to the danger he is in by a ringing telephone that he never answers. It seems that the summons is itself the message: the ring alone reveals that he has been tracked down and singled out for execution. Nor is there any question that the call could be for someone else: he never asks for whom the bell tolls. By refusing to answer the telephone, however, he refuses to be named and thus subjected to the law: he steals a little time to die, as he has lived, equivocally.

When the telephone rings, the outer world bursts into the inner sanctum of the home. This is why Bowen associates the telephone with the shadowy fourth; that is, with the outside that lurks within the inside, the mysterious $n+1$ or one-too-many that renders autonomy impossible. Yet a ringing telephone hails without conferring identity on either the caller or the called: until the call is answered, both parties to the dialogue remain unnamed, unknown. What the ring represents is not therefore a call to subjectivity, nor an invitation to exchange, but a summons to sheer exteriority, beyond the subject and beyond the reciprocity of human intercourse. This is why the telephone is linked to death, though it is also linked to the erotic: Bowen's characters are called to love as they are called to death, and the call comes not from the heart but from 'sheer otherness', embodied in the telephone's peremptory, inhuman summons: 'the telephone stung an intact silence' (*Friends*, p. 45).

In *Friends and Relations*, Laurel, lunching in a restaurant, is interrupted by a call from Janet: 'The messenger, like death, approached. A call to the telephone?' Laurel instantly vanishes, leaving her companions gazing at her 'empty place with the chair awry, the poor sweet-pea lying across her plate', like a floral tribute on a grave (p. 117). We next see Laurel 'shut in with her sister's voice in the strait little telephone box like a coffin upright'. Meanwhile Janet wonders why she has interrupted her own tryst with Edward merely to traumatise her sister with a telephone-call. 'Why speak *now*, at all, to Laurel?' Janet asks herself. 'From now he and she would not feel alone any more' (p. 118). In effect, Janet answers her own question: lovers in Bowen can never be alone together. Love involves at least four persons – and a telephone.

Four plus one make five ...

Notes

My interest in Bowen was first aroused by Andrew Bennett and Nicholas Royle with their daring readings of her work in *Elizabeth Bowen and the Dissolution of the Novel* (New York: St Martin's Press, 1995) and in the *Bowen Newsletter*, and I would like to thank them.

1. *The Heat of the Day* (1949; London: Vintage, 1998), p. 195.
2. Bowen writes of her own war experience that 'I lived, both as a civilian and a writer, with every pore open ... Sometimes I hardly knew where I stopped and everyone else began. The violent destruction of solid things ... left all of us, equally, heady and disembodied. Walls went down ... ' Preface to the American Edition of *The Demon Lover* (1945), in *Collected Impressions* (London: Longman, Green and Co., 1950), pp. 47–8.
3. Elizabeth Bowen, 'Out of a Book', in *Collected Impressions*, p. 269.
4. Elizabeth Bowen, letter to Charles Ritchie, March 1945; quoted in Victoria Glendinning, *Elizabeth Bowen: Portrait of a Writer* (London: Weidenfeld and Nicholson, 1977), p. 150.
5. Glendinning, p. 82.
6. Elizabeth Bowen, letter to Graham Greene, in *Why Do I Write? An Exchange of Views Between Elizabeth Bowen, Graham Greene, and V. S. Pritchett* (London: Percival Marshall, 1948), p. 56: 'I do think conflict essential – conflict in the self (a never quite dislodgeable something to push against), and an if anything hyper acute sense of every kind of conflict, and every phase of any kind of conflict, in society.'
7. Jacques Lacan, 'Of Structure as an Inmixing of an Otherness Prerequisite to Any Subject Whatever', in *The Languages of Criticism and the Sciences of Man: The Structuralist Controversy*, eds. Richard Macksey and Eugenio Donato (Baltimore: Johns Hopkins University Press, 1970), pp. 190–1.
8. 'The Shadowy Third', in *The Collected Stories of Elizabeth Bowen*, intro. Angus Wilson (Harmondsworth: Penguin, 1983), p. 75.
9. Elizabeth Bowen, *A World of Love* (1955; Harmondsworth: Penguin, 1983), p. 37. See also Andrew Bennett and Nicholas Royle, *Elizabeth Bowen and the Dissolution of the Novel*, p. xviii.

10. The term 'at a standstill' is used at least three times in *Friends and Relations* (1931; Hamondsworth: Penguin, 1943), pp. 7, 9, 27, etc. Bowen herself remarks on the restlessness of her characters: 'Someone remarks, Bowen characters are almost perpetually in transit. Arguably: if you are to include transitions from room to room or floor to floor of the same house, or one to another portion of its surroundings' (*The Mulberry Tree: Writings of Elizabeth Bowen*, ed. Hermione Lee [London: Virago, 1986], p. 286).

11. Hermione Lee, *Elizabeth Bowen: An Estimation* (London: Vision Press; Totowa, N J: Barnes and Noble, 1981), p. 69. See also the revised edition of this book, *Elizabeth Bowen* (London: Vintage, 1999), p. 69.

12. Elizabeth Bowen, *Friends and Relations*, p. 119.

13. Quoted in Patricia Craig, *Elizabeth Bowen* (Harmondsworth: Penguin, 1986), p. 59.

14. Elizabeth Bowen, *The Hotel* (1927; Harmondsworth: Penguin, 1943), p. 119.

15. Maurice Merleau-Ponty, *The Visible and the Invisible*, trans. Alphonso Lingis (Evanston, IL: Northwestern University Press, 1968), p. 139.

16. Andrew Bennett, 'Movables: Across *The Death of the Heart*', *Bowen Newsletter*: 2:1 (1993) 4.

17. Alain Robbe-Grillet, 'Old "Values" and the New Novel (Nature, Humanism, Tragedy)', trans. Bruce Morrissette, *Evergreen Review* 3:9 (1959) 100; 'A Fresh Start for Fiction', trans. Richard Howard, *Evergreen Review* 1:3 (1957) 102.

18. 'The whole Past … may be one enormous abeyance', Sydney says in *The Hotel*, p. 35.

19. See Julian Moynahan, 'Elizabeth Bowen: Anglo-Irish Postmortem', *Raritan* 9:2 (1989) 68–97.

20. Elizabeth Bowen, *The Last September* (1929; Harmondsworth: Penguin, 1987), p. 138.

21. Lee, *Elizabeth Bowen* (1999), p. 63.

22. Walter Benjamin, *Charles Baudelaire: A Lyric Poet in the Age of High Capitalism*, trans. Harry Zone (London: Verso, 1983), p. 169.

23. Gertrude Stein, 'What are Master-Pieces and Why Are There So Few of Them' (1940), in *Look At Me Now and Here I Am: Writings and Lectures 1909–45*, ed. Patricia Meyerowitz (Harmondsworth: Penguin, 1971), p. 149.

24. See Susan Stewart, *On Longing: Narratives of the Miniature, the Gigantic, the Souvenir, the Collection* (Baltimore: Johns Hopkins University Press, 1984).

25. Nicolas Abraham and Maria Torok, *The Shell and the Kernel*, trans. Nicholas Rand (Chicago: Chicago University Press, 1994), p. 173.

26. Sigmund Freud, *Jokes and their Relation to the Unconscious* (1905), in *The Complete Psychological Works of Sigmund Freud*, trans. James Strachey (London: Hogarth, 1953–74), Vol. 8, pp. 64–5. Henceforth designated as *SE*.

27. The birth, on 7 June 1899, 'was celebrated at Bowen's Court with great rejoicings; jigs were danced on the kitchen table with still more solemn fervour than after a cricket match, and no one, from the moment the sex was announced, said a word against Elizabeth for not being Robert', Elizabeth Bowen, *Bowen's Court* (1942) in *Bowen's Court and Seven Winters: Memories of a Dublin Childhood*, intro. Hermione Lee (London: Virago, 1984), p. 404.

28. This is also how Bowen describes the 'habitat' of love in *The Heat of the Day*: 'The lovers had for two years possessed a hermetic world, which, like the ideal book about nothing, stayed itself on itself by its inner force', p. 90.

29. James Joyce, 'The Sisters', in *Dubliners* (New York: Viking, 1969), p. 9.

30. 'Elizabeth Bowen', p. 84.

31. W. B. Yeats, 'Byzantium' (1930/32), line 16, in *The Poems*, ed. Daniel Albright (London: Everyman, 1992), p. 298; Beckett, *The Unnameable* (1950/55), in *Molloy, Malone Dies, The Unnameable* (London: Calder, 1994), p. 418.

32. Elizabeth Bowen, 'The Big House', in *Collected Impressions*, p. 197.

33. Elizabeth Bowen, Report to the Secretary of State for Foreign Affairs, 9 November 1940, in *'Notes on Eire': Espionage Reports to Winston Churchill, 1940–2*, eds. Jack Lane and Brendan Clifford (Aubane, Milstreet, County Cork: Aubane Historical Society, 1999), p. 12. The editors of this strange volume take a remarkably vitriolic attitude to Bowen's so-called espionage in Ireland.

34. Sean O'Faolain, 'A Reading and Remembrance of Elizabeth Bowen', *London Review of Books*, 4–17 March 1982, pp. 15–16; quoted in Roy Foster, *Paddy & Mr Punch* (London: Allen Lane, 1993), p. 122.

35. Freud, *Fragment of an Analysis of a Case of Hysteria* (1905), *SE*, vol. 7, p. 120n.; 'Female Sexuality' (1931), *SE*, vol. 21, p. 226.

36. Bowen, *Pictures and Conversations* (Harmondsworth: Penguin, 1975), pp. 48, 12; Glendinning, p. 28.

37. Glendinning, p. 28.

38. See John P. Muller and William J. Richardson, eds, *The Purloined Poe: Lacan, Derrida, and Psychoanalytic Reading* (Baltimore: Johns Hopkins University Press, 1988).

39. The French term for interference on the telephone line is *un effet parasitaire*.

40. Sean O'Faolain, *The Vanishing Hero: Studies of Novelists of the Twenties* (London: Eyre and Spottiswoode, 1956), p. 180.

41. Georg Simmel, 'The Metropolis and Mental Life', in *The Sociology of Georg Simmel*, trans. Kurt H. Wolff (Glencoe, IL: The Free Press, 1950), pp. 413–14.

2

The Wibberlee Wobberlee Walk: Lowry, Hamilton, Kavan and the Addictions of 1940s Fiction

Geoff Ward

1

The literary 1930s had been all about borders. Their narratives of cross-ings-over and trouble at the frontier could be political, psychosexual, traitorous or, more usually, a fusion of these things. Edward Upward's *Journey to the Border* (1938) with its Marxist narrative of conversion, Graham Greene's espionage 'entertainments' such as *Stamboul Train* (1932) and *The Confidential Agent* (1939), W. H. Auden's *Poems* (1930), *The Orators* (1932) and more straightforward travel literature such as *Letters from Iceland* (1937: with Louis MacNeice) are among the myriad examples. In the 1940s the paradigm would change from linear move-ment to homecoming and return. To a certain extent this is presaged by the tendency of 1930s writing to depict movement forward as a pre-lude to ultimate entrapment. The politics of the time on the literary left are progressive yet fatalistic, and a line from early Auden – 'Before you reach the frontier, you are caught' – would stand as an epitaph to that era.[1] Famously, Auden predicted the rise of leaders who would test to destruction the world in which he had only very recently grown up, some time before Oswald Mosley became a name and Adolf Hitler the Chancellor of the German Reich. Just as poems such as the one com-posed in March 1930 and beginning 'Consider this, and in our time ... ' conjure leaders, their agents and admirers – 'those handsome and diseased youngsters' – out from the shadows of 'immeasurable neurotic dread', so the key texts from the turn of the next decade predict the complexities and hauntings of homecoming in a world only newly at war.[2] This essay seeks to locate and open up the tropes of circul-arity, generally speaking broken circles, that recur in the fiction of the period. Addiction, be it to alcohol, heroin or forms of repetitive behaviour, is a crucial factor in the staggering recurrence of these tropes of staggering home.

2

An 'absurd Pierrot song' is chanted by a family of poetic drunks negotiating with studied erectness the 'Hell Bunker' of the local golf course en route perhaps to sexual dalliance and certainly to alcoholic oblivion in the Wirral section of Malcolm Lowry's otherwise overpoweringly Mexican masterpiece, *Under the Volcano* (1945):

> Oh we allll WALK ze wibberlee wobberlee WALK
> And we allll TALK ze wibberlee wobberlee TALK
> And we alll WEAR wibberlee wobberlee TIES
> And-look-at-all-ze-pretty-girls-with-wibberlee
>   wobberlee eyes. Oh
> We allll SING ze wibberlee wobberlee SONG
> Until ze day is dawn-ing,
> And-we-all-have-zat-wibberlee-wobberlee-wobberlee-
>   Wibberlee-wibberlee-wobberlee feeling
> In ze morning.[3]

Those long and knotty signifiers, the 'TIES' of young males, chime with the 'eyes' of the female while holding them in lower-case thrall, a small instance of Lowry's unashamed symbology of power and the masculine. There follows an apparently casual reference (for nothing in this sublimely overtinted epic is truly casual) to the young Geoffrey Firmin's performance with a golf club, another phallic surrogate that becomes an instrument of murder in Patrick Hamilton's *Hangover Square* (1941), another alcoholic classic. 'The abyss yawned in such a position as to engulf the third shot of a golfer like Geoffrey, a naturally beautiful and graceful player ... ' (pp. 20–1). There is the book in miniature, as might be said of many phrases from *Under the Volcano*. The 'third shot' puts a new twist on the trench soldier's superstition about taking the third light for his cigarette, an allusion that recurs in the Consul's cornucopia of signs and portents. The 'abyss' is *inter alia* and proleptically Firmin's alcoholism, the wreck of his marriage, his death at the hands of a fascist goon squad, the *barranca* into which his dying body is thrown, the vagina, hell, the Hell Bunker. Peering into this seething montage, the contemporary critic might wish to ask, though the author would have been horrified, whether it is then a shame that such a 'beautiful and graceful player' shouldn't have been able to talk it like he walked it with other beautiful and graceful young men, in a drunken camaraderie whose border-blurring invites a homoerotic identification? This kind of yearning lies nearer the surface of Hamilton's novel, where George Harvey Bone can only bring his dreams of murdering the female to fruition when prompted 'to throw her out of the window' by the golden boys of the theatre on a drunken spree in Brighton.[4] Uncertain about their own implications for relations between males, these novels may or may not harbour a sub-text of identifiably gay desire. What is certain is that both novels are profoundly misogynistic – in marked contrast to other male-authored fictions of the time, for example those of Henry Green.

The similarities do not end here: these are both books by alcoholic writers, featuring alcoholic, mentally disturbed male protagonists on the verge of suicide (for the Consul brings about his own shooting), who kill the only significant female character in the book. Bone drowns Netta in the bath, while the Consul untethers another symbol of rampant masculinity, a horse, which duly proceeds to trample his wife Yvonne to death in a storm. In both cases it seems that only water can catalyse the release of trapped emotion, contrasted with the dangers of fire (of which Lowry was terrified), and thereby bring the novel to a close. In both cases the apotheosis is romantic with a gothic inflection, and filmic. Killed off as a human, and therefore sexual, and therefore to the misogynist a promiscuous figure, the woman can now be forgiven. Yvonne turns into she-who-forgives, the cosmic Virgin:

> And leaving the burning dream Yvonne felt herself suddenly gathered upwards and borne towards the stars, through eddies of stars scattering aloft with ever wider circlings like rings on water, among which now appeared, like a flock of diamond birds flying softly and steadily towards Orion, the Pleiades...
>
> p. 336

So that's all right then. Meanwhile, having been drowned, Netta can turn into a nice girl, Bone's dead sister Ellen, who appears in a moment of visionary sentiment as the murderer gasses himself at Netta's fire:

> He was under chloroform. It was like that time, years and years ago, when he was a little boy before he went to school, when he had that operation for adenoids, and his sister Ellen was allowed in to hold his hand...
>   He put out his hand to see if Ellen's hand was still there. Yes, he felt it there – amidst all the whorls and tunnels and shafts.

'All right,' she said, as she said in those old days. 'It's all right. Don't be frightened, George. It's all right.'

He died in the early morning...

p. 279

Both Bone and Firmin are thrown – throw themselves – 'down a dark tunnel', as oneiric analogues for the bad vagina become once more that haunt of ancient peace, the womb. This watery sacrament that can transform the pickled alcoholic into an amniotic floater is gothic in the ironic, modern sense. The murders in *Hangover Square* are wonderfully Hitchcockian – appropriately so, coming from the writer of *Rope* and *Gaslight*. And within the celestial romanticism of her ascent through the clouds, Yvonne's demise encrypts a degree of gothic malevolence as Lowry grants her that posthumous place among the stars that Hollywood denied her in life. *Under the Volcano* alludes repeatedly to a horror film, *The Hands of Orlac*, a sort of Pygmalion and Galatea rejigged by themes of modern surgery and old-fashioned strangulation.[5] Of course Lowry's novel is replete with ironies that serve to batten on the Consul's already barnacled guilt and self-loathing, but it is at least arguable that they reveal to the twenty-first-century reader more than was intended.

There are of course many respects in which Lowry's and Hamilton's fictions have little in common. It is significant nonetheless that two texts, emanating from such different locales and cultural backgrounds share an obsession with 'circlings', to pick up Lowry's word. These build outward through literary allusion and accretion while tightening the screw of self-hatred, imaged in the drunk's 'wobberlee' footsteps, staggering home to what is only secondarily a material place. 'It is not Mexico of course but in the heart' (p. 36). Here the Consul echoes Edgar Allan Poe's famous relocation of the tale of terror as not of Germany but of the soul. Home is where the heart is, a climactic moment combining suicide and murder. All the key texts of the decade are in one sense or another tales of terror: Hanley's *No Directions* (1943), Green's *Caught* (1943) and *Back* (1946) are among the most, Charles Williams's metaphysical thrillers such as *All Hallows Eve* (1945) among the less interesting examples. The apocalyptic romanticism of David Gascoyne's poetry is characteristic of this time as well as being associated with his mental world as a (then) drug addict.

The most famous poem of the 1940s is likewise centripetal and centrifugal in its moves:

> The dove descending breaks the air
> With flame of incandescent terror...

The dove of the Pentecost is also a pigeon catching fire during the Blitz, a phenomenon observed by Eliot and Green, both fire-watchers, and it is also a *Luftwaffe* bomber; the spiritual and the material; love and death; forgiveness and the unforgiveable. Eliot's had always been a poetry of broken circles, Dantean spiral ascent in tension with Modernist fragmentation, accretion of meaning pulled back by the painful allusion to a displaced self-image. Famously, and as early as 1919, he wrote: 'Poetry is not a turning loose of emotion, but an escape from emotion; it is not the expression of personality, but an escape from personality.' Equally famously, however, he also wrote: '…only those who have personality and emotions know what it means to want to escape from those things'.[6] The drifting music and the turn of the screw, the outward and the inner movement, are contradictory initially but finally at one, as the fire and the rose of 'Little Gidding' are one:

> What we call the beginning is often the end
> And to make an end is to make a beginning.
> The end is where we start from.[7]

This is literally true of *Under the Volcano*, where we pick up the tale after the Consul's death, to which the remainder of the text will then lead. In *Hangover Square* Hamilton moves in different circles, overplaying somewhat the network of puns in 'Netta', perhaps in an endeavour to mimic the repetitions characterising schizophrenic discourse: 'Netta. The tangled net of her hair – the dark net – the brunette. The net in which he was caught – netted. Nettles.' (p. 24) and so on. After her murder the dragnet will really close in; not only will the police find Bone, but also the amazing net of thread in which he has enmeshed Netta's door-handles and furniture. Hamilton is equally heavy-handed in his use of politics and current events: Netta fancies Adolf Hitler, her fascist boyfriend looks like Oswald Mosley, and the homecoming to death coincides with the annexation of Poland. Yet this is entirely consonant with the determination of 1940s fiction to keep the centrifugal and the centripetal in play.

The 'circlings' are not just the province of high art. The revaluation of 1930s horror masterpieces such as James Whale's *Bride of Frankenstein* (1935) coupled with the undying popularity of Hammer Films following their resurrection of the Creature in *Curse of Frankenstein* (1957) have drawn attention away from the distinctive obsessions of the 1940s horror film. Distinctive, that is, within the genre; for Ealing shockers like the relatively well-known *Dead of Night* (1945) and the less familiar *The Halfway House* (1943) are films in which the end is where we start from. The latter was directed by Basil Dearden and co-produced by Alberto Cavalcanti; they would direct separate segments of the portmanteau *Dead of Night*. Both films starred Mervyn Johns, an actor capable of psychological nuance keyed to the traumas of a population that had suffered *Blitzkrieg*. In both films he can be read as disturbed, and/or as the sane individual in a world gone mad, preternaturally calm in the earlier film, distracted in the second. As innkeeper at The Halfway House he has in reality been killed in an air-raid one year prior to the day of the action: the haunting, eventually revealed as benign, is intended to benefit those about to die or risk death themselves, but who have time to put their house in order. 'There's one world for the living and one for the dead. And we're meant to take them in turn, that's what I say.' These lines are spoken in the film but denied by it. 'You can speak with your Dead' is the title of a pamphlet visible in the same scene, in an Eliotic or Charles Williamsian circularity the film endorses. This is essentially a Christian horror film in which redemption is possible. *Dead of Night* is a circle of hell without explanatory theology, and the segment in which Michael Redgrave as the ventriloquist tormented by his linguistically autonomous dummy begins to speak to camera *in the dummy's voice* has retained its power to shock. The end of the film is literally a replay of its beginning, the *déjà vu* endured by its architect protagonist vindicated as real, but condemning him to perpetual repetition. The earlier film, made when the outcome of the war was uncertain, rallies its characters to effective action. In *Dead of Night* the world is rigged, a nightmare in one sense terminated by death, as Miles Malleson quietly reminds us that there is always 'room for one more inside' his hearse. And yet it is interminable, as all this takes place within a lone consciousness condemned to repeat its moves and granted understanding only in a flash of illumination as the nightmare begins again. The implication, as with Green's *Caught* and even more *Back*, is that the journey home following trauma is a broken circle in which both home and the hero are changed. Green always supplied happy endings, a sign of faith in love and altered circumstances.

Fantastic films of the period, and texts of addiction, are more fated. The next section of this essay will consist of an examination of Malcolm Lowry's best-known work in order to gauge the degree to which it typifies its time, and the degree to which *Under the Volcano* alternately anticipates and fails to preview versions of addiction, writing

and identity with which fiction of the later 1940s and beyond would
be concerned.

3

Lowry was a Ulyssean wanderer who evaded a homecoming. When he
did come home, it was to die. He began on the Wirral peninsula, eventually graduating from Cambridge with a Third: already wobberlee
much of the time, he had to be shepherded through his Finals (by
Hugh Sykes Davies, among others). After the experiences at sea can-
vassed in *Ultramarine*, and a spell of Fitzrovian bar-room heroics, he
travelled to New York, setting of his uncharacteristically terse novella
Lunar Caustic; Canada, locus of the unfinished *October Ferry to Gabriola*;
and of course Mexico, where in an alcoholic haze shot through with
poetic grace his alter ego, the Consul, would stare down the abyss of
his life and imminent death. As stated previously, many sentences and
pericopes in *Under the Volcano* are microcosms of the whole. However
this interchange between Dr Vigil and the Consul does convey the
themes and parameters of the book particularly well:

'But I think if you are very serious about your progresión a ratos you
may take a longer journey even than this proposèd one.' The Consul
placed his glass on the parapet while the doctor continued. 'Me too
unless we contain with ourselves never to drink no more. I think, mi
amigo, sickness is not only in body but in that part used to be call:
soul... Mesh. The nerves are an... eclectic systemë... perhaps un poco
descompuesto, comprenez, as sometimes in the cine: claro?' 'A sort of
eclampsia, as it were,' the Consul nodded desperately, removing his
glasses, and at this point, the Consul remembered, he had been without a drink nearly ten minutes... He had peered out at the garden,
and it was as though bits of his eyelids had broken off and were flittering and jittering before him, turning into nervous shapes and
shadows, jumping to the guilty chattering in his mind, not quite
voices yet, but they were coming back, they were coming back; a picture of his soul as a town appeared once more before him, but this
time a town ravaged and stricken in the black path of his excess, and
shutting his burning eyes he had thought of the beautiful function-
ing of the system in those who were truly alive, switches connected... a peaceful village. Christ, how it heightened the torture... to
be aware of all this, while at the same time conscious, of the whole
horrible disintegrating mechanism, the light now on, now off,

now on too glaringly, now too dimly, with the glow of a fitful dying battery – then at last to know the whole town plunged into darkness, where communication is lost, motion mere obstruction, bombs threaten, ideas stampede …

pp. 144–5

The Consul never slurs his words, and so does not concede audibly that his life is a complete mesh. In a non-slurred sense, his life is a network, a 'systemë' of 'voices … chattering', puns, quotation, memories, all trembling at the edge of lost consciousness, but crossed by the 'eclampsia', the epileptiform spasms, 'now on, now off', of painful illumination. It is curious at first sight how many words on the page of the OED containing 'eclampsia' are relevant to the novel and to this page in particular: echo, eclaircise, éclaircissement, eclampsia, eclat, eclect, eclectic: all of them in fact. Here 'ideas stampede' as shortly the echoic horse will stampede and crush Yvonne in the éclaircissement, the fitful lightning of the storm. Yet it is not curious at all, for the Consul's eclectic systemë is one vast echo-chamber of signs, symbols, sounds, evidence of a propensity to read significance and potential connection into everything.

This propensity can be terminated only by death, if then. As Tom Roder writes in an astute overview of the novel, the 'manic iridescence of Firmin's significance-seeking wordplay' shows an addiction to addition.[8] The world of symbols, notwithstanding the web of references to the Bible, Kaballah, Faust-texts and the rest of the mirroring arcana, is never complete, for Lowry is as much word-drunk as alcoholic and even as the Consul's corpse is launched into the *barranca* there will be a tailpiece. 'Somebody threw a dead dog after him down the ravine.' (p. 375) This reintroduces just as it appears to terminate the sundry references to the pariah dog in the novel – and even that is not the truly last line of *Under the Volcano*, as the reader will find on turning the last numbered page. As Roder observes, this stacking of image and signification can generate fusion or confusion, heaven or hell, the eclectic systemë or the disintegrating mechanism, un poco descompuesto if not completely loco. The blurring of voices and identities in the second part of *The Waste Land* is relevant here, as is the possession of the ventriloquist by the dummy in *Dead of Night*. A collage or montage technique that began in the intrepidity of the avant-garde might be hell if you actually had to live it. This is one of the defining attitudes of literature of the 1940s. So everything is equally meaningful and meaningless, flittering and jittering like the butterfly caught in the cat's jaws then set free during the preceding scene in Mr Quincey's garden, like eyelids that are parapets over vistas of *delirium tremens*, like, well, like lots of things and yet not, for likeness isn't sameness, and the butterfly is just an insect, not a psyche, the papaverous name Quincey a coincidence, all sense of connection a consolatory strategy designed to hide our existential nakedness, as all moments are isolated if truth be told, and then you die. Ends and beginnings are reversible, as a film can be run backwards: 'as sometimes in the cine: claro?' But 'claro' anagrammatises *Orlac*.

In literary terms the book is a considerable achievement, its circulation of multiplied meaning a pleasure to read, and one not easily exhausted. The second part of the passage quoted is less effective than the first, as the spray of puns and signs is succeeded by the tired and conservative metaphor of the mind as a ravaged town. Of course the Consul is a tired conservative, contrasted with the still youthful Hugh, who fights bulls, rolls his own cigarettes, supports the Spanish government against Franco and has adventures, or thinks he's having them. Just as the alcoholic or the heroin addict surrenders to his or her drug the brain's natural capacity to pacify the senses with endorphins, so Lowry yields up the complementary aspects of his four main characters 'in one of the book's meanings, to be aspects of the same man, or of the human spirit', finally surrendering that single 'spirit' by transfusion to the life of writing.[9] The town-metaphor would then not be tired but apt, like the maudlin evocation of Christ, a moment of self-pity typical of drunken remorse, and so a literary detail, got right. But that won't quite do. The trouble is that, despite the equation in the book's phenomenology between the Consul's mind and Mexico, the inner and the outer, hallucination and local colour, the Lowry-Firmin mind is pledged at the end of the day to a sense of order that its most adventurous use of language violates blithely. Why *shouldn't* ideas stampede? New ideas, of which the Consul is terminally in want, might feel like a stampede. And would you really want to live in a peaceful village?

The many photographs of Lowry in Mexico, in Canada, in his cups, give the game away. The settings are breathtaking, beautiful, give without knowing it. The human subject seems locked in himself, the physique a prison. One look at any of the photographs explains his fear of plagiarism. Lowry was not only fearful of being accused falsely of literary theft, but frightened that he had (particularly in *Ultramarine*) really plagiarised certain narratives by Joseph Conrad or Conrad Aiken. He owed a little – but only a little – to both, the author of *Blue Voyage*, his hero and sometime minder, remarking unkindly but accurately that *Ultramarine* could have been retitled *Purple Passage*. Lowry was unlucky to be pipped to publication by the archetypal novel of dipsomania, Charles

Jackson's *The Lost Weekend* (1944). But no one could (though Lowry feared they would) accuse him of mimicking Jackson's terse and mono-chromatic allegory. The underlying anxiety comes from the tension between the flow of language to which Lowry surrendered himself, and the representation of his self inside that language. He wanted always to supplement, with one more image, one more allusion, one for the road, and did not know when to stop – no wonder the books took so long to write and were mostly incomplete at his death.[10] But he also wanted to be isolated, self-sufficient and whole within that, rejecting the dissipa-tion of identity, the negative capability, that brought out his best work.

I can get at this better from an oblique angle before returning to questions of sexuality, addiction and the avant-garde. One text from the 1940s that became influential twenty years later is Jacques Lacan's 'The Mirror Stage' ('Le Stade du Miroir', 1949). It is salutary to recall that its author was a member of the Surrealist group until André Breton threw him out for deciding on a church wedding and issuing the athe-ist *chef d'école* with an invitation.[11] What passes for clinical data is, as nearly always with Lacan, skimpy, and the central concept of the mir-ror stage – the transformation of the infant subject by his or her assumption of a self-image – is by its nature unverifiable, speculative and mercurial, reflecting not a *rite de passage* in the narrative of human development so much as an intervention in certain key intellectual histories of the 1940s expressed through an unusual disciplinary con-nection. By these lights the weird asides about pigeon gonads and indeed the apparent scientificity of the whole may be read as a neo-surrealist variant on the *Verfremdungseffekt*. However Lacan's attack on 'the contemporary philosophy of being and nothingness' is acute and illuminates not only the Sartrean position of the time, but by implica-tion the fictions with which this volume has to deal:

> At the culmination of the historical effort of a society to refuse to recognize that it has any function other than the utilitarian one, and in the anxiety of the individual confronting the 'concentra-tional' form of the social bond … existentialism must be judged by the explanations it gives of the subjective impasses that have indeed resulted from it; a freedom that is never more authentic than when it is within the walls of a prison; a demand for commitment, expre-ssing the impotence of a pure consciousness to master any situation; a voyeuristic-sadistic idealization of the sexual relation; a personal-ity that realizes itself only in suicide; a consciousness of the other that can be satisfied only by Hegelian murder.

Only, Lacan argues, by a dialectic of knowledge that can illuminate the function of *méconnaissance* that characterises the ego in all its moves, including some light to be 'reflected on to the level of fatality', could an understanding be advanced not only of 'the madness that lies behind the walls of asylums, but also the madness that deafens the world with its sound and fury'.[12] He goes on to argue eloquently, showing a retention of the visionary oneirism of the previous decade, that at the centre of both internally and externally driven strategies of control sits the 'knot of imaginary servitude that love must always undo again, or sever'. 'Concentrational' was an adjective coined in the wake of the Second World War to describe not only the regime of the death-camps but also any residual or evolving signs of that mentality: that and the realisation of a certain kind of personality only in suicide, recalling Hitler's death four years earlier, anchor the text historically. However it is not a misuse or an accidental propensity of Lacan's psychosocial diagnoses that gives them an echoic resonance in *Under the Volcano* and for that matter *Hangover Square*, even more than *Huis Clos*.

It can be assumed from the one reference to Patrick Hamilton in Lowry's correspondence that he had read and seen *Hangover Square* but that, preoccupied with his screen adaptation of Fitzgerald's *Tender is the Night*, he was interested only in the degree to which a novel could be recast for a different medium while remaining recognisable. Sartre is mentioned in several of the letters, but Lowry shows no special interest beyond the passing consideration of what was in the air at the time. What is at stake is not a question of literary influence but of literature produced at a shared historical moment, certain facets of which still operate even for the self-exiled writer at a geographical distance from the European theatre of war. In their different ways the Consul and Bone both show 'the impotence of a pure consciousness to master any situation'. The ascent of the dead Yvonne is nothing if not a 'sadistic idealization of the sexual relation'. Both protagonists can realise their personalities only in forms of suicide and murder. Both protagonists ask whether their own mental state would be better served by incarceration, and both authors attempt to relate the alienation of their characters to a world gone mad. All pledge allegiance to love as the instrument that might undo the knots of pain, but recognise the fatality of opting for the knife. The writing that could go beyond these problems was unavailable to either Hamilton or Lowry, but could only issue from an avant-garde practice that had experienced the concentrational form of the social bond but refused to recognise its 'authenticity' as anything other than a self-serving lie. This would be a writing whose authors lived through and wrote in the 1940s, but that could only realise itself fully from a critical distance in time.

4

> Day of the Dead: I got the chucks and ate my little Willy's sugar skull.[13]

The author of *The Naked Lunch* slipped into Mexico in 1949, after charges in New Orleans for possession of heroin and marijuana made the prospect of a day in court 'unpromising'. In retrospect he was to describe Mexico City with a distinctively alienated relish. 'The City appealed to me. The slum areas compared favorably with anything in Asia for sheer filth and poverty. People would shit all over the street, then lie down and sleep in it with the flies crawling in and out of their mouths.'[14] At this time the City had the world's highest per capita homicide rate. William Burroughs did not technically speaking add to this, as his fatal shooting of the mother of his son in a drunken William Tell stunt was talked down from homicide to *imprudencia criminale* after the palms of ballistics experts had been suitably greased. The case collapsed when the author's lawyer, a fellow addict, shot a youth who had bumped his fender and fled the country, at which point Burroughs was seized by a compulsion to do the same.

In the Preface to *Queer* (begun at the turn of the 1950s, and marking a transition from the Dashiell Hammett monochrome of *Junky* [pub. 1953] to the moschiferous carnival of *The Naked Lunch* [1959]), Burroughs recalls Mexico via a series of what he describes apocryphally as 'newspaper stories':

> A man lives in a little house. A stranger asks him how to find the road for Ayahuasca. 'Ah, this way, *senor.*' He is leading the man around and around: 'The road is right here.' Suddenly he realizes he hasn't any idea where the road is, and why should he be bothered? So he picks up a rock and kills his tormentor.
>
> p. 7

The point of these gruesome spurts of local colour is to present Mexico in existentialist cartoon form, as a place where the *acte gratuite* rules, while simultaneously tearing down the Sartrean No Exit sign that keeps the actor in prison. Given the nature of the incident that truncated Burroughs' sojourn south of the border, black jokes about homicide evince a questionable urge to throw stones coming from one who so narrowly avoided the glasshouse. In the Preface to *Queer*, Burroughs does not condone or even claim to understand fully his motives in shooting Joan Vollmer, little Willy's mother. (William Burroughs Jnr also walked a wobberlee walk, addicted to amphetamines from birth but dying of alcoholism.)[15] The father presents as a tragic curse what most would see as an extraordinary capacity for survival and self-reinvention: 'I am forced to the appalling conclusion that I would never have become a writer but for Joan's death ... I live with the constant threat of possession ... So the death of Joan brought me in contact with the invader, the Ugly Spirit, and maneuvered me into a lifelong struggle, in which I have had no choice except to write my way out.' (p. 18) The Preface concludes with the invocation of 1940s aesthete Denton Welch, somewhat unexpectedly Burroughs' favourite novelist.

The novel *Queer* is an intensely fraught narrative of frustrated homosexual desire. Whatever his mixture of motives on pulling the trigger, the crisis this provoked in Burroughs' life would result in a coming to terms with his homosexuality, as well as his becoming a writer. The sense of strain running through the book comes partly from its avoidance of the autobiographical incident to which it is nonetheless driven to refer obliquely, as well as from the asphyxiating cocoon in which the narrator (Burroughs' favourite alter ego, Lee – his mother's maiden name) struggles. In one typical scene with some resonance for the other texts under discussion, Lee and the unattainable Allerton go to see a film, Jean Cocteau's *Orphée* (1950):

> In the dark theater Lee could feel his body pull towards Allerton, an ameboid protoplasmic projection, straining with a blind worm hunger to enter the other's body, to breathe with his lungs, see with his eyes, learn the feel of his viscera and genitals. Allerton shifted in his seat. Lee felt a sharp twinge, a strain or dislocation of the spirit. His eyes ached. He took off his glasses and ran his hand over his closed eyes.
>
> When they left the theater, Lee felt exhausted. He fumbled and bumped into things. His voice was toneless with strain. He put his hand up to his head from time to time, an awkward, involuntary gesture of pain. 'I need a drink,' he said. He pointed to a bar across the street. 'There,' he said. He sat down in a booth and ordered a double tequila. Allerton ordered a rum and Coke. Lee drank the tequila straight down, listening down into himself for the effect. He ordered another.

'What did you think of the picture?' Lee asked.

'Enjoyed parts of it.'

'Yes.' Lee nodded, pursing his lips and looking down into his empty glass. 'So did I.' He pronounced the words very carefully, like an elocution teacher. 'He always gets some innaresting effects.' Lee laughed. Euphoria was spreading from his stomach. He drank half the second tequila. 'The innaresting thing about Cocteau is his ability to bring the myth alive in modern terms.'

'Ain't it the truth?' said Allerton.

pp. 48–9

The spelling of 'interesting', echoing Burroughs' Missouri drawl and used throughout his oeuvre, replays the origins of his writing, in arrest. He is also charting through Lee a painful rupture of his arrested development that will lead to his maturation as an openly homosexual artist. The stilted dialogue in the bar with its silence-filling platitudes about myth and cinema is both the perpetuation of his servitude to a lie, and the beginnings of an exit from despair.

It is appropriate that the odd couple should have gone to see *Orphée*, the work of a gay filmmaker, starring a gay icon, Jean Marais, and concerning a writer, his dead wife, and his new friends a blond male angel and the figure of Death. (One of the arresting things about Burroughs is his ability to bring the myth alive in modern terms.) When Death interrogates Orpheus as to his desires, he announces as his wish 'écrire, et non être écrivain'. To write, without being 'a writer'. This implication of art as speaking through the subject who articulates but does not censor or control is a highly suggestive one, emblematised by the famous image of the car radio as transmitter for poetic signals in Cocteau's film. The two-way relevance back to Surrealism and the ventriloquial nightmares of Modernism, but also forward to post-1945 avant-garde writing, is clear.[16] The film is also memorable for its use of mirrors in special effect sequences that turn them into two-way doors to poetry, dream and death. (To read through each other's glasses darkly Lacan's essay, Cocteau's film and Jackson's *The Lost Weekend* – which makes obsessive use of mirrors – would go beyond the parameters of this essay.)

There is also something curiously suggestive though hard to pin down in the so-do-I response with which Lee meets his own inability to turn the mirror of desire into a window of opportunity. His pronunciation of words with the excessive precision of the elocution teacher is a conscious gesture of inauthenticity, painful in this transitional state, but the starting point for an adversarial writer, after the War. It is also comparable as a psychosocial moment to moments in Patrick Hamilton's, but not Lowry's, characteristic style. Hamilton charts with the sharpness of nails down a blackboard the anxieties that resulted from a sapping of class hegemony in the years between the wars. Drunkenness was not just a personal problem but to be used strategically, both to satirise the mores and repression of the socially insecure, and as a border-blurring agent that fails ultimately, but that still points, however shakily, to fraternal bonding as a Marxist as well as a gay alternative to slaving in solitude. There are positive as well as negative aspects to Hamilton's description of the beer glass as 'the neurotic's microscope'.[17] Burroughs too would wrest positive from negative, not only beating his physical dependence on opiates but turning it into a universalising critique based on addiction as the fosterchild, weapon and feeding ground of capitalism and its discontents. Stilted conversation is a potent weapon for both these addict-writers. When Bone buys affection of a non-sexual kind from Netta with loans by cheque, she replies as follows: ' "Really, this is most accommodating of you, George," she said in that funny crisp way of hers, *in which she as it were parodied formal speech.*' (p. 136: my emphasis.) Both writers have an ear for the inauthentic because each knew that there was no natural language, only discourses approved by power and passed off as organic, inevitable, sanctioned by tradition, linked mystically to blood and soil, there at any rate to keep you in your place and mobilise you when expediency demands it.

Burroughs' influential equation of language with a virus therefore articulates a permanent state of alert vis-à-vis control from outside, together with a recognition of the need for change as essential to identity, as part of the dialectic of knowledge. Lowry cannot move beyond the No Exit sign into any change, or human relationship, whatsoever. *Under the Volcano* contains a mass of detail about 1930s politics, and through the character Hugh, the Spanish Civil War in particular. But the clock has stopped on the Consul's Day of the Dead, global war and the early 1940s pushed into second place by self-obsession and booze. There is no connection possible with his wife Yvonne, who drifts through the book being pleasant and weepy by turns. Sue Vice argues that these turns are simply the symptoms of womanhood; the Consul's self-affirming sorrow, grandly existential, dramatised in drink, and leading to self-comparisons with Hamlet, is regarded by others as out of the ordinary, whereas 'Yvonne, like all women, is always already melancholic, and therefore always already in effect an alcoholic.'[18] There is a textual basis for reading the Consul as a repressed homosexual that more important aspects of his characterisation finally dismiss.

There is Mr Quincey's appraisal of 'his open fly' (p. 134). There is a spate of weird puns on cocks and cockfights, 'each brief as some hideously mismanaged act of intercourse' (p. 287). But to the Consul the whole male apparatus is mismanaged, hanging as it does on the anti-gravitational whims and spasms of 'that hideously elongated cucumiform bundle of blue nerves and gills below the steaming unself-conscious stomach' (p. 207). Fancying himself a Renaissance man, Lowry/ Firmin is a closet Swiftian. The whore in the final chapter beds and unmans him. He submits, mentally elsewhere. Post- rather than homo- or heterosexual, he doesn't really want anybody, and he doesn't want anything to change. He knows everything there is to know any-way: Latin, alchemy, the difference between Cambridge college ties. It's too late for the dialectic of knowledge. He wants a drink.

5

Lowry's is apparently the most learned and wide-ranging of the 1940s classics of addiction. Deep down it is the most stuck in its period (or the period just preceding its period); most a case study. Its romantic use of exotic locations and its preoccupations with identity crisis and hal-lucination give it a superficial resemblance to Beat writing of the 50s that is more of a cul de sac than a link, in the end. Despite their shared and nearly contemporaneous experiences of Mexico, there is no refer-ence to Lowry in Burroughs' published correspondence.[19]

A different but salient case of an addict-writer negotiating the 1940s at personal cost, but as part of a personal and writerly evolution, is that of Anna Kavan (1901–68). Kavan was born Helen Woods, but in the 1920s began publishing novels – essentially of English manners and marriages – under the name Helen Ferguson, after her first husband. She attempted suicide at least three times, and suffered spells in mental hospital, for example after the death of her son in the Second World War. At this time she worked in New York as a researcher in a military psychiatric unit. After a transitional novel appropriately titled *Change the Name* (1941), she took the name of one her characters. Influenced initially by Kafka, her later fiction is intermittently brilliant. The most famous novel *Ice* (1967) is often praised as a deployment of science fic-tion comparable to work by Burroughs and J. G. Ballard, though the more radical but little known *Sleep Has His House* (1948: first published as *The House of Sleep*) is probably her masterpiece. Self-revision, and what might be considered success and failure, operate in perverse ratios across Kavan's life-narrative. In the 1940s she changed her name, her appearance, began writing brilliant fiction and became a heroin addict, though she also used amphetamines when writing. Hooked for life, she went on to establish the successful architecture and design firm Kavan Properties, renovating old houses in London and generating press attention to her work as an interior designer. Just as the life upended categories of success and failure, security and danger, so did the fiction. With Kavan all that is solid melts into sardony, dissolved by the killing touch of the addict-writer and her so-do-I parodies of formal speech, formal life, formal servitude and torpor:

> The dream scene comes to light as a comprehensive view of a garden suburb seen from the air. The whole layout is visible ... It's a high-class residential district. The streets are wide and planted with trees, the geometrical rows of houses stand in neat gardens, there is a busy shopping centre, solid neo-Georgian municipal buildings, a crescent of fake Tudor houses in herringbone brick disguises, business premises. It's summer. A windy and sunny day. All the gardens are spick-and-span with orderly flower-beds and lawns carefully mown. A few have tennis courts; others have pools, rockeries, sundials, effigies of rabbits, toadstools or gnomes. Some, not many, tradesmen's vans and shiny private cars sliding along the roads ... More insistent than anything, dwarfing the whole scene to papier-maché cuteness, the enormous blue undisciplined sky with robustious clouds bucketing across.

Kavan's 'comprehensive view' shows the 'papier-maché cuteness' of the 'whole layout' of a post-war class hegemony embodied in one of the new garden suburbs, whose shopping centre, Tudor houses and gnomes are all concentrational fakes, mocked by the 'undisciplined sky'. I place quotation marks around her phrases, but in truth every phrase already carries invisible inverted commas, anticipating Susan Sontag's famous definition of camp. It is not a shopping centre but a 'shopping centre'. The writing both remembers and projects the fact that all this could be otherwise, and sees a sinister attempt to retain the pre-war status quo rather than a fresh start in this world that suppresses its recent memories of dislocation, genocide, breakdown:

> A dark limousine, an eight-year-old model, but beautifully kept, is being driven along this street by a chauffeur in hogskin gloves. A white gate with THE ELMS printed on the top bar. Appropriate elm trees at each side. The gate is hooked open ... The front door comes into

prominence with porch and flanking hydrangeas in pots. The car stops; chauffeur gets out of his seat, rings the door bell, comes back and opens the door of the car from which emerges a lady of no particular age, dressed for paying a call … A maid in white afternoon apron and cap opens the house door for her. All these people, the lady, the chauffeur, the gardener, the maid, have the same face which they wear as if it were a mask, indifferent, decorous, nondescript, and quietly, negatively repressive. If the chauffeur and his employer were to change clothes no one would notice the difference.[20]

Whether temperament, experience or heroin came first or combined to generate Kavan's icy detachment is less pertinent than the achievements – of political critique, of style – that the detachment made possible. (The novel mobilises a range of styles to which justice cannot be done in this brief coda.) Her characters share a face worn 'as if it were a mask' but it is not, the sameness is real, the surface and the depths are flattened into one. There is no Lowryesque echo-chamber here, but a satire on the compression of signifiers as the outward expression of the 'negatively repressive'. 'Appropriate elms' flank 'THE ELMS' like a fascist revision of Magritte's 'Ceci n'est pas une pipe'. Ironically that insistence on sameness is undermined by a different sameness, the common features of chauffeur and employer that make the difference in social class imposed on them a blatant fiction.

There will be readers for whom this account will seem to have been unfair to Lowry. For them, my argument that he should have let his writing break free of a model of identity as self-sufficient, developing instead the oneirism which is there in his work but which Burroughs or Kavan used to greater advantage, may be taken as the Consul might have taken a tequila, *cum grano salis*. Lowry was made and marred as a writer by an addiction that allowed hallucination, mirrored by Mexico, to flourish, but only within a frame of guilt and masculinist rectitude that held him back from the bequest he might have made. No less ruinous on a personal level, Hamilton's alcoholism nevertheless allowed him a curiously effective glass through which to bring causes of and alternatives to the darkness of his time into the light. For Burroughs and Kavan the syringe became the neurotic's microscope, Kavan using that detachment to see more clearly 'the whole layout', her architect/designer's camera-eye recalling the aerial views of 1930s literary cartography while ushering in the neo-surrealism and science fiction interests of the post-war period. Burroughs would complete his most influential work in that later period, but his writing career only began in middle age, and was shaped, like the work of the other writers with whom this book deals, by a decade of broken or tightening circles encountered at the limits of social and psychic endurance. The dystopias that dominate post-war fiction are instigated by homecomings in the wake of conflict that discover not peace, but more subtle forms of the concentrational whose Cold War rigidity would be scuffed and satirised by the weirdly wobberlee, *descompuesto*, parodic eclampsias of hallucinatory text.

Notes

1. W. H. Auden, 'XXVII', in *The English Auden: Poems, Essays and Dramatic Writings 1927–1939* (London and Boston: Faber and Faber, 1977), p. 45.
2. Ibid., pp. 46–7.
3. Malcolm Lowry, *Under the Volcano* (1947; London: Jonathan Cape, 1976), p. 20. Henceforth page numbers are given in the main body of the chapter.
4. Patrick Hamilton, *Hangover Square* (1941; London: Penguin 1956), p. 258. Henceforth page numbers are given in the main body of the chapter.
5. *Orlacs Hande* (1925: dir. Robert Wiene), a German Expressionist classic, was filmed again by Hollywood as *Mad Love* (1935: dir. Karl Freund). Both versions starred Peter Lorre as the hands-on doctor. That the wandering hands may be the agents *sub rosa* of the murdering phallus is implied by at least one critic: 'Gogol's sepulchral voice, his absolute baldness and his pale, unhealthy plumpness make him seem like an erect lava who has been force-fed, bleached and then smeared in cold grease.' Leonard Wolf, *Horror: A Connoisseur's Guide to Literature and Film* (New York and Oxford: Facts on File, 1989), p. 144.
6. T. S. Eliot, *Selected Essays* (1932; London: Faber and Faber, 1969), p. 21.
7. T. S. Eliot, *Collected Poems 1909–1962* (1963; London: Faber and Faber, 1966), p. 221.
8. Tom Roder, '(Un)reliability and Pan-(in)significance in *Under the Volcano* and *Island*: a preliminary overview', in S. Vice, M. Campbell and T. Armstrong, eds, *Beyond the Pleasure Dome: Writing and Addiction from the Romantics* (Sheffield: Sheffield Academic Press, 1994), pp. 206–16 (p. 211).
9. Lowry, letter to Jonathan Cape, 2 January 1946. In S. E. Grace, ed., *Sursum Corda! The Collected Letters of Malcolm Lowry: Volume One, 1926–46* (London: Jonathan Cape), 1995, pp. 500–1.
10. The argument of this essay could easily have been bolstered by quotation from Lowry's other fiction which (with the partial exception of *Lunar Caustic*, one or two tales and bits of *Gabriola*) offers diluted variants of *Under the Volcano*. No dates of composition and publication are given, out of deference to the peculiar history of those books' gestation, and the (to me, troubling) fact of their having been completed by other hands.
11. Mark Polizzotti, *Revolution of the Mind: The Life of André Breton* (London: Bloomsbury, 1995).
12. Jacques Lacan, *Ecrits: A Selection*, trans. A. Sheridan (London: Tavistock, 1977), pp. 6–7.

13. William Burroughs, *The Naked Lunch* (Paris: Olympia Press, 1959), p. 24.
14. William Burroughs, *Queer* (London: Picador, 1985), pp. 5–6. Henceforth page numbers are given in the main body of the chapter.
15. The source for information regarding the shooting, the trial and Burroughs' family are drawn from Ted Morgan, *Literary Outlaw: The Life and Times of William Burroughs* (London: Pimlico, 1991).
16. For example, the gay American poet Jack Spicer would turn the radio metaphor into a manifesto in the 1950s.
17. Letter, 22 June 1934, as given by Brian McKenna, 'Confessions of a Heavy-Drinking Marxist', in *Beyond the Pleasure Dome*, pp. 231–44 (p. 242).
18. Sue Vice, 'Mourning, Melancholia and Femininity in Malcolm Lowry's *Under the Volcano*', in *Beyond the Pleasure Dome*, pp. 169–76 (p. 169). The thrust of this essay recalls the general relevance of Freud's observations on mourning and melancholia to both addiction and homosexuality, not merely in the famous paper to which Vice's title alludes but also (for example) in 'Some Neurotic Mechanisms in Jealousy, Paranoia and Homosexuality' (1921), highly relevant to the work of Lowry, Hamilton and Burroughs.
19. There are two references to *Under the Volcano* in the letters of Jack Kerouac, whose prose style is closer to Lowry's, and whose late novel *Big Sur* (1962) revolves around its author's irreversible alcoholism; a 1951 letter to Neal Cassady describes the novel approvingly as 'our personal meat' and recommends it as 'the end of the line or at least the best (for you) since Proust and Joyce'. One year on, and the comparison with Joyce is still there, but with a different inflection. Kerouac wrote to Carl Solomon that *Under the Volcano* was 'incomprehensible' like *Finnegans Wake*, and that the way to 'try to understand' lay not in the book but in 'the author's intellect, and passion, and mystery'. This plays into Lowry's hands, and up to Kerouac's commitment to an improvised prose spun straight from the autobiographical moment. Its commitment to an idea of authenticity betrays its limitations. See A. Charters, ed., *Jack Kerouac: Selected Letters 1940–1956* (New York: Viking, 1995), pp. 325, 376. It is just possible that Burroughs' published output contains a reference to Lowry that I have missed. However my thanks go to Oliver Harris, editor of Burroughs' correspondence, for confirming my current sense that nothing meets the eye.
20. Anna Kavan, *Sleep Has His House* (London: Cassell, 1948), pp. 20–1. Kavan originally titled her novel *The House of Sleep*, already the title of a thriller by Frank King (of *The Ghoul* fame). Jonathan Coe's novel of memory and analysis *The House of Sleep* (1997) pays homage to King, though its themes are closer to Kavan.

3
Bombs and Roses: The Writing of Anxiety in Henry Green's *Caught*
Lyndsey Stonebridge

(The firemen saw each other's faces. They saw the water below a dirty yellow towards the fire; the wharves on that far side low and black, those on the bank they were leaving a pretty rose... They sat very still, beneath the immensity. For, against it, warehouses, small towers, puny steeples seemed alive with sparks from the mile high pandemonium of flame reflected in the quaking sky. This fan, a roaring red gold, pulsed rose at the outside edge, the perimeter round which the heavens, set with stars before fading to utter blackness, were for a space a trembling green.)

Henry Green, *Caught*, pp. 76–7

War, she thought, is sex.

Caught, p. 119

Roses are not generally thought to be objects of anxiety. They are objects of desire, or better, objects that arrest desire by their invitation to aesthetic contemplation, but only for the phobic could a rose be said to be an occasion for dread. Writing during the Second World War, the British writer Henry Green ('a trembling green') suggests otherwise. In this description of the London Blitz from his 1943 novel *Caught*, everything comes up roses.[1] First among literary clichés, roses lend themselves to this kind of figurative estrangement (by virtue of which, in literature, a rose is in fact only very rarely a rose), and Green is by no means the only British writer in the Second World War to note that the fire and the rose are one.[2] In *Caught*, however, Green's roses wreath desire and dread together so tightly that the psychoanalytic cliché – war is sex – snaps back into the tautology that Freud, perhaps, always intended.

46

The idea that war could be sex was, of course, the scandal of Freud's theory of the traumatic neurosis during the First World War. As is well known, only a de-sexualised version of psychoanalysis was admitted into the field hospitals and into the officers' convalescent homes that sprung up in upper-class houses all over Britain. One of those was Green's childhood home, which, he later said, opened up its doors, like those of many of the overprivileged, to the wounded and traumatised in a calculated act of class preservation.[3] One does not have to think too hard to appreciate why, for some at least, it was preferable to see those torn and shocked bodies as seized by a dreadful – but after all perfectly understandable – fear in the face of war, rather than gripped with a less comprehensible anxiety that carried with it a dangerous and potentially lethal sexual charge.

The temptation to unsex trauma theory is still with us today. It is not quite that something has been occluded in contemporary debate and that this something is sexuality. It is more accurate to say that, from a psychoanalytic perspective, the *agon* of sexuality – and particularly of the drives – is right at the heart of trauma, and that this, especially in the recent alliance of psychoanalysis and history, causes a certain awkwardness. One of the strengths of contemporary trauma theory lies in its articulation of a nuanced and subtle historicity, read through both psychoanalysis and literature, which allows the humanities to reconnect with historical violence, without (supposedly) falling into the pitfalls of a naïve historicism.[4] The awkwardness comes because sexual antagonism is both clearly historical (the violence is well documented) *and* structurally necessary to psychoanalytic theories of trauma. The two, the historical and the psychic, are clearly not analogues, but they remain stubbornly and infuriatingly intertwined.[5]

Faced with this theoretical tangle, two options present themselves. The first is to privilege historical trauma over sexual trauma. Psychoanalysis, hence, provides an account of the multiple difficulties of historical representation while escaping the age-old accusation of sexual determination. War, thus, is not (only) sex. For all its hermeneutic power, this new historiography runs the risk of producing a trauma theory without, paradoxically, a psychoanalysis (an Orphics without Eurydice). The second option is to insist on the structural necessity of sexuality and, in particular, of sexual difference, not as the ahistorical referent that lurks beyond representation but, as Slavoj Žižek has reminded us recently, as the 'very obstacle' to symbolisation and representation. This approach has the distinct virtue of keeping sex in trauma theory and of insisting that the labours of historicity will always, de facto, be a matter of sexuality in some form.[6] War, thus, is (still) sex. But what kind of sex is war? Is the kind of sexual *agon* that causes us to stumble over the representation of historical trauma always and invariably the same – not so much ahistorical as unhistoricisable? In what follows, I want to approach some of these questions by taking a step back to the London Blitz and to Henry Green's novel *Caught*, written in the early stages of the war. War, we know, both threatens and provokes narrative. It threatens, as Walter Benjamin pointed out, because it degrades experience to the extent that narrative communication itself is thrown into crisis; and it provokes for precisely the same reason.[7] Silence from the writer during wartime, thus, is often less a sign of pious reticence and more a mute token of exasperated difficulty. Not so for Green, who wrote three novels during the Second World War; *Caught* (1943), *Loving* (1945) and *Back* (1946).[8] A writer who insisted from his schooldays until his death that art was emphatically *not* about representation, Green was one of the handful of British writers during the war to risk an encounter with the limits of the novel form.[9] Fascinated by the misheard, the unspoken, and the oblique (his word), Green is a trauma writer not before, but very much of his time. He is so, foremost, because like those of other modernist writers, Green's novels are not so much monuments to historical consciousness, as poetic elegies to historical unconsciousness. It is precisely what cannot be consciously realised in wartime that attracts Green; and it is from the wounds in time and experience – anxiety, death and sex – that his writing draws its understated power. Green's writing is, however, in no sense some pained lament to the inexpressible; what is registered as traumatic in his work is also, and often exuberantly, erotically charged. War – bizarrely, achingly, stupidly – is sex, not just for the inappropriately named Prudence from *Caught* (whom I quote above), but for Green too. To this extent, Green offers us an opportunity to consider, from an earlier chapter of trauma theory, how it is that there can be no trauma writing that isn't caught up with sexuality; and how it might be – and this is perhaps a more difficult proposition – that it is precisely what appears so non-historicisable about sexuality (as drive, not gender) that becomes the precondition for a way back into history amidst the rubble of the Blitz.

1   A rose is a...

It has become something of a commonplace to note that war is a threat to narrative memory. Anxiously waiting for war, however, is another matter. In his autobiography *Pack My Bag* (1940), written in the crazy days of the Munich crisis, Green notes: 'There must be a threat to one's skin to wake what is left of things remembered into things to die with.'[10] To anticipate death in the company of one's memories is, at least, to have something to give form and place to what, otherwise, would be the nowhere of anxiety. But, as Green observes, such memories are not just cushions of existential support; in shock we awaken memories from yesterday so that we can die with them tomorrow. The past runs into the unthinkable future; narrative chronology gives way to an anxious historicity: 'a rose blossoming into a bud' is how Maurice Blanchot later describes it.[11] This anxious historicity is the thematic and structural principle of *Caught*. Conscripts to the defence of the Home Front, Green's Auxiliary and Regular Firemen, cooks and members of the ARP (Air Raid Precaution) are caught in the interminably anxious time that came to be known as the Phoney War. This was the irreal space between the declaration of war and the first air-raids on Britain in the summer of 1940. The lines of civil defence were drawn and the papier-mâché coffins for the anticipated thousands of air-raid victims were made to order; for ten months the civilian population looked to the sky, but still the bombs did not fall, while from the east and south the relentless destruction and Nazification of Europe moved closer. It is, writes Green in his frontispiece to the novel, 'the effect of that time that I have written into the fiction of *Caught*'.

For the novel's two central characters, the working-class, newly promoted Fire Station Officer Pye, and the middle-class, volunteer auxiliary fireman Roe, the effect of that time of waiting is the incursion of the past into the anxious present. Both are caught by memories – memories of incest, in the case of Pye ('I got a fit of rememberin' back' [p. 166]), and for Roe, of the death of his wife and the abduction of his son ('absorbed by what was left to him of the sights and sounds' [p. 63]), that flare up in the text in intense and vivid image-clusters. It is these persistent image-memories that come to index the horror of the future, barely disguised in the two characters' anagrammatical py(e)ro(e)technic coupling, the technological hellfire that was the Blitz – narrated only twice in the entire novel. To write 'the effect of that time', hence, is not to be understood (prosaically, we might say) as producing an epic account of how war affects people, but as a way of registering the effects of a suffocating national historicity. One must look to the montage techniques of a film such as Humphrey Jennings's *Fires Were Started* (1943), and not, say, to the wholly successful tragi-pathos of *Mrs Miniver* (1942), to find the visual equivalent of Green's literary practice. *Caught*, then, is not only a psychoanalytically informed genealogy of trauma, an exploration of the belated effects of the past upon the present lives of war-anxious characters who are all, in their way, different traumatic 'types'. It is also a text which, in the tradition that Benjamin associated with Baudelaire and Proust, gives poetic form and shape to the trauma, not of the told, but of the telling.[12] How can one tell an anxious historicity? What does it take to imagine a rose blossoming into a bud? A passage towards the end of the novel suggests how (and what it might take), and is worth looking at in some detail, not only because it hints at how *Caught* might be read, but because it prompts certain questions about that reading. On sick leave recovering from the effects of the Blitz ('A bomb came too close. It knocked him out...They called it nervous debility' [p. 172]), Roe tries to explain to his evacuated sister-in-law, Dy, what it's like to live through a Blitz:

'I never felt so alone in all my life. Our taxi was like a pink beetle drawing a peppercorn. We were specks. Everything is so different always from what you expect, and this was fantastic. Of course, we couldn't hear for the noise of the engine, and we had shut the windows so as to get more inside...Yet I suppose it was not like that at all really. One changes everything by going over it.'

'But the real thing,' she said, getting her teeth into this, for she liked arguments, and the bit about the beetle had drawn her attention because she thought it vivid, 'the real thing is the picture you carry in your eye afterwards, surely? It can't be what you can't remember can it?'

'I don't know,' he said, 'only the point about a blitz is this, there's always something you can't describe, and it's not the blitz alone that's true of. Ever since it happened I feel I've been trying to express all sorts of things.'

'I expect that's the result of your being blown up.'

'No,' he said, exasperated suddenly, 'there's an old fault of yours, you're always trying to explain difficult things prosaically.'

'What's prosaically?' she asked. She did not understand.

pp. 179–80

This quarrel will be familiar to anyone who has attempted to track debates within recent trauma theory. Dy wants a referential theory of experience; Roe tells her that the point about traumatic experience is that it is not simply something that cannot be immediately understood.[13] Dy clings to the idea that the 'real thing' is the perceptual photographic picture 'that you carry in your eye' after the event; for her, Roe's problems with expression are the predictable outcome of the mechanical violence of shock. For Roe, the exasperated trauma theorist, the image – far from being a handy retinal mnemonic imprint awaiting later development – was compromised to begin with. It is not only that 'one changes everything by going over it'; just before this exchange, Roe had already explained that to witness an event is not to have any unmediated access to the 'real thing': 'One's imagination is so literary'; it is 'more like a film, or that's what it seems like at the time' (p. 174). This common modernist complaint about the already written nature of experience opens up a place for a kind of writing that traces the residues and negatives of that experience; a writing that begins with what 'you can't remember' and 'what you can't describe'. For the point about a blitz – and the point about trauma – is that it marks the difficulty of catching the 'real thing' within the limits of whatever representational means are at hand, in this case the filmic and the literary. This much is as familiar to contemporary trauma theory as it is to modernism and psychoanalysis. But why (to ask a prosaic question) is it a woman who gets to play the naïve referential historicist here? How come it is she who can't get the point about the eloquent historicity of the unspeakable in trauma?

One would indeed have to be literal-minded to miss the point that it is precisely the filmic image ('We were specks') and the literary imagination ('Our taxi was like a pink beetle drawing a peppercorn'), or the 'vivid' parts of Roe's account, that draw Dy's attention in the first place. Both accounts of the Blitz in *Caught* are similarly vivid rosy colour-fields; the burning docks, for instance, are 'a mosaic aglow with rose' (p. 181). It is the intensive build-up of colour words that gives the text, and the war, its erotic charge. It would have been better, the narrator notes at one point, for the grey fire engines to have been painted pink, 'a boudoir shade, to match that half light which was to settle, night after night, around the larger conflagrations' (p. 149). In this, it is not only the Blitz that is a mosaic of rose, but *Caught* itself. Green (a chosen pen name) was by no means the only modernist to fold experience into chromatic pockets.[14] Freud had already suggested that while 'the linear outlines like those in a drawing or in a primitive painting' cannot do justice to the characteristics of the mind, 'areas of colour melting into one another as they are presented by modern artists' can.[15] Benjamin, too, as Howard Caygill has demonstrated recently, looked to 'chromatic infinity' as an internal limit point within the modern organisation of experience.[16] Green shares Benjamin's fascination with word and image and with the distinction between colour in painting and colour in fantasy. He shares with Freud the idea that chromatic melting can index the non-temporality of the unconscious and, by implication, of unconscious desire – which is why Green's roses can, within the same verbal space, light up the horror of a blitz and turn boudoir-pink. What I referred to earlier as an anxious historicity emerges in *Caught* as a chromatic montage that flowers into the text at periodic intervals, turning narrative time into erotic space. But what has such chromatic montage got to do with prosaic women?

Where contemporary trauma theory is concerned, in Cathy Caruth's phrase, with 'permitting history to arise where immediate understanding may not' (*Caruth*, p. 11) – the eloquent historicity of trauma – in Green's writing, women arise where history cannot – eloquence purchased at a gendered price. Female flesh, as translucent as a rose petal, stretches over the absence of historical experience. To be 'caught' in anxious expectation, to wait for war, is to flesh out the gaps in 'immediate understanding' with a fantasy of sexual difference. In this sense Roe is not only the sophisticated theorist of the unspeakable in trauma, he is also something of a fetishist. Roe supplements the threat to his skin, the aching 'dreading forward' towards a war which stubbornly refuses to unfurl into an event, with graphically *imagistic* memories of his dead wife.[17] He 'could not keep his hands off her in memory … the touch of her rose petal skin' (p. 33). Like a fetishist, Roe substitutes overevaluation for absence. He also has a penchant for the banality of the sexual, as well as of the literary cliché. Lawrentian passages dehisce into exuberant profusions of roses:

> He thought he saw the hot, lazy luxuriance of a rose, the heavy, weightless, luxuriance of a rose, the curling disclosure of the heart of a rose that, as for a hornet, was his for its honey, for the asking, open to him to pierce inside, this heavy, creamy girl turned woman … the opulence his darling had carried about in her skin, sheathed for his display to his sense, in the exuberance of his mother's garden. Her bare legs had been the colour of the white roses about them, the red toenails, through her sandals, stood out against fallen rose leaves of a red that clashed with the enamel she used, the brick paths had been fresh, not stained, as the walls here, by soot-saturated rain.
>
> p. 65

This is not Rilke colour-musing with Cézanne; it is Green giving a literary reply to the thick brushstrokes, the rich build-up of oil on canvas, of his friend (and at the time, his rival in love), the painter Matthew Smith.[18] Just as in Smith's paintings, where surface texture lights up the colours of his series of women and their metonymical roses, here too perceptual mimesis is arrested by opulence.[19] These painterly and literary surfaces are as much part-objects as roses and painted toenails. Sentimental author of his own desire, Roe faces the threat of the future by erecting an image-memorial to the past. But such 'things remembered' also reveal the traces of the threat they are intended to conceal. Barely two pages later, Roe is called to his first fire-drill of the war. Again, he recalls his wife, but this time her image is only barely distinguishable from the future menace he anticipates:

> They were mute in a vast asphalted space. The store towered above, pile after dark pile which, gradually, light after light went darker than the night that was falling. For twenty minutes at dusk the scene was his wife's eyes, wet with tears he thought, her long lashes those black railings, everywhere wet, but, in the air the menace of what was yet to be experienced, the beginning.
>
> p. 37

A rose blossoms into a bud, the yet-to-flower terror of the Blitz.

Green, then, makes time flow backwards and forwards in *Caught* through a flowery chromaticism that turns images of anxiety into images of desire – and vice versa. But for Roe, the middle-class male hopelessly socially adrift in the homosocial class-mix of the Fire Brigade, this anxious, tenacious (and sometimes tedious) heterosexual desire is wholly self-referential: rosy pictorial memory-making, as the missing 's' in his own name indicates, is an act of narcissistic self-making. Sexual difference, in this instance, is a structure that allows this self-authoring to work: by incorporating the dead other into the self, Roe also subsumes the threat of difference, which is also the menace of the war, into the logic of the same. The relation between war and sex here is not so much tautological as supplementary: the menace of war, the nowhere of anxiety, is supplemented by the dead woman and the somewhere of heterosexuality. This heteroerotic memorialising is about as non-historicisable as literary or aesthetic form, or indeed fetishism. Roe's voluntary memories made up of surface texture and cliché are clearly embedded within the necrophilic tradition of literary modernism – but this isn't necessarily what makes them historical. What makes both Roe's sentimental authoring and *Caught* itself symptoms of their time is, as we will see, the *failure* of these opulent image memories, and so the failure of sexual difference, to make up for the absence of meaning occasioned by war.

Where Roe's roses swell up, so to speak, from the inside, for the working-class Pye, sex, or more precisely sex *as* traumatic memory, comes at him from the outside. In the anxiety of the present, Pye is 'caught' by the revelation of incestuous sex with his sister (currently locked up in a mental asylum, charged with having abducted Roe's son). No more than Roe can Pye live in the present; but where his bourgeois underling takes fetishistic solace in the past, Pye compulsively imagines forwards by constructing fantasy situations in which he has the authority denied him in real life – what one does in one's head in *Caught* is a matter of class as well as of sex. Half asleep, dreaming up a scenario in which he goes to visit his sister (taking with him 'a comb with rose briars painted on top'), Pye 'pictures himself' in a confrontation with the family doctor: '"Is there any history in your family, Mr Pye?"' asks the doctor, to which Pye responds, '"Istory, what do you mean by 'istory?"' (p. 87) – a question that might well be asked of the text, as well as of Pye. Pye does have a history, but he doesn't encounter it in his dream (unlike the father in Freud's famous example of the dream of the burning son, Pye puts out fires for a living; like the father, he sleeps to keep trauma at bay). It is only towards the end of the novel that he keeps this belated appointment:

> Without any warning, and with a shock that took all his breath, Pye saw the dry wood shaving creep, bent in the moonlight, the back way to their cottage. He saw it again as though it were before his eyes, which he now tried to draw away from the doctor's...In a surge of blood it was made *clear*, *false*, that it might have been his own sister he was with that night. So it might have been her voice, thick with excitement and fright and disgust that said 'Will it hurt?' So in the blind moonlight, eyes warped by his need, he must have forced his own sister.
>
> p. 140, my emphasis

In contrast to Roe's memories, Pye's revelations are not illuminated: the memory is 'clear, false' in the *blindness* of the moonlight. That cognitive equation is inherent in the traumatic act that is half-revealed here. Incest, famously, is taboo because it thwarts the means by which cultural meanings are made. In this context, incest is like war; not because they are taboo (war clearly isn't), but because both cause problems for instantiation: neither the meaning of war nor the meaning of incest reside in concrete acts, but outside them, in symbol-formation (or in the symbolic exchange of women and signs).[20] Roe's trauma-theory-as-fetishism is one way of keeping something like a symbolic exchange going: as war is to woman, so dread is to a rose, so the threat to one's skin is to an enamelled toenail, so formlessness is to aesthetic opulence, so blindness is to vision. By contrast, Pye's exchange mechanism fails him completely. Nothing is illuminated. It is misperception, not perception, that prevails in the black-out: '"What"', he asks Roe just before his death, '"d'you make of this moonlight, I mean the black-out … D'you mistake objects in it, 'ave you taken one person for another?"' (p. 157). Here the tautology – war is sex – is grotesquely operative; wandering through the black-out, 'too disturbed to notice the invasion of Norway' (p. 133), Pye finally sticks his head in a gas oven before the first bombs fall.

2   … rose is a rose …

Green was not the only observer to note that surreally particular to the British Home Front was the uncanny way in which the anxious space of a nation under siege, ghosted by phantoms half-glimpsed in the black-out, exteriorised the unconscious, made fantasy look like reality and war look like sex. Many psychoanalysts too worried about this erotically charged public sphere, as indeed did the ministries of Health and Information.[21] As in *Caught*, this worrisome desiring anxiety manifests itself most clearly in terms of vision: war, like sex and indeed like art, is a matter of the image, of what can and ought to be seen. The psychoanalyst Melitta Schmideberg, Melanie Klein's daughter, for example, noted how scopophilic impulses played their part in the Blitz in the following description:

> During the day, ruined buildings revealed to the curious their inmost secrets. Here two walls were gone, but a table laid with cutlery and glass stood intact. There nothing remained but a single wall with a suspended bath aloft. A patient was astonished because so many nice houses looked so incredibly dirty, and he gleefully described a house of which only one wall was left and where, above the mantelpiece, one could see a number of pornographic pictures.[22]

War blasts apart the home to reveal its sordid secrets to the world (this, too, is Pye's tragedy). The ruins of a city, the rubble of the civic, are, of course, powerful metonymies for the death and wounding of its inhabitants. In descriptions such as this however, as in *Caught*, it is as if sex, in the form of the image, begins to arise at the precise moment when the phenomenologisation of the wound becomes, apparently, impossible. There is a correlative moment to Schmideberg's account of the pornographic imaginary of wound culture in *Caught*. Ducking down to a shelter amid the chaos of the first raid on London, Roe is 'gleefully' astonished to stumble across a couple in rapt, forgetful union: 'He had been kissing her mouth so it was now a blotch of red.' That 'blotch of red' however quickly begins to bleed into other images and to literally spew out of the wounds that the pornographic image (or primal scene) connotes, but cannot contain: 'The twisted creature under a blanket coughed up a last gushing gout of blood', 'Two police brought past a looter, most of his clothes torn off, heels dragging, drooling blood at the mouth' (p. 97).

Just as in the first war, when the response to this eroticisation of the wound was to take the sex out of trauma theory, so too in the second. In radio broadcasts and in the medico-psychiatric press, the advice was to separate 'realistic' anxiety from 'neurotic' anxiety, to pin anxiety to a proper 'empirical' referent and hence to sweep fantasy off the streets.[23] Ego psychology, with its influential ideology of adaptation, found a foothold here. Britain, Anna Freud suggested some years later, found a way of 'adapting' to trauma.[24] By contrast, when Jacques Lacan visited Britain at the end of the war, looking for something other than the compensatory fantasies of greatness that had marked the per-fidies of Vichy, what he found was a 'rapport véridique au réel', 'a more truthful relation to the real, that [Britain's] utilitarian ideology barely understands [and] that the term adaptation betrays completely'.[25] This is not (yet) the Lacanian real that is so crucially important to contem-porary trauma theory, but it is on its way. It would be a gross over-simplification to argue that it was the war that finally radicalised psychoanalysis. Far from it: for many, the symptomatic response to the overwhelming experience of trauma was a renewed faith in the so-called 'reality principle'. But for others, the experience of the Blitz (in Britain) and the *Blitzkrieg* (in the rest of Europe), served to confirm what they had long suspected: that anxious desire cannot be autho-rised under, to borrow a phrase from Leo Bersani, 'the collective will of the ego', but comes at the ego from elsewhere. In anxiety, one does not 'adapt' to the real; like Pye, one is 'caught' by it – just as one is caught by a picture, or (possibly more disturbing) by an image.

This 'anxious elsewhere' is precisely where Green's perspicacity about sexuality and the image ends up, as will I, after a short psychoanalytic detour. So far we have seen war turn into 'sex' in two different ways. Roe, the anxious fetishist, supplements the thought of death with a kind of compulsive citation of literary and painterly rose-coloured images that turn anxiety into desiring memory. Where Roe recollects pictures in order to collect himself, his anxious alter-ego Pye is subject to traumatic memory images which shatter meaning and identity by bringing desire and anxiety together. Green is not, however, comparing anxious character-types. *Caught* itself resembles what it describes. The text compulsively assembles image-clusters, pockets of chromatic prosody, as if to give some kind of temporary stability to a narrative that otherwise risks the same dissolution of meaning and identity that it adumbrates. For good reason, perhaps: Green wrote the novel while serving as an auxiliary fireman on the Home Front between, as the last words of the text inform us, June 1940 and Christmas 1942. Like many, Green was convinced that he would not survive the war. One way to approach *Caught's* anxious textual production, then, is as a meditation on the extent to which the anticipation of death can be folded into narrative representation. I have begun to suggest this anxious anticipation emerges as a kind of sexualisation, or eroticisation, of lost and anticipated experience.

Caught shares much with Freud's final theory of trauma, and in particular with his inter-war text *Inhibitions, Symptoms and Anxiety* (1926). To some extent, the Freudian theory of anxiety can be read as a metapsychological companion to Green's text – not because it interprets *Caught's* manoeuvres but because, in a backwards sort of repetition, it anticipates them. Anxiety cuts in two directions for Freud. On the one hand, it is a 'signal', a protective action which warns the ego of a potential danger to come; the signal, like an air-raid siren, announces 'I am expecting a situation of helplessness to set in'.[26] But this warning, on the other hand, is efficacious because it is predicated on the repetition of a past trauma: anxious anticipation, thus, has the potential to plunge the ego into traumatic anxiety anew and to devastate its defences. 'Dreading forward', for Freud too, carries the seeds (or the bud) of a past trauma; one which can either protect the ego (Roe) or shatter it (Pye). André Green later described that traumatic anxiety in terms of 'real instinctual impulses from the id which have broken the ego's barriers and are advancing in force towards the heart of the ego in the manner of a *Blitzkrieg*'[27]; thus neatly underscoring the way in which, although it might appear that Freud is trying to set up an opposition between 'realistic' signal, adaptive anxiety and 'neurotic', traumatic, drive-invested anxiety – an opposition between war and sex, no less – anxiety continually calls into question the oppositions that are set up to contain it.[28] It is precisely because the id can advance on the ego in the manner of a *Blitzkrieg*, and, for that matter, because a *Blitzkrieg* can advance on the ego in the manner of an id, that an apparently realistic anxiety can flower into an eroticism, as Henry Green has demonstrated. What is more important for some of the arguments I have been trying to advance here, however, is Freud's definition of that traumatic anxiety – a definition that turns on death, sexuality and the image.

Traumatic anxiety cannot arise out of a fear of death, for the well-known reason that there is no representation of death in the unconscious.[29] As Freud puts it in *Inhibitions*, in yet another rebuttal of the unsexing of trauma theory in the First World War, 'The unconscious seems to contain nothing that could give any content to our concept of the annihilation of life' (*Inhibitions*, p. 138). The thesis that the shell-shocked soldiers of the first war were reacting to death threats to their instincts of self-preservation falls to the ground, as Freud pointed out as early as 1918, once it is understood that our relation to ourselves is libidinised, that is, narcissistic.[30] The image of the absolute annihilation of the self is simply off limits for the subject of psychoanalysis: if I picture my own death, I am still there, still watching and so representing myself to myself, and therefore I am not dead. This may be why when we feel a threat to our skin we awaken memories to die not only with us but, perhaps, *for* us, vicariously. Anticipating death, therefore, is not what traumatises the subject; rather, it is the unmitigated repetition of an experience that feels *like* death that overwhelms the ego. Thus, says Freud, 'fear of death should be regarded as analogous to the fear of castration' (*Inhibitions*, p. 138) – and this may be why imagining things to die with reinstates sexual difference with such forcefulness. If the signs of anatomical difference for the heterosexual male are taken as proof positive of the reality of castration, one way to fend off the threat to oneself is by demonstrating – over and over again – that it will not happen to you, because it has already happened to her. The fetishist takes a less prosaic and less murderous approach: finding roses in place of wounds, he affirms sexual difference at the point where he denies it ('for', as Freud puts it barely one year after *Inhibitions*, 'if a woman had been castrated, then his own possession of a penis was in danger').[31] Both reinstating and muddling the terms of sexual difference, in other words, are also ways of dealing with death.

But castration anxiety itself has another prototype in Freud's history of the anxious ego, in the trauma of 'separation anxiety' or 'object loss'.

As Freud is careful to point out, it is not so much the loss of the mother *qua* object that causes traumatic anxiety, but more precisely 'the loss of the perception of the object (which is equated with the loss of the object itself)' (*Inhibitions*, p. 170). This distinction is crucial, because it allows us to understand why anxiety, and trauma, can never be 'realistic' (or prosaic), but will always be a matter of the image in relation to the ego, or, as Weber puts it, of 'the production and maintenance of stable cathexes, in particular of a visual nature' (*Return to Freud*, p. 155). Neither is the lost perception to be understood as referring directly to the presence or absence of the object (to 'the picture you carry in your eye afterwards', as Dy puts it); anxiety has what Freud calls 'a quality of indefiniteness', because although its presence can be signified or imaged, its object cannot be represented. Images, or 'perceptual identities', for Freud, are far from veridical; rather they betray the extent to which the subject of anxiety is always at one remove from its objects. That 'at one remove' is also the mark of sexuality: the first situation of helplessness – separation anxiety – is also the first articulation of the gap between the intolerable tension of neediness and the hallucination of the image of the object that (or so we fondly imagine) can fill that need. As Jean Laplanche has argued, this misperception at the core of the ego is the very definition, not only of anxiety, but of the sexual drive.[32] Thus it is not only the case that sexuality somehow gets into the image; traumatic anxiety ('drive attack', Laplanche calls it) both makes – and breaks – the images by which the ego constitutes itself. As well as thinking of images *of* sexuality (as pleasant as that is), it is also, therefore, just as important to understand how anxious sexuality itself becomes the condition of the image in the first place.

What, then, might be erotic about the image-clusters that swell up in *Caught* is not only their content, but the way – as if obeying the synthesising laws of Eros – they give form, recathect as it were, to the image as a protective reaction against the loss of perception signalled by anxiety. And what might (more accurately) be fetishistic about Roe's opulent rose-memories is the way in which their artifice works to retain perception, erect the image, only through (as Freud puts it in 'Fetishism') 'a very energetic action' ('Fetishism', p. 353). The thickness of the painterly surfaces of these images lets us know that the object is not so much perceived as actively made, just as the citation of cliché tells us that this active making is also an active repetition. One might be tempted to call this relation between sexuality and the image non-historicisable, always arising in the constitutional trauma of sexed subjectivity. But that would be to forget where we started. If sexuality looks

non-historicisable here it is surely because it is doing the historicising –
giving us images not *of* historical violence, but images which respond to
the threat of that violence. The 'fear of death should be regarded as analogous to the fear of castration'. 'War, she thought, is sex.'

3   ... is *not* a rose

> I too was not, nor my understanding, that resolves things out of the
> images of the senses. I was not the one who saw, but only seeing.
> And what I saw were not things ... but only colours. And I too was
> coloured into this landscape.[33]
>
> Walter Benjamin

To be 'caught' in anxious historicity, then, is to be caught up in a relation to the image. Actively remembering things to die with is also a
protest against death, or, at the very least, part of an effort to master it
through the authoring of images. Much of the pleasure of reading
Caught derives from the way that, psychoanalytically speaking, its
symptoms are also its sublimations: the sensuality of the novel's images
offers a temporary aesthetic resolution, small moments of sense-making, in a novel which – quite literally – has no image of a future in
which its tensions could be resolved. But much as Green is as caught up
in the lure of fetishistic image-making as his character Roe, *Caught* also
undoes its own already tenuous claims to authority. In the same way
the image can only arise in relation to trauma, there is a wound in the
rose which, Green suggests, has to be allowed to bud if there is to be an
alternative to a fetishistic form of historicisation. In this sense, it is Pye's
fate – the fate of one who is traumatically caught by images not of his
own making, whose eyes are 'warped by need' in the 'clear, false' blindness of the London black-out – that thematises a more troubling and
difficult relation to the image than we have seen so far.

Just as object loss lies at the core of Freud's theory of trauma – the loss
that underwrites the difficulty of living historical trauma and the sexual
trauma that follows from that difficulty – so too in *Caught*. The novel
opens with Roe trying to imagine the abduction of his son, Christopher,
by Pye's sister. It is this act of violent separation which wreathes the lives
of the novel's characters together in a melodrama (melotrauma?) of
unhappy coincidences; without Pye's incest, there would have been no
abduction, whereas for Roe himself the abduction prefigures the death of
his wife and so is caught up with his rose-memorialising. By opening
a war novel with the abduction of a child, Green confirms what Freud

sixteen years earlier had begun to explore: that trauma is less the effect of shock than an anticipated repetition of primal separation. By 1940, this thesis had not only been accepted by psychoanalysts and psychologists, but for many it was being lived historically: 'this separation that war had forced into their lives', as Green puts it elsewhere in the novel (p. 10), a separation that feels *like* death, was repeated again and again over mainland Europe. And in Britain the evacuation of children away from the city centres was felt by many to be at least as violent as an abduction.[34]

But Green is not thematising history here: once more, he writes the 'effect of his time' into the fiction of *Caught*, through a meditation on the historicising potential of the image in relation to anxious sexuality. So far we have seen how images in *Caught* eroticise anxiety; how a dreaded absence turns into a rose, then into a woman, and finally into a picture that can make sense out of anxiety. In the opening scenes of the novel, however, Green runs this series backwards, and returns us to what can be described as the origin of the image in relation to anxiety – to a kind of vertigo of the image. If roses are Roe's fetish, fear of falling is his phobia. Roe joined the auxiliary fire service because 'he had for years wanted to see inside one of these turreted buildings and also because he had always been afraid of heights' (p. 27). In classic psychoanalytic terms the taboo on the desire to see (inside one of those turreted mothers, Melanie Klein might say; inside one of those blitzed buildings, her daughter might add) is the motivating force behind the fear of heights. The anxiety of vertigo is above all an anxiety about the image – note again, not about what the image denotes, but about a drive that might overrun the sense-making properties of the image. It is not the mother we fear, but her loss – which we equate with the image – coupled with our overwhelming need.

It is significant then that in a text where all the mothers are either dead, deranged or dangerously bogus, Roe imagines his way into his son's trauma through his own vertigo. What, Green notes, was 'fatal' about the scene of Christopher's abduction was that the department store in which it took place 'had been lit by stained glass windows in front of arc lamps which cast the violent colours of that glass over the goods laid out on counters' (p. 11). As for the son, so too for the father, who falls into this chromatic violence by recalling a childhood vertigo attack during a visit to Tewkesbury Abbey, where

> He had that terror of the urge to leap, his back to deep violet and yellow Bible stories on the glass, his eyes reluctant over the whole grey stretch of the Abbey until they were drawn, abruptly as to a chasm,

inevitably, and so far beneath, down to that floor hemmed with pews, that height calling on the pulses he did not know why to his ears, down to dropped stone flags over which sunlight had cast the colour in each window, the colour it seemed his blood had turned.

p. 12

The terror of the urge to leap lies not in the death that awaits one on the stone flags beneath ('the unconscious [contains] nothing that could give any content to our concept of the annihilation of life'). The terror, rather, lies in being 'caught' between the 'deep violet and yellow' of the windows, and the reflection of the colours on the stones; of being caught, in other words, between two images. What is 'traumatic' about the image here is not what it denotes but the extent to which it dissolves the opposition between a perceiving subject (one who gives form to the image of colour) and perceived image. As the light on the stone flags turns into 'the colour it seemed his blood had turned', Roe's body bleeds into the image he not only sees, but is 'caught' or seen by. It is as if the connotational properties of the roses that elsewhere flower up *in media res* are sucked dry; only a kind of visceral colour – the zero-degree point of signification of any image – remains. One cannot catch these colours, actively perceive them as a whole image, erotically bind them into pictures to fend off death; one is caught between them. This too is Christopher's fate who, while 'held to ransom by the cupidity of boys', 'lost in feelings of this colour' (p. 13) thrown by the light of the department store windows onto goods laid on the counter, is abducted, not so much by a woman posing as a mother, but by fantasmatic colour:

> Words were not means of communication now … when she pulled at his jacket, he did look up and saw nothing strange in how she was, *caught* full by the light from those windows, so that her skin was blue and her orbs, already sapphire, a sea flashing at hot sunset as, uneasy, she glanced left, then right … At the angle she now held herself she lost those rose diamonds in her eyes, these were shaded and so had gone an even deeper blue. He became dazzled by the pink neon lights beyond her features. *Caught* in another patch of colour, some of her chin was pillar-box red, also a part of the silver fox she wore … she *caught* full at him with her eyes that, by the ocean in which they were steeped, were so much part of the world his need had made, and so much part of it by being alive, then he felt everything must be natural, and was ready to do whatever she asked.
>
> p. 14, my emphases

'So much part of the world his need had made', and yet Christopher is dazzled, caught by the infinite vertiginous contrast of colours that only barely let the form of Pye's sister come into focus.

If it is true, as Mark Cousins has suggested, that pictures are defences against the return of traumatic images, then in the opening scenes of the novel it is as if Green is diagnosing what will later become the text's own defence mechanisms.[35] The threat that such images pose is that of not being able to 'occupy' them with a representation – with a rose, for instance. And if that trauma, psychoanalytically speaking, marks the heterogeneity of the sexual drives in relation to representation, so too, for Green at least, does the violence of the Blitz. The abduction scene ends by firelight. Christopher yells. 'She put both hands over her mouth, which was wide open, and so left, in the shadow, a dark hole between firelit fingers over a dark face' (p. 16). Compare this to the passage with which I began:

> They saw the water below a dirty yellow towards the fire; the wharves on that far side low and black, those on the bank they were leaving a pretty rose … This fan, a roaring red gold, pulsed rose at the outside edge, the perimeter round which the heavens, set with stars before fading into utter blackness, were for a space a trembling green.

The 'dark hole between firelit fingers' now 'pulses rose' in the fires of the Blitz; just as the 'blotch of red' in the scene in the air-raid shelter haemorrhages into the wounds of war. Green's colour words beat a circuitous path between the body and the world, thwarting the opposition between the two. This dissolution of boundaries is repeated in the organisation of the text. *Caught* begins with an abduction scene and ends with a description of the Blitz; the two blocks of narration are typographically and stylistically equivalent; both cut up Roe's free indirect discourse, for example, by putting areas of text in parentheses, not in order to establish a narrative hierarchy, but to mark off (to cite Freud once more) 'areas of colour melting into one another'. These chromatic pockets do not 'make sense' in the same way as Roe's opulent rose-memories. They are, rather, assaults on the senses. What the Blitz and Christopher's abduction share is a break-up of images – a kind of anti-cathexis, to use psychoanalytic terms. Words, the psychoanalyst and army medical officer Wilfred Bion noted later, can be hallucinations; images which appear, he says, as 'evacuated objects' (there were more ways than one of being evacuated in the Second World War).[36] The point about a blitz, Green seems to be saying here, and what perhaps makes it so difficult to describe, is the way its lurid sensuality sends those 'evacuated objects' back to us, destroying the opposition between inside and outside (evacuating the subject) and thus attacking the ability to categorise or describe experience. Another name for such an attacking force is the death drive – 'the extreme of sexuality'.[37] Leaving 'a pretty rose' beyond the synthesising powers of Eros, Green (trembling) finally gives us something to die with. Unlike Céline, whose work he admired intensely, Green is not, I would argue, aestheticising the death drive here. Rather, he writes 'the effect of his time' by marking a moment when it no longer becomes possible to fend off the effects of history with a fetish. This, it seems to me at least, is a thoroughly historical endeavour.

4   Goodbye England's Rose

Green's meticulous attention to the workings of anxious desire and the image might be thought of as a late chapter in a modernism which (certainly since Baudelaire) tracks the peripateticism of human sexuality as a way of marking the trauma of modernity. It is as if Eros began to falter at some point; or perhaps it is more accurate to say that psychoanalysis – like the literary history it parallels – has provided us with a language that can make that failure visible and, to some extent, intelligible. It was the First World War that prompted Freud to consider what kind of representational economy lay beyond the synthesising powers of Eros. The speculative daring of *Beyond the Pleasure Principle*, its stops and starts, its leaps and equivocations (remember Freud's famous 'limping' metaphor), mean that it has a justifiably canonical place in contemporary trauma theory. It should not be forgotten, however, that the concept of the death drive has had something of a chequered history over the last eighty years. Rejected at the time by the majority for its speculative excess, and embraced by others because it seemed to offer psychoanalysis a new foundation (for the Kleinians) or means of critique (for the Surrealists), the death drive's various manifestations – as the repetition compulsion, as the Nirvana principle, as aggressivity, as the 'extreme of sexuality' – are always partly (but perhaps only partly) contingent upon the historical exigencies it is brought on to account for or to answer to.[38]

   With this thought in mind, one final word about Henry Green. Green's next but one novel, *Back* (1946), tells the story of a returning soldier's anguished and deluded mourning for his dead lover. Her 'name, of all names, was Rose' (p. 4). Coincidentally, Green's anti-hero, Charley Summers, limps because he 'had lost his leg in France for not noticing the gun beneath a rose' (p. 3).[39] Whereas Roe in *Caught* erected rose-memorials to his dead love in order to imagine an unimaginable future, in *Back* Charley is unable to make a fetish out of his Rose's absence. Rather, as he begins to 'awkwardly search for Rose, through roses', her name comes at him from the outside world; from shop windows ('in a secondhand booksellers with a set of Miss Rhoda Broughton...his eyes read a title, *Cometh up as a Flower*'; 'also in a seed merchant's front..."Carter's patent Rose"'; 'from a wireless shop, a record through loudspeakers of "Honeysuckle Rose"' [pp. 63–4]); in the words of others ('Mrs Frazier spoke of rising prices. "Why," she said, "they rose, they've rose"' [p. 39]); in time itself ('only to find roses grown between the minutes and hours and so entwined that the hands were stuck' [p. 7]), and finally in the form of Rose's half-sister, Nancy Whitmore, whom Charley doggedly pursues convinced that she is his lost love.

There is no space for interiority in *Back*: no imagistic memorialising as self-authoring. Charley's fate is wholly determined by the agency of the roses that relentlessly pursue him through the text. The unconscious in *Back* is structured like the language of a wartime economy – a language of rations, shortages, rising prices and of dead, missing and evacuated persons. Lovers, like the workers and tools in the wartime industry that Charley helps administer, can be replaced. But the most striking aspect of this novel is Green's commitment to a sense of the ordinariness of the trauma of the missed encounters that get tangled up in the letters of his novel. In the end it simply doesn't matter much if Charley's life is scripted beyond his conscious desires. That script, in this sense, *is* what lies beyond Eros (or beyond Rose). To live a life in which one's history and one's fate are so cruelly beyond the limits of one's wishes (beyond the ego, Lacan would say) is painful, but the results are not always fatal. The death drive can play comedy as well as tragedy, as Charley finally explains to Nancy:

'Anyway, it took a bit of forgetting, but I've forgotten now all right.'
'All's well that ends well, then.'
'Least said, soonest mended,' she agreed.

p. 188

This, perhaps, is something like what Lacan may have meant when he spoke of that 'rapport véridique au réel' on the British Home Front.

Notes

1. Ewan Smith, sceptic of all matters psychoanalytic, first introduced me to Henry Green. He will not approve of what follows, but I thank him. I am also indirectly indebted throughout to Rod Mengham's *The Idiom of the Time: The Writings of Henry Green* (Cambridge: Cambridge University Press, 1982).
2. T. S. Eliot, at the end of 'Little Gidding'. For a strikingly different twist on the same comparison, see Elizabeth Bowen's short story 'Look at all those Roses' (1941).
3. 'In the war people in our walk of life entertained all sorts and conditions of men, with a view to self-preservation, to keep the privileges we set store ... after those to whom we were kind enough to win the war for us'; Green, *Pack My Bag* (1940; London: Hogarth, 1979), p. 68.
4. See Cathy Caruth, *Unclaimed Experience: Trauma, Narrative and History* (Baltimore: Johns Hopkins University Press, 1996).
5. For a rigorous argument as to why the historical and the psychic cannot and should not be thought of analogically, see Joan Copjec, *Read My Desire: Lacan Against The Historicists* (Cambridge: MIT Press, 1994).
6. This approach gets risky when the analysis of psychosexual structures of fantasy starts to roam into the domain of historically lived experience. The intricacies of interpassivity and fantasy, for example, are clearly not the only reasons why women write more papers than they publish. It is one thing to insist, rightly, on the sexualisation of trauma, but another to do so by eliding the extent to which trauma, like fantasy, is always historically mediated. For the quotation above, see Slavoj Žižek, *The Plague of Fantasies* (London: Routledge, 1997).
7. See Walter Benjamin, 'The Storyteller: Reflections on the works of Nikolai Lestov', in *Illuminations*, trans. H. Zohn (London: Jonathan Cape, 1970).
8. Green saw the war as presenting new stylistic opportunities for writing. In a defence of C. M. Doughty, he notes: 'Now that we are at war, is not the advantage for writers, and for those who read them, that they will be forced, by the need they have to fight, to go out into territories, it may well be at home, which they would never otherwise have visited, and they will be forced, by way of their own selves, towards a style which, by the impact of a life strange to them and by their honest acceptance of this, will be as pure as Doughty's was, so that they will reach each one his own style that shall be his monument?' 'Apologia', originally published in *Folios*, no. 4 (1941), reprinted in *Surviving: The Uncollected Works of Henry Green*, ed., M. Yorke (London: Chatto and Windus, 1992).
9. Others belonging in this hand include Elizabeth Bowen (*Look at all those Roses* [short stories], 1941; *The Demon Lover* [short stories], 1945; *The Heat of the Day*, 1948); Patrick Hamilton (*Slaves of Solitude*, 1947); Inez Holden (*Night Shift*, 1941); William Sansom (*Fireman Flower and other stories*, 1944); and Virginia Woolf (*Between the Acts*, 1941).
10. *Pack My Bag*, p. 54. The search for 'things remembered' had, of course, become formulaic by the time Green and other second-generation Modernists were writing. Compare William Sansom's narrator in 'Fireman Flower': 'One wishes to envisage the future; one cannot; one casts around

for a substitute; one substitutes the picture of the past, sufficiently alien from the present, a vision – yet one that can be controlled' (p. 150). By contrast, from the first generation, Virginia Woolf despairs at the way the turbulence of the present war prevents the easy interpenetration of past and present: 'But to feel the present sliding over the past, peace is necessary. The present must be smooth, habitual.' 'A Sketch of the Past', in *Moments of Being*, ed. J. Schulkind (London: Grafton, 1982), p. 114.

11. Maurice Blanchot, *The Writing of the Disaster*, trans. A. Smock (Lincoln and London: University of Nebraska Press, 1995), p. 36.
12. See Walter Benjamin, 'Some Motifs in Baudelaire', and 'The Image of Proust', in *Illuminations*.
13. Caruth, *Unclaimed Experience*, pp. 10–11.
14. 'Henry Green' was the pen name of Henry Yorke. Rod Mengham notes how Yorke settled for Green only after toying with Browne.
15. Sigmund Freud, 'The Dissection of the Psychic Personality', *New Introductory Lectures on Psychoanalysis*, trans, J. Strachey (London: Penguin, 1988), p. 112.
16. Howard Caygill, *Walter Benjamin: The Colour of Experience* (London and New York: Routledge, 1998), pp. 9–13, 82–6.
17. 'Dreading forward' is a phrase Green used in his unfinished actual account of firefighting, *London and Fire 1940*, extracts from which were published under the title 'Before the Great Fire'; reprinted in *Surviving*. See also Green's short story of interminable waiting, 'The Lull' (1943), also reprinted in *Surviving*.
18. The woman was the indomitable and beautiful Mary Keene, and the rivalry was amicable. After Smith's 1944 show at the Redfern Gallery, Green wrote to him: 'Why we must all be grateful to you all our lives is that you have put into women everything that goes to make up our loves and have made a glory out of what is glorious … I came away feeling as though my self had been restated'; quoted in Alice Keene, *The Two Mr Smiths: The Life and Work of Sir Matthew Smith 1879–1959* (London: Lund Humphries, 1995), p. 68. Note how putting into women restates the self: it is this kind of gendering as self-engendering that I am tracing here.
19. Elaine Scarry has recently argued that 'perceptual mimesis' is the common property of literary vegetation. It is much easier, Scarry notes, to recall a flower to mind than a face. By comparison, Green's writing blocks such perceptual mimesis both through the profusion of the flowers themselves and by a stylistic imitation – or by literary rather than a perceptual mimesis – of similar passages in the work of the key progenitors of the flowery funeral tradition in literary modernism, Baudelaire, Proust and Lawrence. See Elaine Scarry, 'Imagining Flowers: Perceptual Mimesis', in *Representations* 57 (Winter 1997), pp. 90–115.
20. Mengham, *The Idiom of the Time*, p. 85. Gayle Rubin was the first to reveal the feminist implications of the structure of exchange for anthropology; Elizabeth Cowie and Luce Irigaray did the same for psychoanalytic theory. See Elaine Scarry's *The Body In Pain: The Making and Unmaking of the World* (Oxford: Oxford University Press, 1987) for a thorough analysis of the referential instability of war (pp. 60–157).
21. For an account of these worries see my article 'Anxiety at a Time of Crisis', *History Workshop Journal*, 45 (Spring, 1998), pp. 171–82.

22. Melitta Schmideberg, 'Some Observations on Individual Reactions to Air-Raids', *International Journal of Psycho-Analysis*, 23 (1942), pp. 146–76.

23. See for example Edward Glover's BBC radio broadcasts reprinted in *The Psychology of Fear and Courage* (London: Harmondsworth, 1940).

24. Anna Freud, 'Comments on Trauma', in *Psychic Trauma*, ed., S. Furst (New York: Basic Books, 1967), p. 238. However, she goes on to caution against over-hasty judgements about the status of historical trauma. 'This', she notes, 'happened during the war when Americans, from the greater safety of their home scene, thought of their British friends under bombing as exposed to continuous traumatisation, or as 'heroic', while in Britain at this time stimulus barriers had been raised to include the danger as a familiar, non-traumatic item' (p. 239). For a chilling account of how Americans might be educated to see the threat of nuclear war as a 'familiar non-traumatic item', see I. L. Janis, *Air War and Emotional Stress: Psychological Studies of Bombing and Civilian Defense* (New York: McGraw Books, 1951). Janis's study is based on accounts of the civilian bombing of Europe and Japan in the Second World War.

25. Jacques Lacan, 'La Psychiatrie anglaise et la guerre', in *Evolution psychiatrique*, vol. 1 (Paris, 1947), pp. 293–318.

26. Sigmund Freud, *Inhibitions, Symptoms and Anxiety*, Standard Edition, vol. 20, p. 166.

27. André Green, 'Conceptions of Affect', in *On Private Madness* (Madison, CT: International Universities Press, 1986), p. 206.

28. The argument about anxiety refusing to fit into the oppositional structures that are established to contain it is Samuel Weber's. See his 'The Witch's Letter', in *Return to Freud: Jacques Lacan's Dislocation of Psychoanalysis*, trans. M. Levine (Cambridge: Cambridge University Press, 1991), p. 157.

29. Melanie Klein, by contrast, did believe that there was an unconscious representation of death. For accounts of how that belief was implicated in the theoretical discussions that virtually tore apart the British psychoanalytic community during the Second World War, see Jacqueline Rose, 'Negativity in the work of Melanie Klein', and 'War in the Nursery', in *Why War? Psychoanalysis, Politics and the Return to Melanie Klein* (Oxford: Blackwell, 1993).

30. Introduction to *Psycho-Analysis and the War Neuroses*, Standard Edition, vol. 17.

31. Sigmund Freud, 'Fetishism', in *On Sexuality* (London: Harmondsworth, 1987), p. 352.

32. Jean Laplanche, 'A Metapsychology Put to the Test of Anxiety', *International Journal of Psycho-Analysis*, 62 (1981), p. 89.

33. Walter Benjamin, *The Rainbow: A Dialogue on Phantasie*. Quoted and trans. by Howard Caygill, *Walter Benjamin: The Colour of Experience*, p. 11.

34. For responses to the evacuation, see Tom Harrison et al., eds, *War Begins At Home* (London: Chatto and Windus, 1940).

35. Mark Cousins, 'The Traumatic Image: Vertigo', unpublished paper presented at The Society for Humanities, Cornell University, April 1998.

36. Wilfred Bion, 'On Hallucination', in *Second Thoughts* (New Jersey and London: Jason Aronson, 1993), p. 75.

37. Laplanche, 'A Metapsychology', p. 86. Or as Henry Green himself remarked, 'any work of art, if it is alive, carries the germs of its death, like any other living thing, around with it'. 'An Unfinished Novel', in *Surviving*, p. 254.

38. I argue this point in more detail in 'From Bokhara to Samarra: The Destructive Element in Psychoanalysis and Modernism', in *The Destructive Element: British Psychoanalysis and Modernism* (London: Macmillan, 1998).

39. In an uncanny act of identification – or appropriation – it was in fact Green's lover, Mary Keene, who had a prosthetic leg.

4
The Timeless Elsewhere of the Second World War: Rosamond Lehmann's *The Ballad and the Source* and Kate O'Brien's *The Last of Summer*

Phyllis Lassner

The place and reputation of 1940s British fiction has remained elusive, both as a location in modern literary history and as a definable tradition. Until very recent studies, especially of women writers, it has been the unhappy fate of the 1940s to languish in the shadow of modernist experiments of the 1920s and early 1930s.[1] For critics searching for political or ideological substrata, the 1940s also seem to pale in comparison with the 1930s and 1950s. The 1930s have been reclaimed for their seething rebellions against the exclusionary cultural values of high modernism, and the 1950s for their discontent with the diffused material values of suburbia.[2] Right in their midst and yet distinct from these traditions, the 1940s have yet to gain a firm foothold in the modern literary canon. Even as postmodernist critics are building bridges of literary experimentation to connect contemporary writing and modernism, the span leaps with great agility over the 1940s, producing the effect that its literary production doesn't matter or lacks sufficient experimental cachet to be taken seriously.[3] Certain key texts, like T. S. Eliot's *Four Quartets*, are showcased as exceptions and incorporated into the modernist canon, because it is taken for granted that his continuing oeuvre erases boundaries of formal definition and ideology.[4] These critical strategies ignore what could be explored about the fiction of the 1940s as both historically and literarily distinctive, not to mention interesting.

Part of the problem is the contested literary critical term – historical. For formalist critics of modernist literary history, this has suggested a range of narrative experiments that reflected a philosophical break from the nineteenth-century acceptance of and reliance on empirical observations of human behaviour and motivation as both psychologically accessible and stable enough to follow a comprehensible development from childhood through adulthood. For postmodernists, this break extends to questioning whether social scientific hermeneutic and epistemological perspectives are themselves reliable or stable. As a result of this break, historical boundaries are constantly being crossed, defying the viability of historically documented events and monuments that distinguished one literary movement from another. When history is invoked by both modernists and postmodernists what is meant are the ideologies that framed, perhaps shaped, and helped define historical events and periods, and rarely the events themselves.[5]

These approaches to literary history cannot but have helped to efface the 1940s, a decade synonymous with a historical event whose material realities overwhelm any debates about uncertain hermeneutics or epistemology. The Second World War, with over 100 million casualties, the Holocaust and unambiguous evil empire, has, in its destructiveness and destabilisation, left historians with so little ground to destabilise themselves, that in the wake of the Nazis' industrialised death camps, philosophers and historians have agreed that there is only one meaning to be gleaned from the waste, that it must never happen again.[6] The questions that remain can only address how to understand the nature of complicity with Hitler's evil and how to take in the magnitude of his destructive intentions, means and ends.

Because the victory over the Axis powers exerted a sense of finality, of justice finally if woefully won, there seemed very little left to say about it except to rebuild Europe and hopefully in a more progressive temper. That this feeling is reflected more in the critical assessment of the literature of the 1940s than in the literature itself is very revealing. For only when war ended and post-war reconstruction began did many writers find perspectives and voices in which to memorialise, analyse and reimagine events that at the time had left them only enough psychic energy to live through.[7] In particular, British writing of the 1940s constitutes a literary history that remains compelled by the war that provided the material without which characterisation, settings, temporal and spatial structures, and linguistic and formal experiments could not be imagined. From the Phoney War, through the Battle of Britain and the Blitz, with the evacuations of women and children from the cities to the country, to the last gasp invasion of German buzz bombs, the experience of the Second World War was total and yet affected literary imaginations in less dramatically apparent ways than we might assume. If the First World War had produced a literary revolution in modernism, it was because it ultimately came to be seen as a terrible and futile loss of meaning from the abstractions that had upheld a class-riven society and culture.[8] By contrast, the Second World War was seen at the time and, indeed, ever since as a just battle against the probability of universal enslavement and death. It may very well be that the particular horrors of this necessary war were not so much conducive to formalist revolution as they were to psychological and moral introspection.

Even as the human terrors of the Second World War became inescapable for ordinary civilians as much as for writers, there remains some very serious writing of this war that isolates itself from its material realities. In its historical context, this isolation produces the effect of a radical change from war-writing traditions, especially those representing women's experiences on the home front and behind the lines in the First World War.[9] These fictions, moreover, cannot be catalogued with those labelled either as modernist experiments or as escapist or popular romance. Rosamond Lehmann and Kate O'Brien had, by the 1940s, already established themselves as writers who addressed and represented serious issues in forms which, though not modernist in experimentation or ideology, were adopted with self-conscious and serious attention to literary traditions and methods. Lehmann's 1944 *The Ballad and the Source* and O'Brien's 1943 *The Last of Summer* are not only interesting novels individually and as part of a strong tradition of 1940s British women writers, but also extend and complicate that tradition with peculiarly elusive, if illuminating, representations of the Second World War. Lehmann's novel, set on an Edwardian country estate, and O'Brien's, in 1939 rural Ireland, are so far removed from the war temporally and geographically that they could be said to be performing a kind of denial of the war itself. The two novels utilise conventions associated with romance, evoking a timeless elsewhere, even where references are made to or feature a recognisable topical event. Such references are typically made in the service of heightening the tensions paramount to romance, whether it be lovers who are threatened with separation by war or the foreshadowed and haunting losses of fine young men. These novels challenge the ethos of both wartime romance and epic with a technique that produces an ironic effect. Each novel deploys stock romance emotions and melodramatic plot turns in order to de-romanticise the rhetoric of national stability and identity and the problem of political isolationism. In so doing they raise challenging questions about domestic and national ideologies that prevail and come under fire during this Second World War.

Written a year apart, at a time when it was not clear when the war would end, and news from all fronts was ambiguous at best, Lehmann's and O'Brien's novels are particularly interesting for similarities that highlight their responses to the Second World War by keeping it at bay. The more critically renowned, Lehmann's *The Ballad and the Source* is also the more dramatic in its elision of the war. So successful is this absence that no critical response to the novel mentions the war, despite its publication in the year of the Normandy invasion.[10] An obvious reason for this neglect is that Lehmann's narrative offers no invitation to consider the war. Instead, the novel constructs a world of Edwardian-country-house morals and manners, but one that increasingly foreshadows the onslaught of the First World War. As Gillian Tindall notes, 'the sense of imminent doom, the cutting off of a life just beginning to flower, is more closely derived from the First World War than the Second'.[11]

In the genteel insularity of the Landon and Jardine Thames riverside homes, the novel's central drama seethes with violence, but its relation to war is for much of the novel only suggestive: what is foregrounded instead is a series of conflicted relationships based primarily on and bounded by the characters' intense emotional responses to their needs of each other and bitter disappointments. Where in the past, as she violated Victorian domestic codes, Sybil Jardine had desperately sought solace and help from her best friend, Madrona Landon, so in the present her story obsessively seeks affirmation from Madrona's grandchild. But even as this emotionally intense interplay is fixated on the past and remains fixed in the present, repeating itself with variations on one emotional theme and pattern – 'liar begot liar; and all their road, forward and back, far back, was cratered with disastrous pits of guilt, haunted by ruinous voices crying vengeance' (p. 79) – it suggests the self-referentiality and fragmented characters of modern fiction. This is especially apparent as the novel engages psychoanalytic models of mother-daughter attachment and father-daughter incestuous relations. Despite each of their attempted escapes and searches for self-definition, Sybil and her daughter Ianthe are locked into a desperate hold on each other, a mutually self-cancelling obsession that precludes the emergence of psychological wholeness and rationality in either one. Within this fixed emotional pattern of relations, the novel represents mother and daughter and all those who become ensnared by them as consequently destabilised, both in perspective and behaviour, so they defy any unified conclusions about their relations and individuality.

This decentredness has had the critical effect of encouraging new and changing interpretations of the novel's compelling protagonist,

Sybil Jardine. And while one would expect this of conventional literary discourse, the combined effect of critical debate is that as her multiple name suggests, Sybil Anstey Herbert Jardine is quintessentially modern in her ultimate unknowability. Even as Sybil's powerfully affecting presence imprints itself indelibly on the other major characters' fates, by the end of the novel it is elusiveness that defines her character. This effect derives from the varied and mutually inconsistent perspectives and testimonies of the novel's narrators – the child, Rebecca, Sibyl's grand-daughter Maisie and others Sibyl lures into her web of intrigues. Co-operating fully in this effect of elusiveness, critics of the novel have maintained that Sibyl is self-deluded, a monster, a proto-feminist, a victim of her time and a timeless mythological creature.[12] On the one hand, there is no doubt that she both manipulates her story and therefore the sympathies of her primary listener, Rebecca, and that her ennobling portrait of her husband Harry Jardine belies his alcoholic, 'vaporous' and wounded insubstantiality, while her daughter dives into a weir rather than be rescued by Sibyl (p. 43). Then again, her fall from Victorian grace can be viewed either as a strike for freedom from the repressions of her first husband, Charles Herbert's household, or a wilfully narcissistic abandonment of her maternal responsibilities. Her florid outbursts on behalf of women's rights conflict with her equally impassioned claim that 'women need men' and must learn 'how to please, how to keep them' (p. 137). Her attempts to regain her daughter are just as ambiguous: are her machinations driven by maternal devotion and concern or by revenge and the desire for authority through domination?

Sibyl can of course be seen as embodying qualities of all of the above, and so even larger than the life granted by any one of these prototypes, or even, as Rebecca situates her near the end of the novel, 'Enchantress Queen in an antique ballad of revenge' (p. 233). Grounding Sibyl's opaque character in the stylised and ahistorical convention of myth and ballad does not, however, address the novel's own position in either the literary history of the 1940s or in the literary historical context of its own plotting. The title, in fact, grants the novel two locations, ballad and source. And even though Sibyl identifies the source as something transhistorical, almost mystical – 'The fount of life ... the quick spring that rises in illimitable depths of darkness and flows through every living thing from generation to generation' (p. 97) – the novel as a whole leads us back to a more specific source, a specific generation and historical moment.

All too many references to and reflections on the coming of the Great War make it impossible to read the novel as the timeless elsewhere of romance or of psychological nightmare. Though Sibyl's elusive character may be seen as congruent with the novel's historical evasiveness, the combination grants the novel an urgency that neither its romantic mysteries nor disillusionments effect. The Jardines's idyllic garden setting, with its invasion of sexual temptation and betrayal, may figure a primordial fall, but it also suggests another myth, that of Edwardian stability ruined by the violence of the Great War. This stability, while it derives from Britain's imperial power, also has domestic roots and expression, as it participates in the Victorian romantic icon of the morally fit middle-class home and family. Kathleen J. Renk discusses this icon as 'a metashrine that serves as a transmitter of English culture and as an apparatus that exerted control over what the patriarchy considered the "unmanageable"'. Renk sees the family becoming 'further mythologised as it became associated with the enclosed garden, a place of serenity overseen by the "queen of the garden", as defined by John Ruskin. In addition, this enclosed garden became associated with the notion of England as a heaven on earth'.[13] In Lehmann's novel, the 'queen' has helped construct the idea of the garden as a corner of quiescent moral authority, but she also serves as the tempter who is all too comfortable there.

The myth of England as a garden of domestic felicity may be threatened by the violently patriotic spirit of the Great War as much as by its actual violent losses, but throughout *The Ballad and the Source*, despite the fact that the war doesn't enter the narrative until halfway, its mythology is present as another tempter in the garden. This is a war that has been figured as powerfully mythical in English cultural consciousness, combining deeply felt romantic evocations of national identity. One dominant image, as it crosses boundaries of literature and propaganda and denies those between the social and economic classes, effects national unity in the form of a haunting elegy – England's youth snatched from the promises sown into the nation/garden, the green and gentle isle. In a critical move conjoining both myths, that of the war and of the garden, Lehmann's novel encodes the seeds of the war's violence as part of the social and sexual repressions that constitute Edwardian stability. Though the novel's depiction of repression has been discussed mostly as Sibyl's experience, another experience that relates repression to violence, one which because of its ephemeral quality is easily overlooked, casts another ominous shadow over hers. On the novel's very first page we are introduced to the shadowy Harry Jardine through a statement that may be suspect because it comes from Sibyl's pen but that works to demystify any sense of Edwardian stability: 'Harry's torn roots in England' may refer to his homesickness, but on an anti-sentimental note, its suggestion of a violent rent is corroborated by the novel's bracketing of wars past and present. As Judy Simons observes, Harry's 'embodiment of Victorian militarism' is substantiated by the novel's pervasive military imagery which connotes 'warfare on both a domestic and an international scale'.[14] Simons's concern with the novel's historical context is based on seeing that framework as defined by its explicitly stated narrative past and present, that is, the gentlemanly virtues of Victorian wars torn asunder by the 'moral confusion' of the First World War.[15]

Lehmann, however, makes it clear that those gentlemanly virtues were already in trouble long before the Great War violated their codes. Sibyl's explanation of Harry's instability, that his health broke when he fell off his horse and had to leave the Army, may be mythic embroidery, but the admission of war violence into the narrative in this first chapter establishes a pattern wherein the military imagery dramatising violence on and off the Home Front suggests that this is a society and civilisation that has won and maintained its authority and hegemony by doing battle. What Harry's infirmities signify in this sense are the costs of this confluence of domestic and international warfare. If Victorian and Edwardian societies were ruled by demonstrations of patriarchal dispensation, Harry exhibits the symptoms of battle fatigue that result from an ongoing history of defending and maintaining the barricades on behalf of patriarchal authority. In Lehmann's novel the threat is both external to patriarchal management and an enemy within its gates, materialising as the kinds of plots that are driven by, and do not deny the intense emotion disguised by, Harry's alcoholism, Charles Herbert's locks, and patriotic myths. The presence of war in this novel occurs as the backfire or boomerang effect of this denial. When the First World War breaks out as an interruption to Sibyl's romance plot of obsessively driven intense emotion, it also disrupts the narrative's ongoing search for a rational explanation about the past in the novel's present. This combined rupture, however does not signal change, but rather the most violently logical consequence of a history of war. In Lehmann's narrative logic, war figures as an omnipresent ghost – the return of the repressed as total war.

The novel's attention to war in general and the First World War in particular casts a defining shadow over a novel written during the Second World War. If Harry Jardine's disabilities stand for the crippling costs of warfare, his gated homestead represents the pre-war values which, despite war's continuity, prevail to justify the cost. When August

1914 is first mentioned, Rebecca's parents respond with gratitude that they were not 'caught' in France, but are safely ensconced in their island nation (p. 212). For Lehmann's characters this is not merely physical safety, but the civilisation where one can 'feel safer' because it rejects 'anything on any pitched-up level' as being 'too difficult, too exposed' (p. 241). What England stands for is the 'ordinary' (p. 241), a Victorian patriarchal myth of domesticated emotion. In contrast, the heightened emotional tenor of Sibyl's plotting, with its desperate consequences and her haunting presence, is portrayed as both tempting and threatening to male characters and their need for the mythical garden retreat. When Sibyl bolts from Charles Herbert's home, he attempts to reconstruct the home's moral authority by barricading the door against her and her transgressive desires. As the plot thickens, however, it becomes clear that patriarchy alone cannot reconstitute the serene garden. Even as Charles takes a home in the country, neither he nor his daughter thrives. His hold on Ianthe tightens into incest and her frozen subordination, and he deteriorates and dies. Lehmann seems to be suggesting that there is no Eden without the presence of a woman who in her melodramatically expressive form as its fiercely protective nurturer assumes a threatening role. Paradoxically, the woman nourishes the garden into life, but with a lushness that in its gothicised romanticism is not only overwhelming to the Victorian and modern imaginations, but ultimately unfathomable. When Sibyl leaves, and Charles must assume the role of nurturer and moral authority, the idea of the garden withers as his authority assumes the masculinist rhetoric of translating and subordinating heightened emotion to violent domination.

The double threat, of war and women's emotional plots, cohere in the novel as the haunting myths of the Great War. In a narrative shaped by romantically violent conflicts, about 'the Cumaean Sibyl', a 'Snow Queen' whom critics see as the vengeful wife Clytemnestra and the obsessed mother Demeter, in a plot resembling Sleeping Beauty or Snow White (Siegel, p. 144), the myth-making that created a literary tradition out of the horrors of the First World War provides a model for the creation of meaning out of the novel's futile struggle for domination. If Sibyl tempts all the characters, male and female, with her melodramatic pitch, with its promise of an adventure of uncharted emotional life, her narratives are ultimately defeated by the master narrative of the Great War. The search for meaning in *The Ballad and the Source* stands in ironic relation to the Great War's literary tradition, especially as so many modernists were compelled by the war's exposure of duplicitous and false meanings in the abstractions that supported its futile battles. As the war kills off Sibyl's grandson Malcolm and, shortly afterwards, Harry dies of a chill, 'putting up no fight at all', the rallying cry of 'honour, patriotism, duty' that enlisted so many is killed off as well.

If the realities of the Great War demolished the shared meanings of patriotic war, Lehmann's novel appropriates the Great War literary tradition to assess the costs and meanings of a second world war. For all its grief and autumnal sadness, the literary construction of the First World War provides a vocabulary and rhetoric through which unfathomable and unnecessary loss can be processed. The process consists of rejecting the ethos of all war, a totalising vision commensurate with the absolute, all-encompassing poetics of mythic explanation. At the end, Rebecca narrates a dream which takes the form of a mythic representation of the total destruction threatened by all the novel's political and emotional, internal and external forces. Invoking a Götterdämmerung that is the opposite of genesis, the dream is nonetheless an act of imaginative generation. The young interlocutor spins a commentary of her own that envisions 'the lightless clay world before the end: a cemented grief, sealing the excavations of an extinct human territory' (p. 312). The generative power in that apocalyptic vision for Lehmann lies in the comfort of what is already known and what is emotionally manageable because its horrors had been sheared and tamed into the mythic tradition of the Great War. According to the logic of Rebecca in the act of dreaming, the darkness of 'the lightless clay world' derives from her closed eyes, shutting out the harsh realities of daylight by transforming them into a 'cemented grief', fixed forever, but as make-believe. As Gillian Tindall asserts, this mythic presence becomes a coping strategy:

> It is as if the war which had blighted her later childhood and rooted in her creative consciousness the image of the splendid but doomed young men – 'lost boys' and 'dream figures', as she has described them – had simply been biding its time, lurking there continually below the horizon in the 1920s and 1930s, and when it showed its face again in 1939 the sense of disaster was mitigated with a degree of relief. The hidden enemy had returned, and one could face it after all.
>
> Tindall, p. 106

The ballad form of Lehmann's novel attests to the comforts of mythologising the destructive force of personal and political domination as it expresses itself through charismatic personality. At the moment of writing this novel, when another world war is all too real, seems interminable, and is also piling up incalculable losses, the mythic tradition of the Great War grants certainty. The new war, for which in 1943–4, the period of the novel's production, there is as yet no literary or historical tradition, is present in *The Ballad and the Source* only in its absence. In an inversion of past and present, the presence of the Second World War is felt only as the future haunting the present of a novel set in the past. This past, moreover, by 1943–4, is a safe place, situated by a canonised literary tradition as the 'ordinary' and by now timeless Great War, and by political history as the dénouement of an anachronistic world – the violent culmination of old rivalries among ruling families.

Against Lehmann's ballad of a violated garden, the Second World War stands as a change in the very meaning of war. I would argue with Tindall that the 'extinct' horrors of the First World War are no preparation for Hitler's unique terror. As many British women writers of the 1940s attested, though they had become pacifists as a result of the moral chaos of the Great War, when they learned of Hitler's racist policies and practices, his invasions of Austria and Czechoslovakia, they were convinced that this was a very different kind of war.[16] Unlike the emotional, political and geographic distances between the battle lines of the Great War and the insular Home Front, the Second World War invaded Britain's Home Front, and in Europe and beyond it created victims who shared no role in the causes of the war's political conflicts. It was because of their sympathy with these victims – Jews, gypsies, the handicapped – that so many British women writers found this war on fascism just and necessary.

It may very well be that because this war is not yet won as *The Ballad and the Source* is being written that it ends paradoxically with a vision of unending but safe terror. At the very end of the novel, Rebecca's dream ends as well, with the terrifying image of 'a figure folded in a blue cape, faceless, motionless, watching me' (p. 312). This is the ghost of Sibyl Jardine, menacing but comforting as well. Though there is a great deal of psychological realism portrayed in Sibyl's relations with her daughter, in her recurring rivalries with other women, and in her need to have her story validated as the authoritative version, analytical approaches to her psyche, as other critics have testified, are subordinated to the unstable powers of narrative itself and to the novel's insistence on dominating archetypal relationships. If in narrative tradition myth and irony are viewed as incompatible, this novel's staying power derives from the tension its characterisation of Sibyl constructs between the two forms. Sibyl's larger than life, ominous omnipresence is ultimately tamed by association with the conventions of fairy-tale and mythically threatening women. If the powers of these threatening archetypes are always defeated by the rescuing turn of the narrative, here they are defeated as well by the novel's invocation of the mythic Great War. Rebecca's dream plot, which encompasses the vision of the vigilant Sibyl, consists of Harry, only apparently helpless, announcing that Sibyl can no longer get in because he has set against her with 'lock and bolt' (p. 312). Repeating the earlier plot turn of Sibyl's being locked out of her first husband's home and her daughter's life, the novel here opposes Sibyl's emotional power with the more dominant force of patriarchal legacy, culminating in the Great War mythic tradition. Like the grand narratives of the Great War, the painful stories told about Sibyl are relieved by realising one's ability to wake and emerge from the nightmare. And like Sibyl, the Second World War is an elusive presence, but as inscribed in the novel's ending it is the nightmare that continues and cannot be assuaged or relieved by myth.

It is the fear as well as the necessity of facing this living nightmare that drives the decisive actions of Kate O'Brien's characters in *The Last of Summer*. Featuring a mother as formidable and manipulative as Sibyl Jardine, O'Brien's novel, published in 1943 and set in 1939, also deploys a domestic plot in which to situate the war's coming violence. Despite the time-frame which points to the outbreak of war, the setting of this novel is as removed from wartime experience as that of *The Ballad and the Source*. Waterpark House, an Irish Catholic manor farm, deep in the rural countryside, represents the final barricade against the incursion of Britain's defensive war against Nazi conquest. What Waterpark cannot lock out is a domestic conflict that is equally threatening to its stability. The domestic war, waged within Waterpark's Kernahan family, is also about keeping outsiders at bay and enacts a revenge tale in which personal desire becomes an instrument of emotional violence and an emblem of historical memory, the latter working as an anti-historical sense of the fatedness of Ireland. As this Irish Catholic homestead fights for its right for insular independence, it memorialises the struggle for home rule against British domination. With Eire's nationhood now assured, what remains is to resist British pressure to help Britain, their former coloniser, avoid becoming colonised itself, by the rising empire of the Third Reich. Instead of armed insurrection, however, the political strategy of the Irish Republic, represented here by its domestic counterpart in Waterpark, is passive aggression.

Mother Ireland in this novel is ruled over by Waterpark's matriarch, Hannah Kernahan, with 'silence, pride, and shabbiness', but her hallmarks – 'an arrogance of austerity, contempt for personal feeling, coldness, and perhaps fear from idiosyncracy' – reveal her tactics to be the reverse of Lehmann's Snow Queen (pp. 6, 8). Suggestive of those gentlemanly Victorian virtues that evaporate in Lehmann's Great War, these qualities provide the bulwark not only against violence to Hannah's domestic order, but against that which is 'seductive to the imagination' (p. 24). Like an imperial power herself, holding sway over her own enclosed garden, Hannah rules through emotional manipulation. Here Sibyl's narratives radiate with the imagination that incites violent feeling and inspires the work of narrative interpretation; Hannah's rhetorical resistance to imagination produces entropy, passivity, and either alienation or utter dependence. Where Sibyl's feelings are reconstructed and constructed through her storytelling, Hannah's feelings are expressed in her silences, in the withholding of her story. If Sibyl's listener, Rebecca, is able to sift through various versions of Sibyl's story and form her own conclusions, Hannah's primary target, her son Tom, is manipulated by not having her story. Unlike the varying interpretations of Sibyl's character, there is total agreement about Hannah's both from other characters and from critics. Indeed, this singleness has been seen as a weakness of the novel, though as we shall see, it is suggestive of a kind of coherence that O'Brien is criticising as dangerous in its implications. Hannah's withholding, her resistance to admitting the complicated truth of her past relationships, produces a stranglehold on her son's ability to imagine a connection that would take him outside Waterpark. As the novel extends this meaning, Hannah's resistance is akin to the nation's unwillingness to reconcile its unforgiven past with the responsibilities it must assume for its future in the world. At a time not only of Britain's national emergency but that of all nations threatened by Nazi Germany, this imagined consequence of Ireland's resistance to Britain also narrates a condemnation of Ireland's neutrality during the Second World War, the subject of which questions the role of her younger generations in defining their nation and building its relationship to the outside world.

The novel's political debates are embedded in a tale of seduction, betrayal and revenge that has lain dormant in an otherwise tranquil present until the appearance of an outsider. Angèle Maury (Kernahan), the French daughter of Hannah's brother-in-law, is touring Ireland with an acting troupe and impulsively decides to look up the aunt and cousins she has never met. Angèle is recognised immediately by Hannah as a threat to her dominating power, especially as both her sons become smitten with the self-assured Frenchwoman. And so in the guise of sympathy for her niece's identification with the fate of France, Hannah convinces the son to whom Angèle becomes engaged that the younger woman belongs elsewhere, and being an artist, would only feel 'trapped' in her Irish exile (p. 255). What drives this revenge is another story that intertwines desire and domination, one that only gets narrated as a memory, and because it remains undisclosed to Angèle and to Hannah's sons and daughter, dramatises the power of the unmediated and unresolved past to shape desire in the present. Just as Angèle's cousins, Martin and Tom, vie for her love, so in the past Angèle's father, also named Tom, and his brother Ned both desired Hannah. What might have made a difference to Hannah and Ned's sons was the knowledge that belies the myth of Hannah's rejection of Tom – the fact that Tom found he had to escape from the woman he discovered was made of 'hollow-ground steel' (p. 67).

As in Lehmann's novel, intense parent-child relationships encode the violence that erupts as war. O'Brien's portrayal of Hannah's hold over her son Tom functions as an Oedipal attachment that resonates in Eire's cultural consciousness as the maintenance of the mother country's psychological hold over the sons.[17] Isolated on their estate, with only a skittish relationship with the neighbouring village to which they have ancestral ties, Hannah has raised Tom in a vice that consists only of themselves: the 'assurance which possessed this family...depended on no living will but only on a sense of place and on the sunken years' (p. 51). As radio broadcasts invade Waterpark's insularity with news of Hitler's invasions, Ireland's retreat into neutrality is represented in Hannah's inability to imagine a political interdependence with the world outside. The violence she does to her son, an heir to Ireland, portends barren results for the young republic. Probably because they have not been blessed with Hannah's favoured attentions, her other two children are able to escape, though into circumstances about which the novel expresses concern. Hannah's daughter Jo, having won the right to a university education, commits herself to a nun's life, while Martin, the younger son, with a perspective that can only thrive outside the Oedipal web, analyses his nation with an irony that allows him to see the dangers in political and psychological mythologies. Eire may be imagined as an enclosed and safe garden, but external political realities expose this myth as a dangerous delusion: 'This country is Heaven's anteroom...whether we like the idea or not' (p. 53). At the end of the novel he makes his break complete by announcing that he is going off to France like his uncle before him, but this time to fight for her life, not only his.

The seductive power of Eire's rootedness, 'austere and proud and extremely regional', is depicted as dangerous for the nation through its temptations for Angèle (p. 69). Her intuitive reaction to Hannah's 'tranquil dissociation of her and hers from everything else on earth' is to find it not only 'curious', even 'unattractive', but to be 'chilled' by it and to press the integrity of her own dual identity (p. 21). And yet the French-woman allows herself to fall prey to an austerely domesticated romantic myth, translating her love for Tom into fulfilling the inherited responsibility of generating Eire's children.[18] Like Lehmann's novel, which implicates myths of nationalistic regeneration in the desires of men and the restrictive fates of women, O'Brien's constructs the romantic love between Tom and Angèle as imprinted on the myth of national character and destiny. Debunking any notion of romantic love as a unique and safe haven constructed by two individuals, the attraction and commitment between Tom and Angèle is assessed by the narrator as a 'perilous isolation in each other' (p. 142). Ominously suggestive of Tom's ties to his mother, this is a personal desire that ultimately cannot escape becoming implicated in the novel's political drama. Instead of love conquering all, the myth of national destiny prevails, necessitating constant vigilance against threats to cultural uniqueness and superiority. As it drives Hannah's desires, the myth is domesticated as 'their quiet, united, harmonious, loving life' (p. 148). The primacy of national fate intrudes on Angèle and Tom's love story by working as an imperative on the characters' consciousness of selfhood; it forms a recognition that the destinies of their nations are what must constitute their personal desires. When Angèle reflects on her future with Tom, she realises that not only would she 'cease to be French', she would be 'like an exile', a condition that the narrator argues is 'perilous' and not just because she would relinquish her own national identity (p. 141). Choosing exile in Waterpark House means subjecting herself to replicating its suffocating pattern of psychological and cultural isolation. In psychological terms, the novel employs Racine's *Phèdre*, a mythic romance story, to show another dangerous temptation for Angèle. If she fulfils her mother's desire to perform the role of Phèdre, she will have to rehearse it obsessively and so will fail to construct her own desires. If Angèle performs Phèdre's incestuous longings, she will also enact a fatalism that resists the possibility of contingency and open-endedness. In so doing, she would undo her father's escape into chance and change.[19]

As O'Brien's narrative performs a historical critique of the ideologies of nationalistic mythologies, the romance plot cannot survive historical contingency and the external pressures of national interest. Jo, who will preserve her integrity by retreating from this myth into another, recognises how romantic love is itself a myth that nourishes cultural desire. She is the one to notice that 'Tom, the innocent dreamer, had come home to full desire in such a myth' (pp. 180–1). From the perspective of her own dual identity, rebelling against her mother's dictatorship of narcissistic power and desiring the chaste and collective identity of Catholic sanctuary, Jo will rescue herself from a woman's fated fecundity and submission to the sacred myth of Irish motherhood. She will also escape the self-imprisoning role of fulfilling her desires vicariously, as Hannah has chosen to do. At the same time, however, O'Brien is not sanguine about Jo's choice. As a nun, Jo will be able to retreat from 'a world of increasing savagery and vulgarity and personal passion', but unlike Angèle's initial commitment to Tom and Waterpark, she will have chosen to become part of a pattern that disallows contingency (p. 193).[20]

The novel's embrace of historical contingency is part of its literary history. By the 1930s, the Catholic landed gentry and upper middle-class portrayed in the novel are well on their way to inheriting an assured place, 'to succeed historically'.[21] O'Brien, according to Roche, is 'diagnosing the failure of a revolution, the betrayal of the promise of Ireland to gain full and meaningful independence'.[22] The 1939 setting, only two years after Ireland's Constitution was enacted on 29 December 1937, marks a watershed for Eire's independence and for O'Brien's ongoing critique. For it is at this moment, when Europe's independence is threatened, that Eire withdraws into a position of neutrality which is tantamount to rejection, not only of Britain's cause, but that of non-fascist Europe. For O'Brien, a sign of the developing political maturity of the Irish republic would be recognition of its interdependence with the struggles of democratic Europe to continue to develop.[23]

By 1943, when *The Last of Summer* was published, O'Brien had already been chastised by Irish officialdom when her 1942 novel, *The Land of Spices*, was banned for its 'immoral' representation of convent life. As Mary Breen shows, this novel was not only 'a subtle threat to the narrow isolationist and xenophobic politics that ruled Ireland in the 1940s', but, like *The Last of Summer*, 'it questions and criticises the whole ideology of that period in Irish cultural history', including the tacit agreement between 'Church and State' that 'at the time identified virtue with ignorance'.[24] Representing this deadly identification, Hannah refuses to know anything about Hitler's invasion of Poland and distances herself even further by equating France with Germany – 'A plague on both their houses' (p. 213). The novel's identification of Hannah's personal view with that of the nation enacts O'Brien's fear, as Walshe explains, 'of a devouring and controlling authoritarianism, which would lead to the usurpation of private morality', and 'the rise of cultural fascism'.[25] Most insidiously, the delusion that neutrality preserves the nation's integrity accords with the national myth of a unifying harmony. Both positions support the submission of political progress to an unquestionable myth. Hannah's insistence on Irish neutrality then engages a sense of the word that stretches across the novel's geopolitical stance to questions raised by the narrative about the roles of violence and change.

Unlike Lehmann's novel, which keeps the exigencies of a necessary war at bay, O'Brien engages them through her characters' discussion, their ways of relating to each other, and the narrator's direct and indirect discourses. Where militaristic language is invoked by Lehmann to condemn connections between the violence in personal relations and that of war in general, O'Brien's references achieve the effect of endorsing the historically specific case of the Second World War.[26] Near the end of the novel, when Angèle realises that her relationship with Tom must end, she uses the language of war to express her loss. In the compressed space of two pages, she is given to evaluate her position in a love story as a combatant in two related wars:

'A fighter would stay and fight. So would I – if it weren't for the war, if it weren't for wanting to be at home for the war. It's hopeless, anyway, against her … I hate the fighting, filthy world. And I hate your mother.'

p. 260

On the Irish Home Front, where she is an unwelcome alien, she realises that she has been outflanked by Hannah and must cut her losses. Hannah has manipulated the language of love all too well, with all the expert knowledge of reigning myths about national identity and allegiances that she knows Tom has internalised in his character. Appealing to the lack of imagination she has imprinted on him, Hannah uses Tom to convince Angèle, personifying imagination in her artistry, that if she stayed, she would only be '*trapped*' (p. 260, italics in text). In effect, the love Angèle represents is a catalyst for change, with her French connection akin to the infusion of a new blood type. But with Hannah's primordial hold on her son, Angèle's difference would be rejected by being suffocated in the closed-off corridors of Waterpark's power. Angèle's realisation of defeat, however, occurs congruently with recognition that her love is already 'trapped' by an ambivalence which defies the univocal cultural identity so threatened by imaginative change: ' "I love you," ' Angèle tells Tom, ' "But I'll go home all right. After all, I love France too" ' (p. 261).

This dual identity and love on two fronts, Irish and European, would mark a commitment to change, one sign of which is characterised by Martin, for whom the war against Nazi Germany 'now had long plagued his imagination' (p. 205). Opening his mind to the history of Europe, he learns that 'ideas', which comprise the tense juggling of multivalent personal and political interests, contravene 'conventions' and 'the pompous certainties of ideologists', the combination of which leads to fascism (p. 207). A sign of political regression, like the Oedipal politics supported by Waterpark House, is Eire's frozen antipathy to change inspired by outsiders. In the novel, it is not only Angèle who is the outsider, but in a more complicated characterisation, Martin and Jo, who with their university education and European travels have embraced the cultural influences and political cause of non-fascist Europe, and so have won the disaffection of their mother. Hannah's garden, in this sense, is easily associated with a fascist hold on imagination. Even if her convent-like domain serves as a site of resistance, where she can assert her power in a male-dominated society, Hannah, in O'Brien's view, has only succeeded in mimicking the oppressively static culture which made her what she is. Like the nation itself, in its detachment from the defensive wars of others, Hannah's regime achieves neither self-sufficiency nor neutrality.[27] Relying on its own conventionalised certainties demonstrates subjection to myths, which because they are committed to the past, represent a life-denying confinement. In its most politically static permutations, this dependence on a dominant past undermines the nation's struggle to define itself on its own terms and reject its historic designation as Other. Eire's political neutrality, which is supposed to prevent violation by external powers, is also self-defeating in O'Brien's novel. Its justification supports a meaning of the word neutrality that may save the nation from the chaos of international politics, but aligns it with an equally oppressive politics. Jo's presentation of the religious argument for convent life resonates with the politics of Irish neutrality: 'its rightness, the persistent purity and detachment of its exaction in a world of increasing savagery and vulgarity and personal passion' (p. 193). For O'Brien, 'savagery and vulgarity and personal passion' represent the political and emotional realities that constitute the changing history in which one must live. To remove oneself from the world at war represents a failure of political imagination that threatens not only to kill off those whom fascism designated as expendable, but the moral imagination which gives life to Eire.

The political and moral urgency argued so vociferously in *The Last of Summer* is no less present in the more reticent *The Ballad and the Source*. Sybil's gothic plotting and narratives may make it look as though the novel denies the historical moment of its creation, but the violent reactions of all its characters, expressed in a continuous thread of battle imagery, suggest that the novel is a response to the war which is never far from Lehmann herself. While it could be argued that the timeless elsewhere of its long-ago setting elegises the unhealed losses of the past war, for Lehmann, as for other British women writers, those losses remain coterminous with what is anticipated and feared in the current war that has defied all boundaries – political, ideological, topographical, social and psychological.

If both O'Brien and Lehmann utilise conventional literary forms to express their sense of urgency, what remains distinct in these narratives, as in so many by British women writers, is the complexity and rigour of their fictionalised arguments against 'pompous certainties' and conventional thinking about the Second World War. For them, as for Storm Jameson, Phyllis Bottome and Elizabeth Bowen, among others, what matters is the confluence of values enacted in family life and the lives of their nations that create victims from the exercise of unlimited and, perhaps even more ominous, charismatic power. In turn, their analyses of power and victimisation are imprinted on the literary forms they use, altering them and creating a new genre of war writing. Unlike the literary tradition of the Great War, the writing of the Second World War recognises that by 1943–4, it has become impossible to universalise the subject of war. Knowledge of Hitler's total war on those he labelled Other makes the fictional figure of the outsider more than an individual portrait or a symbolic gesture, but vulnerable in a new, collectively tragic fate. Unlike the tragic losses of the First World War, the unfathomable exterminations of the Second World War Two can be eulogised but not elegised. The writing of British women during the Second World War challenges us still with the problem of confronting this collective threat and tragedy.

Notes

Page references in the text are to the New York editions of Rosamond Lehmann, *The Ballad and the Source* (Reynall and Hitchcock, 1945) and Kate O'Brien, *The Last of Summer* (Doubleday, Doran, 1943).

1. See my study, *British Women Writers of World War Two* (London: Macmillan, 1998), and also Jenny Hartley, *Millions Like Us: British Women's Fiction of the Second World War* (London: Virago, 1997).
2. On rediscoveries of 1930s literature, see for example Patrick Deane, *History in Our Hands* (Leicester: Leicester University Press, 1998) and Janet Montefiore, *Men and Women Writers of the 1930s* (London: Routledge, 1996). On writings of the 1950s, see Niamh Baker, *Happily Ever After?* (London: Macmillan, 1989), and Deborah Phillips and Ian Heywood, *Brave New Causes: Women in British Postwar Fictions* (Leicester: Leicester University Press, 1998).
3. Definitions of modernism have expanded with feminist discovery of the way women's writing performed experiments beyond the canonised forms of their male colleagues. See for example Bonnie Kime Scott, in *The Gender of Modernism* (Indiana: Indiana University Press, 1990), who, while including writing from the 1940s, excludes that about the Second World War.
4. Keith Alldritt, in *Modernism in the Second World War* (New York: Peter Lang, 1989), presents Eliot, Pound, MacDiarmid and Bunting as modernist war poets of the 1940s in their 'common belief in the art of language and its power to sustain in terrible times' (Preface, n.p.).
5. On ideology as history, see for example Linda Hutcheon, *The Politics of Postmodernism* (London: Routledge, 1989).
6. Though histories of the war and of the Holocaust have been written separately, there is this agreement. See for example the three volumes edited by Peter Hayes, *Lessons and Legacies* (Evanston: Northwestern University Press, 1990–99).
7. Elizabeth Bowen is a case in point. Her powerful novel *The Heat of the Day*, about the day-to-day terrors of the Blitz, was published in 1949, with the sense that its disorienting effects were psychically illuminating but needed peacetime to cohere intellectually and creatively.
8. Paul Fussell's *The Great War and Modern Memory* (Oxford: Oxford University Press, 1975) is considered the key work, but since he omits women writers, one must turn to Claire Tylee, *The Great War and Women's Consciousness* (Iowa: Iowa University Press, 1990) to complete the study. An example of women's fiction of the First World War battleground is *Not So Quiet*, by Helen Zenna Smith (pseudonym of Evadne Price).
9. Among the many who wrote of these experiences, Phyllis Bottome, Elizabeth Bowen, Olivia Manning and Storm Jameson are noteworthy.
10. Most critics of this novel don't mention the Second World War, but Ruth Siegel cites Raymond Mortimer's review as 'a meditation on the war' (Ruth Siegel, *Rosamond Lehmann: A Thirties Writer* [New York, Peter Lang, 1989], p. 148). Hartley finds concerns of 1940s fiction in the novel: 'bad mothering and the fatal seductions of charisma' as associated with Hitler (Jenny Hartley, *Millions Like Us*, p. 115). Gillian Tindall argues that, like Lehmann's short fiction of the 1940s, collected as *The Gipsy's Baby* (London: Virago, 1982), war is a powerful presence despite its absence (Gillian Tindall, *Rosamond Lehmann: An Appreciation* [London: Chatto and Windus, 1984], p. 106).
11. Tindall, Rosamond Lehmann, p. 118.
12. See discussions by Siegel, Hartley, Tindall and Harriet Blodgett, 'The Feminism of Rosamond Lehmann's Novels', *University of Mississippi Studies*

in English, 10 (1992), 106–21; Sydney Janet Kaplan, 'Rosamond Lehmann's *The Ballad and the Source*: A Confrontation with "The Great Mother"', *Twentieth Century Literature*, 27 (1987), 127–45; Judy Simons, *Rosamond Lehmann* (New York: St Martin's Press, 1992). Wiktoria Dorosz's realist perspective on Sibyl's character leads her to a balanced assessment of her flaws; *Subjective Fiction and Human Relationships in the Novels of Rosamond Lehmann* (Uppsala: Uppsala University Press, 1975).

13. Kathleen J. Renk, *Caribbean Shadows and Victorian Ghosts*, (Virginia: University of Virginia Press, 1999), p. 8.
14. Simons, *Rosamond Lehmann*, p. 101.
15. Simons, *Rosamond Lehmann*, p. 102.
16. I discuss such writers as Storm Jameson, Phyllis Bottome and Rebecca West in *British Women Writers of World War Two*.
17. Anthony Roche points out that Irish Catholic women help create an Oedipal triangle in order to withdraw from their husbands and so 'transfer to the son, the male body over whom she may (as mother) exercise power'. 'The Ante-Room as Drama', in Eibhear Walshe, ed., *Ordinary People Dancing; Essays on Kate O'Brien* (Cork: Cork University Press, 1993), pp. 85–100. Adele M. Dalsimer sees Angèle's childhood need 'to come first with her father' mirroring not only Hannah's hold on her son, but Angèle's attraction to the younger Tom. *Kate O'Brien: A Critical Study* (Dublin: Gill and Macmillan, 1990), p. 76.
18. Anne Fogarty sees the novel in terms of psychological and social 'family romance', with Angèle fulfilling the cycle begun in the previous generation and continuing 'the stagnation of a backward-looking and repressive Irish society' (p. 114). Although she mentions 1939 as 'the backdrop', she does not discuss the coming war as part of the novel's subject. ' "The Business of Attachment": Romance and Desire in the Novels of Kate O'Brien', in Walshe, *Ordinary People Dancing*, pp. 101–19.
19. Patricia Coughlin reports that O'Brien's writings oppose 'the general cultural narrowness, prudery and ruralist exclusions of Free State Ireland', but challenge its oppression of women. 'Feminine Beauty, Feminist Writing and Sexual Role', in Walshe, *Ordinary People Dancing*, p. 60. Dalsimer puts it more strongly, finding Ireland's neutrality to be 'immoral isolationism in political terms and pathetic self-absorption in human terms'. *Kate O'Brien: A Critical Study*, p. 73.
20. Eibhear Walshe shows how in two other novels by O'Brien, *Mary Lavelle* (1936) and *The Flower of May* (1953), the convent cell or woman's private study can become 'a site of tacit resistance to the dominant discourse of the novel's world'. 'Lock Up Your Daughters: From Ante-Room to Interior Castle', in Walshe, *Ordinary People Dancing*, p. 158.
21. Roche points to O'Brien's political critiques which noted discrepancies between this success and the exclusion 'of women from that promised liberation'. In Walshe, *Ordinary People Dancing*, p. 95.
22. Roche, ibid., p. 95.
23. O'Brien's support for Spain's Republican cause inspired her 1936 novel, *Mary Lavelle*, and her 1937 travel book, *Farewell Spain*, both banned by Franco who then banned her from Spain.

24. Breen, in Walshe, *Ordinary People Dancing*, p. 169. See also Lorna Reynolds, *Kate O'Brien: A Literary Portrait* (Gerrards Cross: Colin Smythe, 1987), whose inside view of Ireland shapes her agreement with O'Brien, p. 75.

25. Walshe, *Ordinary People Dancing*, p. 151.

26. During the war O'Brien lived in England. Her work for the Ministry of Information activated her support for the war.

27. Weekes argues that O'Brien's comparison of domestic and international families requires that 'we apply the same standards' to both, and that according 'dignity' to individuals within the whole is 'more radical ... than that to which Irish nationalists aspired and aspire'. Ann Owens Weekes, *Irish Women Writers: An Uncharted Tradition* (Lexington: University of Kentucky, 1990), p. 132.

5
The Novel Sequences of Joyce Cary

Howard Erskine-Hill

1

If the term novel-sequence means something more than a continuity of character and action through several book-length fictions, in the manner of Anthony Trollope, John Galsworthy, and C. P. Snow, it is to Ford Madox Ford we should look as its founding father in English. Ford's 1914–18 sequence, *Parade's End* (1924–8), carries the reader through the period from before to after the Great War in broadly chronological fashion, but the fictional mode alters radically within the sequence from the wide social survey associated with omniscient-narrator fiction and used to present pre-1914 society, to a point-of-view narration appropriate to the rendering of individual experience in the apparent collapse of the public realm after the war.[1]

After Ford the emergence of the modernistic novel-sequence can be plainly seen. It is found in Grassic Gibbon's (Lesley Mitchell's) *A Scots Quair* (1932–4), Wyndham Lewis's *The Human Age* (1929–55), Beckett's *Molloy*, *Malone Dies* and *The Unnameable* (1951–3), to continue in the work of Lawrence Durrell, Anthony Powell, Robertson Davies, Paul Scott and William Golding. It is characterised, I have argued, by sharp contrast and counterpoint, or strongly articulated evolution, between different constituent novels of the group. Sometimes significant contrast is conveyed through the use of unchronological time, whether through the associative remembrance of a particular mind, or the radical unexplained decision of the novelist himself. Creative difficulty is posed for the reader who, enticed into attempting to interpret the sequence as a whole, is rarely assisted in this act of synthesis. It is this which distinguishes novel-sequence from saga, or, to put it the other way, the modernistic novel sequence from the sequences of Trollope in the nineteenth century and Snow in more recent time.[2]

In the middle of this new development the two separate trilogies of Joyce Cary stand out. Less well-known today than thirty years ago, they comprise: *Herself Surprised* (1941), *To Be A Pilgrim* (1942) and *The Horse's Mouth* (1944); *Prisoner of Grace* (1952), *Except The Lord* (1953) and *Not Honour More* (1955), and share a series of special features which mark them out from other examples of the novel-sequence. For a start, it is clear that Cary studied to be readable, homely and unpretentious. 'The judge, when he sent me to prison, said that I had behaved like a woman without any moral sense' (*Herself Surprised*, p. 1);[3] 'Last month I suffered a great misfortune in the loss of my housekeeper, Mrs Jimson' (*To Be A Pilgrim*, p. 1); 'I was walking by the Thames. Half-past morning on an autumn day. Sun in a mist. Like an orange in a fried fish shop' (*The Horse's Mouth*, p. 1): these are the openings of the novels of the first trilogy. In each the first person singular, the fictional 'I', is found. Indeed, on opening *Herself Surprised* to read of the trial of Sarah Monday and how she seemed to have become criminal without really willing it or knowing it, the reader might suppose that Cary was modelling himself on the Defoe of *Moll Flanders*. Only when one arrives at *The Horse's Mouth* is it clear how radically Cary is using first-person, point-of-view narration. For while the trilogy is undeniably one work, by virtue of a large overlap in circumstance and salient characters, the viewpoint of each character is so markedly different from the others, so *sui generis*, as to make comprehensive interpretation appear dauntingly difficult if not impossible.

More striking still is the outward resemblance of the two trilogies to one another. In each case the opening novel is narrated by a woman who, in one way or another, practically, psychologically, or both, is not in full control of her life. In each case the second and third novels are narrated by two rival men who, in one way or another, compete for the woman, win her support and enjoy her favours. In each case the middle novel reaches further back in time than the other two, and in each case the final novel is almost frenetically present-focussed, reading sometimes almost like a running commentary, albeit in the past tense. There are minor similarities also; for example in the retrospective middle novel of each trilogy, the protagonist, Thomas Wilcher in the first, Chester Nimmo in the second, each caught in different ways between present and past, has a strong-minded elder sister better able to make painful decisions than himself. All this suggests that Cary embraced a characteristic configuration for the novel-sequence. The two trilogies are different attempts to get something right, to mount a challenge in its full strength, or at least to discern a common pattern in different areas of experience. It has been generally accepted that the second trilogy is more explicitly political than the first, though each, in its middle novel, takes a long troubled look at the social history of England.

2

Let us consider the 1940s trilogy. Of this Cary wrote that it was 'designed to show three characters, not only in themselves but as seen by each other' (Preface to the Carfax Edition of *Herself Surprised*). In keeping with his familiar human idiom, the debate about Sarah may be thought to open with the injunction to 'Know thyself', said to her by the prison chaplain after her trial for fraud and theft. What more deceptively easy introduction could there be to a vision of human experience of the most disconcerting kind? Sarah is also the easily recognised unreliable narrator. When she explains how her first master, Matthew Monday, came to propose marriage to her, his cook, or how Monday's friend, Hickman, came to seduce her, or how her later master, Thomas Wilcher, seemed to be proposing marriage when he was really only asking her to be his mistress, which she became; or when she explains, as a brief afterthought, that she has regularly salted a bit of money away from Wilcher's household accounts, or when we learn from *The Horse's Mouth* that she has quietly stashed away certain paintings and drawings by her second 'husband', Gulley Jimson, the reader is hardly disturbed. The reader understands at once that Sarah's narrative seeks to put the best face on things without being comprehensively mendacious. Sarah, a woman who owns to not knowing herself, has many things more prominent in her mind than her crimes, if crimes they be. She loves religion and the old practice of daily household prayers; she loves kitchens and cooking; she loves to be a good servant. Her crimes, one may think, come down to her being a generous sexual woman, who steals either to support her best lover, Gulley Jimson, or to put a bit by for herself for a rainy day. Since, however, there is no governing narrative in this or any other trilogy novel of Cary, the reader cannot really know. If Sarah massages the facts of her life as she tells her story may she not be thought to lie about the whole thing? For the moment (at the end of *Herself Surprised*) this possibility is not salient in the reader's mind. It is the later novels which raise doubts.

Sarah herself writes of her 'double way of life' (*Herself Surprised*, p. 70). There is a morally quite acceptable sense in which Thomas Wilcher, protagonist of *To Be A Pilgrim*, also has a double life, or a double consciousness. He is an intelligent traditionalist, passionately in love with old ways, his old country house of Tolbrook, and the religion and history of England. In this he has, apparently, much in common with Sarah. He is painfully aware, however, that the very traditions of England have demanded the courage to change. He recalls how, as a young intellectual from Oxford studying Kant, he hears the Benjamite preacher Brown roaring out the words of John Bunyan's hymn:

> *No foes shall stay his might,*
> *Though he with giants fight;*
> *He will make good his right*
> *To be a pilgrim.*

At these words I felt my heart turn over ... Brown had no arguments that did not fill me with contempt. But when he sung those verses from Bunyan, his favourite hymn and the battle cry of his ridiculous little sect, then something swelled in my heart as if it would choke me, unless I, too, opened my mouth and sang. I might have been a bell tuned to that note, and perhaps I was. For the Wilchers are as deep English as Bunyan himself. A Protestant people, with the revolution in their bones.

To Be A Pilgrim, p. 7

The hymn is 'deep English', but it sings of leaving behind the things of this world. It is Robert, Brown's son and Wilcher's nephew, who breaks the marvellous Adam architecture of the saloon at Tolbrook to accommodate a threshing machine (pp. 145–6). At the end of the novel the tragic Wilcher must confess to himself that he is:

'an old fossil, and that I have deceived myself about my abilities. I thought I could be an adventurer like Lucy and Edward. I shouted the pilgrim's cry, democracy, liberty, and so forth, but I was a pilgrim only by race. England took me with her on a few stages of her journey. Because she could not help it. She, poor thing, was born upon the road, and lives in such a dust of travel that she never knows where she is.

> *Where away England, steersman answer me?*
> *We cannot tell. For we are all at sea.'*

To Be A Pilgrim, p. 155

quoting an epigram of his brilliant political brother, Edward. Cary's rendering of the pilgrimage motif, from Bunyan and Chaucer, encompasses Wilcher's generation of English middle-class society from pre-1914 Liberalism to the rise of Hitler. Few other English novels of the twentieth century render so rich an account of English middle-class life, at once heroic and bathetic (consider the deaths of Bill and Amy: chapters 119–20, 151), all marvellously assimilated into and seen through one reminiscent mind.

But there is another feature of Wilcher's life which emerged, with the convincing casualness of Sarah Monday, in *Herself Surprised*: his propensity, at one stage in his life, to go out at night to 'exhibit' himself with pocket torches, or to tickle women on seats in Hyde Park (*Herself Surprised*, 71). Wilcher's version of himself seems thus in danger of being seriously selective – if the reader is disposed to believe Sarah. The careful reader, indeed, is here inclined to do so, since Wilcher himself narrates, in more harmless form, an encounter with a girl on a seat at Hyde Park Corner: '"I should think you'd better have someone to look after you"', says the girl (*To Be A Pilgrim*, p. 136). The question is then implicitly posed as to whether Wilcher's image of himself, self-critical within conventional bounds as it is, may be unsupported by other evidence in the trilogy. Robert Bloom, Cary's best but most severe critic, in the course of demonstrating the novelist's morally and aesthetically culpable indeterminism, has even suggested that Wilcher may be mad.[4]

The ambiguous Sarah, by Wilcher seen as the source of the old-fashioned love and support he needs, is seen quite differently by Gulley Jimson, the protagonist of *The Horse's Mouth*. To Gulley, Sarah is at once an opportunity and a peril: an opportunity because he is sexually attracted to her, and because she intermittently sends him money; a peril because he thinks she wants to domesticate him with her nest-building instincts, and thus blunt the sharp edge of his restless artistic vision. This is close to Gulley's approach to the world in general: receive but resist. Like Sarah and Wilcher, Gulley has his own 'double way'. The constant stream of passages from William Blake that flows through his mind intimates to us the independent visionary power to which he is drawn. But as an elderly and unscrupulous survivor in an indifferent and philistine society he is, as Robert Bloom points out, the archetypal rogue and picaro.[5] Even his own art, now an increasingly ambitious series of uncompleted paintings of sacred subjects, seems to be growing comic and surreal. Jimson's increasingly desperate impulse to express his vision in paint comes to its tragi-comic climax as the wall on which he is painting his 'Creation' is demolished by workmen for the local borough council. 'And just then the whale smiled. Her eyes grew bigger and brighter and she bent slowly forwards as if she wanted to kiss me…the whole wall fell slowly away from my brush' (*The Horse's Mouth*, p. 44). Thus creation and demolition meet in a single paradoxical resolution.

The chief issues in the study of Joyce Cary, indeterminacy and sequentiality, can now be seen together. Because Sarah is an ambiguous figure, coming late to a self-knowledge that may in any case be only partial, we can with difficulty use her testimony to establish the truth about Wilcher; equally her understanding of art is rudimentary,[6] so that a question such as whether Gulley Jimson is a rogue or a genius can hardly be settled by her. Wilcher and Jimson, themselves ambiguous, thus remain even in their ambiguity so different in their vision of the world as to confront the reader with an impossible choice. For what Wilcher loves is regarded by Jimson with an exasperation running to suppressed hatred.

It may be seen that Cary's trilogy pattern has almost the elegance of an equation about indeterminacy. This is a direct consequence of Cary's resort to sequence rather than saga. The very contrasts between book and book, narrator and narrator, which is to say protagonist and protagonist, preclude a continuous vision of the world. Rather we are given a formalised, symmetrical, triptych, containing in high relief three radically different figures, each turning in her or his direction, creating his or her own world, held so closely together by the novel-sequence that their unintegratable autonomies can never be shaded into a single view. On the contrary: Cary has achieved a maximum diversity of vision with a maximum definition in form.

3

Despite his hard-won method in the first trilogy, Cary apparently experimented repeatedly with the presentation of Nina Latter (previously Nina Nimmo) in *Prisoner of Grace*.[7] He eventually reverted to a first-person narrative, additionally articulated by parentheses which constitute a minor counterpoint within her story. Far more than Sarah, Nina is acted upon, and torn between the two men in her life, James Vandeleur Latter, soldier, colonial administrator and yachtsman; and Chester Nimmo, radical politician, evangelical preacher and cabinet minister under Lloyd George. Each of these men seems to display something of the best and much of the worst of the Tory (Latter) and

Liberal (Nimmo) positions of the time in which the trilogy is set. Because Nina's autonomy is so much more constrained by Latter and Nimmo than Sarah's by Wilcher and Jimson (Sarah had other lovers and husbands and managed to deceive all of them to some extent), Nina alters the balance of our judgement. She is more skilled in casuistry than Sarah, but is at her most casuistical when defending Chester Nimmo's own casuistry. Seemingly more honest than Sarah, she is less decisive, identifying equally well, at one time or another, with the conflicting views of Nimmo and Latter. Their competition for Nina seems even more relentless than the conflicts of public affairs; indeed, Cary may use this domestic triangle to convey more forcibly the prolonged and bitter competition of politics. Nina's helpless position, if so, at least prompts us to make a generalisation about political life.

It is the middle novel, *Except the Lord*, that constitutes Cary's boldest and most surprising fictional stroke. For Nimmo's narrative reaches so far back in time in recounting his working-class childhood and youth in the West Country, and breaks off so early, that in its content it scarcely touches the lives of Nina and Latter. Save for the narrative present there is but one moment in Nimmo's narrative that mentions Nina at all: his first meeting with her when she was a child (*Except the Lord*, p. 32; cf. *Prisoner of Grace*, p. 4). This is never recalled by Nina herself, or by Latter.

What can the reader make of this extraordinary démarche, in which Cary almost seems to exaggerate the configuration of his earlier trilogy? In itself *Except the Lord*, which brings Nimmo from his childhood through trade unionism to a resumed religion (Psalm 127 being the allusion of the title) is a rich, detailed, moving and memorable piece of working-class autobiography. Its account of hardship and faith in the later nineteenth-century West Country is worthy to be put beside Wilcher's story of the middle class. But how does it relate to the Nimmo we see through the eyes of Nina and Latter? It does not explain the opportunism, twists, turns, lucky escapes and corrupt contrivances of his main political career, as we learn of it from them. Does it then express a religious penitence for all this from his last days? Hardly, when at the very time he is working on these memoirs he is also seducing his former wife, now Mrs Latter, in Latter's own house. Is it a wholly conscious attempt to put a good face on a bad life, designed perhaps to promote his final bid for political power in the crisis of the 1926 Strike? Or is Nimmo's story the formative experience which, cunning and corrupt though he has been, he sincerely thinks was the ground of his career? The reader also notes that Nimmo's memoirs are unfinished.

There are letters between him and his wife which he proposed to use, which Latter urges her to destroy, but which she has been unable to do so before she dies at the hand of her husband. All the reader can say is that Nimmo's narrative reads as something extraordinarily authentic. If the experience it recounts was *not* the root of a radical political and religious faith, it could have been and should have been.

Not Honour More, Jim Latter's story, plunges us back into the crises and contrivances of the present, the period of the 1926 Strike as experienced in the West Country. It is, as previously noted, unreminiscent, present-centred. Latter, the one-time soldier, is brusque, and dismissive to a high degree of 'the talky boys' and wanglers, the corruptions of politicians and the selling out of good traditions, decent people, fidelity and 'Honour'. Unsubtle and impatient, Latter is still capable of circumspection and caution. Had the reader read *Prisoner of Grace* alone before this, he could hardly have disagreed with Latter's condemnation of Nimmo, while Latter's direct competitive attempts to regain Nina for himself also accord with Nina's story. Latter's vision of the world is thus an effective foil to the later career of Nimmo, though it is certainly challenged by Nimmo's account of his own early days.

There is a case (it has been put by Robert Bloom[8]) for thinking Latter the one figure in the second trilogy who stands for integrity, truth and honour. The difficulty, however, is that Latter, like Jimson, is allowed to slide into near-caricature, in this case that of the retired military man, easily ridiculed, who sees all change as decay. This, together with the convoluted plot of political comings and goings, of contrivances and betrayals, means that the one major point of congruence in the entire trilogy – Nina's assertion, perhaps rhetorical, 'Jim can only shoot me dead' (*Prisoner of Grace*, p. 126), and Latter's closing statement – 'I finished the thing in one stroke. She fell at once and did not struggle at all' (*Not Honour More*, p. 47), displays a chilling logic, certainly recalls *Othello* ('it wasn't a murder. It was an execution', Latter says), but refuses to express the desperate emotion which the whole trilogy strongly implies.

What can we make of Cary's second trilogy? Its broad resemblance to the first (the Cary configuration) only throws into relief its several differences. Above all the time-scheme of *Except the Lord* defines a significant silent space: what Nimmo himself might have said about his period as a major politician when he was also the husband of Nina. It is the silence at the centre of the work. It prompts speculation, but it cannot be filled any way the reader likes. The possibilities are limited by the trilogy's other accounts, ambiguous or partial as these may be. Next, the very weakness of Nina, yielding so much to Latter and Nimmo and never, apparently, choosing between them, says much about her two rival lovers. Here her testimony tends to confirm a self-deceiving egoism in Nimmo, and to portray Latter in a more rounded, less stereotyped way than the reader finds in *Not Honour More*. There is somewhat more congruence, perhaps between *Prisoner of Grace* and *Not Honour More* than between *Herself Surprised* and *The Horse's Mouth*. Against that, the counterpointed, even disjunct, status of *Except the Lord* strongly challenges the wavering trend towards congruence in the first and third novels. While Nimmo might utterly delude himself in seeing his early years as the key to his career (we don't know), those early years still seem to offer more ground for human faith, despite their several false dawns, than the worlds rendered by the narratives of Nina and Latter. But the reader is in a strange situation here. Is any of Cary's protagonists in this trilogy sane? Is not Nina's frame of mind virtually schizophrenic? Not quite, perhaps, since she can reason of it. Is not the intense moral resentment of Latter, as lover and husband continually betrayed, obsessive beyond sanity as he becomes Nina's executioner? But then the discrepancy between the earlier Nimmo he himself tells us of, and the later Nimmo of whom Nina and Latter tell, teeters on the far verge of sane explanation. Cary's second trilogy is more disturbing than the first; and while there is much cruel farce, especially in *Not Honour More*, the tragi-comic aspect of the earlier trilogy, which cast in the end would-be reconciling light on its diverse protagonists, is hardly found here. Nina who, perhaps from weakness, perhaps from love, or both, cannot make up her mind who she is, ends up murdered. Latter, limited but if anyone the man of integrity, cannot be so in all senses of the term since he ends up a murderer. As for Nimmo, opportunist, egoist, master of rhetoric, the apologia and the confessional mode, he seems unlikely to know who he is either.

In his essay 'The Way a Novel Gets Written' (1950) Cary wrote: 'I don't know any misery like that of the artist whose work has gone out of fashion.'[9] What would the shade of Cary say today if he were to look back on the reputation of his best novels since his death in 1957? Would he not be struck by the irony that the best book on his novels, Robert Bloom's *The Indeterminate World* (1962), criticised him for a quality which literary fashion was just about to applaud extravagantly: indeterminacy – you pay your money and you choose your meaning? Coherence and closure were in that time disapproved. Did this rescue Cary from the reproofs of Bloom? Not at all. Cary has been largely forgotten or neglected, perhaps because critics find his reader-friendly style embarrassing by comparison, for example, with the rigours of Beckett's *The Unnameable*. The twenty-first-century reader should not, however, be beguiled by the homely if slippery idiom of Sarah, or the painful candour of Nina, into thinking that Cary has a simple, warm, old-fashioned message to convey. Despite his inviting, reader-friendly approach, despite his frequent production of intelligent comedy, the novelist who appears to have started out on his trilogies by putting character above all has, more than most modern novelists, brought his readers to question the integrity or continuity of character as a category with which to attempt to interpret the world. This challenge to conventional assumptions hardly could have been delivered through the single novel. Only through Cary's brilliant and radical management of the novel-sequence, an achievement of the 1940s and earlier 1950s, could this have been done. If these contentions are right, Cary's two trilogies, and his other fiction, deserve a comprehensive reassessment.

Notes

1. This argument is made in Howard Erskine-Hill, 'Ford's Novel Sequence: An Essay in Retrospection', in *Agenda*, vol. 27 no. 4/vol. 28 no. 1 (Winter 1989/Spring 1990), Ford Madox Ford Double Issue, pp. 46–55.
2. Erskine-Hill, 'Ford's Novel Sequence', pp. 46–7.
3. In quoting from Cary's trilogies, which are available only patchily in various editions, it has seemed more useful to give *chapter* numbers (chapters in the trilogies are very short) than page numbers. These references are in the text of the essay.
4. Robert Bloom, *The Indeterminate World: A Study of the Novels of Joyce Cary* (Philadelphia: University of Pennsylvania Press, 1962), p. 96. I am much in debt to Robert Bloom, and to the earlier critics of Cary, notably Andrew Wright, Barbara Hardy, and several others whom Bloom draws into his debate.
5. Bloom, *The Indeterminate World*, pp. 103–4.
6. Cary, in his important Preface to the Carfax Edition of *Herself Surprised*, describes how he had to cut out Sarah's opinions about art and history because they seemed to dilute her character.
7. Bloom, *The Indeterminate World*, p. 41 (citing Cary's *Art and Reality: The Clark Lectures*, 1956, published 1958).
8. Bloom, *The Indeterminate World*, pp. 180–91. Bloom's total discussion of *Latter* is not fully satisfied with the case.
9. 'The Way a Novel Gets Written' (1950), in A. G. Bishop, ed., *Joyce Cary: Selected Essays* (London, 1976), p. 125.

6
Wild Soldiers: Jocelyn Brooke and England's Militarised Landscape

Mark Rawlinson

Although a coeval of Auden and Spender, Jocelyn Brooke's public literary career was post-Second World War, and indeed it followed on from an episode of re-enlistment. Brooke bought himself out of the Army and in the last three years of the 1940s he published two novels, *The Scapegoat* (1948) and *The Image of a Drawn Sword* (1950), another pot-boiling fiction for children, three volumes of fictionalised autobiography later collected as *The Orchid Trilogy – The Military Orchid* (1948), *The Mine of Serpents* (1949) and *The Goose Cathedral* (1950) – and a book of poems. Two further memoirs, another novel and much literary critical and editorial work (on Firbank, Bowen, Welch and Huxley) would follow by 1955.

Brooke's writing in the late 1940s is haunted by soldiers, though in a manner that makes it stand apart from the war literature of the latter half of the decade. Contemporaries were writing fiction about the war years – the Home Front (Elizabeth Bowen, Patrick Hamilton), resistance and prisoners of war (Charles Morgan, Nevil Shute), D Day and after (Alexander Baron, Colin MacInnes) – or their immediate aftermath; demobilisation (J. B. Priestley, Henry Green) and the Allied occupation of Germany (Graham Greene, Jack Aistrop). But, as the first Cold War set in, Brooke published an interlocking sequence of prose works in which the militarisation of civil life correlates not with the disasters and triumphs of resistance to Nazism, but with the formation of sexual identity. In *The Orchid Trilogy* wartime service in the Royal Army Medical Corps is a comic resolution of the trials of a personality divided since childhood, a 'ninetyish' aesthetic sensibility longing for, and fearful of, the masculine ideal embodied in the enlisted man, an ambivalent figure which points up the subject's difference. Furthermore, the troubling of masculinity and of normative symbols of the military elicited by Brooke's work is rooted in a writing of region, the coast and uplands of the author's east Kent birthplace.

In the context of the conservative sexual and gender paradigms which were articulated alongside national and anti-communist identities in the period after 1945, notably in literary and cinematic representations of the collective and individual endeavours of the late war, Brooke's novels and autobiography now appear unmistakeably radical. However the volume and generic diversity of his published output suggest a ready accommodation with post-war literary institutions. In the light of these observations, Brooke's precariousness and marginality in the history of twentieth-century writing (despite notable reprintings since the early 1980s) indicates a reception which has conveniently identified Brooke with the figure of the belated outsider ironised in his *Orchid Trilogy*. The description of his fiction as Kafkaesque, aligning it with a European modernist tradition, is an act of saving compartmentalisation which underplays the way his work is affiliated to, and reconstellates, traditions of English regional and topographical literature. It is in these terms, and attending to the ways in which Brooke's fictional recasting of the private myths of his sexual identity presents England as a militarised landscape, that this essay will seek to place his work.

The pleasures of Brooke's autobiographical writing lie in the subtly self-debunking narration of difference and failure, the ironic candour with which he treats the theme of the child as 'polymorphous pervert', and above all, in the uniquely libidinal and numinous renderings of actual and imagined topographies.[1]

Horn Street led not only to Pericar Woods but also to the mysterious territory, where, as I was told, 'the soldiers lived'; bugles called sadly over the hillsides, beyond the woods, and one was apt to encounter, suddenly and without warning, groups of red-faced men in khaki who would sometimes laugh at us or shout rude remarks as we passed. They terrified me – but only for so long as they were in sight; once we were safely past them, my terror gave place to excited imaginings: I liked to think of myself as one of those laughing, devil-may-care heroes inhabiting the high, wind-swept plateau of Shorncliffe Camp. How old did one have to be (I would ask) before one could be a soldier? At least eighteen, I was told. I was seven – I had eleven years to wait; my ambition, I felt, would hardly survive for as long as that. Besides (as I knew perfectly well), I wasn't that *sort* of person: I was 'different'.

I resigned myself to less exacting phantasies; and the red-faced, swaggering heroes of Horn Street were duly translated into smaller, more manageable versions of themselves; nesting in the undercliff, or confined in wire cages in my private 'Zoo' – half human, half-animal, smooth-faced fauns with putteed legs and (protruding from their khaki-covered buttocks) small white tails like the scuts of rabbits.[2]

Brooke's represented places, largely confined to Kentish downland and the Mediterranean scenes of wartime service, are invariably enchanted or haunted by the presence of soldiers, a presence that he turns to strange and dissonant effects.

Joseph Bristow has written illuminatingly about the personality unfolded in *The Orchid Trilogy*:

He remained mesmerized by soldiering. It was not just that he, like so many aesthetes of his class, was attracted to the military. Brooke eventually realized that he could not only *have* the kind of man he desired, he could *be* one himself.[3]

He was also mesmerised by his own writing. To an extent which can have few parallels, Brooke repeated himself. In his six books from the 1940s, motifs recur from one to another, if not verbatim, then with a disconcerting similarity of lexis, idiom or cadence. These patterns suggest, by turns, obsession or a shameless economy of invention (*The Wonderful Summer* of 1949 recycles the botanical and pyrotechnical reveries of the contemporary *The Military Orchid* and *A Mine of Serpents* in a formulaic children's novel). These first two volumes of fiction-alised autobiography are themselves 'two sets of variations upon the same or similar thematic material'.[4] Prefacing the third volume, he wrote: 'To force my material into novel form would involve a Procrustean distortion of the theme', blithely passing over the fact that this is precisely what he had done in his two contemporary novels.[5] *The Scapegoat* and *The Image of a Drawn Sword*, set, respectively before and after the Second World War, have the same ending, which is twice an artistic failure, to some extent justifying the preference for the 'hybrid' form of the trilogy, and perhaps explaining the oversight. But each novel is also a tremendous and fantastic topographical extrapolation of the subjects and phrases of his poetry and autobiography.

There is something hermetic or closeted about Brooke's work, which a biographical reading might seek to explain in terms of his homosexuality, his near life-long habitation of East Kent, or of the belatedness of a writing career that began in his forties and not a little of which is devoted to examining his failure to become a writer twenty years earlier. Anthony Powell has called Brooke's oeuvre 'an art not like that of any other writer known to me in its manner of marking out a region, both actual and imagined, a magical personal kingdom'.[6] It is a world of limits, of the circumferences of remembered juvenile experience. In the concentrically expanding but egocentric territory of the self's contact with others, the most pregnant places are the margins of the landscape, where 'the soldiers lived'. But, especially where these limits appear to be limitations in his work – geographical and thematic repetition, inescapable self-citation – they are also the source of a vision of England which is not ultimately private at all. The 'afternoon land' of remembered childhood in the hinterland of Folkestone (renamed Glamber in his fiction), a region 'not marked on the ordnance map', strikes up complex resonances amongst more familiar literary treatments of the symbolic matrix of English nature and twentieth-century war.[7] Bugles 'that called sadly over the hillsides' do more than just echo Owen's 'bugles calling them from sad shires' from 'Anthem for Doomed Youth' or Keith Douglas's cynically sentimental 'Sportsmen', written in Tunisia in 1943: 'Listen/against the bullet cries the simple horn'.[8] The martial sounds reverberating across Brooke's imagined England bring a military-pastoral nexus to a state of excess which can only serve to draw its contradictions into the light of day.

'Landscape near Tobruk', by B. J. Brooke (born 1908, educated at Bedales and Oxford, and serving in the RAMC in Italy) was published in *Penguin New Writing's* Poetry Supplement in 1944. On the face of it, Brooke's appearance as a wartime author, a serviceman-poet, amounted to just another lyric about campaigning in North Africa over terrain that swiftly covered up the traces of war. The desert is a 'lunar land' which inhibits the mind's 'habitual/And easy gestures', particularly its emotional investments in 'green/And virginal countryside'. This 'hard/And calcined earth' is, as Adam Piette suggests, 'pure abroad', resistant to the kind of domesticating vision that transformed Flanders, in the words of David Jones, into 'South English places'.[9] Even the living disappear into the featureless landscape:

> The soldiers camped
> In the rock-strewn wadi merge
> Like lizard or jerboa in the brown

And neutral ambient: stripped at gunsite,
Or splashing like glad beasts at sundown in
The brackish pool, their smooth
And lion-coloured bodies seem
The indigenous fauna of an unexplored,
Unspoiled country ... [10]

Full of such surprises, the desert required of its many wartime poets a concerted effort to read it as a battlefield.

Four years on, in *The Scapegoat*, Brooke's first published novel, the scene is pre-war Kent:

He leaned over the gate, his eyes fixed on the distant woods. Presently a sound of heavy, regular footsteps in the road distracted him. A column of soldiers was coming round the corner: one of the battalions in training at the neighbouring barracks. Weighed down with the cumbrous webbing-equipment, sweating in spite of the cold, their raw, meat-red faces surly beneath steel-helmets, they passed heavily down the narrow lane. To Duncan, the soldiers seemed an integral part of the landscape, the indigenous fauna of an unexplored, unfriendly country.[11]

That Libya is 'unspoiled' was a commonplace, but the unfriendliness of Kent is more puzzling, until we learn more about the significance in Brooke's work of the actual and imagined presence of soldiers. Their indigenousness is a different matter. That they appear native to the Libyan wadi conforms to an irony familiar to readers of war poetry: nature is not merely indifferent to the fate of soldier males in battle, it treacherously camouflages their intentions to injure each other. But their niche in the ecology of Kent conspires to transform English nature into a militarised realm which is at once seductive and terrifying.

There is something else troubling about this repetition, which is worth lingering over, and another wartime poem helps to clarify the issue. The nude figures in F. T. Prince's much-anthologised 'Soldiers Bathing', it is often assumed, are sporting in warm North African waters. But the men Prince wrote about were plunging into the North Sea near Scarborough.[12] If the habitual mislocation does not significantly revise interpretations of the poem, it does suggest the extent to which, no less than is the case with 1914–18, apprehensions of the violence of the Second World War are mediated by landscape and place. Brooke's reiteration of the image of 'indigenous fauna' is offensive to this reflex of geographically compartmentalising the events of 1939–45 (which has been a key factor in the selective displacement of larger historical and political meanings in the national memory of war). The repetition appears too blatant a suppression of contexts.

Of his wartime service in Italy, Brooke wrote: 'Here, as in Africa, the flowers were near enough to those of Northern Europe to strike a familiar note.'[13] (Auden, too, mapped the scenes of an English childhood onto Italian terrain in his exactly contemporaneous 'In Praise of Limestone'.) But the psychic impacts of these places are distinct; Southern landscapes 'had none of that mysteriousness, that hint of the *au delà*, which lurks always in the English countryside'.[14] Where the desert refused the mark of military presence, the English countryside in Brooke's writing is a truly militarised space, one that bears indelible traces of soldiering. The Army does not despoil the landscape, as many mid-century conservationists would have it, but is integral to the 'vague, rather frightening yet perversely seductive aura of evil' with which its limits are associated.[15] Brooke was not carelessly relocating an image of overseas conflict in a weary and incomplete demobilisation of the wartime imagination. He was bringing military fauna back home to an environment in which the camouflaging of its violent purposes was not a tactical necessity but a culturally-coded vision of Englishness. Whatever Brooke's motives, his books from the late-1940s reactivate and transfigure the peculiarly parochial gloss which English culture has placed on twentieth-century war. And they invite us to reassess that culture's residual, contradictory but by no means redundant articulations of the military and native soil.

Ronald Firbank, a writer in whom Brooke recognised his own atonal counterpoint of the sentimental and the self-mocking, had a habit of collecting phrases: 'he was a careless worker in some respects – he would inadvertently use them twice over'.[16] But when Brooke echoes himself verbally, literally returning over the same ground, he does so with a self-consciousness that recalls another maker of lists, James Joyce. 'Landscape near Tobruk' resurfaces six years on in an account of Brooke's period of post-war re-enlistment:

> 'What's to do?' I said.
> 'F—all, at the moment. There's a pile of eleven-fifty-sevens wants checking sometime, but that'll do after dinner.'
> 'I'm easy,' I said.
> Corporal Bradnum settled down to the *Daily Mirror* crossword; his mate read a very old number of *Illustrated*.

'Word of seven letters beginning with C, meaning "heat to a high temperature"', said the corporal.[17]

The answer, which the educated Brooke can of course supply, is calcine, the alchemical term that as clap-wallah-poet he had used to describe the burnt desert earth. The anecdote underlines a determination to go into exile from a literary world to which he has yet to gain admittance, and to evade the certainty of failure. In the manner of T. E. Lawrence's enlistment as Aircraftsman Shaw, he submerges self in a deliberate return to an impersonal disciplinary culture. Freedom from responsibility in the Army is preferred to the 'prospect of becoming a professional *littérateur*':

> I knew the booksy racket too well: a *succès d'estime* with a first novel; reviewing for the *Statesman* or the *Times Lit. Supp.*, a talk or two on the Third Programme. Then another book: not so successful. ('I confess to being disappointed with Mr. X's new novel ...'); more reviewing, more talks; an essay or two on some obscure minor writer for the *Cornhill*; and then the gradual decline, through anthologies, 'introductions' and light middles, to a weekly *causerie* in *John O'London* or a staff-job in the BBC ... No, no, I thought: I would as soon be helping Corporal Bradnum with his crossword.[18]

Burying his own published words in the laconic exchanges that pass time in the battalion store while inventorying the kit of demobbed soldiers, Brooke purports to resist his *belle lettriste* destiny. The fiction he was writing at the time does little to challenge the self-critical reserve manifested by this fantasy. 'Blackthorn Winter', a story of unconsummated and unpatriotic heterosexual desire, is banal even by the uneven standards of *Penguin New Writing*:

> She sat down by the window, twisting her handkerchief in her hand (sic), but dry-eyed: looking out across the rain-sodden fields, and the hedges with their falling blossom, towards the row of empty Nissen huts which were all that was left of the camp.[19]

But within a year, and the appearance of *The Scapegoat*, 'truck with the soldiers' – which raises only ripples of village gossip in 'Blackthorn Winter' – has become, in the words of the gay novelist Peter Cameron, 'almost unbelievably subversive and kinky'.[20] Later, in *The Image of a Drawn Sword*, those empty Nissen huts are translated into a numinous site with immemorial military associations, the scene of a 'queer caper': intimacy between men is mysteriously bound up with a bizarre eruption of the phantasmagoria of soldiering which sees the imposition of martial law across Kent. The compelling but disquieting qualities of the scenery on which Brooke writes and rewrites his personal myths are the most striking aspects of his literary efflorescence. In Woolf's *Mrs Dalloway*, Peter Walsh, the returning imperialist functionary, is overtaken by the patter of English militarism, 'like the patter of leaves in a wood':

> Boys in uniform, carrying guns, marched with their eyes ahead of them, marched, their arms stiff, and on their faces an expression like the letters of a legend written round the base of a statue praising duty, gratitude, fidelity, love of England.[21]

The visages of Brooke's 'bum-faced' soldiery connote another kind of love, and his writing is a sexual subversion of bellicose nationalism.[22] Arguably, these dissonant meanings are most potent where they are rooted in a landscape which is not bucolic but militarised, as if some native hydra's teeth had sprouted khaki troopers in every valley and rockery.

In *The Scapegoat* secret places are a margin between civilian and military life, and Kent becomes a highly sexualised and liminal realm. Fantasy is literalised in a struggle which, against the background of an environment pregnant with threat, builds up to an alarming brutality. Brooke concatenates the imaginative perversity of adolescence and the disappointments of maturity (which are subtly played off against each other in *The Orchid Trilogy*) in a generational war: 'sexual abnormality, though it may seem a bearable misfortune in youth, is less easy to come to terms with in middle-age.'[23]

Orphaned at thirteen, Duncan Cameron is transplanted from the 'rounded and perfect world' of his West Country childhood to the 'masculine hardness' of Kent, duplicated in the 'austere masculinity' of his uncle Gerald's farmhouse.[24] An only son of a widowed mother, Duncan's rite of passage is the 'logical conclusion' of childhood 'crazes': botanising, fireworks, 'the rabbit-scutted soldiers in the shrubbery' (p. 28). Duncan's wild soldiers reappear in Brooke's memoir *Private View* as the imaginary inhabitants (toy soldiers, sometimes airmen) of 'closely guarded and anonymous "places" – those countries of the mind which lay, now, remote and unapproachable, beyond the Iron Curtain of puberty'.[25] *The Scapegoat* narrates sexual awakening as a penetration of a militarised landscape which, no longer just a projection of childhood play, materialises as the source of subversive compulsions. Brooke's Cold War metaphor for the land of lost content is characteristic of a sceptical relegation of public events to the status of private alibis. But the cumulative effect of this refracting of modern military history through the remembered rural scenes of early upbringing is, oddly, to remind us of the facility with which English literary culture has pastoralised its memory of war. The reiterative figuration of the soldier as object of homosexual desire in Brooke's writing creates a landscape at once peculiar and familiar, its subversive character not accountable to the erotic subtext alone, but in significant measure to the way national ideologies of war are made literal. Autochthonic myths of the defence of the island realm – resistance springing from the soil in a spontaneously militant patriotism which contrasts with the modernity of post-Napoleonic standing armies on the continent – have come true, with soldiers sprouting up everywhere.

At first Duncan cannot avoid them, then he seeks them out. Entrained for his new home, he falls in with a soldier posted to the hinterland of Folkestone, Brooke's birthplace. In a hastening of his destiny, Duncan is invited to share a cigarette in a rehearsal of the kind of exchange that traditionally cements the strangely domestic camaraderie of the other ranks:

> And we stretched out, unbuttoning our braces,
> Smoking a Woodbine, darning dirty socks...[26]

Brooke's Woodbine – with its appropriately floral name – is the olfactory complement of the bugle's call, one of the author's Anglicised versions of the Proustian *madeleine*:

> The pungent flavour of the cigarette seemed to him a concentrated essence of that fainter, more diffused odour which exhaled from the soldier himself – an alien, mysterious smell, partly tobacco, partly the warm body-reek of sweat and stale urine; to Duncan it seemed the very odour of heroism, an exhalation from the battlefield.
>
> p. 10

In *The Orchid Trilogy* sensations are chronologically promiscuous, they do not only cast the mind back into a lost past, but symbolise the core conflicts of adult experience. *The Scapegoat* collapses these temporalities to produce a more direct confrontation between libido and repression. The plot is a contest between the seductive appeal of the objects of youthful imaginative investment and avuncular authority. Gerald, striving to make a man of Duncan, is no longer himself man enough: at forty-five his physique is collapsing, he can only regret resigning his commission, and the coming war appears on the horizon as a relief from agricultural depression and psychological ennui. He imposes on his nephew the discipline to which he would submit himself, but the boy is already crossing to the other side in an 'undeclared war' (p. 108). Watching troops in 'skin-tight singlets' running cross-country, Duncan experiences a 'sense of fulfilment' realising they 'were no longer the strange fauna of an alien country, but co-habitants, comrades in a world to which he himself now irrevocably belonged: a hard world, but no longer hostile, a soldier's land' (p. 47).

This sense of affiliation comes upon him in a 'bad place', a barren wood-enclosed field called California, its scarry mysteriousness almost ludicrously overcharged by the presence of a trilithon (shades of Hardy's Stonehenge in *Tess*), piles of dead vermin, a maggot-infested sheep's carcass and stinking hellebore with its 'unpleasant mousy tang of hemlock'.[27] Duncan awaits its occupation by military allies in his struggle against his uncle's punitive regime. His thieving from his uncle for Jim Tylor, the soldier on the train, brings the repressed world of the farm to crisis. But visits to the camp also provoke a horrifying materialisation of the vague content of his 'secret phantasies', in the vulgar, physical, unself-conscious and highly ambiguous sexual charge that envelops the regimented community of soldier males. Tylor's tattooed white flesh, bearing a variant of the serpent mark that represents an atavistic bond of service in *The Image of a Drawn Sword*, proleptically figures Duncan's blood-smeared corpse at the novel's end.

More subtle previsions are compelled by the interanimation of imagination and topography. Duncan's state of fearful libidinousness makes him sensitive to an 'abnormal' landscape echoing with indistinct sounds of horns or singing: 'there *weren't* any soldiers – not then, when I first heard it' (p. 99). These unaccountable signs are Gerald's first clue that there is something hidden in the local terrain; disputing the source of Duncan's noises, it was 'as if their souls ... [were] meeting each other nakedly, shamefully, in a setting of some shared, secret degradation' (p. 99). Gerald had earlier found the boy 'exhausted with misery and terror' in California, and brought him back to his bed, where Duncan dreams of verminous attack and 'Gerald was somewhere in the dream, too' (pp. 76, 84). The uncle, shrinking from the unconscious pressure of Duncan's body, sits out the night, rising with 'a creeping disgust, a sense of degradation' as the radio relays news about the Germans entering Prague (p. 85). In the novel's closing pages, he will again rise at dawn, only this time 'the mysterious landscape had revealed its secret' in a recollection of travelling 'in a strange country' whose horizon had seemed uncannily familiar (p. 122). The remembered numinousness of place is a catalyst for assembling clues – ' "voices" in a wood, and a light where no light could be' – and for a pursuit of Duncan, who has fled from punishment to the now deserted camp by the standing stones (p. 123). But the ensuing struggle – Duncan biting like a stoat, Gerald beating him lifeless with a riding crop – pitches the story towards melodrama and puts its suggestiveness at risk from bathetic explication:

> From far away, at the barracks over towards Glamber, came the faint nostalgic note of a bugle, sounding reveillé. Gerald turned away, seeing everything clearly at last: knowing that the long initiation was over; the rites observed, the cycle completed.
>
> p. 128

This deterministic cancelling of an incendiary relationship (incestuous, paedophilic) is bound to disappoint readers, who, like Peter Cameron, have an eye to the comic and domestic treatment of homosexuality by later generations of writers: he views this unsatisfactory denouement as a self-censorious obfuscation. It is true that there are uncertainties in enunciating and relating the conscious and unconscious states of Duncan and Gerald. This problem arises from Brooke's ambition to assemble the warring components of an identity across personal and historical time, and to create a perspective from which to relate the mental and affective lives of the adolescent and the adult. *The Orchid Trilogy* migrates between eras apparently dissociated by a historical process (one that makes Brooke a writer out of his time, a survivor from the 1920s). The perversity of the aesthete's fulfilment in wartime and post-war Army service is motivated by delicate, almost mandarin elaborations on the desired military Other which haunted his youth. In turn, the eruption of the figure of the soldier into the bucolic scenes of childhood is given a critically ironic gloss by juxtaposition with the crude banalities of barrack life and pox-doctoring.

But in *The Scapegoat*, the relationship between naïve libidinousness and self-conscious inhibition is handled in a form that is ultimately less flexible, portentously tragic rather than ironic. The titular symbolism of atonement – Duncan the sacrificial victim, Gerald the scapegoat – suggests that the nephew is in a sense father to the uncle. The 'faint nostalgic note of a bugle' which coincides with the closing of the circle of initiation implies that he is arrested back into a crisis of identity akin to that into which Duncan has been drawn by his new environment. The approaching hostilities which may relieve Gerald from the onerous failures of civilian life hold out the self-obliterating appeal of Army discipline, but it is hard to say whether the secret of the landscape he has intuited represents access to the dangerous enchantments that overtook Duncan or just the means by which to bury them.

In his discursive poem 'California', Brooke makes explicit the connection between liminal place and disturbances in the foundations of identity:

> A centre that is, in fact, no centre, but
> A shifting objective, like the sexual dreams
> Of puberty ...

In the 'exile' of adulthood 'the attraction and repulsion/ Of the mad kingdom' flickers indifferently between the transcendent and the banal:

> The tree becomes a woman, the rare orchis
> A kilted soldier, and the jankerwallah
> Finds in the bum-faced sergeant's naked grin
> His love's objective, and a Venusberg
> In scrubbed and blancoed guardroom ... [28]

Orchid-hunting is one of the ruling figures for what lies beyond in *The Military Orchid*. Botanising becomes a quest for a fugitive symbol of the idea of the soldier and of the sense of inferiority that the 'appurtenances of soldiering' so self-destructively yet deliciously incarnate. Apparently extinct in Britain by the Great War, *O. militaris* – 'its name ... a *cor au fond du bois*' – was rediscovered only in May 1947.[29] The story of the guarding of the colony's location by voluntary naturalist organisations like the Chiltern Military Orchid Group – coded telegrams, round-the-clock surveillance, wardens with shotguns – reads like a story of the Home Guard in the manner of Isherwood and Upward. This concealment was effective until long after Brooke had stopped writing. In *The Military Orchid*, the plant's extinction is mourned alongside the passing of 'the concept of soldiering as a chivalric and honourable calling':

> Behind the drum and fife
> Past hawthorn-wood and hollow
> Through earth and out of life
> The soldiers follow ...[30]

Brooke's ellipses silently modify Housman's period-stopped quatrain: the precariousness of Brooke's militarised landscape – a scene of ambiguous quest and self-division – is of a different order to the immemorial trials and ironies of Housman's Shropshire: 'Then 'twas the Roman, now 'tis I.'[31] Brooke called Elizabeth Bowen a '"landscape with figures"' novelist, interested in the '"cracking" or "heaving"' of the ground upon which they so perilously exist', but as in much of his critical writing, he seems also to be describing himself.[32] His soldiery compel psychogeographic upheavals which are not end-stopped by the 'free land of the grave' but drawn out in ambivalent submission to the alien ethos of embodied military discipline.[33]

Brooke advertises the failure of psychoanalysis to explain the love of flowers, but we do not require Freud's account of flower symbolism in *The Interpretation of Dreams* (and the analysis of his dream about authoring a botanical monograph) to recognise the indigenous and abiding association that underpins Brooke's floral emblem of military fauna. The Military Orchid, or 'Soldiers Cullions' as Gerard's *The Herball* of 1597 names it, is a testicular icon. The anthropomorphic significance of its tubers (resembling a bulky scrotum) is in the case of this hybrid amplified by the ginger-bread-man form of a prominent, pink labellum (the 'kilted soldier' of 'California').[34] *O. militaris* symbolises not a world that has disappeared, but one of childhood's 'rehearsals, incomplete or abortive attempts at the real thing', which Brooke would know in his periods in the Army in the 1940s.[35]

The Image of a Drawn Sword is a fantastic variation on the affective connections between the romanticising fantasies of the militarised landscape of childhood and the submission of selfhood in enlistment. The absence of specification in the early pages – set on the terrain beyond Glamber, but consisting of a series of tropes rather than topoi – is in the nature of a clue: the novel's plot progressively concretises a topography which emerges initially as a correlate of psychic states. English landscape, in a line from Wordsworth via Hardy to Edward Thomas, is the sounding board of the self's questioning, and a screen on which intellectual and moral ambitions are projected. The pathetic fallacy, whose relation to the patriotic fiction of an essential English topography is grounded by the 'handful of English earth' with which Thomas affirmed what he was going to France to fight for, is given new implications in Brooke's novel.[36]

Reynard Langrish is in a state of incipient disintegration, the boundaries of his person are dislocated. This dispersal, akin to a failure of proprioception, is signified by a leakage of the punctual self into the numinous beyond: the 'several parts of himself' appear to lie 'scattered about the perimeter of a gradually widening circle'.[37] This unfixedness is both a consequence and a characteristic of his environment: 'it seemed to him that the very countryside itself was exerting upon him an invisible, indefinable pressure... At the same time, the features of the landscape took on a peculiar appearance of unreality, as though seen through a distorting lens, or reproduced by some inferior photographic process' (p. 14).

This loosening of identity is answered by a summons to resume a wartime military personality. A young Army officer, Roy Archer, turning up lost at the cottage Langrish shares with his mother, is a source of exaltation and fear, a 'larger than life' masculine ideal and the locus of an inscrutable authority (p. 19). The military invasion of Langrish's life temporarily galvanises him out of lassitude but exacerbates his sense of suspension, for Archer's behaviour implies that the matter of re-enlistment and retraining has been decided, their purpose already understood. Langrish is redivided across the boundary between the normal world of work and the alternately virtual and real world of a remobilised Britain. His initial dilemma is made more acute by the conjunctions that arise in his consciousness between the enigma of the political emergency to which Archer confidentially alludes and residual childhood fears and desires mapped onto Kent.

Chief among the places 'not marked on the ordnance map' is Clambercrown, a stretch of downland that in Brooke's memoirs is a *terra incognita* on an egocentric cognitive map of the enlarging world of his childhood. In *Image*, the name stirs a 'vague childhood memory' which referred to 'nothing so definite' as a human habitation but to 'an ill-defined woodland district, never delimited'. This 'mysterious territory' is restored to the adult Langrish as 'a landmark for military manoeuvres' in overheard 'Army "shop"' (pp. 28–9). This is not so much a case of the individual coming under the sway of social space (the cartographic representation of Britain being, historically, a primarily military project) but of the military having insinuated itself into an unobjectifiable, private topography. Secret places represent the possible field for manoeuvre of military units whose preparations are publicly inadmissible. But there is more to what is going on here than Brooke using the military (a culturally and officially countenanced homosocial sphere) to provide cover for a story that explores a crisis of sexual identity, or externalising psychic breakdown as a political pathology (the neurotic's willing submission to militant authoritarianism).

Brooke's vision of rural England modifies the relationship between the pastoral and war. Nature's apparent duplicity in occluding the presence of agents of military violence is a hallmark of the canon of twentieth-century English war poetry, from Owen and David Jones to Henry Reed and Keith Douglas (only post-Hiroshima would war acquire the power to change the weather). Brooke's soldiers are not aliens in a landscape otherwise indifferent to man, they are indigenous features of a culturally and psychologically represented space that is distinguishable from both objectified nature and the objectifying grid of the ordnance survey. Geoffrey Matthews's poem 'Modern Deceit' (1941) exploits the ambiguities of this kind of landscape – in which khaki colonises English verdure – to question the hegemonic purchase of patriotic bellicism on servicemen. The inscrutable gap between the militarised identity displayed by the temporary soldier's uniform and his private motives is paralleled in a scene which oscillates between war naturalised and nature militarised:

> The farm where I work has ivy at the windows
> And filaments of smoke climbing like convolvulus,
> But there are no sties nor ploughlands there, the cattle are sham,
> The nesting-boxes are a guard against gas.[38]

In Brooke's writing this military transformation of place, in which topographical appearances become dangerously deceptive, is not contingent on wartime exigency, it is made an abiding feature of the landscape. The military presence becomes natural, or rather a core element of English nature in its function as a component of cultural identity.

Langrish's troubled assimilation to the conspiratorial scheme of enlistment and training, which seems to be an outgrowth of a locale no longer familiar, is bound up with the resurgence of earlier confrontations with the militarised limits of his birthplace. The far cry of a bugle restores an 'older memory' of searching fruitlessly for the Dog Inn at

Clambercrown. Then he had found himself surrounded by soldiers, and had fled their 'red, grinning faces', pursued 'by laughter and catcalls' (p. 40). The inability, for long after, to revisit that scene (Brooke himself, as we have already seen, returns to it in *The Goose Cathedral*) is echoed in his present concealment of the 'sense of well-being' that ensues from participation in the 'esoteric tribal rites' of running and sparring conducted on the site of the Roman Camp and from the sense of 'obligation' to re-enlist. It is an obligation that is impossible to resist because it is unverifiable: the more Langrish tries to pin it down, the further it transforms his personal crisis into a mode of subliminal conscription. As the day appointed for re-enlistment nears, his contrary responses to the summons cast him back to a fear as if he was starting school and an excitement 'comparable to the vague stirrings of sexuality in an adolescent' (p. 65). Archer's desertion of Langrish (the authority which he detests but is compelled to submit to will not acknowledge him) furthers the process by which the occulted militant emergency is internalised as a possibility of escape from a sense of dissolution. Langrish assumes the role of the inferior adolescent of Brooke's autobiographical writing, drawn to the musty, muscular and brutal camaraderie of the military. His inhibitions are figured in the elusiveness of the conspirators. Like *O. militaris*, this mysterious force evades his attempts to locate it.

When Langrish retraces the 'gymnasium' in the Roman Camp above Glamber the only occupant is a vagrant. Although this old soldier is branded with the serpent tattoo that distinguishes members of the training battalion, he dismisses Langrish's 'wishful' account of military preparations as a 'queer caper' (p. 69). Back on civvy street next morning, minus his wallet, Langrish recalls this encounter – 'the tramp's rough kindness, his offer of the cocoa and a "kip", the sudden birth of trust and a brief, transient affection' – as a 'precocious flower' that had 'withered in the bud' (p. 72). Brooke doesn't permit his hero to articulate the queerness of his seduction by an unofficial military enterprise which explicitly seeks to restore the virtues of the 'old-fashioned' swaddie after all the wartime 'pansy nonsense' about the superiority of the educated 'citizen-soldier' (p. 46). As in the autobiographical texts, the rough appeal of the virile trooper to the self-conscious bourgeois is narrated topographically.

Joining up in Archer's increasingly invisible force comes to seem a lost chance of escaping a 'monotonous, circumscribed life' (p. 75). However the novel sustains the inner conflict arising from idealisations of military service by tracing Langrish's inhibitions and yearnings onto the altered terrain of the 'uncharted region' of Clambercrown. Never-occupied defensive positions from the late war possess 'an odd air of expectancy, as though their disuse were merely temporary' (p. 74). The disquieting effort required to explain signs of more recent military occupation is symptomatic of a loss of will that accompanies the receding hope of freedom from self-consciousness in Army discipline. But when the zero-hour for enlistment has passed it is these barbed-wire barriers which provoke the 'motion of irrevocable surrender' which translate him from civilian into soldier. The fenced-off dug-out which Langrish explores in a return of the 'old curiosity' is a tunnel which debouches into a terrain ruled by military law. Penetrating the residually militarised landscape, he irrevocably enters a khaki world.

The novel, despite Brooke's disavowals, has been called Kafkaesque (p. 10). But Langrish's futile attempts to object to his forced enlistment before a military hierarchy whose procedures do not admit the possibility of non-military prerogatives, draws on native responses to mobilisation and militarisation in the Second World War, processes whose autotelic manifestations struck many as unrelated to any stated or coherent war aim. Julian Maclaren-Ross's stories in *The Stuff to Give the Troops* (1944) are the most entertaining and caustic contemporary narratives about conscripted civilians ensnared in the regulations of an autonomous and sovereign military regime. In homage to 'I had to go sick', Maclaren-Ross's best delineation of the de-humanising miasma of red tape and chickenshit into which the onetime-person is jettisoned, Langrish is denied recourse to medical redress because 'the Army no longer recognises the practice of psychotherapy' (p. 112).

By turning Langrish's dilemma from getting into the Army to trying to escape its claims on him, Brooke brings the alternation of submission and repulsion to a new pitch of desperation, reconfiguring the ambivalent motives behind his own sequence of enlistments as a political nightmare. The fantasy militarisation of England's flora and fauna is literalised, and a psychological division is turned into a state of emergency in which 'all law is martial': 'There's surely not much distinction nowadays between being at war and being at peace' (p. 110). Under this law, Langrish's loathing of the 'inescapable crude intimacy' of barrack society, 'a lewd phantasmagoria of squalor' weakens in proportion to his submersion to regimentation and the 'monotonous patois of the Army...a crude, homespun fabric of friendliness'; 'enforced servitude' becomes 'a perverse and inexplicable joy' (pp. 103–05).

But Langrish's disorientating experience of sharing control of himself with his military Other is unsatisfactorily resolved in a crudely Oedipal struggle. *The Image of a Drawn Sword*, like *The Scapegoat*, suffers from the requirements of novelistic denouement. A return to his mother's cottage is a last act of resistance against external authority. Running away from punishment, he seems to awake from the 'confused, duplicated world' of occupied Kent (p. 137). But it is the past that has vanished: home has been visited by 'years of neglect', ghoulishly rendered in a 'putrefied' meal laid out for him by his mother, and the vestigial features on her decayed corpse (pp. 139–40). Langrish's own flesh is altered also, inscribed now with the tattoo of 'the fanged and terrible serpent coiled about the naked sword' (p. 137). This is the brand of an abiding homosocial community, cutting across class boundaries, for even members of the officer-caste like Archer sport it, and across time, resembling a supposedly Druidic amulet in Glamber museum, and a full-dress uniform portrait of Langrish's father, his hand 'clasping the sword-hilt ...' (pp. 18, 44–5). Langrish's 'native indecision' is dispelled as the cycle of initiation into that collective is completed. Archer comes to the cottage a second time bearing news that 'the other lot ... are moving up' and forming their HQ in the old inn at Clambercrown (p. 141). Langrish, prepared to repel the soldiers he expects to arrest him, shoots his recruiter. The killing of the authority figure who revealed then blocked the portals of the khaki world, together with the exaction of a promise 'to go through with it', is a crashing deflation of the novel's carefully wrought and cleverly sustained enigmas. Langrish's 'serene happiness' in the operation of an unflinching will as past and future are fused in 'the living moment' verges on a parody of contemporary war fiction, such as Jack Lindsay's *Beyond Terror* (1943) with its endorsement of violence and the violent death: 'Living this fight with an awareness of the issues, one lived the after-struggle and achievement, one lived at the heart of life'.[39] In Lindsay's book, the issues are ideological, political ideals which turn killing into a mode of transcendence. Brooke's version of consummation is an equally partial and idealised resolution of profound contradictions, which, however, exist at the level of psychological attractions to authoritarianism.

Brooke's oeuvre cannot be read solely as an aetiology and taxonomy of sexual difference (though he returns to these themes in later novels about the margins of 1930s 'homocommunist' literary culture, *The Passing of a Hero* [1953] and *Unconventional Weapons* [1961]). By writing back onto an English rural childhood the sexy appeal of Auden's 'Soldiers who swarm in the pubs in their pretty clothes' (in Folkestone's louche and dangerous neighbour Dover), Brooke's work is suggestive of the complex relationship between ideas of English landscape and fantasies of the military. He tantalisingly literalises the poet's intuition that 'all this show/ Has, somewhere inland, a vague and dirty root'.[40]

Superficially, *Image* resembles contemporary fictions concerned with the precarious fate of individualism in a society where a condition of war or the supersession of military authority have become normal, like Warner's *The Aerodrome* (1941) or Orwell's *Nineteen Eighty-Four* (1949). But the political scenario which Brooke invents as a correlative of Langrish's buried desires (and as a variation on his own surrenders to military authority) is not helpfully thought of as a prophecy of an emergent militant collectivism. In its fantastic extrapolation of something already latent in the imagined countryside, the novel refracts both the historical invasions of rural England by a military whose territorial needs were swollen by the mass-mobilisation of the world wars and by mechanisation, and the ironic cultural inscription of high-tech war within pastoral conventions.

'Kent and Sussex have always been particularly liable to invasion' wrote Sheila Kaye-Smith in 1937, viewing the suburbanisation of the South East between the wars in terms of Norman incursions and Napoleonic threats.[41] But E. M. Forster saw the military as the sharp end of urbanising and industrialising modernity:

> The fighting services are bound to become serious enemies of what is left of England. Wherever they see a tract of wild, unspoiled country they naturally want it for camps, artillery practice, bomb-dropping, poison-gas tests. I remember Salisbury Plain thirty years ago, when the cancer was beginning to gnaw at its eastern lobe, round Bulford, but all the rest was pure. Now the plain is infected from side to side; there is machine-gun practice behind Heytesbury, and flags lolling their tongues of blood up the lanes to Imber-in-the-Down. In Dorsetshire, Bere Heath (Hardy's Egdon) has been attacked by the Tank Corps, which is also responsible for the ruining of the land near Lulworth Cove.[42]

This apparently unequal struggle could be reversed in wartime allegories of fascism (Warner's *The Aerodrome*, or Ealing Studio's 1942 *Went the Day Well?*) and of the People's War (Powell and Pressburger's *A Canterbury Tale* of 1944). This was not because Forster's fears were unwarranted, but because the English village landscape had become a symbol of the civil and ostensibly libertarian militarisation celebrated in C. Day Lewis's Local Defence Volunteer poem 'The Stand-To':

> Last night a Stand-To was ordered. Thirty men of us here
> Came out to guard the star-lit village – my men who wear

Unwitting the season's beauty, the received truth of the spade –
Roadmen, farm labourers, masons, turned to another trade.[43]

Perhaps the most surprising symbol of post-war opposition to military
jurisdiction over tracts of England (for the ruralist tradition has been in
many ways defiantly masculinist) is the Greenham protest of the 1980s.
But in the Army's recent 'conversion to conservation' the firing range is
represented as a defended natural environment, secure from popular
transgression. To Patrick Wright this 'affinity between green activism
and military power' marks a clear break with the 'cultural and anti-
statist valuation of English rural life' which flourished in the 1930s.[44]

Wright's account of the Royal Armoured Corps' as-yet-unrescinded
occupation of the Dorset village of Tyneham (just east of Forster's ruined
Lulworth Cove) during the Second World War reveals the complexity of
cultural construction of natural heritage. But while military encroach-
ments provided a rallying point for nostalgic rhetoric about a violated
English countryside, we should not overlook the impress of war on the
reproduction of ideas of rural tradition. Inter-war ruralist groupings like
the Wessex Agricultural Defence Association, the English Mistery and
even the Soil Association had their ideological roots in fascism and a
militant anti-modernity.[45] That this constellation of rural and militant
values does not wither away in post-war Britain has much to do with a
process by which English place is hallowed by the memory of wars
which were fought elsewhere. One significant strand in this survival is
the work of Henry Williamson, notably his *roman fleuve*, *A Chronicle of
Ancient Sunlight* (1951–69), in which an authoritarian politics born of
the community of the trenches is sublimated in nature writing and
efforts to reverse a declining agricultural economy. For Philip Maddison,
the 'obliteration of the country adjoining London' is a less ambiguous
breach in the continuity of his life than the Great War. His Wessex
Gartenfeste, or Garden Fortress, is an iconic element in Williamson's
mapping of war onto rural England: the sequestered countryside is the
only environment in which the reconstructive vision that the veteran
draws from his war experience can be preserved from dissolution.[46]

Literary English landscapes and the cultural meanings of twentieth-
century wars converge in ways that require us to build on Fussell's
observation that 'there are moments in war memoirs when vignettes of
rural irony seem the result of a conflation of Hardy and Housman'.[47]
The process is bipolar: while literate servicemen learned to refract
Flanders through a mordant poetry of English landscape, later generations of readers annexed the tragedy of the Great War to the scenery

vacated by the athletic territorials of *A Shropshire Lad*. Thomas's 'As the teams' head brass', with its rueful annotation of war's disruption of the husbanding of English soil, is emblematic of the way the war came home as its literature's ironic conventions were reversed. War would be inscribed on rural England not only via the iconography of memorials in churches and on village greens but also, more gradually, as a precarious landscape became a metonym for the loss of a generation. Rupert Brooke's famous conceit of alien soil reterritorialised, 'some corner of a foreign field/ That is for ever England', is turned on its head. 'The corner of a corner of England is infinite', observed Hilaire Belloc: the numinousness of landscape is amplified by its association with historical crisis.[48] When Alun Lewis complained, two years after Dunkirk, about 'England's pastoral army', he intended a slight against sedentary and distinctly unbellicose garrison duties.[49] But in describing the 'unreal trauma' of the Army's continuing phoney war in this way he also registered the strange affinity between the idea of the military and the countryside: Lewis's soldiers belong there.

Brooke's wild soldiers might be considered an uncanny literalisation of a latent presence in English literary topography. The perverseness of his imagination comes to seem indigenous itself, not because it perpetually returns to the same east Kent terrain, but because its ramifications are entangled with the broader imprint of war on rural heritage. But in envisaging servicemen as native fauna, Brooke's writing is also a source of illumination, casting into relief perceptions of the countryside which naturalise a strain of militarist ideology purportedly alien to a modern England which has, 'traditionally', fought its wars abroad.

Notes

1. Jocelyn Brooke, *Private View* (1954; London: Robin Clark, 1989), p. 1.
2. Jocelyn Brooke, *The Orchid Trilogy* (Harmondsworth: Penguin, 1981), pp. 339–40.
3. Joseph Bristow, *Effeminate England: Homoerotic Writing After 1885* (Buckingham: Open University Press, 1995), p. 156.
4. Brooke, 'Author's Note' to *A Mine of Serpents*, p. 112.
5. Brooke, 'Author's Note' to *The Goose Cathedral*, p. 309.
6. Anthony Powell, *The Strangers Are All Gone* (London: Heinemann, 1982), p. 18.
7. Jocelyn Brooke, *The Image of a Drawn Sword* (Harmondsworth: Penguin, 1983), p. 28.
8. Jon Stallworthy, ed., *The Poems of Wilfred Owen* (London: The Hogarth Press, 1985), p. 76; Desmond Graham, ed., *The Complete Poems of Keith Douglas* (Oxford: Oxford University Press, 1979), p. 110.

9. Adam Piette, *Imagination at War: British Fiction and Poetry 1939–1945* (London: Macmillan, 1995), p. 20.
10. Jocelyn Brooke, 'Landscape near Tobruk', *Penguin New Writing*, 21 (1944), p. 149.
11. Jocelyn Brooke, *The Scapegoat* (London: The Bodley Head, 1948), p. 31.
12. Communication with the author.
13. Brooke, *Orchid Trilogy*, p. 92.
14. Ibid., p. 91.
15. Jocelyn Brooke, *The Dog at Clambercrown* (1955: London: Sphere, 1990), p. 53.
16. Jocelyn Brooke, *Ronald Firbank* (London: Arthur Barker, 1951), p. 12.
17. Brooke, *Orchid Trilogy*, p. 320.
18. Ibid., p. 422.
19. Jocelyn Brooke, 'Blackthorn Winter', *Penguin New Writing*, 31 (1947), p. 183.
20. Ibid., p. 174; Peter Cameron, 'Afterword' to Jocelyn Brooke, *The Scapegoat* (New York: Turtle Point Press, n.d.), p. 171.
21. Virginia Woolf, *Mrs Dalloway* (Harmondsworth: Penguin, 1972), p. 57.
22. Jocelyn Brooke, 'California', *December Spring: Poems* (London: The Bodley Head, 1946), p. 48.
23. Brooke, *Firbank*, p. 82.
24. Brooke, *Scapegoat*, pp. 6, 17, 41.
25. Brooke, *Private View*, p. 35.
26. Alun Lewis, 'All Day it has Rained', *Raiders' Dawn and other Poems* (London: George Allen & Unwin, 1942), p. 16.
27. Richard Mabey, *Flora Britannica* (London: Sinclair-Stevenson, 1996), p. 41.
28. Brooke, *December Spring*, pp. 46–8.
29. Brooke, *Orchid Trilogy*, p. 21.
30. Ibid. p. 53; A. E. Housman, *Collected Poems and Selected Prose*, ed., Christopher Ricks (Harmondsworth: Penguin, 1989), p. 104.
31. Housman, 'On Wenlock Edge the wood's in trouble', *Collected Poems*, p. 55.
32. Jocelyn Brooke, *Elizabeth Bowen*, (London: Longmans, Green & Co., for The British Council, 1952), pp. 6, 9.
33. Housman, 'Crossing alone the nighted ferry', *Collected Poems*, p. 169.
34. Mabey, *Flora Britannica*, p. 446.
35. Brooke, *Scapegoat*, p. 28.
36. Eleanor Farjeon, *Edward Thomas: The Last Four Years* (Stroud: Sutton, 1997), p. 280.
37. Brooke, *Image*, pp. 17–18.
38. Geoffrey Matthews, *War Poems*, ed., Arnold Rattenbury (Reading: Whiteknights Press, 1989), p. 73.
39. Jack Lindsay, *Beyond Terror: A Novel of the Battle of Crete* (London: Andrew Dakers, 1943), p. 311.
40. W. H. Auden, 'Dover', *The English Auden: Poems, Essays and Dramatic Writings, 1927–1939*, ed., Edward Mendelson (London: Faber, 1977), pp. 222–3.
41. Sheila Kaye-Smith, 'Laughter in the South-East', in *Britain and the Beast: A Survey by Twenty-Six Authors*, ed., Clough Williams-Ellis (London: Dent, 1937), p. 32.
42. E. M. Forster, 'Havoc', ibid., p. 45.
43. C. Day Lewis, *Word Over All* (London: Jonathan Cape, 1943), p. 28.

44. Patrick Wright, *The Village that Died for England: The Strange Story of Tyneham* (London: Jonathan Cape, 1995), pp. 364–5.
45. Ibid., pp. 171, 175.
46. Henry Williamson, *The Phoenix Generation* (1965; London: Panther, 1967), pp. 125, 146.
47. Paul Fussell, *The Great War and Modern Memory* (Oxford: Oxford University Press, 1975), p. 164.
48. Wright, *The Village that Died for England*, epigraph.
49. John Pikoulis, ed., *Alun Lewis: A Miscellany of his Writings* (Bridgend: Poetry Wales Press, 1982), p. 152.

7
Broken Glass

Rod Mengham

Broken glass fills the streets in James Hanley's *No Directions* (1943). The novel opens with a scene in which a drunken sailor stumbles around in the black-out, believing that the 'sea of glass' beneath his feet is actually a shifting sea of ice. The physical fact of glass debris, the sailor's phobic reaction to it, and his imaginative transformation of the entire scene, encapsulate the historical crisis of literary writing during the Blitz. This essay will explore the specific problems of representation encountered by novelists and short-story writers attempting to capture the experience of the Home Front.

For several years during the 1940s, the image of broken glass served as a motif for a whole range of issues that were interrelated in the cultural products of the period. Physical broken glass was, of course, an ubiquitous obstacle during the London Blitz; it was literally inescapable. The various media of the time concentrated on two main settings within which it might be experienced. There was glass in the street: shards of transparency choking the arteries of communication; and there was glass in the home, representing the final invasion by the war of the space which is personally, individually, organised, and in connection with which personal memory is organised. Broken glass acted as a reminder of how insubstantial the dividing-line is between the self and everything that threatens to overwhelm it.

Ideas about broken glass also circulated in ways that stimulated arguments about methods of composition and communication across the whole range of the arts. Broken glass became the implicit corollary of an entire series of critical comments and propositions issued in a cultural climate where the key terms were those of fragmentation and transparency. Interruption became both the subject matter and the condition of artistic production. Since the beginning of the war, there had been something of a hiatus in the writing and publication of novels, for example. As Robert Hewison's study of wartime London demonstrates, 'the actual number of fiction titles published fell from 4,222 in 1939 to 1,246 in 1945, which, taking into account the total decline in book production, means a fall from about a third to a fifth of the total of all volumes published annually'.[1] Many prominent novelists failed to publish a novel during the war. Elizabeth Bowen, for instance, stated publicly that she felt unable to produce fiction in any sustained form because

> these years rebuff the imagination as much by being fragmentary as by being violent. It is by dislocations, by recurrent checks to his desire for meaning, that the writer is most thrown out. The imagination cannot simply endure events; for it the passive role is impossible. Where it cannot dominate, it is put out of action.[2]

The novel is put out of action by fragmentation, discontinuity in the social life it is asked to reflect. Its form is, understandably, being identified with coherence and continuity. And it loses its accustomed role not simply through the overreaction of literary sensibilities to the new conditions; the editors of Mass-Observation, monitoring the hopes and fears of a broad cross-section of the populace, could speak of a general sense of there being no more continuity than could be found in the 'future of the next second'.[3] The present was felt to be radically disconnected from the past and future. Britons found themselves in a vacuum where their tried and trusted ways of giving shape and sense to their lives no longer applied. They were experiencing a gap, or lull, in meaning itself. The feelings of aimlessness, of 'no directions', that this engendered are reflected brilliantly in the work of Henry Green, perhaps especially in the short story to which he gave the rather obvious but apt title 'The Lull'. Novels continued to be read. But there was an interesting preference for writers such as Tolstoy and Trollope, whose attitude towards place and time was staggeringly comprehensive and unifying. Such books would compensate readers for the lack of wholeness felt in their own lives, but could only make the gap between fiction and reality wider. Among the novels still being written there were also conspicuous trends. Henry Reed, surveying the fiction produced between 1939 and 1949, insists on the frequency of childhood themes.[4] Infantile security is the most reassuring of all. One way or another, an uncontrollable present was being eclipsed among reversions to a past that could be effectively controlled.

The silence threatened by the lull in meaning was most effectively filled by a new enthusiasm for short stories. Collections of stories by one author and anthologies of stories by several suddenly grew in popularity where there had been no substantial demand for them before. This made sense not simply because the story was categorically the form of the part as opposed to the whole but because a certain kind of story predominated: it was the kind that did not present an understanding of what was happening *now*, but which merely provided a record of events to be used as material for a reading *later on*, after the 'lull'. Whatever it all meant could only be understood *then*. 'When to-day has become yesterday, it will have integrated.'[5]

Hewison justifiably associates this documentary kind of story with the enormously influential *New Writing*, edited by John Lehmann. It prompted a method of reading that would tolerate incompleteness, fragmentariness, on the understanding that a real and satisfying completeness would eventually supervene; and as such, it legitimated the abandonment of the novel as a means of articulating the real. It was a literary method of dealing with the puzzlement of discontinuity that was given a powerful boost by the example of T. S. Eliot in *Four Quartets*. (Eliot returned to 'Burnt Norton', treated it as incomplete, and included it in a larger structure whose protracted writing over a period of time constantly looks forward to its own recapitulation.) To speak in general terms of the literary scene in the early 1940s: the novel was writing itself into the past, while the short story was writing itself into the future.

But the most interesting short fiction of the period, if it did not resist utterly the demands of transparency and fragmentation, issued from a recognition of the need to complicate the terms of photographic realism and of radical presentness. William Sansom's short stories 'The Wall' and 'The Witnesses' both examine the limits of conventional perception and imagine a kind of vision that is wholly incommensurate with that of the camera: 'In that single second my brain digested every detail of the scene. New eyes opened at the sides of my head so that, from within, I photographed a hemispherical panorama bounded by the huge length of the building in front of me and the narrow lane on either side.'[6] The fireman narrator of this story, 'The Wall', describes at impossible length the multitude of perceptions that crowd in on him during the fragment of time in which the collapsing wall of a burning building descends on top of him and his two colleagues. Paradoxically, the three firemen are saved by being framed by a window space, reproducing the shape of the photograph or slide that would not have preserved the meaning of their experience:

> Lofty, away by the pump, was killed. Len, Verno and myself they dug out. There was very little brick on top of us. We had been lucky. We had been framed by one of those symmetrical, oblong window spaces.
>
> p. 111

In 'The Witnesses' even the relationship between eye and brain is not taken for granted. The story is narrated in the first person plural, supposedly by the eyes, registering phenomena without being able to introduce coherence into the scene, without being able to bring things properly into focus: 'Everything flashed into being. Light evaporated the mist, so that each corner of the architecture, each detail of the pump, each line of the operator's uniform leapt into abrupt definition, like objects switched suddenly onto a screen' (p. 85). Just as space is filled with an impossible amount of detail, so the fragment of time in which the crucial event occurs is saturated with incident. However brief the interval, it is charged with a density of information that makes it almost inconceivable as part of an eventual whole:

> Before every great catastrophe there is said to be a pause, a terrible imagined silence. Threatened men for the first time in their lives become aware of certainty. The quicksilver sets, time freezes solid... The hypnosis is absolute. Each muscle freezes, not so much with dread as with knowledge. And then, in the least part of the last second, the will to movement reasserts itself. In any direction – they will run, strike, jump...
>
> p. 86

The documentary reflex cannot access data at this level of operation; the attempt to concentrate on the moment is undermined by the realisation of time moving at different rates beneath the anecdotal pace of narration.

In the less experimental fiction of Elizabeth Berridge, the bombing and ransacking of houses is what prompts a desire to narrate in characters for whom storytelling provides a means of imaginatively controlling the upheaval in their lives. Or it would do, if the urge to formalise these accounts of disruption did not have to contend with the absence of a satisfactory audience. Conventional storytelling means a retreat into solipsism rather than a positive act of communication. The intended addressees are either deaf ('To Tea with the Colonel') or killed off before those who have worked out their stories can actually tell them ('Tell it to a Stranger').[7] Of all Berridge's wartime fictions, the most eloquent in linking these narratorial frustrations to other, more haunting forms of loss is 'The Notebooks', which concerns a widow's dilemma over the disposition of her husband's fragmentary writings. She clings to his notebooks as a faithful representation of their time together, but donates them after the war to a local museum where she knows they will be framed in a way that will lend them more coherence than they possess. This story shows an unusual insight into the psychology of wartime discontinuities; it recognises the illusory, artificial nature of the delayed act of completion and faces up to the reality of loss threatened by the disintegration of private life and the space and time it inhabits.

Henry Green's short stories take the refusal of literary integration as axiomatic; not only are the *New Writing* assumptions not built into them but they deliberately reject the dynamics of the story whose resolution is deferred. Both 'A Rescue' and 'Mr Jonas' are definite that the whole question of completeness is one they simply do not care about – the ending of each story is demoralisingly vague:

> The injured man was taken away in an ambulance. We have not heard anything of him. He may have died.[8]

> When the other crew took over we had fought our way back to ... that hole out of which ... had risen, to live again whoever he might be, this Mr Jonas.[9]

'The Lull' goes further, revolving different modes of representation whose project is to try to come to terms with the conditions of the Blitz.[10] The reader is obliged to move from writing which discounts the need to probe beneath the surface of its descriptions to writing which necessarily does so with self-conscious success, then on to writing whose knowledge of experience consists of what it knows is unfathomable. These different modes of approach to the text all interfere with each other so that readers do not know where they stand; they cannot feel at home for long with the documentary style, nor can they comfortably revert to the expectation of full meaning, nor even abandon themselves to despair in the face of no meaning at all. 'The Lull' keeps them on the move, made aware of the relative strengths and weaknesses of the different viewpoints they might have assumed.

What throws the writing into confusion is of course the threat of meaninglessness: the lull, the abeyance in every way of making sense. The meaning of the lull is an absence of meaning. And yet the text runs through a whole series of characters who narrate, who persist in constructing the type of story that is no longer adequate to the historical moment. The exploratory movement of the writing shows how this tendency can lead from a partial to a total eclipse of reality. With its lack of conventional development, its inconclusiveness, and its awareness of the conditions of meaninglessness, 'The Lull' makes naked the motives behind the production of story and plot during a respite from ordered coherence.

For Elizabeth Bowen, the failure to shed redundant, outlived habits of mind induces what she refers to memorably as a 'rising tide of hallucination'. She writes in 1944, in a 'Postscript' to a volume of her own short stories, *The Demon Lover*, of the pressure of subject matter building up behind the inadequacy of traditional methods of making sense: 'The simple way to put it was, "One cannot take things in." What was happening was out of all proportion to our faculties for knowing, thinking and checking up.'[11] The result was a spectacular failure of realism. Bowen describes her own stories as 'disjected snapshots', records of the time, attempts to capture the moment whose objectivity has been fatally compromised by the sheer burden of affect they fail to contain: 'It seems to me that during the war the overcharged subconsciousness of everybody overflowed and merged. It is because the general subconsciousness saturates these stories that they have an authority nothing to do with me' (pp. 190–1). Bowen makes a direct connection between the experience of collective fantasy and the material conditions in which the boundaries and partitions that separate individual lives are brutally shattered:

> Sometimes I hardly knew where I stopped and somebody else began. The violent destruction of solid things, the explosion of the illusion that prestige, power and permanence attach to bulk and weight, left all of us, equally, heady and disembodied. Walls went down; and we felt, if not knew, each other. We all lived in a state of lucid abnormality.
>
> p. 191

The stories in *The Demon Lover* are filled with houses that have boarded-up windows and door frames that have shifted; that is when the houses are not missing altogether. The house that is featured in 'In the Square' is the property of an upper-middle-class family now obliged to share their rooms with members of the working class. Privacy is a thing of the past, since the building now functions as a 'sounding-box'. There is fierce competition over the keys to these semi-derelict lodgings; the necessity to share and the simultaneous unwillingness to share accentuates the tension which accompanies the shifting of these social boundaries, a tension which finds expression in the release of fantasy or hallucination: 'life...had to complete itself in *some* way. It is a fact that in Britain, and especially in London, in war-time many people had strange deep intense dreams' (p. 192).

In the fiction of Bowen, Sansom and Hanley, the subject matter of documentary realism begins to turn strange, so that what can be seen starting to infiltrate the writing is the logic of dream or nightmare. In the title story of the collection *The Demon Lover*, the female protagonist is introduced checking the condition of her empty London home, a bomb-damaged edifice with boarded-up windows, a front door that is warped, and a lock that is 'unwilling'. She has the feeling that the place is haunted by an indefinable presence, and is then stunned to discover a letter from a long-dead fiancé last seen during the First World War. The letter proposes a meeting in the next hour or so. This menacing reminder of a past the heroine thought she had left behind takes even more concrete form in the shape of the taxi-driver she enlists to help her make her escape. As the car speeds further and further into the deserted, war-ravaged areas of the city, the heroine, increasingly con-cerned, leans forward to 'scratch at the glass panel'. When the driver turns round, revealing his identity, the terrified woman falls to beating 'with her gloved hands on the glass all round'. This is a story about breakable and unbreakable kinds of glass, about the invasion of the self by a memory that cannot be brought into a manageable relation with the present. The past is represented by a hidden memory that can never enter into an avowed continuity with the present.

This critical negotiation is also at the heart of Sansom's story 'Fireman Flower'.[12] The protagonist, who is seen fighting a fire during the London Blitz, penetrates further and further inside a large, factory-like building, in pursuit of what is referred to several times as the 'kernel' or 'seat' of the fire. What he finds there is a surrealistic vision of his own past, which takes the form of an encounter with a childhood friend inside a room that is miraculously immune to the flames. The encounter could either bring him face to face with an aspect of his past that he needs to deal with and resolve, or it could offer the basis of an infantile form of security, the substitution of a comfortable past for a troubling present and an uncertain future: not so much the seat *of* the fire, as a seat *by* the fire:

> The past was more real than the present because the picture was clearly defined. It was secure, rounded off, a complete picture that was finished and which he knew nothing could now alter: nothing like the unstable present, which one could hardly understand at all … One wishes to envisage the future: one cannot: one casts around for a substitute: one substitutes the picture of the past, sufficiently alien from the present, a vision – yet one that can be controlled.
>
> pp. 149–50

Just before entering the mysterious room, Flower is presented with an image of himself in a tall mirror; its reflecting surface locates him with reference to the time, as well as the space, he has just come from: 'In front the reflection of his past masqueraded as the darkling ghost of the future' (p. 146). This is an image that needs to be shattered; glass that needs to be broken. Flower rejects nostalgia and engages with the workings of desire in trying to project a viable future. When he leaves the room, the mirror has vanished: 'Life as he had known it had been broken down. From the elements a new world had been moulded. Iron, fire, brick, smoke, and water from the huge hydrants were patterned into a new choreography that enlivened fiercely the blood and the spirit' (p. 156). The ability to create a new world out of the broken fragments of the present depends on the protagonist's love for his fiancée, Joan, and on something alluded to, somewhat mystically, as the operations of spirit.

From the story as a whole it is clear that what is being described here is an engagement with the subconscious. The illusion of completeness, of integration, that is retrieved from the past or deferred until some point in the future, is replaced by the 'will to create' something meaningful out of the disjected present. It is precisely a responsiveness to 'strange deep intense dreams', to the pressure of affect, that leads to an acceptance of disintegration as a necessary prelude to reorganisation: 'so that he loved a single rusted nail as he loved the Gioconda smile, the factory's timeclock as he loved the mould of autumn leaves, a mausoleum as he loved the crèche, a cat's head in the gutter as he loved the breasts of Joan' (p. 163).

The absence of focus in conventional terms, of a perspective that would impose order on this array of details, is what preoccupies the painter, Clem, in Hanley's *No Directions*.[13] He and his wife inhabit a house rocked by explosions and surrounded by broken glass, where the doors no longer fit, where it is impossible to control the infractions of private space. Every time the air-raid sirens sound, Clem struggles to carry down to the shelter in the basement the huge painting on which he believes he has captured the 'depth' that is otherwise missing from their lives. But the novel culminates with a much more spectacular, and wholly symbolic, demonstration of the role of fantasy in providing this much-needed 'depth'. Clem runs outside into a world that is literally raining glass, only to encounter a runaway horse that he wrestles with and eventually manages to control. This dream-like element resembles closely the strange appearance of a powerful white horse that erupts momentarily through the surface of documentary realism in Humphrey Jennings's contemporaneous film about the Blitz, *Fires Were Started* (1943).

Hanley's novel begins with a 'rising tide of hallucination', the illusory sea of ice that the drunken sailor substitutes for the street full of broken glass, and it ends with a recognition of the role of the subconscious in coming to grips with – or 'taking in' – the Blitz: with a situation in which the conventional means of imaginatively organising space and time no longer apply. As Molly Panter-Downes expressed it in a story written in 1941: ' "Safe as houses" was a maxim which meant nothing nowadays.'[14] Broken glass signalled the dereliction of old structures and required a response from fiction in an urgent, shared project: the reimagining of history and its locations.

Notes

 1. Robert Hewison, *Under Siege: Literary Life in London 1939–1945* (London: Weidenfeld and Nicolson, 1977) p. 83.
 2. Elizabeth Bowen, 'Contemporary,' review of *In My Good Books* by V. S. Pritchett, *New Statesman*, 23 May 1942.
 3. Mass-Observation, *War Begins at Home*, edited and arranged by Tom Harrisson and Charles Madge (London: Chatto and Windus, 1940) p. 187.
 4. Henry Reed, *The Novel Since 1939* (London: British Council, 1949)
 5. Bowen, 'Contemporary'.
 6. William Sansom, *Fireman Flower and Other Stories* (London: Hogarth Press, 1944) p. 109. Subsequent page references are to this edition.
 7. Elizabeth Berridge, *Tell it to a Stranger: Stories from the 1940s* (London: Persephone Books, 2000). Subsequent page references are to this edition.
 8. Henry Green, 'A Rescue', in *Penguin New Writing*, 4 (March 1941) p. 93.
 9. Henry Green, 'Mr Jonas', in *Penguin New Writing*, 14 (July/September 1942) p. 20.
10. Henry Green, 'The Lull', *New Writing and Daylight*, 3 (Summer 1943) pp. 11–21.

11. Elizabeth Bowen, *The Demon Lover and Other Stories* (London: Jonathan Cape, 1945) p. 193. Subsequent page references are to this edition.

12. Sansom, *Fireman Flower*.

13. James Hanley, *No Directions* (London: Nicolson and Watson, 1943)

14. Molly Panter-Downes, 'Fin de Siècle' in *Good Evening, Mrs Craven: the Wartime Stories of Molly Panter-Downes* (London: Persephone Books, 1999) p. 67.

8
Lying, Cruelty, Secrecy and Alienation in I. Compton-Burnett's *Elders and Betters*

Barbara Hardy

I. Compton-Burnett – she preferred the initial to 'Ivy', and some of her first readers assumed the author was a man – has been insufficiently analysed and praised. She has admirers, including many novelists, but her work is not obligatory in studies of modernism. The critic of twentieth-century fiction can't take a step without mentioning Proust, Joyce, Mann, Lawrence, Woolf and Beckett, but Compton-Burnett may be left out, reduced to the status of minor or cult or eccentric author.[1] Any discussion of her work has to mention this relative neglect, and before looking at one of the novels written in the 1940s, *Elders and Betters* (1944), I shall make some general comments.

She is original, experimental, difficult but not obscure. A possible reason for her neglect is her structural difference from the other original, experimental and more obscure modernists who conspicuously dislocate language, character and narrative: she doesn't fit into the usual categories of innovative fiction. Her radical change is to throw narrative responsibility on to dialogue, pushing to an extreme the dramatic concentration of Henry James. As she increases the proportion of dialogue to narrative and description, the result is an extreme stylisation of conversational exchange and discussion: everyone is highly articulate, the very young and the very old, the foolish and the wise. She rejects the large looseness of the baggy monsters James so economically nicknamed but sets her novels in their period, enjoying friction between old time and new style.

The acclaimed modernists, Joyce, Proust and Woolf, make time elastic and sequence wayward; she keeps fiction's temporal conventions, though affection for unities of time and place makes her streamlined narratives even more conspicuously compressed than James's. Joyce and Woolf make new syntaxes to record the irregular flow of conscious and subconscious mind; she writes crystal-clear expressive dialogues in a traditional, elegant and immaculate prose which offers pleasures and rigours. (Both welcome to us whose prized fiction is often unself-critically banal or over-written.) D. H. Lawrence sometimes smashed the old stable ego; she creates psychologically realistic characters, individualised in body, mind and power, socially and professionally typed, defined by idiolect and act. Woolf and Lawrence recreated styles of feeling in fiction; her one and only world is the family with its traditional loves and hates, revised in a Victorian or Edwardian time-frame. Her novels peel off the rich varied surfaces of Joyce, Lawrence and Woolf, but also avoid deep symbolism. Hers is a world of family talk, its flow, clash and collaboration exaggerated, extended and isolated. Her stripped minimalist conversation-novel makes considerable demands on the reader's attention.

Repetition of character and plot is another cause of relative neglect. Among her negligent critics are readers like myself who love her originality and functional mannerism, but do not teach or write about her because of a difficulty, even after rereading, of possessing the novels and keeping them in mind.[2] I find it hard or impossible to identify and locate her characters, let alone scenes and words, at will, as everyone does with Mr Woodhouse, Jaggers, Klesmer, Ralph Touchett, Lily Briscoe, Watt and Molloy. Charles Burkhart dismisses Pamela Hansford Johnson's comment on the unmemorability of Compton-Burnett's characters; there are about six she remembers without text or hard memory-search: he has no such problem; my experience is closer to hers. I have been rereading the novels since the 1950s, have a reasonable literary memory, can retrieve events, persons, objects and speech from novelists I know less well – Balzac or Scott – but except with a novel I am currently reading, I need to check text to verify or identify her people and actions.[3] She creates her own world, to use the convenient metaphor, by concentrated talk, but it is not a world I hold in my head, her characters not those I call from the mind's file and project on the mind's screen, to distinguish without textual reference, as I can after one or two readings of most novels.

Her titles, locally relevant but often interchangeable, don't help. Nor does a tendency to withhold details of clothes, food and objects, all important in her novels. Her characters, settings and plots are markedly similar to each other, though each novel has a strong vivid particularity and as one returns it seems impossible it should have been forgotten. There is something not yet defined about her repetitions and minimalism that inhibits the process of recall, and the local unmemorability or inaccessibility is an obstacle to full critical appreciation.

If we were to project a god of human creation, its viewpoint might be similar: though we seem to each other and ourselves so distinct, so uniquely fingerprinted, from a divine or extra-terrestrial view we could be indistinguishable – minds, bodies, emotions, relationships, vices, virtues, lives, deaths and all. (As people of an unfamiliar colour look alike until colour is familiarised.) Compton-Burnett withholds the author's – or a surrogate's – narrative presence, and perhaps there is a link between her impersonality and a felt distance between reader and character.

One characteristic may certainly repel romantic or easy-read readers. She offers no sublimities and no point of identification, as other modernists do, except Brecht (and occasionally he does too, for instance in *Mother Courage and her Children*). She creates the alienation which was his dramatic aim, the avoidance of identification, catharsis, and exaltation in the interest of rational response. *Elders and Betters*, her second novel of the 1940s, is an extreme illustration. Apart from comic appeal, there are few novelistic treats on offer.

Like her other novels, *Elders and Betters* presents a small world. Compton-Burnett is such an original novelist that her language and storytelling make an implicit critique of previous and contemporary novels: her writing throws into bold relief the formal, moral and metaphysical simplifications of others. This is not to say that she doesn't simplify: she famously neglects the news of the world. To think of Balzac, Zola, Dickens or George Eliot is to think of the post-Napoleonic period, wars, industrial and rural distress, workhouse legislation, litigation, city sanitation and the first Reform Act. Jane Austen, still sometimes seen as a creator of private worlds, can tell a background story of the Navy and war. Compton-Burnett said the only world she knew ended in 1912, and as a novelist of the succeeding half-century she conspicuously omitted parliament, legislation, war and foreign affairs. There is defined social background, but presented allusively, not through social narrative or generalisation. Her novels illustrate the decay of landed gentry, and problems of inheritance and cash are prominent, but kept personal. There are doctors, teachers, writers, clergymen, lawyers and civil servants, but no institutional life. People make visits or professional journeys (even to South America) but there is no foreign detail. Politics are conspicuous by their absence.

Our attention is occasionally and subtly drawn to the absence. In *A House and its Head* interest in the news is affected by Duncan

Edgeworth, a tyrant aggressively holding up his departure, for which the family longs:

> He put his burdens down, and taking a chair picked up the paper. 'I should not have left the paper lying idle, when I was your age,' he said, smiling. 'You have very little curiosity about the nation's affairs.'
> 'True, when they are swamped by an acute private anxiety,' said Grant.
> 'You don't think this election business will follow that course...'
> 'No, Uncle, I scarcely think it will.'
> Duncan continued his perusal with an air of alertness and interest, pausing to comment or quote.
>
> Chapter VI

Duncan's pretence, Grant's defence and the narrative ellipses make a specialised tease for the reader. Similar teasing occurs in *Elders and Betters* when the witty Terence Calderon boasts in his laid-back Wildean dandaical style of irony, exaggeration, affectation and candour, that he doesn't want to read *The Times*:

> 'I cannot bear news. It is all about foreign countries that are sepa-rated by the sea, and that is so cheerless for a lover of an English fireside. And I am always afraid of meeting some sort of heroism; and that seems to consist of finding some dreadful situation and throwing oneself in it, or of finding oneself in it and wilfully remaining there. And then I imagine myself in it, behaving in just the same way, and my emotion is too much for me.'
>
> Chapter III

'I cannot bear news'. This playful passage works as a cool allusion to the novelist's and the novel's omission of the larger scene. She knows con-temporary readers intent on foreign news may expect the novelist to read her *Times* and show it, but she puts them straight, using an intelli-gent idle reader as an oblique, ironic and highly subtle defence, which is also a rare reflexive allusion to the famous moral and aesthetic experi-ences of empathy and identification, absent thrills in Compton-Burnett.

Compton-Burnett's Terence is charming, clever, amusing and decid-edly unheroic. He makes a mercenary marriage to an unattractive woman because she inherits a fortune and he doesn't want to work. He is rather like Mary Crawford in *Mansfield Park*, but his author refrains from rebuking his moral levity. 'I imagine myself in it': he would enjoy that author's novels, where we are never invited to imagine ourselves heroic in dreadful situations and where characters refuse complicity with heroics. Her austere style of long articulate talk is their expressive medium. The conversation-novel in which characters speak their mind and question each other closely, which we must follow slowly and carefully, is the demanding form of a story refusing heroics and cant. (It entertains us, however, with sparkling dry wit and rational comedy.) The austerities of an alienating form and content may also have something to do with the novelist's neglect, though they should be admired as moral and intellectual virtues.

In *Elders and Betters* there are neighbouring families, the Donnes and the Calderons – Compton-Burnett often blandly and amusingly names characters after famous authors. The families are two generations of siblings and cousins, one group served by a contented housekeeper and two critical servants, another by four happy invisible servants and a well-to-do governess. Benjamin Donne and his adult sons are civil servants, his brother-in-law Thomas Calderon a critic, journalist and writer who would like to just be 'a writer', whose wife and invalid sister-in-law have small private incomes. There are bright children, Reuben, Dora and Julius, the only wholly sympathetic characters. All characters might belong to the present day but are placed at the beginning of the twentieth century by the size of families, the unemployment of upper-middle-class women, and the class gap – sometimes discussed – between servants and employers.

The plot events are the deaths of Benjamin's sisters, Sukey Donne and Jessica Calderon, Anna Donne's engagement to her cousin Terence Calderon, Thomas Calderon's brief engagement to Florence the governess's niece, her re-engagement to Esmond Donne, and Tullia Calderon's engagement to her cousin Bernard. These events form a narrative armature but are not the crises. Deaths and engagements are only causes and effects of the crucial psychological events: Anna's three wicked deeds, her burning of Sukey's will to gain an inheritance and Terence, her cruel brainwashing of Jessica, and her lie about Jessica's last wish, with Thomas's realisation that he wants his daughter Tullia more than second marriage. Action is intensified by being kept within the family, as is made explicit by the characters, and by the unities of action, time and place which remind us that Compton-Burnett read Classics (at Royal Holloway College, University of London).

The unity is mentioned in two of many reflexive moves, characters observing that family engagements don't bring in anyone new, and a child told very close relatives can't marry because of the need for fresh blood. In several novels there is incest, or the danger of incest because of clandestine love affairs. The recycling of relationships within a small circle adds to the sinister atmosphere – a family loucheness – which comedy enhances rather than diminishes: for instance, *A House and its Head* ends with a three-year-old child's innocent 'good bad' joke about incest. Cousin marriage is almost the norm: *cousinage* is indeed a dangerous *voisinage*, but filial relationship is hazardous too, the more fascinating when we don't know how far it goes: after Thomas tells his daughter Tullia she is irreplaceable in his affections they are seen locked in each other's arms. There are favouritisms and close pairings in the Calderon family, as in most Compton-Burnett homes and households. There is more animosity *chez* Donne – no one does familial rudeness as well as Compton-Burnett.

There is a Greek use of chorus. The first conversation with the complexly paired servants, Ethel and Cook, concludes with a high-styled comparison of Anna and Jenny and a neglect of amusing, vain, ironic and marginal duenna-cousin Claribel. This is the beginning of the chorus, important in the novels though also a source of what the novelist saw as unnecessary padding. Occasionally downstairs action has an elaborate plot of its own, as in *Manservant and Maidservant*, but here it is pure chorus, with Ethel and Cook as individualised enigmatic characters, barely named, strictly private, history and relationship untold. As in drama, the chorus of 'ordinary' citizens may be a source of information, and in *Elders and Betters* and *Manservant and Maidservant* an underground network of servant and tradesman transmits news at top speed. The news is the narrative of family life, self-styled creative gossip.

The Calderon children form a chorus, important in their own right, spotted as the same species as the adults – funny, pathetic and eloquent, inventing religion, language, play and protection, loving, fighting, fooling and getting the giggles as children do, over-loved and fearful, desperate for security and space – patronised by their elders but not their author. Their self-aware innocence and fiercely seized detachment from adult troubles are choric qualifications: like the servants, children tell their stories from the verge of action. Their make-believe, mime, exaggeration and critique inform and provoke the reader.

Idiolect and action bring out moral qualities. Stylised verisimilitude throws style into relief. This is evident in a preliminary flow of domestic event and routine, which introduces character and moral type and fills the interstices of later sensational developments. The Donnes arrive at their new house in four stages, criticise it to Anna who has chosen it, with her father, and show complacency, self-importance, insensitivity, sensitivity, humour, humourlessness, altruism and egoism. The preparatory domestic events are the stuff of everyday life: meals, talk of a lost bag which isn't really lost and of Ethel and Cook's payment and tip for transport from station to house, questions about the dead wife and mother, visits to the Calderons with family chat about growth, age, looks, money, servants, illnesses – Sukey, Jessica, Reuben and Cook are variously afflicted – the Donne children's secret world, games and lessons. After character is fixed in this diurnal flow the crucial actions follow. Narrative and description give way to dialogue, though the key action occurs in solitude and secrecy, dramatised for the reader.

This is Anna's purloining of the will in her favour which Sukey, dying of heart disease, asks her to destroy, just before her death:

> Anna read aloud … Sukey listened with her eyes closed and gave no sign of the moment when she slept. Anna read until the sleep was sound, and then closed the book and rose to go, taking the scroll from the table. It seemed as if Sukey knew what she did, for her face settled into youth and calm. Anna looked at her, and looked again; stood as if she hardly knew where she was; approached her and touched her hand and her face; made a movement to the desk, and drew back and glanced round the room, as if to make sure she was alone.
>
> Chapter VII

The topos of supposition in the three 'as if's reminds us that we see surface and infer mind. We read Anna's first impulse to obey Sukey's instruction, next, her realisation that Sukey is dead; then finally her temptation to take the other will from the desk. There follows a similarly behaviouristic description of action and expression as she leaves, carrying the will home: 'showing neither haste nor fear', she 'seemed prepared'. When she burns the first will Sukey has asked her to preserve, 'She still maintained her usual air; she might have been acting to herself'. There is a rare narrative penetration of thought: 'Anna remembered that walls have ears and eyes', permitted because the author knows the reader knows the guilty action. The free indirect style points an excess of performance, sharpening Anna's banal idiolect with 'and eyes'. Matter-of-fact precision and description is doubly performative, marking character and pacing reader. Until she burns the will Anna is prepared to meet people and adapt: 'glancing about in readiness to exchange a greeting', and 'Her word was ready for anyone who asked for it'. She meets no one, and her future acting is public lying and keeping her secret. We are in it with her, her only observers, and feel the burden.

Greek tragedy suggests itself because of the unities, the family wrongs, the choruses and ambiguous references to tragedy. What makes Compton-Burnett's action and plot original is the sustained privacy and secrecy of moral event. In tragedy proper, and in much fiction, there is no moral act which does not get a public exposure and a public punishment. (Punishment may not be institutional, hence 'poetic' justice, designed for Bill Sikes, Carker, Casaubon and others.) Edmund in *King Lear* gets poetic justice when his brother kills him in formal combat, and for much of the play his villainy, like Anna's, is a secret between him and the audience, with all the dramatic irony and tension that follow. But with his deathbed confession comes revelation and recognition, an anagnorisis which the conventions of Elizabethan and Jacobean drama lead us to expect. Compton-Burnett transforms this convention, and the guilty, though publicly exposed within the family or sometimes in the larger, never more than village-sized community, are unpunished by the judicial system and often by society, family and conscience.

In *A House and its Head* Sibyl Edgeworth commissions a murder which is discovered by the family, but not repented or revealed outside the family, and she ends up satisfied with her marriage and money. *Men and Wives* shows the agonised crime of Matthew Haslam, which gets a little more than family publicity, but though he does not get off scot-free and loses his fiancée, he survives, preserved for the medical career his murdered mother planned. There is little or no poetic justice for these family criminals. In *Elders and Betters* there is no poetic justice at all, and in a further turn of the screw, Anna's faults are not only never punished, never regretted, and highly successful, but never discovered. The reader's knowledge stays isolated.

Anna succeeds like Sibyl and survives like Sibyl and Matthew, but with no distress. Only the author and reader know the secret. *Elders and Betters* comes close to tragedy but misses it, not only because the good are destroyed and the bad do well (and Anna is too bad for an Aristotelian tragic hero), but also because only author and reader recognise causality. To most of the characters purpose is disguised or hidden, so the end can be happy – in a way – but speciously, not for the reader. No one inside the novel knows that Anna is guilty of theft, deception and killing, and it ends with three pairings. The narrative works, originally, as a secret unilateral communication, straight from author to reader, and so does its ending.

Anna is unusual amongst Compton-Burnett's characters not only in her successful secrecy but in her total immorality, totally revealed to the reader as she rises and never falls. Sibyl is a nasty character and motivated solely by money, but the murder, also nasty, is her only bad act, and we are held back from too much feeling by not knowing the victim or seeing much of Sibyl. We know Matthew Haslam – and his victim – only too well, as a character driven desperate by intolerable possessiveness. Horace Lamb in *Manservant and Maidservant* is a miserly, mean, cruel and unjust tyrant who ruins his children's childhood, but he is exposed, punished, and – exceptionally – undergoes a kind of conversion. In *Two Worlds and their Ways*, two parents and their two children lie, steal and cheat, but are justified, forgiven and left essentially unpunished, even consoled, while the more moral headmistress of the girl's school is insensitive, self-seeking and unlovable. In every novel almost everyone is likely to steal, lie, plagiarise, deceive, cheat, betray and seduce, without being punished, blamed, or even categorised. The novels say and show that we are mostly self-seeking, egocentric and afraid to die. In *Elders and Betters* there is a great exemplary scene in which hosts and guests at a luncheon party avoid being the first to sit down because they think they are thirteen at table: it amusingly and sharply brings out our unheroic egoisms.

But some self-seeking is more villainous than others. At the heart of *Elders and Betters* is heartless Anna, looming large from the start, charmless, clumsy, self-centred, rough, hard, deceitful, destructive, callous and cruel. After she destroys Jessica, the good woman for whom the vice of deceit is so appalling that other vices are said to seem virtues in comparison, we watch her getting away with it, gaining, flourishing and subverting all traditions of poetic justice and discovery. Other writers appear sentimental and untruthful in comparison.

Anna is not brilliant, no Machiavellian planner like Richard of Gloucester, Iago and Edmund, but a fortunate opportunist. She is a determined, bad-but-lucky liar, and the nature of lying is unfolded in conversation-scenes in which we concentrate on words. After the major lying scenes in which she says her aunt died feeling neglected, we watch her stumble in storytelling as she does in physically clumsy movement. She is not a good improviser and there are clues which people nearly pick up: after she lies about her aunt burning papers Reuben mentions a smell of burning in the Donne house, but she gets away with the explanation that it was a coal on the rug, after a further slip and retrieval:

> 'There was a live coal on this rug…It spurted out of the fire. It was a good thing I was there to stop it from smouldering. I had just come back from Aunt Sukey, and could have dispensed with being startled at that moment.'
>   'But you didn't know that she was dead,' said Rueben.
>   'No, but I knew she was ill and exhausted. It gave me a sort of nervous feeling to be with her. It seems that I ought to have guessed more than I did.'

Chapter VIII

Compton-Burnett is one of the best psychologists of the lie, and dialogue conspicuously isolates Anna's recovery, then her later redundant and over-imaginative lying, headily undertaken after getting away with the first big lie. Lie generating lie – as it did for Odysseus – she gratuitously invents a story about Sukey's promise of a photograph, surprising Jessica, 'She never had her photograph taken', to wriggle out with self-characterising self-deprecation:

> 'Or have I got it twisted in some way? That would be rather in my character. I asked her if she would have her portrait painted. And she said she would give me a photograph of it, if she ever did. I think that was it.'

Chapter IX

Pressed to describe Sukey's end in detail, she pushes her luck, and when an invented hand-folding is rejected – ' "Sukey never folded her hands", said Jessica, with no touch of pouncing on a weak point; simply in expression of her thought' – fumbles her way into an acceptable story, warming to the work:

> 'Oh, well, idle in her lap. I don't suppose she did fold them. Actually they were working in her lap, but there did not seem to be any need to drive that home. They were closing and unclosing, if you must have the scene as it was. You make it quite impossible to save you anything.'

Chapter X

The generation of lying circumstance generates aggression: ' "And how can you say so positively what it was? You did not watch her so faithfully, or that was not her impression"', and the revisionary lying works: '"I can imagine her hands working," Jessica said, once again speaking to herself' (Chapter X). Dangerous corners which in other fictions trip or betray are successfully rounded and left behind, and Anna's first successful wicked act is consolidated by her second, in which she demoralises and destroys Jessica. It is all done in and by conversation.

Like many novelists, Compton-Burnett is an expert on the varieties of narrative imagination and makes Anna an uninventive storyteller who works on a grounding of fact. She uses her imagination effectively when offered a truth for her false construction: her best story, the killer, is one of those lies which is a part-truth. The truth is her aunt's dark brooding susceptible self-doubt. By imaginative elimination of psychological impossibilities, Jessica comes to suspect Anna and innocently gives her a dangerous opening by suggesting she has something on her mind. Once more she spurs her niece to attack as the best defence. Anna receives and revises Jessica's idea during the 'just perceptible pause' – which we must read and understand – in this dialogue, and during the next pause, in which Jessica looks at her face, she diverts Jessica's attention and moves in for the kill:

> 'Anna,' said Jessica, in a tone that held no sudden difference, but seemed to come from gathering purpose; 'if you ever wanted to tell me anything, you would not be afraid? ... You would not hesitate?'
> There was a just perceptible pause.
> 'Indeed I should,' said Anna, almost with a laugh. 'You are the last person I would face in such a situation ... You would make anyone feel a criminal, indeed might make anyone be one. I begin to feel my mind reflecting your own. It must be ghastly to have such seething depths within one.'
> Jessica looked into her niece's face.
> 'I wonder if other people see me like that.'
>
> Chapter X

What is the relationship between the form of dialogue and the subject of successful crime? Along with the lack of moral consequence goes the advantage of conversation, the isolation of speech, the lack of moral commentary. We follow the long devastating dialogue, four pages long, in which Anna generates her imagined story about Jessica, to destroy her aunt's confidence, without observations by the author, who presents the reader with characters and actions and stays impersonal, outside the story. Anna's destructive pressure on Jessica is effective because it is imaginative, all performed by words, shown by this word-expert to break bones as effectively as sticks and stones. The aggression is the more hideous because the artist is imagining imagination. It is formed like, or as, an artist's self-generated reading, starting in spontaneous self-defence and culminating in elaborately generalising sensuous imagery, allusion and paradox: 'You are like some dark angel, honestly and unselfishly serving the cause of evil', even luxuriously daring truths when asked for precision: 'It is all vague and nameless to me', and 'So, if you like, say I have imagined it.' In a brilliant comic characterisation of another liar, Bertha Mullet, a nursemaid in *Parents and Children* who delights her disbelief-suspending charges with social fantasies of tragic falls from high life, the author points out the liar's use of truth, but here she leaves it to her hard-pressed and controlled reader to note.

The reader infers feelings which are not described. (Feelings are sometimes described within dialogue, where the description does not come from the novel's chief narrator but is in character and so may be dishonest.) But tone is frequently indicated, as in an early conversation when Anna, Jenney and Claribel arrive at the new house: 'in her rather rough tone', 'in a tone of speaking to a child', or 'in a tone of appreciation' are clues to feelings, attitudes and relationships. In that last dialogue between aunt and niece the behaviouristic directions are ironies suggesting that tone is only tone-deep, reinforcing the reader's recognition of the difference between surface and depth, as by now we have inferred Jessica's honest doubting and her gradual susceptibility (like Othello's honest doubting and susceptibility) and have observed Anna's falsity and effectiveness (like Iago's falsity and effectiveness). The novelist preserves the distinction between what we have inferred and what we have observed.

'"Anna," said Jessica, in a tone that held no sudden difference but seemed to come from gathering purpose'; 'Jessica looked at Anna almost in wonderment, seeming to return from the world of her own thoughts'; '"We will leave the matter of the will," said Jessica, as if her thoughts had been elsewhere'; '"A cloud would be lifted from the household if I were gone," said Jessica, using a tone between question and statement'; 'Anna rested her eyes in a new wonderment on her aunt.' Once more, the novelist is scrupulously using the topos of supposition, 'seemed', 'as if' and 'seeming', and here only of Jessica, since the reader knows Anna's insincerity, having observed her actions.

Her third and conclusive lie is to clever, lazy Terence, the cousin she falls in love with and can buy. (In a rare and perhaps mistaken explanation, the narrator says he is the motive for her lying and cheating.) Once more, luck plays into her not very dextrous hands. What she achieves in wooing Terence is as unlikely as Richard of Gloucester's winning courtship of Anne over the corpse of her father-in-law, but unlike Richard she needs an opening and seizes it when Terence lightly, seriously, charmingly and conveniently says his father has cruelly told him to earn his living:

> 'But cannot you really do something for yourself?'
> 'A breadwinner is born, not made. My mother quite understood it.'
> 'Then that is what she meant by what she said to me,' said Anna, as if to herself.
>
> Chapter XII

Her customary slack style of cliché stands her in good stead:

> 'Did she ask you to adopt me?'
> Anna glanced at him for a moment.
> 'You are pretty warm,' she said.

She trips again and recovers again when Terence, smart reader of surfaces, wonders why his reportedly unkind mother 'kindly' wanted her for a daughter-in-law, and quickly perceives Jessica's reported comment on Florence is not in 'the tone of my mother's speech'. Anna again enjoys the luxury of using truth for lie: '"Oh, no, no, it is mine ... I am not quoting your mother. I should not dream of it ... "' (Chapter XIII).

A little later Anna clears 'the way between' Terence and Florence, 'as if by a carefully unconsidered movement', sits at a distance, 'her eyes on the pair'. She joins a coded conversation about work and marriage, 'And you don't take very kindly to labour, do you?', staging, observing and relishing the end of the unmentioned rivalry which we, like her, decode. By the end of the triangular conversation-piece we know it's all over with love: bright but physically and morally indolent Terence will ignorantly allow himself to be 'adopted' in the 'way a woman adopts a man' by the not-so-bright woman who drove his dearly beloved mother to death. By the beginning of the next chapter Anna announces her engagement to her unflattering astounded family.

The novelist presents us with moral action which we must read for ourselves, carefully and without mediation. She presents us with a moral world in which there are no punishments, where Anna enjoys only pleasure and success after she destroys Jessica, keeps her stolen inheritance and gains money, man and marriage. One of Compton-Burnett's best critics, Burkhart, arguing that Anna is sympathetic in some ways, praises her bluntness, but her banal parade of bluntness is surely a convenient medium, not an alleviation, of her deceit.

'I expect I am still the blundering innocent I always was' raises the dangerous subject of crime; cliché-puncturing Miss Lacy asks why the innocent are said to blunder when it is criminals who are noted for it, and Terence's wit and paradox sparkle in response. The conversation teems, like much of the novel, with dramatic irony. Anna, less clever than either but clever enough to get Terence by criminal deceits he and Miss Lacy do not even begin to imagine, points the innocence of their witty, idling conversation, in which her silence and speech are not idle, though her tone is. Terence reminds us of Wilde again:

> 'We are very unfair to criminals,' said Terence. 'They only make one blunder out of so many. They ought nearly always to have the credit of the crime. What right have we to be so exacting, when we are only criminals at heart?'
> 'What kind of things do we hide within us?' said Anna, in an idle tone.
> 'Bad things, but not that the world calls wrong.'
> 'Hasty judgements, self-satisfaction,' said Miss Lacy. 'Too little understanding.'
> 'Those are not bad,' said Terence. 'They are the stuff of life itself. Which no doubt means that they are very bad indeed.'
> 'You are being clever,' said Anna.
>
> Chapter XIV

He is, but as we read the commonplace which cheapens paradox and abstracts wisdom, we observe, with Anna, the limits of clever talk.

Burkhart says Anna's dominance dwindles at the end, and in a sense it does, having succeeded. But though the loves of Thomas, Florence and Tullia move into the foreground, Anna's lies, which will never stop, never stop. We are constantly and consciously reading her duplicity, success and total lack of any sign of remorse, reading the secret life running beneath the full, frank and public drama. The text has become sub-text, but is the more ironically pronounced – if only they knew! – because so much else is made public in the almost ceaseless flow of conversation. The reader is made sharply aware of the reading process.

Florence rapidly exchanges daughter-loving unimaginative Thomas (whom she preferred – we infer – to self-serving Terence) for Anna's brother Esmond, who has a job in the Civil Service and is the next to make an offer. The cynical spinsters, Claribel and Miss Lacy, detached fascinated outsiders and observers, prefer celibacy because the grapes of the marriage feast are sour. And they really are sour. But nothing sweeter is on offer, in this novel. Jenney is sweet but sentimental, undiscriminating, easily satisfied, and asking nothing for herself, like many of Compton-Burnett's nice and good people who make such excellent carers. It is a bleak world, in spite of the jokes, the wit and the fools.

Compton-Burnett's world has something in common with Hardy's imagining of tragic imagination but is fundamentally unlike Hardy's, which is marked by tragically angry and compassionate hankering after the lost providence, admiration and pity for the imaginative life of the thwarted creature. Compton-Burnett's fiction is neither angry nor compassionate, tragic nor optimistic, simply austere and stoical. It is also unlike Hardy's fiction because its reader is made to see the point without narrative guidance and interiority. The reliance on dialogue, though accompanied by description and full stage-directions at the beginning of the story, makes the reading process one of constant and conscious attention and inference, intellectually exhilarating, emotionally and morally disturbing.

In this novel, for instance, the absence of narrative has an especially unnerving effect in Anna's lies and secrets. This is marked in those dialogues with Jessica, as we read and realise the language of a terribly unscrupulous lying and a terribly susceptible listening. Perhaps the successful shock of this act lies in its process in dialogue, direct speech. It is murder by language, and more startling in its direct moral impact – because it is strange, and because we follow it closely, word-by-word – than the off-stage murder of the infant Richard Edgeworth in *A House and its Head* or the beautifully staged matricide in *Men and Wives*. The language of the unusual aftermath of crime's success is effective too.

The episode creates a loneliness for the reader, an enforced self-reliance, along with the shocking absence of fictional consolation, in these reading acts. Sibyl Edgeworth and Matthew Haslam are absorbed back into the resilient community, not hampered or not hampered for long by their murders, but what is shockingly different and differently shocking in *Elders and Betters*, where Anna's destruction of Jessica is not technically murder, is the permanent secrecy, both subject and form. The violence and lying ends with us, and involves us, not romantically or sublimely or cathartically or pornographically, but coldly. What strikes us is not just the absence of commentary and conclusion, the un-ideal truth of unpunished unstoppable destruction and lying, but the contrast with the flattering and consoling lies literature usually tells and we usually lap up. Compton-Burnett is so different from other writers that we are invited to reflect on difference. And the lies in the novels may make us reflect on the lies of novels. The secret cold communication of knowledge, especially in *Elders and Betters*, can reproach the usual pleasant warmths of fiction.

Hardy's guidance is not only that of an omniscient teller, somewhat less marked than in Thackeray, Dickens and George Eliot; it offers the interiority of characters, so we sympathise and identify with the imaginative pressures, dismays and raptures of Marty, Tess and Jude. The norm of imaginative penetration, soliciting sympathy or empathy even in unromantic unchristian post-metaphysical artists like Hardy, is lacking in Compton-Burnett. She places us outside the consciousness of characters, without authorial reassurance and interpretation, leaving speech to speak and shock on its own. We are denied the pleasures of exalted identification in a strong writerly invitation, assertive in *Elders and Betters* because the novel is so character-dominated, by Anna. In none of Compton-Burnett's other novels is there such concentration on the power and viewpoint of one person: only some scenes with the children are free from Anna's presence.

We are denied certain treats, but humour, wit and irony contribute to our entertainment, though they don't alleviate the pains and rigours of reading. Though she did not publicise her intention as Thackeray did, and avoids his occasional sentimentality and idealism, Compton-Burnett makes the reader thoroughly uncomfortable. She also makes the reader see the simplifications and solaces of other writers. But is it possible to say that the four novels of the 1940s, *Parents and Children* (1941), *Elders and Betters*, *Manservant and Maidservant* (1947) and *Two Worlds and their Ways* (1949) are particularly dark? Their action is less physically violent than that of several other novels, including those in which murder occurs, and apart from Anna Donne, Iago's rival, the other 1940s characters who deceive, steal, lie and betray are no more and no less morally and personally wrong than Compton-Burnett's earlier or later villains.

Her favourite figure of the domestic tyrant, absent in *Elders and Betters*, has long been read as political synecdoche. (Its author disclaimed such intention, while admitting the common element in tyranny.) The period of her major work, 1925 to 1971 – she wished to suppress her first, *Dolores*, published in 1911, after which followed a long gap – was marked by disturbance and violence. Anna's unmediated callousness and triumphant destruction appear in the 1940s.

The novel has another topical resonance, an allusion to Jewishness which I bracket with Anna's secret cruelty and Terence's conspicuous distaste, 'I cannot bear news.' Accidental or not, allusion is magnetised by history. The tone is relaxed:

> The family had a faintly Jewish look, and biblical names had a way of recurring amongst them, but they neither claimed nor admitted any strain of Jewish blood. The truth was that there had been none in the last generations, and that they had no earlier record of their history.
>
> Chapter II

Whether by design or not the reader is alerted: 'neither claimed nor admitted' and 'history'. The calm is impartial: like her relaxed treatment of homosexual relations in several novels, these sentences say and show that group prejudice is not entertained. One way of being anti-racist and anti-sexist is to be anti-anti-Semitic and anti-homophobic; her way is to regard stereotyped bias as unthinkable. When one recalls the casual and less casual anti-Semitism of many pre-war writers her tone is especially effective and welcome.

This book is an extreme image of the stoical, austere and unreligious view of life directly or indirectly expressed in all her novels. Beside them other literature – Christian or humanist, realist or naturalist – is romantic, exalted and idealist. We can understand that Compton-Burnett admired the radical ironist Jane Austen, but she is more astringent, without Austen's romantic streak or her Christian hope and consolation; what Jane Austen might have been if born later to find happy endings harder to contrive, less intellectually congenial.

Compton-Burnett is not the novelist of the happy ending, but not of the unhappy ending either. That is what is disconcerting. Her imaginative achievement is not only to be candid about human wickedness, but to shock us quietly and rationally, to show cruelty and greed without an outcry. The artist she sometimes reminds me of is Samuel Beckett, but he is agonised, as well as amused and bewildered, by life and death, and though she is amused, she is never agonised or bewildered. There is no darkness or vastation or irony at the end of this novel, but a return to the closely observed flow of family life and conversation. Life goes on. It is important that Anna's story ceases to be central towards the end, as in Compton-Burnett's other novels which turn on a wicked act; the murderers Sibyl and Matthew go on too. The novelist avoids a grand unhappy ending, to show the social assimilation of the guilty act and the guilty person, their dreadful ordinariness, avoiding a flattering tri-umphalist conclusion, light or dark. Observing the cleverness of the non-stop talk in *Elders and Betters*, Jenney observes that it 'is all about nothing'. It may seem to be but it is not.

Compton-Burnett's style is lucid, stoical and astringent. She does not show faults or guilts as banal but shows them and their successes as native to everyday life. Implications are rationalist and anti-metaphysi-cal, and might be unbearable were it not for strong comedy. She is not writing a polemic against sublimities, and can only be called didactic if a call for reason is didactic. Brecht wanted to inhibit aesthetic identifi-cation and encourage reason. Compton-Burnett has no political pro-gramme but wants us to see life rationally, or writes so that we read rationally. A love of clarity explains her distaste for lies and secrets, but the average sensual reader prefers social critique prettily packaged, optimistic *Bleak House* and *Ulysses*, melioristic *Middlemarch*, not com-pletely pessimistic *Germinal*. *Gulliver's Travels* is metamorphosed into a child's story. The compulsory rational attention Compton-Burnett requires is unglamorous and tiring. Alienation is not attraction.

The acknowledgement of lying, secrecy, cruelty and destruction seems appropriate in a wartime book. Its relevance doesn't stop with its decade. The 1940s ended in the destruction of Nazism and concentra-tion camps, but not of money-culture, torture, tyranny, racism, war and the lies that deny the faults of their existence or the existence of their faults.

Notes

1. See Charles Burkhart, *I. Compton-Burnett* (London, 1965)
2. I gave up teaching Compton-Burnett because I could hardly ever make spon-taneous reference to a novel.
3. Burkhart, *I. Compton-Burnett*, p. 64.

9
Away from the Lighthouse: William Sansom and Elizabeth Taylor in 1949

N. H. Reeve

During the American Civil War there were numerous reports of a phenomenon which became known as an 'acoustic shadow'; at a certain distance from the battlefield the sounds of war could not be heard, although the action was clearly visible. An odd silence rather like this seems to hang over William Sansom's *The Body* (1949). Of course the recent war infiltrated all the fiction of its immediate aftermath; its presence had, in some sense, to be 'taken for granted', as Lawrence said the Great War should be in *Women In Love*, whether it were referred to directly or not. But Sansom's work appears peculiarly marked by the pressure of experience and feeling associated with the war, at the same time as the war itself has been erased altogether from the characters' lives. Everything else in the novel reflects the period in which it was written; there are passing mentions of atom bombs and rationing, and there is an attempted revival of the boating parties of 'ten years ago at least', pre-catastrophic idylls regarded with both nostalgia and suspicion, reinspected for evidence of a corruption that may have lurked unnoticed within them. But apart from these brief allusions, it is as if an inhibition about confronting the war directly – Sansom once wrote that 'the dreadful performance of modern battle ... is too violent for the arts to transcribe'[1] – has brought about a curiously surreptitious registration of its impact. This story of mid-life crisis and jealousy is given much of its edge and momentum by a set of motifs and fantasies which belong in their most characteristic, intensified forms to the history from which the text turns away: the fascinating threat of invasion, the chance for cleansing adventure, for spying, for the thrill of pursuit and evading capture, the upheavals and defamiliarisations of the domestic world, the opening of potentially radicalising glimpses into the lives of one's neighbours, all accompanied by a frayed kind of disorientation and nervous blankness; the whole set in a sense borrowed from a stock whose origin is not acknowledged, and reinforcing the impression that the experience dramatised in the novel is really a substitute or screen for something else that is being missed or evaded.

The novel is narrated by Henry Bishop, a middle-aged, middle-class, utterly conventional London suburbanite who lives off the proceeds of an inherited hairdressing business. One afternoon in the garden he sees, or imagines he sees, his wife Madge being lasciviously stared at through her half-open bathroom window by his next-door neighbour, Charley Diver, a hearty, practical-joke-playing garage owner with 'the air of an ex-officer, of a man of action'. Bishop's world spontaneously collapses into jealous obsession, his every moment thereafter devoted to strategies for collecting information, interpreting signs and confirming suspicions; he breaks into Diver's house; he arranges assignations with Diver's would-be girlfriend Norma; he tells Madge he has gone to a conference while renting a room a mile away so he can burst in and surprise the 'lovers'; he contrives the extravagant boating party in order to sit Madge and Diver together in a skiff so he can study their behaviour from behind. He admits quite early in the narrative how much he is enjoying the experience, the sensation of power given him by the hidden ulterior motive behind all his relationships with others, and he becomes so committed to the new life his jealousy has forged for him that when he has finally to accept that he has been mistaken, his existence seems to lose all meaning: far from being able to respond to his wife's loving and faintly amused compassion, he can only look forward almost wistfully to the possibility of a further outbreak of mistrust.

The opening sequence in the garden sets a tone:

> To hold the syringe gently, firmly but delicately – not to squirt, but to prod the sleeper into wakefulness with the nozzle ... only to stir a movement, to initiate a presence from such a deep dead sleep. Gently, gently – lean thus into the ivy, face close in to the leaves, bowed in yet hardly daring to breathe, not to shake a single leaf, hand held far away up the wall, but face now close, secret, smelling the earth underneath the ivy like a smell close to earlier days, intimate the eyes and closed the world ... then carefully prod, no tickle – tickle the long dead leg on the leaf.
>
> p. 5

These comic-sinister, slightly destabilising suggestions of interrogation, or truth-drugs, or experimental torture in which the victim is deliberately aroused so as to feel more intensely the coming pain, throw a little shadow from the world they allude to over everything that follows in the book.

A reminiscence of childhood is awakened in this extreme juxtaposition of power and helplessness, this last-minute savouring of what one is about to destroy; it sets up an extended sado-masochistic structure, pursued with all the myopic, meticulous attentiveness that characterises Bishop's narrative, in which Bishop himself, Madge and Diver will be allotted alternating roles of victim and tormentor, in a fantasy of identities overflowing and crossing into others'.

In the jealousy which overtakes Bishop the erotic component is blended with an acute territorial anxiety; his space appears thrillingly vulnerable to invasion from below ('I nudged the leaf with the nozzle. The whole ivy shook – such a shaking at human level would have meant an earthquake, an upturning of houses and a crumbling of lives' [p. 6]); from the side ('The stranger came into the garden. I cannot say "calmly", he made a sudden sprinting jump over a narrow bed of small flowers' [p. 11]); and especially from the sky: as he is about to squirt the insect, 'the air above clapped loud with sound' (p. 6), and not only does Diver have a photograph of a jet fighter on the wall of his room, but when they all find themselves at a party there while a thunderstorm rages outside and Bishop is summoning up the nerve to confront his supposed rival, 'just at that moment Madge's hair shone gold and glinting in the glass all over the blue aeroplane, it was like some baleful sunrise above the clouds' (p. 46). When he does share sexual intimacy with his wife, his conviction of her infidelity produces uneasy sensations of excitement and recoil as he feels his own body turning into another's:

> I felt the warmth of her body against my hand, the shape of her flesh as I put my arm round her: but then my hand was Diver's hand, and the darkly sensed shape the same that Diver might feel, this body I knew so well yielded now not to my touch but to Diver's. So as we made our love … I tortured myself with a rediscovery of her body through Diver's red-haired arms.
>
> p. 125

The intensity with which he imagines his life being torn open seems to register an unacknowledged desire that it should be so; 'rediscovery' involves slipping from the protective, self-protective 'put my arm round her', to a previously unthinkable primitive aggression of 'red-haired arms'. Moreover, by transforming his life into a quest for evidence, Bishop can act as the dedicated amateur scientist he had always wished to be, but for which he had never been able to summon the energy and concentration. He at last seems able properly to emulate his father, to sink back into the 'reassuring maleness' (p. 64) of the library-cum-study in the house he has inherited along with the business, books on physics and architecture, microscopes, labelled cases of moths and rock fragments – 'reassuring' not least for providing a refuge, for father and son in turn, from the lingering ambivalences of a professional life spent among cosmetics, fashions and hair colour, an expertise in feminine detail involving a mixture of dispassionate appraisal and furtive absorption, as if in long preparation for the crisis of self which now spills over. Bishop's new investigative purposefulness gives him the chance to explore all kinds of taboo sensations, while passing them off to himself as accidental by-products of his justified, almost disinterested search for truth. He probes around in his wife's bedroom:

> What a strange, secret life a woman must live among such secrets… this unfamiliarity seemed to stimulate me… Now into the lower drawers, feeling with my hands among the silk things folded there, among stockings and soft underclothes and the hard carapace of a corset. Then – in the bottom of the bottom drawer, tucked far inside – I felt a box…
>
> p. 66

– while a few days later, dancing at a café with Norma, he is so overcome by the frankness with which 'as soon as she was in my arms she thrust her thighs against mine, clamping herself immovably' (p. 101), that he tries to turn their steps into a tango so he can stand away from her for a minute.

More exhilarating still, and more spiced with anxiety, is the sensation of having broken into the enemy camp and become a spy blending in among unsuspecting strangers. Although Bishop has lived in the same place all his life, he has never entered the house next door or given it a second thought. It looks much plainer than his own turreted and ornamented property, but it conceals riches; a constantly shifting population of bedsit tenants with weirdly colliding tastes and habits: the thriller-writer Bradford 'smelt of incense and macintoshes' (p. 105), Diver's patio 'contrived a mixed appearance of Mediterranean courtyard, derelict garage, and pixie glen' (p. 34); his flat is awash with the lurid colours and kitsch bric-a-brac so resonant of the years of austerity, of lemon essence served with tea, of Vintrex, a kind of ersatz port, of plastic dogs with lightbulbs for eyes, of cigarette boxes pretending to be books bound in vellum. This house rapidly becomes for Bishop a loathsome and enticing alter-ego: 'More and more I thought of the two houses as a single entity, with a passage between but nevertheless joined' (p. 93) – a place not only harbouring the supposed sexual secrets he is trying to sniff out, but seeming to represent a compendium of everything of which his own existence has been deprived. There is a powerful evocation throughout this novel of a special suburban sensibility, one for which a minor deviation from one's usual route, or a district perhaps only half a mile away, appear threateningly alien; where, starved of nourishment, the imagination responds by searching for the exotic in the banal (Bishop walks towards the pumping station with 'its acid emerald cupolas clustering low among the roofs and brown brick. It was always like descending from the hills to some fabulous citadel of the east' [p. 73]), or conversely by prizing the overlooked and the disregarded, the patches of waste ground still precariously surviving amid the uniformities; private havens of fantasy or regret, like miniature versions of the London bomb sites which, in another novel written at this time, Rose Macaulay's *The World My Wilderness*, allowed a maquisard existence, with its deceptively simple, utopian definitions of 'friend' and 'enemy', to carry on a little longer after the actual war had finished. There are moments in *The Body* when the visions that most animate it, the sudden exposures of things previously hidden, the adrenaline rush and the wary curiosity as walls and barriers start to collapse, are seen almost as if it was indeed bomb damage that made them possible:

> Like a storm subsiding, the room abruptly grew quiet…only the smoke remained. Scattered sentences shot in and died on what was almost silence. I noticed people looking at each other as if they had never really looked before. Only the smoke hung still deeply clouding this extraordinary non-movement.
>
> p. 58

Estranged absorption in detail, of the kind which gives Bishop's narrative its compulsive character, was the most powerful feature of the stories of the Blitz for which Sansom was most celebrated, such as 'Building Alive' and 'The Wall'. Such absorption seemed both a defence against and a symptom of the mind's inability to grasp fully what was facing it. The pressure of crisis creates a kind of collision in those writings between a laconic, professional risk-appraisal, a heightened awareness of hidden fault-lines:

> The house, suddenly stretched by blast, was settling itself ... Walking in such houses, the walls and floor are forgotten; the mind pictures only the vivid inner framework of beams and supports, where they might run and how, under stress, they might behave; the house is perceived as a skeleton.[2]

and an erotically charged, almost ecstatically gratifying sense of the inadequacy of words, of the experience being somehow protected by the cognitive doubt it engenders:

> The wall ... sprang out at my eyes, bulging round, then snapped back into its flat self. That happened, distinctly. Whether ... it had actually expanded into so round and resilient a curve, or whether the noise and the windclap of the explosion jarred this round illusion within my own round eyes – I do not know. But that happened ...[3]

('The Wall', incidentally, recounts as an incident in the lives of Blitz firefighters the same situation which, adapted from a Buster Keaton film, became a recent Turner Prize-winning installation by Steve McQueen: a wall falling forwards on top of a man standing at just the right distance for the empty window frame to pass over his head and leave him unhurt – although I did not come across any mention of Sansom's work in the accounts of this one.) In *The Body*, what appears to be an analogous combination of defence and symptom produces a recurrent aggressiveness of description, as the mind attempts to reclaim in one area the control which is dissolving in another. When Madge laughs at one of Charley's witticisms, it sounds to Bishop 'as if a row of metal bells, verdigrised but game, had suddenly become galvanised behind her nose' (p. 31) – a remark presumably designed to screen him from his fear of what her laughter might mean, but which makes the fear more apparent by violently compressing together many of the most intense concerns of his mental life: bodily impurities, automatisation, the decaying-genteel accoutrements of suburban villas. When a storm interrupts the boating party, Bishop kills time with an extraordinarily protracted account of the different ways in which rain can rain: as if, just before the moment which was going to settle his suspicions about Madge and Diver one way or the other, a space had opened up for all the conflicting desires aroused by those suspicions to pool themselves – on the one hand the urge to classify, to maintain absolute distinctions and to prevent adulteration, and on the other, the yearning for experience to multiply indefinitely, for more and more variegations to expand over the horizon. Eventually the intervals of suspense, suspense never fully resolved, allow his habitual immersion in tiny particulars to release visions of movement and instability inside the most familiar things, whether they be his own body:

> I suddenly grew conscious of my living body. Inside those black boots there were feet and toes and on the toes greyish-yellow hairs … all the time, motionless in a motionless room, my body was slowly, slowly falling to pieces. A gradual, infinitesimal disintegration was taking place … Pores … were now drying up, hairs were loosening in their follicles … my fingernails were growing, phlegm accumulated itself on the membranes of my throat and nose – all the time steadily, relentlessly.
>
> p. 128

– or, increasingly, and adding all the time to the deepening feeling of mortality in the novel, those houses, persistently seen as if blown open and their insides exposed, a hidden, coiled disorder underpinning all the life lived in them:

> Pipes … ran everywhere … curling and branching and forking like things alive and waiting; some suddenly bulged, like snakes digesting a swallowed prey … And as I looked up at all those windows, there sprang out distinctly from the façades those pipes again, gutter-pipes and drain-pipes winding fantastically over the otherwise ordered house-fronts of grey plaster: many had been picked out in bright paint, others took on a depth of shadow cast by the lowering evening sun.
>
> pp. 205–11

So much of his imagination is caught in a struggle between solid and liquid; watery images are recurrent, not only in the comic-Freudianisms of pumping stations, bursting dams, flushing sewage and the gleefully enraged destruction of Diver's goldfish tank with a poker, but in more general visions of the whole suburban landscape being built upon water – 'the clipped lawns, the low square clumps of golden privet and green laurel – it seemed that these evergreens were suckled wet by the great wealth of water underneath' (p. 73) – and sinking back into it by degrees.

There is bubbling up as well as sinking. The most curious feature of Bishop's own house is halfway down the garden, a 'strange tumescence':

> A circular brick cylinder...rises almost in the centre of the lawn...The curved brick is creepered with wistaria...and like a skirt to the tower there is set, in stony folds, a rising accumulation of marble and blue-grey rocks green with thick-leaved rock plants. To this promontory I walked – it was a place to which I would often walk with absent mind, an attracting pillar.
>
> pp. 145–6

This phallic tower with its feminine surround involves a symbolic convergence of so many shaping forces in his life that it begins to resemble a parodic miniature of Woolf's lighthouse; father and mother and a suggestion of the sea; childhood sensations evoked by the sight of the young men next door marking out a tennis court ('I...felt again in memory the supple freedom of my own youth' [pp. 146–7]); his overwhelming fear of exclusion reignited as the young men ignore him (this is the moment when, in a desperate attempt to allay his neighbours' suspicions of his behaviour, he invites them all to the boating picnic). There are few signs, however, that his little voyages to the 'attracting pillar', his moments of mental refreshment, can produce any conciliation between the present and the past, or the balance of elegy and enfranchisement on which Woolf's novel came to rest. On the contrary, it is primarily a place of disturbance and antagonism. The brick cylinder both offends and draws attention to the symmetry of the lawn, the tidiness of the entire household, by being set 'a trifle to one side of the exact centre'. Rather than transmitting comfortingly regular beams of light, it blasts out acrid smoke from an underground railway at unpredictable intervals (it would certainly make alfresco entertaining rather hazardous). These blasts always induce Bishop's 'bitter and impotent disapproval' (p. 149): everything about this bizarre object graphically reinforces his awareness that the very ground of his existence is outside his control, that from the beginning he has shared his tenancy with alternative, random, anarchic powers. There could be some comic tribute paid here not only to Woolf but to Forster, who in 'The Machine Stops' used a very similar railway tunnel ventilation shaft as the focal point of the hero's rebellion, the passage leading from anaesthetised conformity to wild Nature, since Henry's

entire narrative effectively constitutes a half-conscious, hopeless protest against the life he has inherited, a life so arranged and laid down
for him in advance as to leave no room for manoeuvre. His
jealousy of his wife itself seems like the eruption of some subterranean
ambivalence towards everything he claims to have loved. Perhaps it
was really provoked by her apparently happy acceptance of the role of
mother-substitute, which marrying him and moving into his house
entailed. She seems never to have wanted to alter anything, except
on one occasion when she redecorated his mother's bedroom,
now her own, and Henry – Henry Bishop was the name of the com-
poser of 'Home, Sweet Home' – is at least as agitated by this minimal
sign of independence and rejection as by the textures in her
underwear drawer: agitated almost to the point that his search for evidence of her adultery becomes merely a pretext for creeping in and out
of her room and feeling its power ('I breathed relief … that I was out of
that new shiny bedroom and in the sympathy of the friendly
old landing' [p. 144]). Similarly, his clumsy attempt to pump the
frustrated crime-writer Bradford for incriminating information about
Diver only opens the way for a wild attack, as it were on Henry's
behalf, on the whole way of life of which he has imagined himself the
custodian:

> 'This crumbling borough, this decrepitous mark of Victoria's great-
> ness … You – Mr Bishop – have I believe an establishment in the
> parade called Seychelles? … Seychelles Parade! And does anyone here
> dream of enquiring into that name … and finding it to designate no
> less than ninety glittering islands set like jewels in the blue tropical
> ocean of India … and the names, the names, Bishop, of those islands –
> Praslin, Silhouette, Curieuse, Félicité, Bijoutier … Rename your estab-
> lishment, Monsieur Bishop, call yourself Maison Curieuse, Coiffeur
> de Seychelles Parade!'
>
> p. 86

– a vision of naming and renaming all too bitterly out of reach of those
condemned to be virtually exact replicas of the previous generation:
parodies of continuity but, like Henry and Madge, without children of
their own, with their own futures blocked off and uncertain. It seems
to me that this kind of sardonic pathos taps into the contemporary
mood as tellingly as anything in the most conspicuous novel of that
year, Orwell's *1984*.

Elizabeth Taylor's novel of 1949, *A Wreath Of Roses*, is also a study of mid-life crisis, jealousy and the fear of ageing, of the questions asked of a life by the sudden intrusion of violence into it. The war and its aftermath feature more explicitly than in *The Body*, but Taylor's novel takes a comparably oblique approach to the way in which the war has fuelled and provided packaging for certain self-pitying fantasies of empowerment. *A Wreath Of Roses* also involves a confrontation with Virginia Woolf, more earnest and protracted than Sansom's, with the same underlying feeling of the second generation's having been cheated out of the chance their elders had to lay post-war ghosts and to open new horizons. Taylor had begun to reuse some Woolfian motifs in her previous novel, *A View of the Harbour* (1947), with its lighthouse, its fishing imagery and its unfinished painting, and *A Wreath Of Roses* returns to them with an ambivalent fascination, seeming to oscillate between yearning for a harmonising vision, a bridging of differences, however temporary, and an exasperated dismissal of the falsity of any such thing in its own times. In some respects *A Wreath Of Roses* looks back on Woolf, as representing the world before 1939, in much the same spirit as Woolf herself had looked back on the world before 1914; except that in the late 1940s what one of Taylor's characters, Richard Elton, describes as 'a sort of tired horror' (p. 7) seems to have permeated so deeply as to have corroded recollection itself. Camilla is trying to give Richard an account of her first love:

> But how could she? The nineteen-forties impinged on the nineteen-twenties; such darkness lay over the nostalgia that it seemed not sweet but meaningless. Ugliness has the extra power of making beauty seem unreal, a service beauty seems rarely able to return.
>
> p. 158

Debarred nostalgia emerges immediately as a presiding theme; the opening chapter sets up a series of images of homecoming disrupted by shock and violence. Camilla, an unmarried school secretary in her thirties, meets Richard through their jointly witnessing a man committing suicide on a country railway station, an event which 'broke the afternoon in two ... What had been timeless and silent became chaotic and disorganised' (p. 3). The trauma releases an array of part-echoes, apparent doublings and circularities, uncanny and disconcerting effects which take away the calming powers of repetition just as Camilla was most in search of them. Her annual reunion with her old friend Liz, a vicar's wife with a new baby, and Liz's former governess Frances, an elderly painter, is always the highlight of her drab, frustrating year. Camilla's return journey now finds itself intruded upon by someone else's, as Richard claims to be coming back to his home town after a long absence to write a book about his wartime experiences. The sense of familiarity which this train ride should bring her becomes skewed by flashback; as they pass the next station, it turns into a replica of the suicide site – 'the same deserted platform, the geraniums; as if they had completed a circle' (p. 5). Everything seems indefinitely stained; 'the death she had witnessed was not to be so easily left behind... it would go along with her' (p. 4), in the same way that the larger-scale disturbances of wartime seem to have gone along with Richard:

> He looked up and down the station, uncertainly, she thought: but there seemed plenty to account for that – his loss of nerve which he had described, or simply the fact of returning after a long interval to a once familiar place. There are usually changes; and if there are not it is even stranger.

p. 10

This comment touches with a minimum of fuss on the key tropes of dislocation and readjustment that dominate so much 1940s writing. At the same time, there is a sense in which Camilla is relying on the stock generalisations of the day, when uneasy-homecoming syndrome is so ubiquitous as to have become a virtual cliché, to help her re-establish a distance from this man, to screen off the more complex disturbances which his behaviour has aroused in her. Most of the novel's characters use words to fend things off, to build shelters or to secure little temporary advantages over whatever seems threatening; Taylor's writing repeatedly probes the self-deluding manoeuvres which the mind employs to pretend it is in charge of what is overwhelming it. The story Camilla tells herself about her developing relationship with Richard – that, jealous of Liz's baby, she is taking revenge by having a little arm's-length holiday romance with a man 'of the kind that she... believed she despised' (p. 1) – has some truth in it, as many such manoeuvres do, but it glosses over a deeper problem: that the aura of mystery, violence, callousness and psychological damage which he brings with him has an alarming erotic appeal, magnetising something repressed and reciprocal in her which is harder to face or be articulate about. Meanwhile, the play of sameness and difference, the doublings and mirror-effects which keep rippling out from the initial trauma, reinforce the tantalising sensation she has of being half in control of her experience and half adrift in it.

In one oddly contrived but still intriguingly charged instance, Camilla finds herself using, in conversation with Liz, the remarks Richard had made about the suicide – 'I wonder why?' and 'Upsetting!' – only for Liz to answer in the same words with which Camilla herself had then rebuked him: 'Something more than upsetting.' Such an eerie re-encounter with her old self, just as she had begun to experiment with a new one, could either increase her sense of estrangement, or lull her into believing she could limit its extent, that a safe retreat was never too far away (like all Taylor's novels, this one exposes with surgical precision the kind of complacency which partly acknowledges that it may be blundering, and becomes more complacent as a result). When, not long afterwards, she and Richard meet in a pub and watch each other in a mirror:

> Alone in the looking glass they seemed. They watched, with a steady fascination, as if those two other selves would commit some action independently of them; would ... turn to one another in the closest intimacy, make some violent impact upon one another which could not be made in actuality.
>
> p. 26

The terms 'as if' and 'actuality' seem to be trying rather nervously to redraw the distinctions which in Camilla's mind are starting to blur; and by now the text is returning almost obsessively to the question of whether, once departure has occurred, home would still be there to come back to, and what it would look like if it were.

The general concern to re-establish continuity with the past at a time of dislocation emerges in the frequent discussions of childhood and the consequences of upbringing – discussions for which the novel seems to reserve a special irony. Liz's baby, the main subject of meditation, is alternately spoilt or neglected while the adults meditate, and the person who draws the most plausible connection between what happened to him as a child and what he has become, is, unbeknown to the rest of them, making it all up. Richard (it is never clear whether this is his real name) appears both to embody and to exploit the confusions of the time and the cravings for meaning which they induce. He is one of those in whom the war seems to have stirred up an unappeasable hunger for authentic sensation, leading him subsequently not only to fantasy but to murder; at the time he meets Camilla, he is not returning to his home town at all, but is on the run from the police. He has reached the point of half-believing his own stories about himself, stories of a fluency and consistency which might ordinarily make them suspect, but which for precisely those qualities exert a seductive power over the unfulfilled or the embittered by change, in search of similarly watertight narratives for themselves. He fabricates images of a cruel and deprived childhood because he wants to gain Camilla's sympathy, but she just as eagerly laps them up because they give her the illusion of regaining control over the very tensions in her that have drawn her to him:

> The same thing happened to us both, she thought ... starved as children, but he (perhaps because he is a man) reacting to violence, inviting danger, attempting everything and everyone. While I am stiffening into an old maid, recoiling fastidiously from life.
>
> p. 89

If, as she comes to believe, the two of them are really the missing halves of each other, then the attraction between them is no longer perverse or incomprehensible, as her friends see it, but the uncovering of some long-hidden and confidently rationalisable need: a summing-up which simultaneously takes her close to the truth and miles away from it. Richard manipulates to the full the post-conflict stereotypes to which, for all her caustic intelligence, she is deeply susceptible – the ones that offer her an empowering role: the demobbed soldier in search of a nurse for his bruised sensitivity, the young man needing help to fight his way out of his parents' shadow; and when he takes her to see what he tells her is the house where he grew up, all the motifs that come into play in their relationship, the illusory doublings and replicas, the false returns, the private resentments, the striking combinations of blindness and insight, build up to an almost vertiginous climax:

> 'Here it is!' he said. He knew at once that he had been clever in choosing his house; for she stopped, her face grew intent, her eyes narrowed dreamily. He took her arm and drew her closer to him ... 'Yes,' she said softly. 'I can imagine it all going on inside such a house.'
>
> p. 193

The woman who lives there welcomes them in – a man evading arrest, pretending to be showing his 'fiancée' round his 'old home'; the 'fiancée' humouring one pretence while ignorant of the other, distressed on his behalf at the squalor of a place she believes to hold so many poignant memories for him; he acting, with just the right measure of existential ennui, the part of the weary veteran struggling to find surviving fragments of his old life among all the changes; the householder, presumably a war widow, moved to tears by this spectacle of youthful intimacy and reconnection with the past – an extraordinary and impressively *noir* concatenation of cynicism, loneliness and hopeless desire, in which true feelings and manufactured ones seem to have interpenetrated so tightly that neither could avoid contamination by the other.

The painter, Frances, is full of anxiety over impurities like this; she wants her painting to effect a clear distinction between the beautiful and the ugly, something the rest of the novel insists cannot be done. Having devoted herself in the past to what she now calls a ladylike charm, she is currently responding to what she takes to be the spirit of the times by painting uncontaminated ugliness, trying to turn herself from a Vuillard into a Francis Bacon. As she approaches the end of her life, she remains deeply unsure whether or not she is satisfied with it; sometimes she tells herself that her painting is her true joy, sometimes that its cost in lost human intimacy has been too great, sometimes that what she has produced is not only worthless but corrupting:

> 'I committed a grave sin against the suffering of the world by ignoring it, by tempting others with charm and nostalgia until they ignored it too.'
>
> p. 169

Her increasingly histrionic self-accusations, almost reminiscent of contemporary show trials, are like so many other pronouncements in the novel, motivated as much by an exhausted wish to simplify as by real conviction. She is trying to fend off the disturbance aroused by the arrival of Morland Beddoes, a man she is meeting for the first time after years of correspondence, a man who admires her work for reasons she can no longer accept, and whose presence reminds her of all the companionship she has forfeited. Their relationship is also, in its way, organised around the motifs of war, homecoming and change; they wrote to each other while he was in a German prison camp, and formed ideas of each other which they are now rather doubting the wisdom of testing. He prizes her paintings precisely for having transcended the contemporary violence and agitation which she criticises them for excluding; he relied in the camp on his memories of the serenity and order in her work, the expression for him of an idealised femininity which the war did so much to throw into crisis – intensifying its appeal for men just as women were finding new opportunities to break its shackles. The debate between Frances and Morland, as Niamh Baker suggests, touches on the difficulties created for female artists by the post-war pressures on women to resume forms men found less threatening; Morland is as much implicated in the search for omniscient maternal figures as is Richard Elton.[4] But at the same time he puts his finger on something her pre-war, 'feminine' paintings possessed which the more recent work, driven more by therapeutic than by aesthetic needs, has lost: a ruthless and unsentimental clarity of vision:

> 'The picture of Liz on the sofa – she was a woman alone in a room; as only God, I should have thought, could ever possibly have seen her. It was the truth.'
>
> p. 170

God may see things undisturbed by accident or surprise, in the light of an absolute knowledge that leaves no room for desire; but Frances by now is too weary and infirm to continue struggling to erase her personality from her work:

> 'This curious light,' Frances began, and then stopped ... 'Oh, it flies away,' she thought, striking her hands together in her lap. 'It can't ever be caught or described ... Life itself is an unfinished sentence, or a few haphazard brushstrokes. Nothing stays. Nothing is completed. I can make nothing whole from it, however small ... The meaning of a painting is a voice crying out: "I saw it. Before it vanished, it was thus."'
>
> p. 222

The intertwining of personal needs and aesthetic values would suggest the presence of Virginia Woolf behind this even without the explicit allusions. Frances sounds more and more like an elderly, dismayed Lily Briscoe, full of doubts about the little miracles she used to believe in, feeling that in the midst of shape there was chaos: 'in the heart of life, in the core of even everyday things is there not violence, with flames wheeling, turmoil, pain?' (p. 42).[5] In the sheer proliferation of its echoes of *To The Lighthouse*, *A Wreath Of Roses* exhibits all the classic symptoms of the fight with the overshadowing predecessor, a predecessor again seeming to hold the keys to a post-catastrophic comfort which is no longer on offer. At times it is almost as if *To The Lighthouse* had so used up the language available for the subjects *A Wreath Of Roses* wants to deal with that it can only be recycled again, in a manner somewhere between homage and sarcastic parody. Frances thinks of how eventually her paintings, 'those manifestos of ours against the indifference of the world will lie, face down ... in attics' (p. 143; Liz's baby spends much of its time asleep in a room stacked with Frances's discarded canvases); Richard writes in his diary that 'we are all like icebergs; underneath where the greater parts are hidden it is dark and unreachable' (p. 94); Camilla (actually called 'Cam' at one point) has been brought up in a donnish Cambridge household among clever and overbearing elder brothers; Frances responds to Morland's remark about the truth of her painting by 'blowing out a match' (p. 170); when they are all making plans for their annual picnic Camilla even says 'I think it will rain tomorrow' (p. 207). The picnic itself is like the one in Sansom's novel, a dishevelled attempt to reconnect with old securities which only exposes how far from them everyone has drifted; a kind of master-image of all the other fractured homecomings, with its ritual associations of fulfilment and closure made the butt of some sardonic comment from Camilla:

> 'It's a lovely day ... the sort of day people remember as the *end* of something – the last day before the war, the last day of peace, the day the Old Queen died, the end of an era. They look back and say: "It was perfect weather that summer. There never was weather like it, before or after. We didn't know it was the last day of our happiness, and that it would never be the same again".'
>
> p. 220; italics in text

The nostalgia beneath the satire here does not seem to be for any particular order of things of which this day marks an end, but rather for a time when a day could seem so inflected; recent history has accumulated so many portentous moments, so many instances of the untrustworthiness of beauty, or of the menace lurking in calm, that any fresh ones have already been ironically discounted and robbed of their chance to be significant, and there is no longer any glamour in the apocalyptic thinking by which so much modernism was sustained.

The novel consistently undercuts the kind of attitudinising which Camilla parodies here. A dappling pattern is built up whereby each character's attempt at epigram is countered by another's elsewhere; there is no faith in summings-up, only an exposure of the restless desire to make them. There is also a good deal of comic leavening: Frances, for example, marks her new-found interest in unpleasantness by acquiring a huge slobbering dog, Hotchkiss, named presumably after the celebrated machine-gun designer, which she forces Camilla and Liz to take with them on their walks, as if to remind them, in the midst of their abstractions, of all the disagreeable practical difficulties of the here and now. The working-class characters are acutely and unpatronisingly observed, making sly, unmalicious fun of their employers and enjoying the drama of the everyday problems which the gentry take so sombrely; the novel even rather self-consciously satirises its own dark agonising by introducing a character called 'Mrs Taylor', Liz's husband's housekeeper – 'that wretched woman: bleak, inexorable, casting sadness about her... with her unalterable time-table... her bad heads, her preoccupation with suicide – "Why I don't put my head in the gas oven and be done with it, I don't know"' (p. 166). There is a distinct period flavour to this, hard to itemise; both Sansom and Taylor seem to approach the world with a special mixture of humour and apprehension. They were exact contemporaries (born 1912), unusual in being relatively late starters, publishing nothing before the war and essentially shaped as writers by it; one boisterous, the other terse and aphoristic, but both employing the kind of insistent, wary precision about place and colour which sees death behind everything it looks at. And certainly an abiding preoccupation with the fragility and porousness of the shelters people build, physical or mental, is something that can be traced in their work long afterwards: one could compare the half-amused fearfulness in some of Sansom's 1950s stories, such as 'Question and Answer' (1956) or 'Among the Dahlias' (1957), with that in Taylor's last writings, a story like 'Sisters' (1969), or her posthumously published novel *Blaming* (1976).

Notes

Page references in the text are to the following editions: William Sansom, *The Body* (London: Hogarth Press, 1949; reprinted for The Reader's Union, London, 1950); Elizabeth Taylor, *A Wreath of Roses* (London: Virago Press, 1994).

1. William Sansom, 'A Fireman's Journal', in *Leaves in the Storm: A Book of Diaries*, eds, Stefan Schimanski and Henry Treece (London: Lindsay Drummond, 1947), p. 141.
2. *The Stories of William Sansom* (London: Hogarth Press, 1963), p. 83.
3. Ibid., p. 85.
4. Niamh Baker, *Happily Ever After? Women's Fiction in Postwar Britain, 1945–60* (London: Macmillan, 1989), pp. 152–3.
5. Since Frances ends her career trying to paint a wreath of roses, in ironic counterpoint to this vision of wheeling flames, Taylor's novel could well be added to the list Lyndsey Stonebridge gives elsewhere in this volume of works from the 1940s which involve a collocation of fire and rose.

10
Souvenirs from France: Textual Traumatism in Henry Green's *Back*

Gerard Barrett

> Is not repetition itself a kind of resurrection of the dead?
>
> Paul Ricoeur, 'Narrative Time'

Set in London during the last year of the Second World War, Henry Green's *Back* (1946) is the decade's finest representation of a condition that has only recently acquired a name. Post-traumatic stress disorder was not accepted as a genuine medical syndrome by the American Psychiatric Society until 1980 and the British Ministry of Defence has been equally slow to recognise its existence.[1] *Back* describes the effect of post-traumatic stress on a repatriated soldier, Charley Summers. The physical trauma that afflicts Charley is evident from the outset: disembarking from a bus by a church in the English countryside, the returning soldier has to move carefully because of his wooden leg. Although his psychological injuries will not become visible until later in the novel, they are foreshadowed in this opening scene. Charley has come to the churchyard to visit the grave of a woman called Rose, whom he had loved before the war began. When he subsequently meets Rose's half-sister, Nancy Whitmore, of whose existence he had been unaware, he becomes convinced that Nancy is actually Rose, that Rose has been alive and deceiving him while he thought her dead. Several comic and nightmarish coincidences conspire to perpetuate Charley's delusion until his gradual recovery leads to an ambiguous resolution: the final scene of the novel has him calling Rose's name as he holds Nancy naked in his arms.

Although the main symptoms of Charley's trauma are clear, Green's account of its origin is clouded with insinuation and reticence.[2] The narrator never explains or allows Charley to admit to consciousness 'something in France which he knew, as he valued his reason, that he must always shut out'.[3] All the narrative offers in this regard is an oblique movement around the figure of a mouse. When Charley meets Rose's mother, Mrs Grant, on his return to London, she mistakes him for her brother John, who died at war in 1917. Charley finds her 'much too neat ... everything was mouse tidy, except it seemed her wits' (p. 16). The figure of the mouse, in this scene, is associated with amnesia and delusion brought on by melancholia. The figure subsequently takes on a sexual connotation. In the fifth chapter, Charley's sexual obsession with his secretary is communicated through his awareness of 'her breasts, which she wore as though ashamed, like two soft nests of white mice, in front. Their covered creepiness, in this hot summer, nagged him' (p. 43). The figure goes through another mutation near the end of the novel when Charley, making his only revelation about his time in the prisoners' camp, tells Nancy: 'I had a mouse out there' (p. 199). Nancy's reply is to relate this to her cat, inquiring: 'You don't hold it against my puss?' (p. 199). Although Charley reassures her that it has never even crossed his mind, the name of Nancy's cat, of all possible names, is Panzer.[4]

The symbolic significance of the cat had surfaced in an earlier chapter, where Charley is woken up in the night by the sound of Mrs Grant screaming in the room above him. Her husband is dying and the cat's ability to sleep through her cries threatens to bring the source of Charley's trauma to the surface:

> And he saw the cat curled up asleep. It didn't even raise its ears. Then, at the idea that this animal could ignore crude animal cries above, which he had shut out with his wet palms, he nearly let the horror get him, for the feelings he must never have again were summoned once more when he realized the cat, they came rumbling back, as though at a signal, from a moment at night in France. But he won free. He mastered it.
>
> p. 186

The feelings that come 'rumbling back', the verb itself suggesting the movement of tanks over a landscape, are never admitted into the novel, but a number of interpretative possibilities present themselves. Charley may have suffered a sexual violation in the camps or an extreme form of deprivation, such as solitary confinement.[5] Another possibility is that Charley's missing leg is a synecdochal expression of a loss that is even more devastating.[6] The only certainty is that the figure of the mouse gathers a number of ideas – melancholic neurosis, repressed sexuality, companionship, the fear of being killed and devoured by a more powerful enemy – into a pattern that resists a definitive decoding. In any case, my purpose in tracing this figure is less to explain Charley's trauma than to demonstrate the oblique intra-textual way it is expressed.

Green is more forthcoming on the origins of Charley's physical trauma. However, his revelation that Charley lost his leg in France 'for not noticing the gun beneath a rose' (p. 5), defies the reader to take it literally. This statement, appearing in the context of Charley's grief for a woman named Rose, suggests that *Back* is a rhetorical text, more interested in symbolic than mimetic values. It effectively inscribes the religious and aesthetic symbol of the rose within the historical context of the war.[7] On the other hand, the rose is also accredited with the power of transcending time:

> The idea had been to make the clock's hands go round. And now that he'd come, he told himself, all he was after was to turn them back, the fool, only to find roses grown between the minutes and the hours, and so entwined that the hands were stuck.
>
> pp. 8–9

These contrasting images suggest that the novel's symbolic, religious, and literary level cannot be cordoned off from its historical and secular dimension; the interplay of the two within the text allows neither to dominate. Delusion becomes as valid as truth in a story where the very distinction between such categories is undermined.

A contemporary critic of the novel complained that *Back*'s nightmarish atmosphere depends on two 'low grade' coincidences, the likeness between the half-sisters and the recurrence of Rose's name as the past tense of a common verb.[8] However, the actual cause of Charley's delusion is not Nancy's resemblance to Rose, but his own morbid wish fulfilment. Green himself, with characteristic understatement, claimed that the novel was 'all about a man whose nerves are very bad'.[9] This description suggests that the novel is not concerned with the objective resemblance between Nancy and Rose but with the traumatised disposition of the man that confuses them. Like Thomas Hardy's *The Well-Beloved* (1897), *Back* is, to borrow Hardy's sub-title, 'a sketch of a temperament'. The likeness between the sisters is beside the point: when Charley tries to expose Nancy by confronting her with Rose's husband, this man says that the two women are not at all alike.

Green's story of trauma and Hardy's tale of migrating platonic love have more in common than might be expected. Both blend realism and fantasy in their explorations of death's power to renew love. The love that the male protagonists feel, in both novels, is not conventional sexual desire but 'that strange form of mediation which is the repetition of one person in another'.[10] Hardy's hero, Jocelyn Pierston, loves three women, the second two being the daughter and the grand-daughter of the first. All three are named Avice and the repetitive series begins when his love for the first Avice is reawakened by her death. A tripartite pattern of loving also takes place in *Back*: the woman that Charley comes to love and marry is neither Rose nor Nancy but a resurrection of one in the other. This 'resurrection' is not simply the final fall into delusion for Charley; it is complied with by the text of the novel itself. The text, like its hero, exists in a state of traumatism; his disorder is mirrored by the morbid condition of the narrative system.

It could, of course, be argued that the idea of Charley's love following a tripartite rather than a binary pattern is less an objective narrative fact than a critical interpretation. Let us look once again at the novel's final scene to see if this can be established more firmly.

> Then he knelt by the bed, having under eyes the great, the overwhelming sight of the woman he loved, for the first time without her clothes. And because the lamp was lit, the pink shade seemed to spill a light of roses over her in all their summer colours, her hands that lay along her legs were red, her stomach gold, her breasts the colour of cream roses, and her neck white roses for the bride. She had shut her eyes to let him have his fill, but it was too much, for he burst into tears again, he buried his face in her side just below the ribs, and bawled like a child. 'Rose,' he called out, not knowing he did so, 'Rose'.
>
> p. 208

Most of Green's critics propose two interpretations of Charley's enunciation of Rose's name: this is either the final regression for Charley into delusion or it is his ultimate exorcism of the ghost of Rose.[11] However, in confining themselves to two possibilities, Green's critics lock the narrative into a binary framework that the text itself renders untenable. The idea of the third love, combining two of the novel's major themes in the sexual presence of Nancy and the linguistic presence of Rose, develops subtly but steadily throughout the later stages of the book. Michael North points to several details in the text that anticipate the final scene:

> When Nancy is invited to help nurse her father and begins to refer to Mrs Grant as 'Mother' (p. 164), it is obvious that she has moved

into a role she has long coveted. To play Rose in the sickroom is finally to possess the legitimacy she has lacked, both legally and psychologically...Charley is virtually dragged back from sanity by the collusion of the family...The obsession Charley conceives on his own and conquers on his own by the middle of the novel is returned to him here by the collaboration of all the other actors in his life.[12]

However, it is not only the characters in the novel who conspire to resurrect Rose in Charley's deluded consciousness: the text itself, through its obsession with tripartite patterns, plays a major role in this 'resurrection'.

The tripartite patterns developed in *Back* contribute to a religious sub-text in the narrative. The first of these patterns is Charley's discovery of 'rose after rose after rose' (p. 5) in the graveyard, where the repetition of 'rose' is less a rococo flourish than a minute formal expression of the novel's tripartite structure. For instance, Charley's three denials of Rose (pp. 13, 26, 151) are set off against Nancy's three affirmations of love for her dead husband, Phil (pp. 88, 145, 198). Linked to this pattern of denial and affirmation are numerous micro-patterns, also of a triadic nature. The most oblique of these is the tricycle Rose's child is riding when Charley sees him for the first time.[13] Elsewhere, the narrator will say that Charley 'saw everything a third time' (p. 70) or that James was saying something 'for the third time' (p. 85). In the space of 'three weeks' Charley calls 'thrice at Miss Whitmore's' (p. 163). Rose lives only three months after she marries James and Nancy's husband gets three leaves of absence before he dies in action. When hoping for a nocturnal visit from Nancy at Mr Grant's, Charley tries the sofa to see it makes a noise: 'He bounced once, then twice, yes thrice, as he lay there' (p. 184). Charley's three denials, however, occupy a hierarchical position in this series. Alluding to Peter's three denials of Christ, they form an archetype that structures the others. The Christian symbolism his three denials evoke suggests that their function is to endow a religious significance to the love that is being denied.[14] In a novel where so much is structured in a tripartite way, can the central issue really be a man's love for *two* women? Everything in the text conspires to resurrect Rose, not just the other characters in the novel.

Back is unique in Green's oeuvre in having this religious dimension. Green's general indifference to religious symbolism makes his use of it in this novel a symptom of the traumatised state of the text. At times, the characters themselves construe events in a religious way, if only unconsciously. Nancy introduces a messianic motif into the story when she reminds Charley (three times) that her husband died fighting for him (p. 88). At another point, Charley speaks of Rose 'as of a rib that had been removed' (p. 145) and in the novel's final scene he buries his face in Nancy's side, 'just below the ribs' before calling out for Rose (p. 208).

The tripartite pattern of desire that connects *Back* to *The Well-Beloved* is reinforced by numerous correspondences of detail and motif between the novels. In *Back*, for example, Charley faints after seeing Nancy for the first time. The next chapter begins with Charley coming round to find 'Rose' kneeling at his head. This recalls the scene in *The Well-Beloved* where Pierston, emerging from sleep, sees the second Avice for the first time: 'during some minute or minutes he seemed to see Avice Caro herself, bending over and then withdrawing from her grave in the light of the moon.'[15] The corresponding scene in *Back* contains a reference to Nancy's 'moon cool hands laid about his temples' (p. 48), in a further echo of Hardy's scene. The theme of pursuit is represented in both novels by the action of following people through streets. Pierston, a sculptor, follows women in the street whose faces seem to 'express to a hair's-breath in mutable flesh what he was at that moment wishing to express in durable shape' (p. 76). At the end of *Back*'s second chapter, Charley gets off a train and follows a woman with red hair 'the best part of three miles, back to what may have been her home, without trying to strike up an acquaintance' (p. 22). Charley's surname, Summers, recalls that of the painter, Alfred Somers, Pierston's friend and confidant. In *The Well-Beloved*, Hardy refers to an immemorial island custom of pre-nuptial union (p. 248); when Nancy asks Charley to marry her at the end of *Back* she makes only one condition, that they have a 'trial trip' (p. 208).

What do these parallels signify? How do they affect the way we read and interpret *Back*? One way to answer this question is to turn to one of J. Hillis Miller's observations on *The Well-Beloved*. The novel, Miller claims, undermines Hardy's claims to authority as the generating source of the story he writes:

> The man and author Thomas Hardy become within the pages of *The Well-Beloved* subject to the long chain of earlier versions of the story written by the various authors he cites, Plato, Shakespeare, Milton, Crashaw, Shelley. The story he tells repeats with a difference stories they have told. This echoing line of citations shows that this novel is only one more naming of 'the one shape of many names'. It cannot be appropriated by a single signature, any more than the well-beloved can be incarnated once and for all in a single shell. Thomas Hardy, life story and all, ceases to be the authorizing source and

becomes himself only one in the middle of a long row. The series
extends after as well as before.

pp. 171–2

Miller extends the series to Proust, pointing out that there is a reference
to *The Well-Beloved*, 'where the man loves three women', in *Remembrance
of Things Past*. Green was an avowed admirer of Proust's work and it may
have been this that directed him towards Hardy's novel.[16] The relationship between the books can be viewed in various ways. Hardy's novel is
a possible source of Green's, undermining Green's claim to authority as
the origin of his own text. Green certainly wanted to undermine his
authorial claim to some degree: his inclusion of a twelve-page extract
from an eighteenth century autobiography in the middle of the novel
(pp. 92–104) is evidence of this. It is as though Green's novel wishes to
blur its own identity and confuse itself with other literary works in a formal equivalent of Charley's condition. It is also possible that a motivation or inspiration in Hardy serendipitously recurred in Green fifty years
later. For Miller, the distinction of Hardy's novel is to have seen so
clearly 'the connections among three strata of human life: erotic experience, unfulfilled religious longing, and the making or reading of works
of literature' (p. 175). As these three strata intersect throughout the narrative of *Back*, it may be this shared perception rather than a conscious
attempt at parody that is the linch-pin of Green's repetition of Hardy.

Language, reading and writing play a pivotal role in the cultivation,
development and resolution of *Back's* plot. Charley's trauma partly finds
expression in linguistic terms. The similarities between some of the
characters' names – James *Phil*ips, *Phil White*, Nancy *Whit*more (my
emphasis) – creates a nightmare of connections in the text, one that
reflects Charley's paranoid belief that everybody is in league against
him (Charley's fellow amputee, Middlewitch, even knows a man called
Charley Rose). Charley finds it impossible to escape the thought of Rose
because her name (in the form of the past tense of the verb, 'to rise')
seems omnipresent in conversation around him. The more paranoid
and deluded he becomes, the more he finds himself at the mercy of
words. Green does not fail to exploit the comic potential of this situation. While in a rage at Rose's father, Mr Grant, for what he perceives to
be his part in the plot to deceive him, Charley suddenly finds himself
by a church:

> He found himself reading a poster stuck up on the notice board out-
> side, which went, 'Grant o Lord', then said something about a faithful

servant. The first word shook him. He cried again, 'The bastard', right out loud.

p. 58

This scene is a *mise en abyme* that parodies the novel's own spirals of free association and ambiguity.[17]

The idea of Rose's 'resurrection' also has a linguistic dimension, being one of the meanings that clings to her name. At one point, Charley's landlady, while talking about rising prices in wartime, says 'they rose, they've rose' and the words, 'because he had not paid attention, the words pierced right through' (p. 35). The presence of the word 'pierced' in this context alludes to the crucifixion that preceded the biblical resurrection of Christ.[18] The culmination of all this is a scene that closely condenses the themes of sex, writing, death and resurrection, when Charley visits Nancy for the first time without realising who she is:

> Then he was outside an inner door, on which was written her name. Her name was there on a card. He read her name, Miss Nancy Whitmore, in Gothic lettering as cut on tombstones. He noticed the brass knocker, a dolphin hanging by the tail. He ran his eye over this door which was painted pink. The wall paper he stared at round the door, was of wreathed roses on a white ground. He looked again. Someone had wiped the paint down so often, it was so clean that the top coat was wearing thin. In the moulding round the panels a yellow first coat grinned through at callers. And her card was held in place by two fresh bits of sticking plaster, pink.
> With a melting of his spine, he felt she must be a tart.

pp. 46–7

When Nancy opens the door to Charley, he sees 'the dead spit, the living image, herself, Rose in person' (p. 47). Charley's act of reading outside her door will be replicated by other, more paranoid perusals of text, all of which relate to his confusion of Nancy with Rose.

The novel's awareness of its own status as a textual entity is visible in the opening scene in the graveyard, where genuine roses are duplicated by 'frosted paper blooms' (p. 5) under glass. At the beginning of the fifth chapter, the arrival of Charley's secretary is described in terms that suggest a transmutation of words into flesh:

> Then, as he went to his room and saw her, he had once again the experience inseparable from government procedure, he had before

his eyes the product of a prolonged correspondence; that is, first the discouraging replies, followed by official consent to there being a vacancy, after which a notification that the vacancy would be filled, then, at last, the name of a person to be directed to fill it, then, finally, that wait, a deadly pause of weeks, before, without warning, these letters, these forms and the reference numbers bloomed into flesh and blood, a young woman, with shorthand, who could type.

p. 37

Charley's relationship with this woman, whose name turns out to be Dot, is mediated through the trope of writing. Later in the novel, when embarrassed at a sexually charged situation, Dot tries to suppress her disquiet by tracing her name with her finger on a bedroom window (p. 123). In this way, the theme of desire intersects and becomes a permutation of the theme of writing and reading, repeating the dynamic that Miller finds in *The Well-Beloved*.

The Well-Beloved, however, is not the primary origin of *Back* as Green's novel has several sources jostling for supremacy within it. Every critic who writes about the novel ends up relating it to other literary works. North considers the whole of *Back* to be an expansion of a scene in Green's earlier novel, *Caught* (p. 123).[19] Edward Stokes views the novel as a modern *Romance of the Rose*[20] while R. S. Ryf, thinking of the presence of bombs as well as roses in the novel, suggests that *Back* may be Green's *Four Quartets* (p. 29). Rod Mengham has found echoes of Keats's 'Ode on Melancholy' scattered throughout the text. In the opening scene, for example, where Charley searches for the grave of Rose, an actual rose falls against his forehead. Mengham reads this as an echo of the prohibition 'Nor suffer thy pale forehead to be kissed/ by nightshade' (ll. 3–4) from the first verse of Keats's poem, but concludes that it does not really matter whether the allusions to Keats are verifiable or not:

> What is important is that there should be some doubt either way. Because in order to be accurate about what it means to read Henry Green, there must be a strong sense of the giddiness of interpretation that this entails.[21]

My addition of *The Well-Beloved* to this list of sources and allusions is not simply an attempt to add to this vertigo. Although the intertextuality of *Back* may well result from an incipient postmodernism that began to emerge in Green's work at this stage, we can come to a closer understanding of the way it works by relating it to the historical conditions in which the novel was written. Intertextuality in *Back* is an aesthetic equivalent of the trauma that afflicts its central character. Green has written the novel in such a way that it can be perceived as a 'double' of other texts, as Nancy, in Charley's traumatised consciousness, is 'the living image' of Rose.

The sense that *Back* is the double of another text reaches its apotheosis with the passage entitled 'From the Souvenirs of Madame DE CRÉQUY (1710–1800) to her infant grandson Tancrède Raoul de Créquy, Prince de Montlaur'. This follows Charley's attempt to expose Nancy by confronting her with Rose's widow, James. When James gets home from London the following evening, he picks up a literary review Rose had liked where he comes across the translation that seems so close to Charley's situation.

> Accordingly he wrote on the cover 'Read, mark, learn, and inwardly digest', signed his initials, drew attention to the story with a cross, and sent the thing to Summers, whom he forgave the moment he had posted the packet.
>
> p. 91

The cross is another example of Green's use of intersecting patterns in his fiction, being an act of writing, a religious symbol and an emblem of a sexual relationship (when Charley sees it he imagines it to be 'an old kiss from Rose') simultaneously.

The extract Charley reads tells the story of Sophie Septimanie de Richelieu whose love for the Count de Gisors was thwarted by her arranged marriage to an older man. The Count is killed at war a few months after his own arranged marriage and Sophie's subsequent love for the Count's identical half-brother results in the young man's murder and Sophie's suicide. Along with the thematic parallels between the extract and the novel, such as mistaken identity and the death of the beloved, there are several correspondences of detail and motif. Sophie, like Charley, faints at the sound of her dead lover's name. The Count's letters to Sophie parallel the letters Rose had sent to Charley before the war. Sophie's enchanting eyes correspond to Charley's 'great eyes' that 'seemed to grow from his head, and float in the air before your own' (p. 36). Roses feature in the extract in the form of flowering rose trees in a Parisian 'dream palace' (p. 95). Even the extract's most eccentric character, the Vidame de Poitiers, has a counterpart in the novel in the form of 'old Ernie Mandrew'.[22]

The part that the extract plays in bringing about the resurrection of Rose provides a further example of the oblique nature of Green's narrative art. Green's translation of the extract concludes:

> All my life I shall never forget this twin attachment, these two extraordinary passions she somehow found a way to lavish on two men who were entirely different and yet at the same time exactly similar, on the living and the dead, on the brilliant Count de Gisors, and an obscure young man. Nor can I ever forget her last moments when, with both lovers gone, she seemed, as she in turn lay dying before my eyes, to fuse the memory of these two men into one, into one true lover.
>
> p. 104

The phrase 'the living and the dead' is Green's interpolation; an earlier version of the same passage by another translator concludes:

> I shall never forget this strange and prodigious affection: two loves inextricably mingled; two beloved objects, absolutely different and yet so alike – the illustrious and admired Comte de Gisors and the obscure and unfortunate M. de Guys.
>
> During her last moments the remembrance of these two brothers were mingled into one sentiment of fidelity and love.[23]

There is a subtle difference between 'one true lover' and 'one sentiment'. The phrasing of Green's version implies that the perceived mingling of the two lovers creates a third, foreshadowing the fusion of Rose and Nancy in Charley's imagination at the novel's end.

Some contemporary critics condemned Green's use of the extract in *Back*. Evelyn Waugh struck the most cantankerous note, on one occasion deriding it as plagiarism and, on other, as a pastiche that wrecks the novel.[24] Even some of Green's admirers view the extract with embarrassment. Jeremy Treglown lists it among the many 'eccentricities of plausibility, organization and stylistic texture' in *Back*, and judges it to be 'perfunctorily incorporated'.[25] Rod Mengham, however, has cannily spotted two 'fastidious and underhand' (p. 171) preparations for the extract in the novel's opening scene that demonstrate the care Green took to absorb it into his text. Charley uncovers the name of the extract's heroine during his search for Rose's grave: 'He had the time to read the one word, "Sophie", cut with no name or date' (p. 8). A page later, the narrator's designation of Charley's artificial leg as 'the long souvenir he had brought back from France' (p. 9) directly alludes to the title of Madame de Créquy's book. Mengham also suggests that the name of the other amputee that appears in the novel, Middlewitch, is a covert reference to the passage from *The Souvenirs*, 'which is in the middle' of *Back*, a point that can be supported by the numerous French phrases that pepper Middlewitch's conversation.[26] Mengham's interpretation, however, can be taken further. It is not coincidental that the extract is foreshadowed by the novel's two amputees: Green's procedure of cutting an extract out of a nineteenth-century text enacts, on a symbolic and formal level, the amputations that Summers, Middlewitch and thousands of their historical counterparts suffered during the war. As an avatar of the motif of amputation, the extract from *The Souvenirs* exemplifies the novel's textual traumatism. If it sits rather awkwardly in the novel then that is exactly how it should be: as awkward and artificial as a peg leg.[27]

The incorporation of the passage from *The Souvenirs* also parallels Charley's mental disorientation. When Waugh read the novel in 1946, he decided that Green had taken leave of his own senses and described the inclusion of the extract as 'very mad'.[28] Such a judgement is not the preserve of Green's detractors. Mengham suggests that madness is the aesthetic milieu of the text, pointing out that the real meaning of the extract 'is a wholly schizophrenic one, irrecoverable without special knowledge. In intra-textual terms this is *unknown* knowledge, and the meaning remains ostensibly hidden, quite precisely *sub rosa*' (p. 172). However, the eccentric, mad or schizophrenic nature of the extract has both aesthetic and historical justification. It is a formal parallel for Charley's delusions and paranoia, being a double of the text that contains him.

There is, however, one other fastidious and underhand preparation for the presence of the extract, which is more cunning than any of Green's preparations in the novel itself. In the summer of 1944, Green published another translation from *The Souvenirs* in the literary review, *Horizon*. This piece, entitled 'The Waters of Nanterre', appeared with a number of other translations under the general heading, 'Varieties of Religious Experience'.[29] The passage, which describes a pilgrimage made by Madame de Créquy to take the waters at the well of a patron saint, revolves around two cases of mistaken identity. The appearance of this comedy of errors in the most widely read literary magazine in England during the war lends an ironic undercurrent to the most contrived aspect of *Back*. For such a piece of writing could have been read, indeed a passage from the same book on a similar theme was read, by the English reading public in 1944. By planting this piece from *The Souvenirs* in *Horizon*, Green ensured that the most fantastic and hallucinatory aspect of *Back* would have an oblique, historical validity.[30]

Far from being perfunctorily incorporated, the extract from *The Souvenirs* is closely connected to other interpolated texts in the narrative. The chapter that follows the extract begins with a text that, in its language, theme and tone, is in marked contrast to the translation that precedes it. This is the business letter to Charley's engineering firm complaining of the non-delivery of parts. Although these two heterogeneous texts initially seem worlds apart, Charley's reaction to the letter forges a link between them. Charley views the letter as an outrageous fiction, a 'try on' (p. 108), something which is simply 'not true' (p. 106). Showing the letter to another official, he suggests that someone may have forged it: 'Silly I know…but I just wondered. Noticed some strange things lately. One of those handwriting experts could tell' (p. 110). Charley's response to the letter echoes that which greeted Madame de Créquy's book when it first appeared in England in 1834: it was dismissed as a forgery.[31] The handwriting motif in *Back* recalls a comment in the translator's preface to the 1904 English edition of *The Souvenirs*: 'Portions of the first part were possibly written by the Marquise herself – indeed they bear the impress of a woman's hand.'[32] Charley's comment also connects the business letter and the extract to the personal letters he receives from Nancy and Rose. When Nancy sends him a note a few pages later, he thinks that Rose must be disguising her hand when he sees the writing on the envelope. This prompts him to send the note, along with Rose's letters, to a handwriting expert. This identification of the translation as one strand of a larger pattern of writing, one that has insinuations of forgery embroidered into it, makes the inclusion of the extract appear more considered than it may seem on a first reading. If we still regard it as schizophrenic, then at least that schizophrenia can be regarded as a narrative strategy of the text itself.

Treglown, who has had access to Green's unpublished papers, claims that Green did not know that *The Souvenirs* was a fabrication (p. xiv), the evidence for this being a letter Green wrote to Evelyn Waugh.[33] The theme of forgery, however, plays too prominent a part in the novel to make this likely. Indeed, the themes of forgery and handwriting become the focus of a textual exorcism of Rose from Charley's imagination that precedes her 'resurrection' in the novel's final scene. The scene in question, which is another *mise en abyme* of Green's aesthetic procedure in *Back*, concerns the five letters from Rose that Charley has treated like sacred relics. The text reproduces Rose's five letters in their entirety. They are all undated, like the tombstone bearing the name 'Sophie' that

Charley uncovers in the opening chapter. Although Charley has resolved to give one of the letters to a handwriting expert to compare Rose's hand with Nancy's, he cannot bear to let one of them go. Then he has an idea:

> He found his nail scissors, got the letters again, and began, without thinking, to cut those sentences out which he thought would not give him away. He worked fast, laying each snippet on a sheet of newspaper to which he proposed to paste the bits like a telegram. And this was the message from Rose that he scissored, almost at random, out of their love letters:
> 'Dear/ go to Redham for me and/ tell them how you saw/ those mules/ coming up to London./ So be a dear/ and go down/ From Rose'.
> He felt he had been exceedingly clever, till, all at once, he realized he had destroyed, cut into ribbons, every letter he had ever had from Rose. Then he despaired, blaming himself... Yet that night he slept very well for once, and did not dream.
>
> p. 122

The literal meaning of Rose's request for Charley to bring some 'mules' is that she wants him to buy her a pair of shoes. However, there is another meaning of the word that Green may have had in mind, one that reflects his definition of prose as 'a gathering web of insinuations'.[34] In numismatics, a 'mule' results when the obverse of one coin is combined with the reverse of a different type. Although this sometimes happens through human error, it is usually, according to one authority, 'intentional though unofficial'.[35] In this interpretation, *Back* is a 'mule' with an English obverse and a French reverse, a fictional artefact that has a reverse side made up of other texts. The intentional or 'official' status of these texts is left to the reader to determine.

The episode as a whole can be read as a symbolic act of vengeance for Charley's own dismemberment: the gun that struck him down was fired beneath a rose. Furthermore, Charley's rearrangement of Rose's words doubles the traumatic intertextuality of the novel itself. *Back* cuts a piece out of an eighteenth-century memoir and pieces it together with other allusions, to Hardy, Keats, Eliot, the Gospels, and Green's previous novels, *Caught* and *Loving*. Although at points these citations threaten to blur the distinction between *Back* and its sources, they ultimately create new patterns and forge another message. The meaning of that message, like that of Charley's 'cut-up', lies not in its distorted and disorientating content but in the traumatised form of its textual production.

Notes

1. See Andrew Buncombe, 'Service Veterans Seeking Millions for Combat Stress', *The Independent*, 22 April 2000, p. 5.
2. Although at one point he is described as a shell-shock case, this is the subjective perception of a character, not a clinical diagnosis.
3. Henry Green, *Back* (London: Hogarth Press, 1946), p. 186. Subsequent references appear parenthetically.
4. How likely would an English war widow be to give her cat a Germanic name that signifies an armoured tank division?
5. As another returning soldier in the novel comments, 'You'd only to go in the guard room and sneeze in front of one of Herr Adolph's portraits, and it was off to the dark in solitary confinement, right away' (p. 118).
6. This could be the reason he seems so unenthusiastic about having children. See p. 202.
7. In the final scene of the film *All Quiet on the Western Front* the hero falls to a sniper's bullet, having been distracted by a butterfly that alights on the parapet. In both cases, a symbol of natural beauty brings about the death or injury of the soldier.
8. Reyner Heppenstall, *New Statesman*, 23 November, 1946, p. 386.
9. Letter to Rosamond Lehmann, 14 March 1945, Library of King's College, Cambridge.
10. J. Hillis Miller, *Fiction and Repetition: Seven English Novels* (Oxford: Basil Blackwell, 1982) p. 175. Subsequent references appear parenthetically.
11. See, for example, R. S. Ryf, *Henry Green* (New York: Columbia University Press, 1967), pp. 31–3.
12. Michael North, *Henry Green and the Writing of His Generation* (Charlottesville: Virginia University Press, 1984), pp. 133–4.
13. Charley believes Ridley to be his own son though he is actually James's child. When he first encounters Ridley, the boy is ringing a bell, the sound of which becomes the occasion for a synaesthetic evocation of Rose: 'For there was a bicycle bell…clustering spray upon spray of sound which wreathed the air much as those roses grew around the headstones' (p. 6). After James sends Charley the story that he hopes will cure him of his delusion, he asks, 'Which didn't ring the bell, eh Charley?' (p. 129).
14. The resurrection of Christ is said to have taken place on the third day after his death.
15. Thomas Hardy, *The Well-Beloved: A Sketch of a Temperament* (London: Macmillan, 1927), pp. 122–3. Subsequent references appear parenthetically.
16. In his autobiography, Green recalled reading Proust at Oxford. 'The last few volumes of *A la Recherche du Temps Perdu* were coming out and anyone who pretended to care about good writing and knew French knew his Proust'. *Pack My Bag* (London: Hogarth Press, 1992), p. 206.
17. The term *mise en abyme* was coined by André Gide, author of *Les Faux-Monnayeurs* (1926). It denotes an internal reduplication of a literary work that creates a sense of infinite interior regression.
18. See John 19: 34–7: 'They will look on the one they have pierced.'
19. 'He turned to her and she seemed his in her white clothes, with a cry the blackbird had flown and in her eyes as, speechless, she turned, still a

stranger, to look into him, he thought he saw the hot, lazy, luxuriance of a rose, the heavy, weightless, luxuriance of a rose, the curling disclosure of the heart of a rose that, as for a hornet, was his for its honey, for the asking, open for him to pierce inside, this heavy, creamy, girl turned woman'. Henry Green, *Caught* (London: Harvill, 1991), p. 62.

20. Edward Stokes, *The Novels of Henry Green* (London: Hogarth Press, 1959), p. 117.

21. Rod Mengham, *The Idiom of the Time: The Writings of Henry Green* (Cambridge: Cambridge University Press, 1982), p. 174. Subsequent references appear parenthetically.

22. The Vidame's antechambers are 'full of liveried footmen drawn up in two ranks' (p. 95); Mandrew's house is 'crawling with domestic servants' (p. 136).

23. *The French Nobelesque of the XVIII Century*, trans. Mrs Colquhoun Grant from *Les Souvenirs de la Marquise [sic.] de Créquy, 1834* (London: John Murray, 1904), p. 126. Grant, incidentally, was Rose's surname.

24. Technically, it is neither. It is not plagiarism because Madame De Créquy's authorship is acknowledged in the text; it is not a pastiche because Green does not parody the extract, he reproduces it.

25. Jeremy Treglown, Introduction to *Back* (London: Harvill, 1997), p. vii. Subsequent references appear parenthetically.

26. ' "*Les grands Mutilés*, that's the name the French have for us" ' (p. 23); ' "In the *Palais de Swim*, or whatever they call the place" ' (p. 115); ' "He's had it Nance, *Il l'a eu*, as our French cousins say" ' (p. 118).

27. The union of nature and artifice is a one of the novel's recurring motifs: in the opening scene, 'a live wreath [of roses] lay fallen on a wreath of stone' (p. 5).

28. Letter to Nancy Mitford, 27 November 1946, Yorke Archive.

29. See *Horizon* 10 (1944): p. 390ff.

30. A scene in Green's previous novel also anticipates the description of the Vidame's palace in *Back*. In *Loving*, the Blue Drawing Room of Kinalty Castle is furnished in the manner of a stable. The 'milking stools, pails, clogs, the cow byre furniture all in gilded wood…was disposed around to create the most celebrated eighteenth-century folly in Eire that had still to be burned down' (p. 203). When Sophie visits the Vidame in his town house she finds herself in 'in a sort of elegant cowshed…The walls were whitewashed, and there actually were five or six cows feeding peacefully in their stalls' (p. 95).

31. There is a theory that *The Souvenirs* were the production of a Breton adventurer, M. de Courchamps, rather than the genuine memoirs of Madame de Créquy. The anonymous reviewer in *The Quarterly Review* claimed that the fabricator had 'very ridiculously mistaken one lady of the family of Créqui for another' and had then built his whole edifice on this fundamental blunder. As Mengham points out, one account of a case of mistaken identity is in itself the occasion for another case of the same mistake. He concludes that the writing in *Back* is itself 'a confidence trick' (p. 172).

32. Translator's Preface, *The French Nobelesque of the XVIII Century*, p. v.

33. 11 November 1946, Yorke Archive.

34. Green, *Pack My Bag*, p. 84.

35. Burton Hobson, *International Guide to Coin Collecting* (New York: Signet, 1966), p. 140.

11

'Quantitative judgements don't apply': The Fiction of Evelyn Waugh and Graham Greene

Peter Mudford

> The dove descending breaks the air
> With flame of incandescent terror…
>
> T. S. Eliot: 'Little Gidding', 1944

The air-raids on London and other cities of Western Europe in the Second World War brought with them an incandescent terror. Incendiary bombs, fire storms, blitzes and saturation-bombing were used by the Allies and the Axis powers in varying ways to terrorise and demoralise civilian populations into a desire for surrender. The propaganda war was fought from the air, and in the air, culminating in the nuclear explosions at Hiroshima and Nagasaki. The photos of ruined cities, of St Paul's standing alone in the midst of urban desolation, or the tower of the *Gedachtnskirche* arising out of the devastation of Berlin became part of a modern apocalypse: an unveiling of a new interpretation of ruins. What had once been admired and visited would as the ruins of Time in Athens and Rome become overlain with another image of ruins. This could no longer be ascribed to Time, with the accompanying and romantic associations of past splendour, but rather to a devastation of another kind, as Graham Greene suggested in *The Ministry of Fear* (1942):

> Now in the strange torn landscape where London shops were reduced to a stone ground-plan like those of Pompeii he moved with familiarity; he was part of this destruction as he was no longer part of the past – the long weekends in the country, the laughter up lanes in the evening, the swallows gathering on telegraph wires, peace.
>
> p. 40

Among these new ruins, there was no possible reconstruction of some greater past, whether real or imaginary, which succumbed to change and the inevitable inscription on all mortal things of time and death. Rather, these new images of our time asked Kent's question at the end of *King Lear*, 'Is this the promised end?' And Edgar's reply – 'Or image of that horror?' Time was to proliferate those images of horror with the films and photos of Belsen and Auschwitz. 'We shan't', as W. H. Auden was to write in *The Cave of Making*, 'not since Stalin and Hitler trust ourselves ever again: we know that subjectively all is possible.' This was to have profound implications for questions of identity, leadership, authority and tradition, whether in the arts or society. After so much destruction, what forgiveness? 'In the uncertain hour before the morning', which Eliot invoked in 'Little Gidding', 'near the ending of interminable night', stories of survival in the 1940s were shaped by the attitudes and beliefs of the past. It has been remarked with some accuracy that the nineteenth century came to an end in 1945.

But, while the war lasted, survival for civilians and those in the forces meant just that. Buildings which had stood the test of time were reduced to rubble. On the night of 10 May 1941, the Law Courts, the Mint, the Tower of London, Westminster Hall and the House of Commons were all hit. Three thousand people were left dead or injured in one night. During 1940 and 1941 one Londoner in six was made homeless. In this period Henry Moore went into the underground where thousands lived a troglodyte existence as their houses were destroyed in the streets above, recording both the squalor and the dignity. Herbert Read described these drawings as 'the most authentic expression of the special tragedy of this war – its direct impact on the ordinary mass of humanity, the women, children and old men of our cities'.[1] Graham Greene recorded these scenes in underground shelters in *The Ministry of Fear*:

> All along the walls the bodies lay two deep, while outside the raid rumbled and receded. This was a quiet night: any raid which happened a mile away wasn't a raid at all. An old man snored across the aisle and at the end of the shelter two lovers lay on a mattress with their hands and knees touching.
>
> p. 64

In various circumstances, survival could be, and often was, what it became for Lord Marchmain at the end of Evelyn Waugh's *Brideshead Revisited* (1945): 'He had no strength for any other *war* than his own solitary struggle to survive' (p. 377: my italic). This was as true for civilians, as for those caught up in many different theatres of war, from the Burma Railroad to the ruins of Stalingrad.

War gives rise to two kinds of writing: the first is documentary, and objective:

> During the march, in order to defend their eyes from the glare of the snow, the soldiers put something black in front of them: against the danger of frostbite the most useful remedy was to keep moving the feet, never staying still, and especially removing one's boots at night … A group of soldiers, who had been left behind because of these difficulties, saw not far off, in a valley in the middle of the snow-covered plain, a dark pool: melted snow, they thought.[2]

This passage, from Xenophon's *Anabasis*, was written in the fifth century BC. The next, written two thousand years later, describes the evacuation from Stalingrad in 1942:

> A large column of refugees left the city heading west into German-occupied territory on 14 September, with their few remaining possessions piled on handcarts or carried in cardboard suitcases. A German correspondent saw civilians caught by shellfire turned into a bloody mess of torso and torn clothes, with a severed hand stuck in telegraph wires overhead.[3]

The refugees from besieged Stalingrad, like the Greek army two thousand years earlier, move through a wintry landscape, without shelter or food, surrounded by the 'supreme indifference' of Nature and Fortune. Both passages create images which have become the domain of film and television, where the haunted despairing looks of those who are far from home and do not know if they will live to see another day to require no further commentary.

But there is another kind of writing about war, where reporting and imagined narrative intersect. A German lieutenant writing to his wife from the siege of Stalingrad asked: 'I often ask myself what is all this suffering for. Has mankind gone crazy?'[4] A century earlier, Tolstoy in his *Sketches from Sebastopol* brought to the notice of the Tsar, and his glittering entourage in Moscow and St Petersburg, the horrors of the Crimean War. His sketches combined courageous reportage with fictional narratives. These portrayed the sufferings of imagined individuals who, like the German lieutenant, questioned the purpose and necessity for all they endured. It is this second kind of writing about war which has become – sometimes directly, sometimes indirectly – the province of the novelist, as it came to inspire much of *War and Peace*.

Thomas Mann, reflecting in California about the unconditional surrender of Germany, wrote: 'If I had taken Hitler's sham victory seriously, if I had taken it to heart, there would in truth have been nothing left for me to do but pass away. Surviving means victory... Hitler had the great merit of producing a simplification of emotions... a clear and deadly hatred.'[5] Unshakeable resolve equally enabled Churchill to unify the nation in the face of the shortages of food, rationing of all kinds, bombing, as well as the flow of telegrams announcing the missing and the dead. But the war not only involved the question of who survived, but also of what was being destroyed and the value of what survived. 'Biffing' could not be, as Evelyn Waugh indicated through the character of Ben Ritchie Hook in the *Sword of Honour* trilogy, a sufficient *raison d'être*, even if it meant temporary survival.

The horror and pity of war is the predominant theme in poetry and prose about the First World War. Massive slaughters on the battlefields of France have their memorials still; and the enemy who is also a friend their most tragic epitaph. In the novels of Evelyn Waugh and Graham Greene, the enemy is usually unseen, and seldom mentioned. The war is often felt as a 'sullen reverberation', or like noises from a play which is being performed elsewhere. This reflected their personal circumstances. Their non-involvement in the fighting (except Waugh for a brief time in Crete) resulted from age, class and education, as well as the process of selection for various types of wartime jobs. But displacing the actual war to the 'wings' left the centre-stage free for another form of conflict: an inner drama not sudden or precipitous, but nonetheless indicative of a shift in the centre of gravity for society as a whole.

In the late 1940s and 1950s, the question was often asked: 'What kind of war did he have?' The answer, 'Oh, he had a very good war' implied more than just survival: not only had he survived the war, but he had done himself good as a result of it:

> 'The great thing is to get into uniform; then you can start moving yourself round. It's a very exclusive war at present. Once you're in, there's every opportunity. I've got my eye on India or Egypt. Somewhere there's no black-out. Fellow in the flats where I live got coshed on the head the other night, right on the steps. All a bit too dangerous for me. I don't want a medal. I want to be known as one of the soft-faced men who did well out of the war.'
>
> *Sword of Honour*, p. 17

The speaker, Lord Kilbannock, proves very successful throughout the war in adapting himself to circumstances, unconcerned as he is with any values beyond his own well-being. At the opposite extreme, those who fought bravely, were promoted and decorated, but often found themselves 'on the shelf', without any role or employment once the fighting was over:

> General Whale gazed at Ian despondingly, uncomprehendingly. Three years, two years, even six months ago there would have been a detonation of rage. Now he sighed deeply. He gazed round the rough concrete walls of his shelter, at the silent 'scrambler' telephone on his table. He felt (and had he known the passage might so have expressed it) like a beautiful and ineffectual angel beating in the void his luminous wings in vain.
>
> 'What am I doing here?' he asked. 'Why am I taking cover when all I want to do is die?'
>
> *Sword of Honour*, p. 616

As Angus Calder remarks in his notes to the trilogy,

> Waugh's touch in this passage is exquisite. Whale has been the target of his satire and it might even seem snide of him to quote here Matthew Arnold's phrases about Shelley...But suddenly Whale reveals a spiritual dimension – despair.[6]

Elsewhere in Waugh's work, characters like Basil Seal and Rex Mottram who completely lack this dimension, survive, and do very well out of the war. In *Put Out More Flags*, Waugh's first wartime novel (1942), Sir Joseph Mainwaring epitomised the type 'whose courtly and ponderous form concealed a peppercorn lightness of soul, a deep unimpressionable frivolity, which left him bobbing serenely on the great waves of history which splintered more solid natures to matchwood' (p. 212).

Mainwaring's words bring the novel, with its ironic title, to its smashing conclusion:

> 'There's a new spirit abroad,' he said. 'I see it on every side.' And, poor booby, he was bang right.
>
> p. 222

This new spirit led first to the 'Churchillian renaissance', but it also led in 1945 to the Labour Party's landslide victory. The Britain which had been bombed needed to be rebuilt in a new way. The time had come for change.

In *Unconditional Surrender*, the final volume of Waugh's trilogy, Everard Spruce founds a monthly review called 'Survival'. He does so despite believing that 'the human race was destined to dissolve in chaos'. Given Government approval, and scattered from aeroplanes in countries still occupied by the Germans, 'Survival' is devoted to the survival of values. Waugh's satire is directed (not altogether justly) at Cyril Connolly's *Horizon*. But it also reflects his own more personal despair. Survival did not necessarily bring with it belief in what had survived. Pragmatic success in wartime society, civilian or military, did not conceal the void beneath the surface.

Against it there is set not an assertion, but a questioning and sceptical comprehension which Waugh ascribes to the elder Crouchback in his trilogy, and Graham Greene expresses with gnomic force in *The Heart of the Matter* (1948):

> If one knew, he wondered, the facts, would one have to feel pity even for the planets? if one reached what they called the heart of the matter?
>
> p. 124

'Release from duty' led to the writing of the one novel which seems as likely to endure as any other novel of the 1940s: Waugh's *Brideshead Revisited, The Sacred and Profane Memories of Captain Charles Ryder*. Waugh described the inception of the novel like this:

> In December 1943 I had the good fortune when parachuting to incur a minor injury which afforded me a rest from military service. This was extended by a sympathetic commanding officer, who let me remain unemployed until June 1944 when the book was finished. I wrote with a zest that was quite strange to me, and also with impatience to get back to the war.
>
> Preface, p. 9

There is nothing surprising about the desire in times of privation and 'threatening disaster' to write about a less imperilled world. The tone and feeling of *Brideshead Revisited* is born of the reflection, 'the true paradises are the paradises which we have lost'. Waugh was later to assert that much of the book was a 'panegyric preached over an empty coffin'. In fact, aristocratic life in a large country house was not doomed to die with the Second World War, or at least not as completely as Waugh anticipated. Nonetheless, there was a corpse in the coffin; and its spirit shapes the contours of the landscape in which Brideshead is enfolded.

The carefree hedonism of Charles Ryder's youthful friendship with Sebastian Flyte is 'remembered with tears by a middle aged captain of infantry'. Chapter One is entitled 'Et in Arcadia Ego', recalling that death too is in Arcadia. Social conventions, religion, marriage, family, integrity of life, art, houses are all dying, or in danger of dying. The shadows closing around Sebastian Flyte in his alchoholism and exile are shadows enclosing a way of life, and the values inscribed on it. The war becomes an end-game.

'My theme', Charles Ryder says, 'is memory, that winged host that soared above me one grey morning in wartime.' (p. 259). And it is memory, increasingly enclosed by the coming war, which creates the particular nostalgia of the book. The shadows of war darken around Brideshead and its world of youth, happiness and pleasure. Like memory which is tangible and elusive, *Brideshead* attempts to recapture something just out of reach. 'Youth? Adolescence? Romance? The conjuring stuff of these things' (p. 163). As Charles Ryder puts it at the end of Chapter One, 'we seemed to be in pursuit of our own shadows'.

The novel is circumstantial and factual. Houses, rooms, furniture, possessions have the solidity which comes from Waugh's detailed knowledge of art and artefact, and reflect his liking for the splendour which falls on castle walls. But like the pleasures of taste, to which, as Waugh admits, in the scarcities of wartime the novel often refers, memory reaches out only to find that what is being remembered has passed away. Sebastian's decline into alchoholism, Lord Marchmain's deathbed recognition of Catholicism, Julia's rejection of marriage to Charles because she cannot put another good in the place of God, are all part of this process of what cannot be grasped and held on to. Brideshead only comes to exist when it is revisited; and Nanny Hawkins has become the last survivor in the Flyte household. Like Firs in Chekhov's *The Cherry Orchard*, she represents the dying spirit of the past.

The war becomes the context in which this dissolution occurs; but the war itself with its actual destruction and violence acts only as the catalyst in the wings, dissolving all that Brideshead has stood for. Charles Ryder, when reflecting on his relationship to Julia, expresses it like this:

'Perhaps,' I thought, while her words still hung in the air between us like a wisp of smoke – a thought to fade and vanish like smoke without trace – 'perhaps all our loves are merely hints and symbols; vagabond-language scrawled on gateposts and paving-stones along the weary road that others have tramped before us; perhaps you and I are types and this sadness which sometimes falls between us springs from disappointment in our search, each straining through and beyond the other, snatching a glimpse now and then of the *shadow* which turns the corner always a pace or two ahead of us.'

p. 346, my emphasis

As the war closes in, so the shadows run faster ahead. Like much about the 1940s, *Brideshead Revisited* exists on the cusp of the old world and the new. Rex Mottram and his friends are having a good war, increasing their power within the new society the war was creating. Mottram has already been described as a 'tiny bit of a man pretending he was the whole' (p. 230). Once war comes Mottram is able to make broadcasts about Hitler, which, as Nanny Hawkins says, will make him feel very small, if he understands English. Rex Mottram, and his friends, are the new 'angels' who have the world at their feet. Hooper, another example of the coming man, believes we could learn a thing or two from Hitler by putting loonies in the gas-chamber.

By the time *Brideshead Revisited* was published, food rationing, utility clothes, Woolton pies and bombs had ground everything down to a dreary uniformity; people were weary of a war which dragged on year after year, laying waste to lives and cities, with little prospect of an end. Against this background the romanticism of the novel had an obvious appeal. But there was also something more distinctive about *Brideshead Revisited*. In February 1945,Waugh wrote of it:

I hope in April everyone's minds will be on great events in Europe rather than novels of the past. But I believe it will go on being read for many years.[7]

In Waugh's estimation, and that of many of his contemporaries, he had succeeded in writing a classic. Italo Calvino in his recent essay 'Why read the classics?' offers two definitions of a classic especially pertinent to *Brideshead Revisited* as a novel of the 1940s, and to its subsequent survival: 'A classic is a work which relegates the noise of the present to a background hum', and 'a classic is a work which persists as background noise even when a present that is totally incompatible with it holds sway'.[8] The contrast between the sacred and profane, the portrayal of all men and women, however blessed by wealth and class, as in an

Augustinian sense 'fallen', raise questions about the nature of society and its values which the noise of war, if foregrounded, would have blotted out. A half-century later, Calvino's second definition points to a continuing concern with what is sacred in a world where information and technology seem neither fulfilling nor sufficient. When Charles Ryder returns to Brideshead, the house has been requisitioned as an army camp. What Brideshead stands for has been changed for ever. He visits the chapel, where the art-nouveau lamp still burns in front of the altar:

> a beaten-copper lamp of deplorable design relit before the beaten-copper doors of a tabernacle; the flame which the old knights saw from their tombs, which they saw put out; that flame burns again for other soldiers, far from home, farther in heart, than Acre or Jerusalem ...
>
> p. 331

It is to the survival of that sacred flame which also still burns at Broome that Waugh will return in *Sword of Honour* where, as the old Mr Crouchback says, 'Quantitative judgements don't apply.'

Evelyn Waugh wrote of his wartime trilogy in the Preface:

> The product is intended (as it was originally) to be read as a single story. I sought to give a description of the Second World War as it was seen and experienced by a single uncharacteristic Englishman, and to show its effect on him.
>
> Preface, p. xxxiv

He belonged to a west-country Catholic family, whose outlook and feelings found little place in the modern age. The war, at least temporarily, offers Guy Crouchback a form of community in the Halbardiers which he has never found in society outside. Against this displacement, about which Waugh writes with seriousness, the events of the war itself come across as episodes in a black comedy or farce, presenting Waugh with plenty of opportunities to display his comic invention, and his talent for creating 'a gallery of comic characters'.

Waugh originally intended to call it just 'honour'; and the sub-text of the novel, its centre of gravity, is concerned with honour, or lack of it, in the contemporary world. The old and traditionally Catholic Mr Crouchback, withdrawn and living in a furnished bed-sitting-room, exemplifies its tenuous survival; Ivor Claire, who saves his own skin, and abandons his troops in the evacuation of Crete (afterwards doing very nicely for himself by using his influence to get a job in India) exemplifies its abandonment.

The title refers to the sword, forged at the King's command as a gift to the 'steel-hearted people of Stalingrad', as a token of homage from the British people. Long queues waited to see it in Westminster Abbey. Though not recorded in the novel, the fate of the sword became blackly comic. Churchill presented it to Stalin at the Tehran Conference in 1943. Stalin lifted it to his lips to kiss the scabbard before handing it to Marshal Voroshilov, who let the sword slide out of the scabbard and clatter loudly to the floor.[9] The novel contains many moments of farce of a similar kind: the blowing up of Apthorpe's portable latrine, the death of the Laird of Mugg and his niece, not through enemy action as reported, but through the Commandos' incompetence in the use of explosives at home, and the faked account of Trimmer's raid on a French beach which turns him into an international hero. But with the exception of the bloody evacuation of Crete (and much more marginally the British involvement with aid to the partisans in Yugoslavia) the war exists as a documentary background: the fall of France, the German arrival in Boulogne, the invasion of Russia, the North African campaign, the surrender of Italy; all are mentioned as the backdrop to events in the life of Guy Crouchback, a thirty-six year old who craves a place in the war, as an antidote to his loneliness and isolation:

> Even good men thought their private honour would be satisfied by war. They could assert their manhood by killing and being killed. They would accept hardships in recompense for having been selfish and lazy. Danger justified privilege.
>
> p. 788

Guy Crouchback, divorced and comfortably off, accepts this as a definition of his own motivation. His non-heroic and essentially passive role has often made him the object of criticism of the trilogy, as a weak and uninteresting character described by his ex-wife with some justice as a 'wet, smug, obscene, pompous, sexless, lunatic pig' (p.149). But as Waugh himself admits, somewhat reluctantly, the centre of his interest in the trilogy turns out not to be the war as such, but the Catholic usage of his youth. As with *Brideshead Revisited*, Waugh's comments on his achievement turn out to be too restricted. The broad scope of the trilogy uses the background of the war to portray the sexual mores and social attitudes of the upper middle class at a time when (in Waugh's phrase) the 'age of the common man' is leaving them, like Guy and

Brigadier Ritchie-Hook, washed up. But the old world is giving way to a new without foundations, and where, as he was later to say, a third world war was most likely to occur out of boredom.

The horrors of the war, except in the evacuation from Crete, are seen through the wrong end of a telescope:

> It all seemed a long way from Tony's excursions in no man's land... far from those secret forests where the trains were, even while the Halberdiers and their guests sat bemused by wine and harmony, rolling east and west with their doomed loads.
>
> p. 64

Here, as often, the action takes place off-stage:

> It was a warm, highly coloured, well-found place far from bombs and gas, famine and enemy occupation; far from the lightless concentration-camp which all Europe had suddenly become.
>
> p. 233

Shells and searchlights over London become 'pure Turner, or is it John Martin?' The homeless and the evacuees become a reproach to those with houses large enough to have nurseries, but personal loss and tragedy rarely dominate the portrayal of generalised chaos which threatens to engulf the civilian population as well as lead to a debacle in battle.

The tears which are shed are shed for civilisation as Waugh sees it, not for individuals in their agony. Some critics see this as Waugh losing his satirical bite; others as a failure to adapt his particular talent for black comedy and farce to the reality of the war. But there is a different way of reading the trilogy arising out of the encounter between the documentary and the fictional. The war is chronicled; we are made aware of its central events and development. But unlike Tolstoy, who stands back from the narrative to give his view of the historical process, Waugh's interpretation of events comes from his characters. They reflect Waugh's own wartime experience, and his outlook on the modern age. Characters based on real life are composite, and the judgements implied of them unreliable – especially of Robert Laycock and Field Marshall Wavell. The war against Hitler's evil comes across as a shambles, with orders given and countermanded, and troops left in the dark as to what is happening, or what they are supposed to be doing. Waugh observes this with sharpness of detail and an omission of comment which allows the callowness of human behaviour to speak for itself, as when Mrs Stitch throws away the red identity disk which Guy has taken from the body of a British soldier killed in Crete (p. 444).

In the scope of the novel, the accumulation of subterfuges and deceits, personal and military, bears out the prophecy made at the outset, 'This war has begun in darkness and will end in silence.' The old Mr Crouchback's equally gnomic conclusion to his son about the Catholic faith, 'Quantitative judgements don't apply', serves at the opposite extreme to offer a view in which something more than a silent void exists within a parody of civilisation. In his integrity of life, unmoved by the criticism or dislike of others, he stands for the man who has not lost his soul, and believes in Catholic practice as he always known it. He stands a little to the side in Waugh's gallery of comic characters, but he is never portrayed with solemnity. His son achieves only the most pallid reflection of his father's authority, living as he does in an opportunistic world. As the final words of the trilogy put it, 'things have turned out very conveniently for Guy'. This convenience involves his one unselfish act, in marrying Virginia again, to act as father for her child by the unscrupulous Trimmer; and after her death in the air-raid, his further marriage to a friend by whom, in the first version, he has two children, as heir to the tradition of the blessed Gervase Crouchback. But these 'nippers', as he refers to them, are eradicated in the final version, as giving a happier ending than Waugh believed in.

Although the older Crouchback has died without an heir, his spirit dominates this trilogy about the Second World War. He symbolises what the struggle for survival is about, against all those who have done well out of the war, to whom survival means just that, and also personal gain. Whatever grace survives in the modern age exists only within individual lives; but without the power to inspire in any general sense the continuities in which Waugh believed. The ending of *Sword of Honour* lacks even the tentative affirmation of the final words of *Brideshead Revisited*.

Graham Greene wrote *The Ministry of Fear* in Sierra Leone in 1942. 'It was impossible,' Greene wrote, 'to forget the menace of submarines – it was part of our everyday life; the reason why so many wives stayed throughout their husbands' tours, the reason why I had no refrigerator – it had been lost on the way out.'[10] But this novel was shaped by Greene's experiences as an air-raid warden in the London Blitz of 1941, especially the Great Blitz of Wednesday 16 April. Greene kept a journal at the time, which he used as a basis for parts of the novel, although much else in it was derived from earlier boyhood experience of his first love, and of psychoanalysis. The ministry of fear is created out of the world of nightmare, and unconscious fear as much as the nightly bombing raid which drove Londoners underground. As often, the strength of the novel results from the crystallisation of experiences which are documentary and fantastic. 'My own village was bounded on the south by New Oxford Street, on the north by Euston Road, on the east by Gordon Square, on the west by Gower Street.' As in the later *The End of the Affair* (1951), the streets of London, pubs, cafés, lodging houses, bombed and burning buildings are evoked through the partly surreal atmosphere of the Blitz, which in the end fuses with Greene's metaphysical obsessions. War provides the context for the novel, but the war on Londoners, not the war of soldiers or on battlefields. As with much of Waugh's and Anthony Powell's writing, that war is felt only as a distant reverberation. Greene illustrates this in what he has to say about the completion of *The Ministry of Fear*: 'So, having finished the book, I began the weary task of typing it out with one finger after dinner, and I was lucky to finish it before the scurry of the North African landings affected even my remote coast with cables at all hours.'[11]

The war which Greene documents is captured like this:

> He caught a number 19 bus from Piccadilly. After the ruins of St James's Church one passed at that early date into peaceful country. Knightsbridge and Sloane Street were not at war, but Chelsea was, and Battersea was in the front line. It was an odd front line that twisted like the track of a hurricane and left patches of peace.
>
> p. 87

It was odd, and very different from the front lines of the First World War. The three flares which Greene, and his fictional character Rowe, saw 'sailing slowly, beautifully, down, clusters of spangles off a Christmas tree', illuminate another London in which the ministry of fear extends beyond the domain of espionage and war, but nonetheless the war is the imaginative space in which this metaphorical exploration occurs:

> A phrase of Johns's came back to mind about the Ministry of Fear. He felt now that he had joined its permanent staff. But it wasn't the small Ministry to which Johns had referred, with limited aims like winning a war or changing a constitution. It was a Ministry as large as life to which all who loved belonged. If one loved one feared.
>
> p. 220

Rowe's own exile from peace of mind and happiness is mirrored in the devastation of the bombed city. What can be rebuilt from the ruins remains uncertain. As the final words of the novel put it: 'It seemed to him that after all one could exaggerate the value of happiness' (p. 221). The submarines which prowl the seas off West Africa, and confine many of those who have been sent there for the duration, become the instruments of change in *The Heart of the Matter* (1948). The sinking of the ship on which Helen Rolt and her husband are travelling leads to her arrival, after forty days in an open boat, in Sierra Leone. The affair of the young widow with the lonely police-officer, Scobie, torn by his loyalty to his wife and his doomed attempt to remain a good Catholic, becomes the heart of the matter.

Once more, and again for autobiographical reasons, the war – apart from the submarines, which are themselves 'off-shore' – is taking place a long way away: its slaughter, its everyday violence and its nightly fear have no place in the novel. But it is still the context in which the novel occurs; and hatred of war creates the border of its territory. Louise, Scobie's unhappy wife, joined him 'the first year of the phoney war, and now she couldn't get away: the danger of submarines had made her as much a fixture as the handcuffs on the nail' (p. 16). The Vichy French are just across the border. Convoys lie at anchor in the harbour; and the smuggling of industrial diamonds, essential to Germany, provide the context for Scobie's downfall. As in Waugh's *Sword of Honour* trilogy, the war also means the time for the next generation is speeded up, the not so young are passed over, as Scobie is. 'Look at all the generals who have been passed over since 1940' (p. 27). Again, as in Waugh, fortunes are being made from the war by men outside it, like Tallit and Yusuf. But as Scobie discovers when he tries to obtain an overdraft to pay for Louise's visit to South Africa, the war is highly selective. His bank-manager tells him: 'We've had orders to be strict about overdrafts. It's the war, you know. There's one valuable security nobody can offer now, his life' (p. 45). Scobie has to borrow money from the Syrian Yusuf, whose war is being fought on the very different front of Muslims against Christians; and for him, as he complains, the war is not going well. The war casts long shadows over the West-African landscape for whites and blacks, enclosing them in an isolated space where their jealousies and hatreds become more extreme.

When Helen Rolt is brought ashore on a stretcher, bringing from the open boat only her stamp-album, she seems little more than something the war has washed up on a foreign shore. When Scobie first goes to visit her in her hut, the sirens are wailing for a complete black-out. He goes to warn her that a light is showing from her hut. It happens about once a month, he tells her, but nothing ever happens. She asks him to stay till the All Clear sounds. The war – again 'off-stage' – creates the opportunity for the affair between two people, each lonely in their different ways. But this war is also the trigger for another war which is about to break out between Scobie and God, or between Scobie and the way his faith tells him he ought to live, but finds he cannot. Survival begins to present itself as a problem in a different form; and this is not a war which Scobie is destined to win. In the context of the novel the two wars are not finally separable. Scobie sees the landscape of his affair with Helen in terms of the metaphors of war, and of a lost peace:

> He went slowly and cautiously on, choosing his words carefully, as though he were pursuing a path through an evacuated country sown with booby-traps: every step he took he expected the explosion.
>
> p. 180

From the time Louise returns safely from South Africa, warned by a friend about her husband's affair with Helen Rolt, the real war is displaced by theological war which Louise exacerbates by her attempt to make her husband a good Catholic. By insisting that he goes to confession and takes communion, she makes him feel that that he is putting damnation beneath his tongue. Scobie's awareness that he loves two women, and that this is incompatible with his Catholic faith, results in his contemplation of suicide, itself a sure way of ensuring damnation. To Helen his Catholicism is anathema, an excuse for not leaving his wife; to Scobie, a belief that he cannot give up. In losing the battle, he is aware that he is giving up peace of mind:

> 'I have left even the hope of peace for ever. I am the responsible man. I shall soon have gone too far in my design of deception ever to go back.'
>
> p. 224

With this loss of peace comes too an increasing tiredness with the struggle, for which the evipan, prescribed for simulated angina, and stored up for his eventual suicide, seems ironically a necessary palliative to pain. As Scobie reflects, 'we are all of us resigned to death: it's life we aren't resigned to' (p. 259).

The desire for a lost peace and the weariness of the continuing war dominate the end of Scobie's life, as it increasingly dominated the feelings of people involved in the actual war. Churchill quoted Clough in encouragement, 'Say not the struggle nought availeth.' Scobie offered up his damnation to God. Whatever the theological objections to this, and Waugh did object, the space of the outer war encloses an inner space in which peace is never won.

The setting of *The End of the Affair* (1951), like *The Ministry of Fear*, is war-time London; but while the earlier novel belongs to the Blitz of 1941, the pivotal events of the later novel occur in 1944:

> It was the first night of what were later called the V1s in June 1944. We had become unused to air-raids. Apart from the short spell in February 1944, there had been nothing since the blitz petered out with the great final raids of 1941. When the sirens went and the first robots came over, we assumed that a few planes had broken through our night defence. All Clear had still not sounded after an hour.
>
> p. 69

Once again, the war of battlefields, of the struggle for Europe, has no place in the novel, and is deliberately held at a distance by the narrator, Maurice Bendrix:

> Even the war hardly affected me. A lame leg kept me out of the Army, and as I was in Civil Defence, my fellow workers were only too glad that I never wanted the quiet morning turns of duty.
>
> p. 34

As a writer, Bendrix needs to discover about the life of a civil servant for his next novel. His cold-hearted search for copy leads to his intense affair with Sarah, Henry Miles's wife. As in *The Heart of the Matter*, war is the context for another kind of war, war in the heart, with its explosions like the V1s which occur unexpectedly, and by stealth after the engines have cut out. The destructive impact of these is reflected in the creative impact of what, at the end of the novel, are no less unexpectedly taken to be miracles. Stealth in the night is characteristic of each. Survival is, to say the least, of a precarious kind; and while Bendrix, unlike Scobie, does not die, his survival is that of the vanquished. In 1946, where the novel ends, he finds one prayer that seemed to serve the winter mood: 'O God, You've done enough. You've robbed me of enough, I'm too tired and too old to learn to love, leave me alone for ever' (p. 191).

The novel which Bendrix is trying to write is held up not by the actual war but by the end of his affair with Sarah, and yet for the reader the two are not separable. Greene's novel is not the novel which Bendrix is writing:

> And all that time I couldn't work. So much of a novelist's writing, as I have said, takes place in the unconscious: in those depths the last word is written before the first word appears on paper. We remember the details of our story, we do not invent them. War didn't trouble deep sea-caves, but now there was something of infinitely greater importance to me than war, than my novel – the end of love.
>
> p. 35

Charles Ryder's last love dies at the start of *Brideshead Revisited*; its survival only suggested at the end by the lamp still burning in the Catholic chapel. For Bendrix there is no such restorative flame. The war will even destroy the places where he and Sarah have made love:

> A week ago I revisited the terrace. Half of it was gone – the half where the hotels used to stand had been blasted to bits, and the place where we made love that night was a patch of air.
>
> p. 44

The ruins of cities stand for the ruins of a way of life, in which both the physical and the metaphysical war are on the point of being lost, and a way of life obliterated, as the title suggests. In a way that is characteristic of the 1940s, the actual war provides the context for this other war, which is located in a landscape of divided belief and uncertainties:

> I wanted Sarah for a lifetime, and You took her away. With Your great schemes you ruin our happiness like a harvester ruins a mouse's nest: I hate you, God, I hate You as though You existed.
>
> p. 191

The war in *The End of the Affair* is fought out, so the novel makes us believe, on a battlefield no less real than those which exist elsewhere between opposing sets of values, and where the stakes in terms of survival are no less high. As in *The Heart of the Matter,* the desire for peace, especially peace of mind, which is always elusive, conflicts with the aggressive emotion of hate, leading in the end only to an immense tiredness at what cannot be resolved or ended. In the fiction of, or about, the 1940s considered here, survival is seen in the context of war, but the battleground lies within, where quantitative judgements don't apply, and surviving does not mean victory, as Thomas Mann had proclaimed.

Notes

All page references are to the Penguin editions of the novels of Evelyn Waugh and Graham Greene:

Evelyn Waugh: *Put Out More Flags* (1942), *Brideshead Revisited* (1945), *Sword of Honour* (1952–61).

Graham Greene*: The Ministry of Fear* (1942), *The Heart of the Matter* (1948), *The End of the Affair* (1951).

1. Quoted in Philip Ziegler, *London at War, 1939–45* (London: Arrow, 1998), p. 136.
2. Quoted in Italo Calvino, *Why Read the Classics?* trans. M. McLaughlin (London: cape, 1999), p. 19.
3. Anthony Beevor, *Stalingrad* (London: Penguin Books, 1999), p. 175.
4. Ibid., p. 200.
5. Thomas Mann, *The Genesis of a Novel* trans. R. and C. Winston (London: Secker and Warburg, 1961), p. 131.
6. Evelyn Waugh, *Sword of Honour*, p. 693.
7. *The Letters of Evelyn Waugh*, ed., M. Amory (London: Phoenix, 1980), p. 200.
8. Calvino, *Why Read the Classics?* p. 8.
9. Beevor, *Stalingrad*, p. 418.
10. Graham Greene, *Ways of Escape* (London: Bodley Head, 1980), pp. 99–100.
11. Ibid., p. 100.

Index